KILKENNEY SOLUTIONS

KILKENNEY SOLUTIONS

JAMES KRIEGER

PROPAGANDA PRESS

KILKENNEY SOLUTIONS

This is a work of fiction. All the characters and events portrayed in this book are fictional, and any resemblance to real people or incidents is purely coincidental.

Propaganda Press, LLC
Please visit us on the web at
https://www.propaganda-press.com/

Paperback ISBN: 979-8-9933977-2-6
E-Book ISBN: 979-8-9933977-0-2

Cover art and Illustrations by: Adolf Riker
Interior Layout and Design by: Kenneth Kroeker

Proudly Made in the United States of America

CHAPTER ONE

The palm trees of Nueva Kalloo burned like birthday candles against the dawn sky, their fronds curling into ash that drifted down onto the cratered boulevard like black snow. What had been the jewel of the Caribbean Federation—a resort world of white sand beaches and crystal-blue waters—was now a graveyard of twisted rebar and pulverized concrete.

The morning humidity hung thick as soup, turning the smoke from burning buildings into a choking fog that clung to the colonial style facades along Avenida Libertad. Parrots that had nested in the royal palms for centuries now wheeled frantically overhead, their bright plumage incongruous against the columns of black smoke. The famous glass-bottom canals that had once ferried tourists through the downtown's underwater gardens were shattered, leaking their engineered ecosystem into streets already ankle-deep in debris and worse.

A Dunkirk main battle tank crushed a decorative fountain beneath its treads—one depicting President-General Cortez as a benevolent father distributing bread to grateful children. The statue's bronze head rolled into a drainage ditch already clogged with propaganda posters promising "Prosperity Through Order." The hybrid beast was wrapped in improvised cage armor welded from construction rebar, designed to detonate shaped charges before they could reach the hull. Barbed wire coiled around the turret and sides like metal thorns. A cope cage of slat armor covered the top, jury-rigged from steel mesh that used to fence in a local school's playground.

The rebels had learned from the urban meat grinders of the old world. Every surface that could mount something did—blocks of concrete hung from chains as improvised reactive armor, view slits gave the crew 360-degree vision. The government markings had been hastily covered with rebel insignia—a broken chain wrapped around a machete—still dripping fresh paint.

Through the tank's periscope, Commander Miguel Reyes could see the Presidential Palace's neo-baroque towers rising above the smoke. Twenty-three years Cortez had ruled from those air-conditioned halls while the shantytown workers who cleaned his pools and served his guests lived without running water. Twenty-three years of watching foreign mining consortiums strip the coastal mountains bare while locals were shot for fishing in "protected" resort waters. The breaking point had been last month's "Paradise Tax"—a levy on anyone living within sight of the beaches, designed to force the poor into the interior so tourists wouldn't have to see them.

Its 140mm smoothbore roared, the autoloader cycling another round as the first impact turned a section of palace wall into powder and flame. Ancient coral stone—quarried by slaves three hundred years ago—exploded outward in pink-white chunks. The coaxial 30mm autocannon chattered in short bursts, walking fire across the palace windows where government snipers tried to find gaps in the urban modifications. Spent brass rained down on the infantry huddled behind the tank's bulk, using it as mobile cover as they advanced through the killing ground.

"Push forward! Push forward!" Reyes screamed into his comm from the cupola of his Dunkirk, his voice crackling through the static of jamming countermeasures. The rebels—farmers who'd lost their lands to resort expansion, dock workers replaced by automation but still taxed for "employment opportunity fees," teachers who'd had enough of teaching lies—surged through the breach behind his armor. Their mismatched gear included everything from stolen military exoskeletons to hunting rifles duct-taped with homemade explosive rounds.

The air itself seemed to burn in the tropical heat, thermite rounds igniting the moisture into brief, wisps of flame. A government loyalist with a rocket launcher popped up from behind a concrete barrier—one of the "Peace Walls" Cortez had built to separate tourist districts from worker neighborhoods. Reyes swiveled the commander's gun and cut him down with a burst of .50 caliber fire, the man's torso separating from his legs in a spray of red mist that hung in the humid air like morning dew. To his left, a rebel squad stormed a machine gun nest built into what had been a beachside café, the lead man taking three rounds to the chest before his homemade satchel charge—agricultural fertilizer and fuel oil—turned the position into a crater. Body parts rained down on the courtyard like confetti at a parade from hell, landing in the ornamental pools filled with imported koi that somehow still swam in circles, oblivious to the carnage above.

The palace guards were fighting hard—these were the elite, the ones who'd gotten rich enforcing Cortez's "rehabilitation camps" for dissidents, who'd machinegunned union organizers on the docks just last year. A rebel with a flamethrower—a repurposed agricultural sprayer filled with petroleum gel—hosed down a doorway where government troops had taken cover. Their screams lasted exactly four seconds before the heat cooked their lungs from the inside out. The smell of burning flesh mixed with cordite and diesel exhaust, overwhelming even the ever-present stench of rotting fruit from the destroyed market district.

Through the smoke, Reyes could see the famous Cortez Towers—luxury apartments built with disaster relief funds after the last hurricane, still empty because only foreign investors could afford them. A government sniper team had set up in the penthouse, their muzzle flashes visible through the floor-to-ceiling windows. He called in coordinates to his rocket teams, who were hauling repurposed anti-ship missiles through the rubble-strewn streets.

The tank gunner traversed the turret toward a tracked government APC trying to flank their position through what had been the Botanical Gardens—Cortez's pride, built while hospitals went without medicine. The 140mm spoke once, and the vehicle's side armor caved in like a crushed beer can. The crew inside didn't even have time to scream before the overpressure turned their organs to jelly. Blood poured from the vehicle's vision blocks like water from a cracked aquarium, mixing with the afternoon rain that had just started—the daily deluge that turned the streets into rivers and reminded everyone that despite the palaces and towers, Nueva Kalloo was still a jungle world that mankind had only borrowed.

"Second platoon, move up the right side!" An infantry commander barked. "Use the fountain for—"

A government soldier with a jury-rigged mine strapped to his chest sprinted from cover, heading straight for the rebel tank column. One of Cortez's "Loyalty Brigade"—men whose families were held hostage to ensure their dedication. The suicide bomber made it fifteen meters before concentrated fire from three rebels literally tore him apart, but the mine detonated anyway. Shrapnel scythed through an advancing squad of rebels, one man's jaw hanging by a thread of meat as he dropped to his knees, trying to hold his face together with blood-slicked fingers while tropical birds sang incongruously in the smoke-shrouded trees above.

Inside the palace's command bunker, President-General Eduardo Cortez stood perfectly still, a stark contrast to the chaos erupting on his tactical displays. His immaculate white uniform remained pristine despite the dust raining from the ceiling with each impact. While his generals shouted contradictory orders and his bodyguards nervously checked their weapons, Cortez's eyes remained fixed on a small holo-projector in his palm.

The main tactical display told the story of his crumbling regime in real-time. Red markers—rebels—had pushed through the Government Quarter and taken the broadcast stations. His Republican Guard still held a shrinking perimeter around the palace complex, but they'd been forced to abandon the Treasury Building, the Ministry of Defense, and critically, the main ammunition depot on the eastern approach. Without resupply, his elite troops had maybe six hours of sustained combat left.

Worse, the blue markers representing his regular army units remained frozen at their positions twenty kilometers outside the capital. The Second and Fourth Infantry Brigades had acknowledged orders to advance three times but hadn't moved a meter. Their commanders were waiting to see who would win before committing—a Caribbean Federation tradition as old as the Federation itself. The yellow markers showing his armor were the most damning: of forty-three Dunkirk tanks in the capital garrison, thirty-eight now displayed rebel IFF tags. His own tank commanders had driven their vehicles straight into rebel lines at dawn, crews intact, announcing their defection over open channels for everyone to hear.

The display showed a simple banking interface: 50,000,000 credits pending. The status bar pulsed amber—processing, processing, processing.

"Sir, the northern wall has been breached!" Colonel Vasquez, head of palace security, shouted over the din, blood trickling from a gash where shrapnel had caught his forehead. "Republican Guard Third Company is falling back to the inner courtyard—they've lost half their strength!"

On the tactical display, Cortez watched the blue dots representing Third Company retreat in real-time, several winking out as he watched. The rebels were using his own tanks against him now, the irony not lost even in this moment.

"Sir, we've lost contact with the airport garrison!" The communications officer's voice cracked—he was barely eighteen, pressed into service just two weeks ago when his predecessor had mysteriously disappeared, probably defected. "Last report had rebel armor overrunning the main terminal!"

Without the airport, even if he survived this, there was no escape route. The navy base had gone dark an hour ago—either destroyed or declaring neutrality.

"Sir, we need to evacuate now!" General Martinez grabbed Cortez's shoulder, his own uniform torn and dusty from a near miss that had collapsed half the command center's ceiling. "The Guard can hold the underground tunnels for maybe twenty minutes—we can reach the submarine pens!"

"The submarines that left for 'training exercises' yesterday?" Cortez asked mildly, not taking his eyes off the holo-projector. He knew Admiral Santos had taken the entire submarine squadron out to sea to wait out the fighting. Another tradition—the navy always survived regime changes.

Cortez ignored them all after that. His thumb hovered over the projector, refreshing the screen obsessively. Outside, he could hear the distinctive whistle-shriek of rocket teams targeting his last remaining loyal tanks—three Dunkirks manned by his personal bodyguard battalion, the only unit he'd paid well enough to ensure loyalty. The rebels had learned—take out the hardpoints first, then flood the grounds.

The tactical display flickered as another section updated: REPUBLICAN GUARD BARRACKS - LOST. SENATE BUILDING - LOST. CENTRAL BANK - LOST. Each update carved away another piece of his twenty-three-year empire.

An explosion shook the bunker hard enough to knock several men to their knees. Through the reinforced window slits, Cortez watched one of his guard towers buckle from a rocket strike—Tower Four, the lynchpin of the eastern approach. Without it, the rebels could bring armor straight up Liberation Avenue. The automated defense turret atop it—a C-RAM system designed to shred drone swarms—was still firing, spitting tracer rounds at 4,500 rounds per minute. Even as the tower's structure failed and began to collapse, the gun continued its relentless barrage, the AI targeting system locked onto heat signatures until the moment it disappeared into the cloud of gray dust and orange fire.

"Eastern approach is compromised!" Someone screamed. "They're bringing up tanks!"

Not tanks—his tanks, with his ammunition, crewed by men he'd trained. The tactical display showed it clearly: eight Dunkirks in rebel colors advancing in textbook formation, exactly as the Republican Guard manual specified.

The holo-projector chimed softly.

Status: COMPLETE. The amber turned green.

Cortez's lips curled into something that wasn't quite a smile. "Gentlemen," he said calmly, causing the pandemonium to pause momentarily, "I believe our salvation is about to arrive."

The tactical officer frowned at his console, momentarily distracted from cataloging their defeats. "Sir, air traffic control is reading a massive energy signature descending through the thermosphere. It's... it's huge."

Through the smoke and flame of the dying city, something descended through the clouds. The rebel advance faltered as soldiers craned their necks skyward. A Tante-class assault carrier, three hundred meters of scarred battlesteel and composite armor, punched through the smoke layer with surgical precision. The ship was a veteran of the Colonial Wars—its hull classification barely visible beneath layers of ablative patches: CVA-447, originally commissioned by the Terran Defense Force before being decommissioned and sold into the gray market where ships like her found new life with private military contractors. PURGATORY was stenciled across its scarred hull in letters twenty meters tall, the name barely visible through the scorch marks of a hundred atmospheric entries.

The carrier's profile was unmistakable to anyone who'd studied military history—a flattened wedge design optimized for atmospheric operations, with reinforced ventral armor that could withstand ground fire during combat drops. Point defense turrets tracked along its flanks, their barrels following potential threats even as the ship descended. The main drives, four massive Krueger-Tesla engines originally designed for deep space operations, had been retrofitted with atmospheric compensation vents that now screamed in the tropical air, turning moisture into steam that wreathed the ship like a burial shroud.

"What the hell is that?" Reyes whispered, his revolution suddenly feeling very small.

Along the carrier's belly, ten hexagonal drop bays began their opening sequence—massive blast doors retracting in perfect synchronization, each one twenty meters across. The bays glowed orange from the heat of atmospheric entry, and through the shimmer, mechanical shadows stirred. These weren't cargo holds hastily converted for mech operations—these were purpose-built deployment systems, with electromagnetic launch rails and shock-absorption systems designed to deliver forty-ton war machines into combat at terminal velocity.

Through the heat shimmer of its descent thrusters, dark shapes began to drop—humanoid, but wrong. Too big. Too angular. Too predatory.

The first mech launched from Bay One with a magnetic acceleration that would have liquefied an unprotected human. It fell for exactly three seconds before its jump jets ignited—four Nakamura Z9 vectored thrust units, two mounted in the back and one on each leg, originally designed for zero-gravity combat but equally effective for controlled atmospheric descent. The jets fired in sequenced bursts, each adjustment calculated by the mech's combat AI to control the descent while maintaining unpredictable lateral movement—standard anti-air doctrine that made them nearly impossible to track with ground-based weapons.

The forty-foot combat frame hit the ground in the palace courtyard with an impact that registered on seismographs fifty kilometers away. Its legs, reinforced with layered shock absorbers and synthetic muscle fibers that cost more than most military vehicles, compressed and released, dissipating the landing energy through the palace's decorative marble. The mech rose from its landing crouch with the fluid grace of an apex predator awakening, wrapped in overlapping plates of ablative armor that had been scarred and replaced so many times the original factory specifications were more suggestion than fact.

Bays Two and Three discharged simultaneously, their occupants firing jets in opposing spirals that looked choreographed. These were lighter variants—reconnaissance and fire support models that used extended jet burns to land on elevated positions. One touched down on the Ministry of Justice's roof with surprising delicacy, its pilot feathering the thrust so precisely that the building's glass skylights didn't even crack. The other landed on a parking garage, its weight distribution automatically calculated to avoid collapse.

More impacts followed in rapid succession. The mechs spread out in practiced patterns—two-unit fire teams with overlapping fields of coverage, exactly as the manual specified. Bay Six disgorged a heavy assault variant that didn't even bother with grace—it fired its jets just enough to avoid crater-making velocity, then slammed down in the middle of a rebel tank formation, crushing a technical under one foot while its weapons were already spinning up.

The drop pattern wasn't random. Within twenty seconds, Kilkenney Solutions had established a perimeter with interlocking fields of fire, high ground secured, and approach routes covered. The mechs moved with razor-sharp precision, their pilots' neural interfaces weaving thought and action in three-dimensional harmony, reflexes sharpened by countless Fringe operations.

Its head—if you could call the sensor cluster that—swept left and right, targeting data streaming across its pilot's vision. The "face" was a collection of optical sensors, thermal imagers, and targeting lasers arranged in a vaguely skull-like pattern that some pilots decorated with paint jobs to enhance the psychological effect. This one bore tally marks along its jaw—sixty-three kills in neat white lines.

Each bore the same marking on their shoulder pauldrons: a Celtic cross bisected by a combat knife. Below it, stenciled in military precision: KILKENNEY SOLUTIONS - NO REFUNDS, NO SURVIVORS.

The lead mech's weapons came online with a symphony of mechanical violence. Twin 30mm autocannons mounted on articulated shoulder hardpoints spun up with a sound like tearing metal, their six rotating barrels glowing cherry-red within seconds. Each gun was fed by a 1,200-round drum magazine housed in the mech's back—depleted uranium-tipped shells that could punch through a meter of reinforced concrete or the frontal armor of anything the rebels had managed to steal. The first burst caught a rebel technical—a civilian pickup truck with a welded-on anti-aircraft gun—as it tried to retreat down the Boulevard of Liberation. The rounds didn't just destroy the vehicle; they vaporized it, turning metal and flesh into a pink mist that painted the white colonial storefronts behind it.

Missile pods on both shoulders bloomed open like lethal flowers, revealing twelve tubes per pod. The micro-missiles inside weren't dumb fire rockets but semi-intelligent munitions with their own targeting packages—each one capable of identifying and prioritizing threats based on heat signature, movement pattern, and electromagnetic emission. The first salvo of six missiles spiraled outward in different directions, each one finding a different target: a rebel sniper team on the Cathedral of Santa Emanuella Alcabú's bell tower (one of the few structures that survived the morning's bombardment), an ammunition truck trying to hide behind the burned-out remains of a tourist bus, three separate machine gun nests that had been carved into the facade of the National Bank, and a rebel command post set up in what used to be an outdoor café where tourists had sipped imported coffee just yesterday.

A plasma cutter ignited on the mech's left arm with a distinctive crack-hiss, the blade of superheated gas turning the air around it into ozone. The weapon was originally designed for ship salvage—cutting through hull plating in zero gravity—but worked equally well on tanks, buildings, or anything else that needed to stop existing. The blade burned at 3,000 degrees Celsius, hot enough that the rain now starting to fall—Nueva Kalloo's daily afternoon deluge—turned to steam before it could touch the weapon, creating a localized fog around the mech's left side. The plasma cutter's containment field kept the blade at exactly one meter in length, though the pilot could extend it to three meters for special occasions or particularly stubborn fortifications.

The mech's right arm carried something more conventional but no less lethal—a 90mm smoothbore cannon, essentially a tank's main gun redesigned for mechanical hands. The weapon's autoloader could cycle through different ammunition types in seconds: high-explosive for infantry and light vehicles, armor-piercing for tanks, canister shot that turned the weapon into a massive shotgun for close-quarters urban fighting, and white phosphorus rounds that were technically illegal under six different treaties that no one enforced in the Fringe.

Around the plaza, the rebels were trying to respond, but their weapons were woefully inadequate. RPGs designed to kill thirty-year-old tanks just sparked off the mech's reactive armor—hexagonal tiles that exploded outward when hit, neutralizing shaped charges before they could penetrate. A rebel tank—one of the Dunkirks that had defected that morning—tried to traverse its turret toward the mech, but the machine was already moving, jump jets firing in short bursts that sent it sliding laterally across the plaza's wet tiles like a skater on ice, maintaining its facing while completely changing position. The tank's shot carved through empty air where the mech had been a second before.

The government loyalists still holding the palace's western wing started cheering, thinking salvation had arrived. They were about to learn that Kilkenney Solutions had been paid to secure the palace, not necessarily to save everyone in it. Collateral damage was a contract negotiation point, not a moral consideration.

Inside the cockpit, Kenney Jaeger's gloved hands gripped the control sticks with practiced ease. The interior was cramped, functional—pure military efficiency. No wasted space, every surface either a display, a control, or armor plating. His combat helmet's HUD painted targets across his vision in overlapping layers of tactical data, the neural link translating his intentions into mechanical motion with millisecond precision. He could feel the mech's weight distribution, the heat building in the reactor core, the subtle vibration of each footfall through the feedback systems built into his pilot suit.

"All units, this is Kilkenney Actual," his gravelly voice crackled across the tactical net through his helmet's comm system. "Let's show this banana republic what some real GDP can buy. And watch those missile expenditures—I'm not eating another contract loss because you trigger-happy bastards wanted fireworks."

"Copy that, Boss," Deadeye's drawl came through from his overwatch position. "Though technically, it is their new year. Regime change and all."

"Shut up and shoot straight, Deadeye."

"Boss, this is Priest," the deep baritone cut in. "Got what looks like a whole rebel company trying to flank through the cathedral. Want me to educate them on the wages of sin?"

"Light 'em up."

"The Lord giveth and the Lord taketh away," Priest replied, his autocannons already spinning up. "Mostly taketh in this case."

"Killjoy, McKnight, you two still playing grab-ass or you ready to work?" Kenney barked, sliding his mech between two burning tanks.

"Fuck you, Boss," Killjoy laughed over the net. "We're already at the palace gates. These Republic Guard pussies are practically crying with relief."

"Yeah, well, don't let them hug you too tight. We're here for the paycheck, not to make friends."

"Boss, Trollibee here. Got three—make that four rebel tanks trying to push up Market Street. They're using civilians as shields, how do over."

"Not our problem. Contract says secure the palace, not run a humanitarian mission. Splash 'em."

"Roger that. Sorry folks, should've stayed home today."

To emphasize his point, Kenney's mech sprinted full-tilt through what had been downtown's financial district. The lead Dunkirk ahead had so much improvised armor welded on—shopping carts, street signs, chunks of ATM machines—it looked like a military vehicle had looted a scrapyard. Kenney's plasma blade carved through it without breaking stride, the molten edges of the cut glowing as the two halves fell apart, crew still strapped inside.

The lead Dunkirk tank, pride of the rebel armor, swiveled its turret toward the nearest mech. Dunkirks—thirty-year-old surplus that half the third world bought when the major powers upgraded—were reliable, cheap, and plentiful. The kind of tank that kept running on prayers and duct tape, that you could fix with a hammer and some swearing. But if that was the heaviest metal the rebels could field, they might as well have brought golf carts to a demolition derby.

The crew inside had exactly two seconds to realize their mistake before Kenney's plasma blade carved through the turret like a hot knife through butter. The ammunition cooked off instantly, turning the sixty-ton vehicle into a brief, brilliant star.

The rebellion had lasted six months.

Kilkenney Solutions would end it in six minutes.

Killjoy and McKnight, two suppression-variant uprights, had landed directly in the palace courtyard like twin hammers of judgment. Their mechs were modified for close-quarters urban warfare—heavier armor plating around the cockpit and joints, additional reactive panels welded onto the legs, and most importantly, the arm-mounted M134G rotary miniguns that gave them their classification. Each arm carried a six-barrel rotating cannon fed by armored ammunition belts that ran from massive drum magazines mounted on their backs—10,000 rounds per gun, 20,000 rounds total per mech. The weapons were already spinning up before their landing struts fully absorbed the impact, the distinctive whine climbing to a roar.

"McKnight, you take the grand steps, I got the fountain plaza," Killjoy called out, his mech's torso already rotating independently from its legs—a disturbing sight that looked like a body breaking in half.

"Copy. These fuckers picked the wrong day to play revolutionary."

The palace courtyard had been designed by some colonial architect who'd never imagined it would become a killing field. Marble fountains depicting sea nymphs, manicured topiary gardens shaped like exotic birds, a mosaic floor showing Nueva Kalloo's founding—all the backdrop for mechanized slaughter. About two hundred rebels had made it through the outer walls, thinking they'd won when the Republic Guard fell back. They were scattered across the courtyard in small groups, some taking cover behind overturned marble benches, others trying to set up machine guns on the grand staircase leading to the palace's main entrance.

Killjoy's mech raised both arms, and the 7.62mm storms they unleashed weren't aimed—they didn't need to be. Each gun fired at 6,000 rounds per minute, the combined rate of fire creating a literal wall of lead that swept across the courtyard. The rebels caught in the open simply ceased to exist from the waist up, their lower halves standing for a moment before toppling into the decorative pools that were rapidly turning red. The sound was indescribable—not the rat-tat-tat of movie machine guns but a continuous roar like ripping canvas amplified through concert speakers.

McKnight was more methodical. His mech walked forward with deliberate steps, each footfall crushing ornamental flower beds that had been maintained for a century. A squad of rebels tried to retreat toward the palace's eastern wing, probably thinking the marble columns would provide cover. McKnight's left arm tracked them with mechanical precision, the minigun's stream of tracers drawing a perfectly straight line that walked through the columns like they were made of cheese. Marble dust mixed with red mist as bodies were literally cut apart by the sustained fire.

"McNight, got a technical trying to be clever," Killjoy reported, his sensors picking up movement. A rebel truck with a mounted ZPU-4 anti-aircraft gun was trying to use the palace's service entrance, hoping to flank them through the gardens.

"Your sector, your kill," McNight replied.

Killjoy's mech pivoted at the hips, the motion so smooth it looked almost human despite being twelve meters tall. He didn't even stop firing—just swept his right arm across in a continuous arc. The technical's driver had enough time to see the stream of tracers adjusting toward him before the cab disintegrated. The truck flipped, its mounted gun spinning wildly as it cartwheeled through a greenhouse, glass and steel and flesh creating an abstract art piece of destruction.

McKnight's suppression mech simply walked through a rebel platoon that had been trying to organize near the grand staircase. They'd been Republic Guard defectors, still wearing their government uniforms with hastily tied rebel armbands. Professional soldiers who should have known better than to cluster in the open. McKnight's massive feet crushed anyone too slow or too terrified to move, leaving red smears across the marble steps that had hosted presidents and dignitaries. He didn't even bother with precision—he just pivoted at the hips and elbows, hosing down entire grid squares while using his jump jets in short bursts to slide the mech laterally, clearing whole sections of the courtyard like a janitor with a pressure washer.

"Jesus Christ, McKnight, leave something for the cleanup crew to identify," Killjoy laughed over the comm.

"Frack 'em. They wanted to play revolution, they can be revolutionary paste."

A group of rebels with RPGs had made it to the palace's second-floor balcony—smart positioning that would have worked against conventional forces. They fired simultaneously, four rockets streaming toward McKnight's mech. His AI controlled point-defense system activated automatically, small lasers mounted on his shoulders burning three of the four rockets out of the air. The fourth hit his left shoulder, reactive armor detonating outward in a shower of ceramic and metal that did nothing to slow his advance.

"Ow," McKnight said flatly, then raised both arms toward the balcony. The entire facade of that section of the palace simply disappeared in a cloud of dust and tracers. When the firing stopped three seconds later, the balcony no longer existed, and neither did the room behind it, or the room behind that.

"Palace is going to need some renovation," Killjoy observed, stepping over what had been a rebel machine gun position and was now just a crater with some metal fragments.

"Send the repair bills to the rebels," McKnight replied. "Oh wait, they're all dead."

The Republic Guard who'd been holding the palace entrance had either fled into the palace's maze of corridors or been reduced to the same red paste as the rebels—at this range, with this much firepower, it was impossible to tell friend from foe. Government uniforms and rebel armbands meant nothing when 7.62mm rounds were arriving at 6,000 per minute. Some had tried waving white flags, others the government's blue and gold banner, but in the smoke and chaos and continuous roar of the miniguns, such distinctions were academic.

"McKnight, we just smoked some guys in government kit," Killjoy noted, his thermal imaging showing rapidly cooling bodies among what had been a defensive position.

"Not our problem. Contract says secure the palace, not play spot-the-difference. They should've gotten the fuck inside when the shooting started."

Several Republic Guard soldiers had indeed made that calculation, barricading themselves behind the palace's massive bronze doors and praying to whatever gods they believed in that the mechs wouldn't decide to come through. They could hear their former positions being obliterated, marble and meat mixing into an unrecognizable slurry. Whether their comrades outside were fighting, surrendering, or switching sides no longer mattered—anyone in that courtyard was becoming part of the landscape.

"Boss, this is McKnight. Palace courtyard is... clear. Nothing moving on thermals bigger than a rat."

"Copy. What about Republic Guard?"

"What Republic Guard? There's just hamburger out here. Some of it might've been on our side five minutes ago, but fuck if I can tell now."

Through the palace windows, surviving government forces watched in horror as the two mechs systematically worked through the courtyard, their pilots treating the operation with the same emotional investment as pressure-washing a deck. This wasn't warfare with its rules and conventions—it was industrial-scale deletion of anything that moved, had moved, or might move.

Three blocks away, a recon variant touched down on the Banco Nacional's roof with surprising delicacy, its lighter frame and jump jets designed for mobility over armor. The twenty-story building groaned under the mech's weight but held—the pre-war architecture built to withstand hurricanes proving useful for supporting thirty tons of military hardware. The pilot—callsign "Deadeye"—was already acquiring targets through the mech's enhanced optics suite.

Inside his cockpit, Deadeye's neural interface translated his thoughts into mechanical motion. The 90mm rifle—essentially a tank's main gun mated to a precision targeting system and mounted on an articulated arm—swung smoothly as his eyes tracked across the city. The weapon was a Krupp-Boeing M90A3, five meters of tungsten-lined barrel with magnetic assist coils that added an extra 400 meters per second to the round's velocity. At this range, with this elevation advantage, he might as well have been God picking who lived and died.

His first target appeared in the scope—a rebel command vehicle, an armored bus they'd reinforced with welded plate steel, racing down the Avenue of Martyrs. Through the mech's optics, he could see rebels inside bent over maps, probably trying to coordinate the assault on the palace. The targeting computer calculated wind speed, humidity, barrel temperature, even the Coriolis effect from the planet's rotation. A perfect firing solution appeared as a green dot leading the vehicle by exactly 3.7 meters.

Deadeye squeezed the trigger mentally through the neural link. The 90mm spoke with a sound like the world's largest sledgehammer hitting an anvil. The entire mech rocked back slightly, stabilizers in the legs automatically compensating. The shell—a tungsten-core armor-piercing round—left the barrel at 1,800 meters per second, a hypersonic crack splitting the air. The massive brass casing, nearly a meter long and as thick as a man's thigh, ejected from the breach in a cloud of smoke and spinning brass.

The casing fell, tumbling end over end. Twenty stories below, a rebel squad was taking cover behind a delivery truck, planning their next move. The brass shell casing—still glowing orange from the heat of firing—crashed through the truck's thin roof and struck the squad leader in the shoulder, the impact shattering his collarbone and driving him to the pavement. His screams were drowned out by the explosion three blocks away as the shell found its mark.

The command vehicle didn't explode so much as cease. The tungsten penetrator punched through the armor, through the rebels, through the maps and radios and dreams of revolution, and out the other side, continuing another fifty meters before embedding itself in an apartment building. The kinetic energy transfer liquefied everything inside the bus. It rolled another ten meters on momentum alone before tilting over, dark fluids pouring from the entry and exit holes.

"Scratch one command element," Deadeye muttered, already tracking his next target. The autoloader was already at work—mechanical arms selecting the next round from the ready magazine, ramming it home with pneumatic precision. Four seconds from shot to ready.

Target two: an ammunition truck trying to resupply the rebel Dunkirks, weaving through debris on Liberation Boulevard. Deadeye switched to high-explosive. The round was different—shorter, fatter, with a proximity fuse that would detonate on impact rather than penetrate. He tracked the truck's desperate swerving, the targeting computer drawing predictive paths based on its movement pattern.

Fire. Rock back. The shell casing ejected in a shower of sparks, falling toward a crowded market street where rebels and civilians were mixed together. A woman looked up just in time to see the brass cylinder spinning toward her. She tried to run but the casing—forty pounds of brass still hot enough to brand flesh—struck her in the back, driving her face-first into the pavement. Around her, others scrambled away from where they thought the next one might land, not understanding that to Deadeye, they were just ants scurrying around his firing position.

The ammunition truck became a fireball that took out half a city block. Secondary explosions rippled outward as crates of missiles and tank rounds cooked off, turning the entire intersection into a pillar of fire that rose two hundred meters into the air. Windows shattered for six blocks in every direction.

"Beautiful," Deadeye whispered, watching the thermal bloom through his sensors.

A captured government anti-air vehicle—a tracked platform with quad 30mm cannons—was trying to elevate its barrels to engage the mechs. The crew had gotten the weapons nearly vertical, probably thinking they had a chance. Deadeye's targeting reticle settled on the vehicle's ammunition feed system, the most vulnerable point. He could have killed them quicker with a center-mass shot, but where was the artistry in that?

The rifle cracked again. Another casing fell, this one landing in a fountain where rebels were trying to fill water bottles. The brass shell sent a geyser of water and blood skyward as it crushed someone's foot, the steam from the hot metal mixing with screams.

The anti-air vehicle's ammunition feed detonated, but the crew compartment remained intact for exactly two seconds—long enough for them to realize what had happened—before the stored ammunition below cooked off. The turret launched straight up like a rocket, spinning wildly, before crashing back down through the roof of a convenience store.

"Deadeye, this is Boss," Kenney's voice crackled through. "Stop playing with your food and clear those approach routes."

"Copy, Boss. Though I'd like to point out that I'm creating art here."

"Create it faster."

Deadeye cycled through targets with mechanical efficiency. A rebel tank hiding behind a parking garage—armor-piercing round through three floors of concrete and into its engine block. Shell casing crashed through a bus stop where rebels were treating wounded. A machine gun nest on a hotel balcony—high-explosive that removed the entire floor. That casing landed in a swimming pool, the water instantly boiling around it. A fuel depot the rebels were using as a rally point—incendiary round that turned two city blocks into an inferno.

Each shot, another massive casing falling like bronze rain onto the streets below, crushing, burning, terrorizing. The rebels had stopped looking up at the mech and started watching the sky for the next falling shell, diving for cover every time they heard the distinctive crack of the 90mm.

"Hey boss," Deadeye's voice crackled over the secure channel, his Confederate drawl somehow relaxed despite the chaos. Inside his cockpit, his hands danced across the control surfaces—left hand adjusting optical zoom on a secondary monitor while his right finger hovered over the trigger. His neural interface highlighted potential targets in order of threat assessment, but his eyes had locked onto something else entirely. Through the smoke of burning buildings, his enhanced optics had picked up the distinctive copper gleam of brewery tanks. "You know that clause you love so much?"

"The one about 'tactical acquisition of opportunity assets and denial of enemy resources'?" Kenney replied, bisecting another tank without breaking stride. His plasma blade carved through the Dunkirk's turret in one smooth motion while his left hand flicked through ammunition selections on his console—switching from armor-piercing to high-explosive for the infantry scattering behind the wreck. His eyes never left his primary display, where thermal imaging showed him the rebels' panicked heat signatures fleeing like ants from a magnifying glass.

"That's the one." Deadeye's fingers pulled up a tactical overlay on his tertiary screen, cross-referencing satellite imagery with real-time visual data. He tagged the brewery with a gold icon—potential asset—while simultaneously lining up a shot on a rebel technical that didn't know it was already dead. "I'm looking at the Kalloo Brewery—three Michelin stars, mostly craft beers but their top shelf whiskey collection is supposedly worth more than some countries.

Minimal rebel presence, probably because they're too stupid to know what they're sitting on."

"And?" Kenney's voice came through slightly strained as he pivoted his mech's torso 180 degrees to catch a rebel RPG team trying to flank him. His thumbs depressed both autocannon triggers simultaneously, turning the team into mist, while his peripheral vision caught movement on his radar display—friendlies inbound from the north.

"And about two blocks south, I've got eyes on the National Reserve Bank." Deadeye was now juggling three different screens—his main targeting display, a street-level tactical map, and a live feed from a commandeered traffic camera he'd hacked into. His cybernetic eye implant, connected to the mech's systems, let him process all three simultaneously. "The rebels are loading trucks with what the net says is about forty percent of the country's gold reserves. They're moving fast but sloppy—I count maybe two squads on security."

Kenney's mech paused mid-step, his hands freezing on the controls. On his tactical display, he pulled up the same data Deadeye was seeing, his neural interface calculating the value—rough estimate, forty-three million credits worth of gold, plus whatever else was in the vaults. His left hand unconsciously reached for the water tube in his helmet, taking a quick sip while his brain ran the numbers. "Deadeye, that sounds like critical enemy resources that need immediate denial."

"My thoughts exactly, Boss Actual. Want me to put a round through their lead truck? Might slow down their withdrawal." Deadeye's targeting reticle was already settling on the vehicle's engine block, his finger caressing the trigger. The firing solution was perfect—wind calm, clear line of sight, the truck stopped while they loaded. His other hand was already selecting the next target, pre-planning the engagement sequence.

"Negative. Mark both locations." Kenney's fingers flew across his command console, tagging both sites on the company tactical net so all units could see them. His other hand was plotting approach routes, calculating time-to-target. He switched channels with a thought through his neural link. "Joker, you monitoring this?"

"Boss Actual, this is Joker," her voice crackled through, the sound of turbulence and engine noise in the background, her Neo-Slavic accent thicker than usual from the concentration required to pilot through the thermals. "Dust-off is inbound, three minutes out. I have forty combat engineers in cargo bay, and they are very eager to do some 'battlefield recovery operations,' da?"

Through the Dust-off's cockpit canopy, she could see the city burning below, smoke columns rising like pillars to heaven. Her hands were steady on the dropship's controls despite the thermals trying to throw the hundred-ton cargo hauler around—she'd flown worse approaches through the asteroid fields of Volgograd Prime.

"Joker, you beautiful salvage queen," Kenney replied, unable to keep the appreciation out of his voice. "Perfect timing. Deadeye's marked a brewery six blocks north of the palace. Kalloo Brewery. Intel says it's got a whiskey collection worth more than this entire operation. I want you to take your engineers and strip it clean—every bottle, every cask, hell, take the copper stills if you can fit them in the hold."

"Spasibo for the compliment, Boss," Joker laughed, already adjusting her approach vector, the massive dropship banking left despite its ungainly profile. "My boys brought hand trucks and cargo nets. We will have that place stripped faster than Siberian winter strips trees, da? Maybe thirty seconds on ground, forty if we are being gentle with bottles."

Her co-pilot, Vex, was already pulling up the brewery's schematics on his display while she fought the controls through another thermal updraft.

"The cargo manifest will read 'recovered cultural materials vital to regional stability,'" Joker continued, her accent making 'vital' sound like 'wital.' "Is good paperwork, Boss. You learn well from your salvage queen."

"That's why you're the best, Joker. But anyone who drinks on the job pays triple market value."

"Boss, you wound me!" She switched to rapid-fire Neo-Slavic over her shoulder to the engineer crew chief, then back to English. "My boys are professionals. They would never... okay, maybe little bit for quality control, da? Is important to verify what we are recovering."

"Priest, I need you to provide security for Joker's loading operation," Kenney continued, switching channels smoothly.

"Copy that, Boss Actual," Priest's baritone rumbled through. His assault mech was currently turning a rebel-held apartment complex into rubble, methodical and thorough. "The Lord provides, and we facilitate redistribution. ETA to the brewery is ninety seconds."

Scott Blake's voice cut into the channel from the Purgatory's CIC, his tone dry as week-old toast. "Joker, Blake here. Make sure the cargo manifest reads 'recovered cultural materials vital to regional stability.' For the paperwork."

"Ah, Mister Blake!" Joker responded cheerfully. "Always thinking about the bureaucracy. Is good—I was going to write 'borrowed alcohol for company morale' but yours sounds more official, da?"

"That's why I handle the paperwork and you handle the flying," Blake replied, spitting tobacco juice into his console-side spittoon with an audible ping. "Keep the receipts straight and I keep us out of customs jail."

"Copy that, financial wizard. Your salvage queen will make you proud."

Joker laughed, pushing the Dust-off's engines harder. The dropship—originally designed for heavy equipment recovery—had cargo clamps that could secure anything from damaged mechs to, say, several tons of premium alcohol. "Though if this stuff's as good as Deadeye says, might have some spillage. Quality control, you understand."

"Anyone who drinks on the job pays triple market value," Kenney warned. "That includes your engineers."

"You wound me, Boss Actual. My boys are professionals. They'd never sample the merchandise." In the cargo bay behind her, she could hear the engineers already taking bets on who could load the most cases. "Thirty-second ground time once we touch down. I want us loaded and airborne before anyone notices the brewery's been converted to our private reserve."

A captured government anti-air vehicle that might have actually threatened the mechs lasted roughly four seconds after Deadeye noticed it, then shifted his attention back to marking targets of opportunity—both military and liquid.

The corporate military contractors who'd trained them would've called it "mission deviation." Kilkenney Solutions called it "diversified revenue streams."

"Streaks, Racer, report," Kenney barked over comms, his left hand dancing across the weapons panel while his right maintained a death grip on the primary control stick. Sweat ran down his back despite the climate control, the neural feedback from his mech making him feel every impact, every near miss.

"Yo, sports complex is totally dead, boss-man," Streaks replied, his breathing heavy through the comm. Inside his cockpit, warning lights flickered amber—minor armor damage from an RPG that got too close. He was tracking six different targets on his display while his mech's stealth systems kept him invisible to rebel thermals. His fingers worked the control sticks in micro-movements, each twitch translating to tons of mechanical force. "Gnarly plot twist, dude—this was like, their backup command post or whatever. Me and Racer are just cruisin' through the leftovers, no biggie."

"Cleanup and collection," Racer added with a laugh that couldn't quite hide his exhaustion. His cockpit was a symphony of data—facial recognition software running on his left screen, tactical overlay on the right, and in the center, his targeting reticle jumping from body to body as his mech's sensors catalogued the dead. "Well I'll be hornswoggled—my AI's havin' itself a regular hootenanny with this facial recognition, y'all. We done bagged ourselves three colonels, a general, and—hot damn and yeehaw, that there's Miguel 'The Butcher' Reyes. That ol' boy had himself a half-million credit bounty from that massacre down in New Honduras, sure as shootin'."

"File them all. Dead or alive pays the same, and dead's easier to transport." Kenney's voice came through strained as he simultaneously engaged three targets—his left hand triggering the autocannons while his right swung the plasma blade through a concrete barrier where rebels were taking cover. The neural interface let him feel the resistance of the concrete, the way it parted before the superheated blade like butter.

Meanwhile, Kenney was turning the main freeway into a shooting gallery. Inside his cockpit, the temperature had risen five degrees despite the cooling systems working overtime. His displays showed him the world in overlapping layers—thermal imaging painted rebels as white-hot signatures against the cooler concrete, motion tracking highlighted anything that moved, and threat assessment tagged every weapon system in order of danger. His hands moved constantly—left hand switching between weapon systems, adjusting shield strength, managing heat buildup; right hand on the main control stick, every movement translating through the neural link into the mech's actions.

Rebel armor trying to retreat or reposition found themselves facing a forty-foot nightmare sprinting at sixty kilometers per hour. Kenney's legs were locked into the control pedals, his thigh muscles burning from maintaining the precise pressure needed for the high-speed maneuvers. Each footfall sent feedback through the neural link—he could feel the road surface, feel when his foot crushed a car versus bare pavement, feel the slight give when he stepped on something organic.

He caught movement in his peripheral—not on the screens but through the neural link's enhanced awareness, that sixth sense that kept pilots alive. An anti-tank team with an ATGM launcher positioned behind an overturned bus. His hands moved without conscious thought, left hand slamming the shield generator to maximum while his right tried to torque the mech sideways.

The missile streaked toward him, too fast to dodge at this range. Through his helmet's display, he could see the warhead's approach in slow motion—the neural interface speeding up his perception even though his mech couldn't move any faster. His kinetic shield flared to life, electromagnetic fields catching the shaped charge mere meters from his cockpit. The warhead detonated against the barrier in a bloom of copper and fire that would have cored him straight through. The impact feedback through the neural link felt like being punched in the chest, his body interpreting the shield drain as physical pain.

Close. Too close. That's what you get for showboating, Kenney. Should've just let it hit. It's what you deserve after—

He crushed the thought like he crushed the anti-tank team beneath his mech's foot a second later. Through the neural link, he felt them die—the brief resistance before bones and organs gave way, transmitted through thousands of pressure sensors in the mech's foot. His cockpit speakers picked up their screams for exactly 0.3 seconds before they were lost in the sound of grinding metal and concrete.

"Boss, you alright?" Deadeye's voice cut through. "I saw that shield flare from here."

"Fine," Kenney grunted, his displays showing shield power at thirty percent and climbing. His left hand was already redistributing power from secondary systems, pulling energy from the jump jets to accelerate shield regeneration. "Just rebels learning that shoulder-fired weapons are last year's tech."

He pivoted the mech—a motion that required both hands on the controls and his core muscles tight to handle the G-forces—and opened up with both autocannons on a building where muzzle flashes indicated a rebel strongpoint. Inside his helmet, targeting solutions appeared as fast as he could think about them, the neural interface translating intention into action faster than his hands alone ever could. Each trigger pull was deliberate but rapid, his fingers dancing between full auto and controlled bursts to manage heat buildup and ammunition consumption.

"Boss, this is Streaks. Stadium's clear, but I'm looking at something interesting on thermal. Looks like a bunker entrance, probably where the rebel commanders were trying to retreat to."

Kenney checked his ammunition counters—autocannon rounds at sixty percent, missiles at forty, plasma cutter fuel at seventy. His water tube delivered another shot of lukewarm water as he considered. "Can you crack it?"

"Already on it," Streaks replied. In his cockpit, his fingers flew across the demolition controls, selecting breaching charges from his mech's loadout. "Give me thirty seconds."

"Sir, spaceport secured," Trollibee's gruff voice came through the comms, accompanied by the sound of autocannon fire. Inside his cockpit, sweat dripped onto his controls despite the cooling system running full blast. His hands worked three different weapon systems simultaneously—autocannons providing suppressing fire, missiles locked onto fleeing vehicles, and his point defense lasers swatting down the occasional RPG. "Purgatory's touching down now. The rebels had a battalion of anti-air and a whole wing of strike fighters on the tarmac."

"Had?" Kenney asked, already knowing the answer. Through his displays, he could see Trollibee's tactical feed—the spaceport looked like someone had taken a giant hammer to a model airplane collection.

"Big Country turned them into modern art," Trollibee chuckled, his massive assault mech stepping over what used to be a F-95 Headhunter strike fighter. The aircraft had been caught on the ground during pre-flight checks—twenty meters of swept-wing interceptor reduced to burning scrap by a single plasma blade stroke through its centerline. "Lots of pretty explosions. The AA crews tried to pivot their guns down to hit us. Didn't work out for them."

The strike fighters had been the rebels' pride—twelve atmospheric superiority craft they'd captured from the government air base two weeks ago. Sleek, twin-engine machines designed to dominate the skies with their 30mm rotary cannons and heat-seeking missiles. They'd been lined up on the tarmac in perfect formation, pilots running for their cockpits when the mechs arrived.

Big Country had walked down the flight line methodically, his mech's plasma blade carving through each aircraft like a chef preparing sushi. Fuel tanks ruptured, ammunition cooked off, and twelve pilots' dreams of air support died in under a minute. One fighter had actually managed to start its engines—the pilot desperately trying to taxi toward the runway. Big Country had grabbed its tail section with his mech's free hand, lifted the twenty-ton aircraft like a toy, and slammed it nose-first into the tarmac hard enough to compress the cockpit into a space the size of a briefcase.

The anti-air battalion had fared no better. Three batteries of modern SAM systems—vertical launch tubes capable of engaging targets in orbit—and six radar-guided autocannon platforms designed to create an impenetrable dome of fire against aerial assault. The crews had tried to depress their weapons to engage the mechs, but the systems weren't designed to shoot at ground targets. Trollibee had walked through their desperately lowered fire, 30mm rounds sparking harmlessly off his armor, before systematically crushing each platform under his mech's feet.

"Purgatory Control, this is Trollibee," he said, switching to the landing coordination channel while his right hand continued to fire bursts at fleeing rebels. "Landing zone is clear. Marking approach vectors now."

His left hand danced across the navigation panel, his mech's laser designators painting four corner points of a safe landing zone—a section of reinforced tarmac originally designed for heavy cargo shuttles. The data streamed directly to Purgatory's navigation computer, creating a virtual landing box in the pilot's display.

"Big Country, give them some smoke," Trollibee ordered.

"Copy." Big Country's mech pulled smoke grenades from his hip dispensers, tossing them in a practiced pattern around the landing zone. Purple smoke—the universal signal for 'safe to land'—billowed up in four columns, visible even through the battle haze.

The Purgatory descended through the smoke, its scarred hull catching the morning light. Inside the carrier's bridge, the pilot—a former Navy deserter named Conway—fought the controls as thermal updrafts from the burning city tried to throw his approach off. His co-pilot called out altitude and drift readings while his hands made constant micro-adjustments to the four main engines.

"One hundred meters, two meters drift starboard," the co-pilot announced.

"Correcting." Conway's fingers danced across the thrust controls, each engine responding independently. The Purgatory wasn't designed for delicate maneuvers—it was like trying to parallel park a building—but he'd done this a hundred times before.

On the ground, Trollibee and Big Country's mechs stood as living landing beacons, their arms raised to guide the ship down. The backwash from Purgatory's engines turned the tarmac into a furnace, paint peeling off nearby hangar buildings, abandoned ground vehicles flipping end over end.

"Fifty meters, one meter drift port."

"I see it." Conway could feel the ship responding slowly, three hundred meters of metal and armor fighting gravity and inertia.

The landing struts deployed with a hydraulic whine audible even over the engines. Each strut was ten meters thick, designed to support the carrier's full combat weight plus a complete mech complement. They touched down one by one—rear starboard, rear port, forward starboard, and finally forward port—each impact sending vibrations through the entire spaceport.

"Touchdown confirmed," Conway announced. "Purgatory has landed."

"Big Country, damage assessment," Kenney ordered over the tactical net.

Inside his cockpit, Big Country was already running through his post-combat checklist while his mech's sensors swept the Purgatory's hull. His displays showed thermal imaging, structural analysis, and electromagnetic scanning all running simultaneously. "Minimal, boss. Few scorch marks on Purgatory's belly from small arms." He zoomed in on one section where rifle rounds had left tiny star-shaped impacts on the armor, none deeper than a few millimeters. "The rebels really thought infantry rifles would hurt a starship. It was almost cute."

"Like kittens attacking a tank," Trollibee added, his mech's foot casually crushing an abandoned anti-air radar truck as he moved to establish a perimeter. "Though I've got to give them credit for trying. Takes balls to shoot at a starship with a rifle."

"Takes stupidity," Big Country corrected. "There's brave and then there's brain-dead."

The Purgatory's cargo ramps were already lowering, ground crews in exo-suits running out to establish refueling lines and ammunition conveyors. The ship might have landed, but the battle was far from over—this was just a pit stop before the next round of killing.

Kenney's vision blurred for a moment. Kira's face flashed before him—not how she looked at the end, broken and bloody in the wreckage, but from their last morning together. Coffee on the balcony. Her laugh when he'd made a stupid joke about—

It's my fault. Should've been there. Should've protected her. It's my fault it's my—

Movement. His combat instincts kicked in a fraction of a second before his conscious mind registered the threat—that primal awareness honed through dozens of battlefields where hesitation meant death. Through the neural link, he felt it as a tingling at the base of his skull, his mech's proximity sensors detecting the threat before his eyes could process it.

His head snapped left, hands already moving. Through his helmet's display, threat indicators bloomed red. A rebel infantry squad—eight men in sweat-soaked fatigues—wheeling an ancient Rheinmetall K-90 into position. The massive kinetic cannon was a relic from the early mech wars, its electromagnetic rails designed to accelerate tungsten penetrators to hypersonic speeds. The rebels had welded crude tracks from a construction vehicle onto its base, turning the emplaced weapon into a mobile anti-mech gun. At this range, that old beast's 90mm kinetic penetrators could punch through his armor like tissue—the tungsten sabot would enter through his cockpit and exit through his reactor, turning him into superheated vapor along the way.

Kenney's left hand slammed the weapons selector while his right torqued the mech's torso fifteen degrees—just enough to bring the shoulder pod to bear. His thumb found the launch authorization, a red safety cover that flipped up with practiced ease. The targeting reticle in his display went from yellow to green as the missile achieved lock. The rebels were cranking the K-90's elevation servos frantically, the twin rails dropping degree by degree toward his center mass. Through his magnified optics, he could see the loader already sliding a tungsten penetrator into the breach, the gunner's hands flying over the firing solution computer.

They needed three more seconds. They had one.

His thumb pressed down. Inside the shoulder pod, explosive bolts fired, releasing the missile from its housing. The rocket motor ignited a millisecond later, accelerating the missile from zero to Mach 2 in the span of a heartbeat. Kenney felt the launch through the neural link—a brief sensation like someone punching his shoulder.

The missile covered the two hundred meters in 0.3 seconds. Its warhead—a shaped charge designed to crack bunkers—detonated on impact. The K-90 and its crew didn't disappear so much as transform. The electromagnetic rails bent backwards like twisted DNA before separating into spinning fragments. The capacitor bank—a solid block of superconducting material—erupted in a secondary explosion of electrical discharge. The crew ceased to exist as discrete organisms, becoming instead a red mist mixed with metal fragments that spread across the intersection.

The shockwave shattered windows for three city blocks. Pieces of the K-90—a track wheel here, part of the rail housing there—rained down on buildings hundreds of meters away. One rebel's helmet, somehow intact, landed in a fountain six blocks north, the head still inside it.

Fuck. Should've let them take the shot. Would've been quick at least.

The thought came unbidden, that familiar self-destructive whisper. His hands hesitated on the controls for a fraction of a second—enough time for his mech to stride past where the gun emplacement had been, his foot crushing what might have been part of the loading mechanism into the asphalt.

"Pilot Jaeger," the mech's AI, designated Foxtrot, chirped in through his helmet speakers. Its voice carried a refined British accent, like a butler who'd seen too much combat. "I'm detecting elevated stress markers, sir. Heart rate irregular—currently at 142 BPM with arrhythmic patterns. Cortisol levels elevated thirty percent above baseline. Might I suggest a mild combat sedative? Five milligrams of Zalphene would take the edge off, as it were."

"Shut up, Fox." His left hand reflexively went to the medical override panel, ensuring the AI couldn't start pumping drugs into his system without permission.

"Very well, sir. Marking your declination in the combat log. Though I feel obliged to mention this is the fourteenth consecutive mission where you've refused recommended pharmaceutical assistance. Rather stubborn of you, if I may say so."

"I said shut up."

"Of course, Pilot Jaeger. Returning to combat advisory mode only. Though you really should consider talking to someone about these death wishes of yours. Frightfully unhealthy."

His displays showed more threats vectoring in—a technical with a mounted gun trying to flank from the east, probable RPG team on a roof to the north. His hands went back to the controls, pushing aside the death wish that whispered in his ear. The autocannons spun up with a whine, tracking toward the technical. He pulled the trigger, feeling the vibration through his entire body as 30mm rounds turned the vehicle into confetti.

But part of him wondered what it would have felt like—that 90mm penetrator punching through his cockpit. Would he even have time to register it, or would he just cease, like those rebels with the K-90? Quick. Clean. No more waking up reaching for Kira's side of the bed. No more seeing her face in smoke patterns or hearing her laugh in distant explosions. Just... nothing. Finally with her again, wherever she was now. Better than the slow burn of guilt that never stopped eating at him.

"Killjoy, McKnight, report," Kenney barked into the comm, pushing the ghosts back down. His hands worked the controls automatically, muscle memory taking over—left hand cycling through damage reports on secondary displays while his right guided the mech through the rubble-strewn streets. The neural feedback showed minor armor degradation across his torso, nothing critical but enough to make his ribs ache in sympathy.

"Presidential complex is secure, boss," McKnight's steady voice came through, though Kenney could hear the exhaustion beneath the professional tone. Through the tactical feed, Kenney watched McKnight's mech methodically clearing the palace's eastern wing. The pilot was using his jump jets in micro-bursts, hopping from courtyard to courtyard while his arm-mounted miniguns swept each area. "Republic Guard actually rallied once they saw us turning the tide. They're mopping up stragglers, trying to look useful for whoever signs their paychecks next week."

On McKnight's display, the palace looked like a giant had taken bites out of it. The eastern facade was gone, replaced by a skeletal framework of rebar and concrete. His mech stepped through what had been the ceremonial entrance, the massive doors now just twisted metal. A squad of Republic Guard soldiers were dragging rebel bodies into piles, their movements efficient but hollow-eyed—men who'd seen their certain death transformed into unlikely survival.

"Killjoy, you intact?"

"Mostly," Killjoy grunted, his transmission crackling with static. Inside his cockpit, red warning lights painted his face in hellish tones—hydraulic pressure dropping in the left leg, actuator response down to sixty percent. His hands fought the controls as the damaged leg tried to drag him off-balance with each step. "Rocket team got clever, moved through three floors of an office building before popping out. Took an RPG to the left knee actuator."

The rebels had set up a textbook ambush. While Killjoy had been focused on clearing the palace's main plaza, a team had infiltrated the Cortez Insurance Building overlooking his position. They'd moved through the cubicle maze, setting up on the third floor with perfect sight lines. The first RPG had caught him mid-stride, the shaped charge detonating against his left knee joint. His reactive armor had absorbed most of the blast, but enough kinetic energy had transferred through to damage the primary actuator.

"Can you make it to Purgatory?"

"Yeah, just don't ask me to dance." Killjoy's mech limped forward, each step sending error messages cascading across his displays. He'd already rerouted power from secondary systems, his mech's computer automatically compensating for the damaged leg by adjusting weight distribution. "Rebels are in full retreat, boss. They're abandoning vehicles and weapons, just trying to get out of the city. Saw a whole platoon throw down their rifles and start swimming across the harbor."

Through Killjoy's optics, Kenney could see the exodus—hundreds of rebels streaming away from the palace district. They'd thrown away anything that marked them as combatants: rifles, ammunition belts, even boots in some cases. The harbor was full of desperately swimming figures, men who'd decided drowning was preferable to facing the mechs. Some were trying to reach the fishing boats moored in the deep water, others just swimming with no clear destination, driven by pure panic.

McKnight's mech moved to the palace's northern wall, where the fighting had been fiercest. His pilot's hands worked the controls with mechanical precision despite the fatigue—seventeen minutes of continuous combat had left his arms burning, sweat stinging his eyes inside the helmet. "Boss, I'm looking at about forty rebels trying to surrender to the Republic Guard near the treasury building. Want me to discourage that?"

"Negative. Let the government sort them out. Not our problem unless they pick up weapons again."

McKnight's targeting systems tracked the surrendering rebels anyway, infrared signatures catalogued and filed. His finger hovered near the trigger—muscle memory from too many false surrenders on other worlds—but he held fire. Through his mech's audio pickups, he could hear the Republic Guard screaming at the rebels to lie face down, the sounds of rifle butts meeting flesh, the beginning of score-settling that would probably last weeks.

"Contract specified defense of the palace and government infrastructure, not pursuit operations. That costs extra." Kenney's mech reached the palace's main gates, or what was left of them. The ornate ironwork had been reduced to twisted metal sculptures, modern art born from violence. His displays showed green lights across the board—objective secured, payment authorized, extraction available.

Killjoy's damaged mech finally cleared the last checkpoint, his miniguns still tracking despite the limp. "Boss, we leaving any stay-behind units? Cortez might want insurance."

"That's what his Republic Guard is for. We did the heavy lifting, they can handle the mop-up." Kenney's hands were already pulling up fuel consumption rates, ammunition expenditure, damage assessments—the tedious mathematics of mercenary work. "All units, begin convergence on Purgatory. Maintain combat readiness until we're aboard."

Through the smoke and devastation, the mechs began their withdrawal. Ten machines that had changed a nation's fate in minutes, leaving behind a palace that looked like it had been attacked by angry gods. The Republic Guard watched them go with a mixture of relief and fear—grateful for the salvation, terrified of the saviors.

"Foxtrot," Kenney said quietly to his AI, "compile combat footage for the after-action report. Cortez will want proof of service."

"Already done, sir," the British accent replied smoothly. "Though I've edited out your more colorful commentary about his parentage during the firefight. Wouldn't do to insult the client."

"Good thinking."

His thermal sensors lit up like a Christmas display—white-hot human signatures packed into the Meridian Commercial Tower, an entire rebel company that had taken defensive positions in the glass-fronted office building. Through his enhanced optics, Kenney could see them clearly: rebels setting up machine gun nests behind overturned desks, RPG teams positioning themselves at corner offices for overlapping fields of fire, snipers taking position near the windows. The twenty-story building—once home to insurance companies and legal firms—had become a vertical fortress. They were probably planning to ambush government forces during the inevitable counterattack, catch them in a crossfire from above.

Kenney's left hand moved to the weapons panel, fingers dancing across the selection matrix. The flamethrower system required a three-step activation—safety release, pressure buildup, ignition sequence. His neural interface showed him the fuel levels: eight hundred liters of promethium gel, enough for forty seconds of continuous spray or several shorter bursts. The nozzle extended from beneath his mech's left forearm armor plating with a hydraulic hiss, the pilot light igniting with a blue flutter before settling to orange.

"Foxtrot, tag that building as hostile," he muttered, his right hand adjusting his position for optimal spray pattern.

"Marking Meridian Tower as legitimate target, sir," the AI responded in its crisp British accent. "Though I should mention there's likely to be civilian presence in a commercial building."

"Not anymore there isn't."

His finger squeezed the trigger. The promethium gel ignited with a soft whump, then roared into a forty-meter stream of liquid fire that punched through the windows like a dragon's breath. The gel was designed to stick and spread—each droplet that hit a surface would continue burning at 1,200 degrees Celsius for minutes. It flowed like water but burned like napalm, pooling in corners, running down walls, spreading across ceilings.

The fourth floor took the brunt of it. What had been a law firm's open-plan office became an inferno in seconds. The rebels' screams started immediately—high, desperate, animal sounds as they tried to escape the inferno. Through his audio pickups, Kenney could hear them clearly for a moment: prayers in Spanish, someone crying for their mother, the crash of furniture as they tried to reach the stairwells.

"Audio dampening recommended," Foxtrot announced. "Activating tactical filter."

The screams faded to a distant static, but Kenney could still see them through his thermal imaging—white-hot figures now surrounded by the even hotter flames, running, falling, some trying to beat the gel off their bodies which only spread it to their hands. The building's sprinkler system activated, but water only made promethium gel burn hotter, turning the droplets into a superheated steam that cooked anyone who breathed it.

Through the smoke and flame, Kenney could see burning figures throwing themselves from windows, choosing the four-story fall over the fire. They tumbled through the air like burning matchsticks, some still alive enough to flail as they fell. One hit a parked car roof with a sound his audio dampeners couldn't quite filter out. Another landed in the decorative fountain in front of the building, the water doing nothing to stop the promethium that continued burning underwater.

"Alright, I think I'm done here," Kenney muttered, more to himself than the comm. His left hand was already retracting the flamethrower nozzle while his right guided the mech away from the building, which was now fully involved—flames spreading up through the broken windows, the glass facade starting to crack and fall in sheets.

"Routing to the bank." His neural interface pulled up the navigation overlay, plotting a path through the downtown financial district. The fastest route would take him down Liberation Avenue, then cut through the Plaza de Armas. His mech's massive feet crushed abandoned cars flat as he walked, each step precise despite the machine's size.

He piloted the mech through war-torn streets at a steady pace, past the ruins of what had been Nueva Kalloo's morning. The Café Domingo where government officials had taken their breakfast—now a crater with espresso machines scattered like shrapnel. The Cathedral of St. Emanuella Alcabú, its bell tower collapsed across the street, bronze bells the size of cars blocking traffic. A kindergarten with its playground on fire, the plastic slides melting into psychedelic pools.

Foxtrot highlighted targets with mechanical precision—threat assessment running constantly. A technical with a mounted gun trying to flee down a side street: Kenney's left hand selected armor-piercing rounds while his right swiveled the torso thirty degrees. The 30mm autocannon spoke in a three-round burst, each shell the size of a beer bottle. The technical's engine block exploded, the vehicle cartwheeling twice before coming to rest upside down, its gunner's upper half no longer connected to his lower.

An anti-tank team setting up in a second-story window, thinking elevation would give them an advantage. Kenney didn't even slow down—his right arm cannon traversed independently from his walking motion, the neural link allowing him to target while moving. A single 90mm high-explosive shell deleted the entire room, along with the apartment next door and the one above. Furniture, rebels, and parts of the building's facade rained down onto the street.

Movement in a storefront—his thermal sensors showing three signatures, weapons hot. His left hand triggered a burst from the autocannons without conscious thought, muscle memory and neural feedback working faster than active decision-making. The storefront exploded outward, whatever the rebels had been planning dying with them.

He moved like a force of nature through the urban devastation, inevitable and impersonal. His cockpit displays showed him the world in overlapping layers of information—thermal signatures, electromagnetic emissions, acoustic anomalies, motion prediction algorithms. His hands worked the controls with the same emotional investment as a pianist playing scales, dealing death with mechanical precision.

"Sir," Foxtrot interjected, "we're approaching the National Bank. I'm detecting multiple vehicles and approximately twenty-three thermal signatures engaged in loading operations."

"Copy," Kenney replied, his hands already adjusting weapons selections. "Time to make a withdrawal."

Kenney's eyes flicked to his ammo counters. Twenty minutes of combat and most of his indicators were bleeding from green to amber to red. The 30mm was down to thirty percent—maybe six hundred rounds left across both guns. Missiles at four remaining. Even the flamethrower's promethium reserves were running low after torching that office building, the gauge showing barely two hundred liters.

"Dust-off Two, get wheels up and start rearm runs," he commanded over the tactical net.

Inside Purgatory's hangar bay three, organized chaos erupted. The ground crew swarmed around Dust-off Two, the modified Hercules-class transport sitting on the deck like a pregnant beetle. Exo-suited loaders manhandled ammunition pallets—each 30mm drum magazine weighing eight hundred kilograms fully loaded. The crew moved with practiced efficiency, but resupply was never fast enough when mechs were burning through ammunition.

In Dust-off Two's cockpit, Hammer was already running through his pre-flight checklist, his co-pilot Jenkins calling out system statuses. The dropship's interior was cramped—every surface covered in switches, displays, warning labels in six languages. Hammer's hands danced across the controls with the confidence of someone who'd flown combat drops for fifteen years across three different wars.

"Boss, we're still loading," Hammer's voice came through, all business. His Confederate drawl only came out when he was relaxed—under pressure, he sounded like a flight manual come to life. "Ground crew's moving as fast as they can, but we need five more minutes. These missile pallets are being temperamental—one of the loading frames jammed."

Through the cockpit's armored windscreen, Hammer could see the crew struggling with a missile pallet. Someone with a crowbar was trying to free a stuck locking mechanism while others held the heavy ordnance steady. Each missile needed individual inspection—one defective round detonating in the bay would turn the dropship into confetti.

"Copy. And Hammer? Load some extra promethium canisters. The fire seems to be working well for crowd control."

"Jesus, boss. Yeah, I got you covered." Hammer turned to Jenkins. "Add two more promethium canisters to the manifest."

"That'll put us over recommended cargo weight," Jenkins noted, fingers already adjusting the load calculations on his display.

"Dust-off Two can handle it. She's hauled worse."

The promethium canisters were the most dangerous cargo. Each one contained five hundred liters of gel that would ignite if it reached forty degrees Celsius. They were triple-walled with cooling systems, but everyone handled them like they were made of prayer and poor life choices. Through the windscreen, Hammer watched two engineers in full hazmat gear carefully loading the canisters into specially designed cradles.

"Three minutes," Jenkins said, monitoring the loading progress. "They're securing the autocannon drums now."

The drums were massive cylindrical magazines requiring special handling frames. Each contained two thousand rounds of 30mm ammunition in linked belts, a mix of armor-piercing and high-explosive in a 3:1 ratio. The engineers locked them into the dropship's automated feed system, which would align with the mechs' loading ports for rapid transfer.

Outside the dropship, KS security forces maintained overwatch. The spaceport might be secure, but paranoia kept mercenaries alive. Guards in full combat armor swept their weapons across potential threat vectors while motion sensors tracked every movement in the hangar.

"Boss, realistically we're looking at five mikes before I can dust off," Hammer reported, watching a crew member wrestling with a stuck ammunition feed guide. "Want me to launch light and come back for a second run?"

"Negative. Full load or nothing. We don't know if we'll get a second chance for resupply."

"Roger that." Hammer's left hand was already gripping the collective in anticipation while his right rested on the stick. His displays showed engine status—the four turbines were in standby, ready to spool up to full power in thirty seconds once they were loaded.

Jenkins was plotting their route on the navigation display. "Best approach is low and fast through the industrial district. Minimal rebel presence and good cover from the factories."

"If we ever get airborne," Hammer muttered, watching the ground crew struggle with the final missile pallet. One of them had brought out a pneumatic hammer, apparently deciding finesse had failed and it was time for percussive maintenance.

"Two minutes," Jenkins updated. "They're making progress."

The dropship's cargo bay was nearly full—eight tons of ammunition and death waiting for delivery. The automated loading arms were prepped and ready, capable of turning Kenney's nearly-empty mech to fully loaded in less than sixty seconds once they reached him.

"Dust-off Two, this is Boss Actual. Status?"

Hammer checked his chronometer. "Ninety seconds, boss. The loading frame decided to throw a tantrum, but we're almost sorted. Then thirty seconds for engine spool-up and we're airborne."

"Copy. Make it happen."

Through the cockpit window, Hammer could see the other mechs scattered across the city—ten metal giants standing among the ruins like mythological titans. Each one would need resupply soon. It was going to be a very busy morning, assuming they could get this damn ship loaded and airborne.

"There!" Jenkins pointed as the ground crew finally freed the jammed pallet. "They got it."

The last missile pallet slid into place with a satisfying clunk that resonated through the dropship's frame. The crew chief was already giving the all-clear signal, ground crew scattering to safe positions behind blast shields.

"Finally," Hammer breathed, his hands already starting the engine sequence. "Boss, Dust-off Two launching in thirty seconds. About damn time."

The National Reserve Bank came into view through his rain-streaked displays, its neoclassical columns now pockmarked with bullet holes. The plaza in front—once home to food vendors and tourist photo ops—had become a makeshift loading zone. The morning rain had turned the decorative gardens into mud, churned up by truck tires and tank treads. Four Dunkirk tanks were arranged in a defensive square around the loading bay, their crews clearly nervous—turrets swiveling constantly, searching for threats.

Through his magnified optics, Kenney could see the chaos in detail. Rebel infantry—maybe forty men—were forming a human chain from the bank's shattered doors to waiting trucks. Gold bars passed hand to hand, each one worth more than these men would see in a lifetime. Some rebels had abandoned discipline entirely, stuffing their pockets with loose bills scattered across the marble steps. One man sat on the ground, laughing hysterically while clutching a single gold bar to his chest like a child with a toy.

Kenney's hands moved across his controls, setting up the engagement. Left hand switching ammunition types—armor-piercing for the tanks, high-explosive for the trucks. Right hand adjusting shield distribution, pushing power to his forward arc. His neural interface painted targeting solutions across all four tanks simultaneously, calculating angles, armor thickness, weak points.

They opened fire simultaneously.

His combat instincts kicked in before the tanks' muzzles even flashed. Kenney threw his mech sideways, left hand slamming the lateral thrust controls while his right torqued the control stick hard. Servos screamed in protest as forty tons of metal moved like a boxer dodging a punch, his body pressed hard against the pilot seat from the G-forces. Through the neural link, he felt his mech's gyroscopes fighting to maintain balance, felt the strain on the knee actuators as they absorbed the lateral momentum.

The first tank's shell—a 140mm HEAT round—carved a molten groove through the air where his cockpit had been. The pressure wave rattled his displays, static flickering across two of them before the systems compensated. He returned fire mid-dodge, his thumb already on the trigger before his targeting reticle settled. The 30mm rounds punched through the Dunkirk's side armor where it was thinnest, just below the turret ring. Inside his helmet, he heard the distinctive sound of ammunition cooking off—a rapid series of pops like firecrackers before the main explosion.

The rebel infantry scattered like roaches when lights came on. Some dove behind the trucks, others ran for the bank's doors. A squad leader—identifiable by the radio on his back—tried to rally his men, pointing at Kenney's mech and screaming orders. A young rebel, probably no more than eighteen, stood frozen with a gold bar in each hand, unable to process what he was seeing.

The second tank tried to track him, but Kenney was already sprinting. His legs pumped the control pedals in rhythm with the mech's strides, the neural feedback making him feel each footfall. His displays showed him everything—speed at forty-eight kilometers per hour, distance to target twenty meters and closing, hydraulic pressure optimal. He got low, his entire body leaning forward in the cockpit as he ducked the mech under the tank's maximum gun depression.

His mech's hands grabbed the tank's barrel—he felt the metal's resistance through haptic feedback, felt the heat from its recent firing. He heaved, every artificial muscle fiber in the mech's arms engaging at once. His own muscles strained in sympathy, the neural link making him feel like he was actually lifting sixty tons of steel. The Dunkirk flipped like a toy, its crew probably experiencing a brief moment of weightlessness before landing upside down with a crunch that flattened the turret into the hull.

Tank three was already rotating to face him, its gunner traversing the turret manually—the power traverse must have been damaged. Kenney's left hand found the plasma blade activation, the three-stage ignition sequence happening in less than a second. The blade erupted from his mech's left arm with its characteristic crack-hiss. His targeting computer showed him the optimal cut angle—forty-three degrees diagonal, avoiding the ammunition storage while bisecting the crew compartment.

He carved through its frontal armor in one smooth motion, his arm following the targeting guide perfectly. The plasma blade left a glowing wound three meters long, the edges still molten. The crew inside had a half-second to see daylight through the breach before the tank's fuel atomized and ignited, turning everything white.

The fourth tank's commander had panicked completely. He'd popped his hatch and was firing the pintle-mounted machine gun, the muzzle flashes lighting up his terrified face. The 7.62mm rounds sparkled across Kenney's armor like angry fireflies on his display, each impact registering as a tiny pressure point through the neural link—like being pelted with rice grains. His damage assessment showed zero penetration, just scorched paint.

The rebel infantry were in full flight now. The loading operation had collapsed into every-man-for-himself chaos. Men threw down gold bars and ran, their boots slipping in the rain-slicked plaza. One truck tried to leave, its bed only half-full, tires spinning as it fishtailed toward the main road. Another rebel was on his knees, apparently praying, while his squadmate tried to drag him to cover.

A staff car—a luxury sedan with rebel flags hastily tied to its antenna—suddenly broke from behind the bank building, engine roaring as it tried to escape in the chaos. Through his optics, Kenney could see officers inside, probably the operation's commanders making their getaway.

Kenney grabbed one of his mech's combat knives from the magnetic sheath on his right hip—a three-meter blade of tungsten carbide that weighed as much as a small car. His targeting computer calculated the trajectory, accounting for distance, vehicle speed, and wind resistance. He threw it like a javelin, his mech's arm following through in a perfect arc.

The knife punched through the fourth tank's armor and deep into its magazine. For a microsecond nothing happened, then the explosion lifted the sixty-ton vehicle five meters off the ground. It tumbled lazily through the air, shedding pieces of track and armor, before crashing down on two of the gold-laden trucks. The secondary explosions set off the trucks' fuel tanks, creating a chain reaction that turned the entire loading area into an inferno.

The staff car never had a chance. The pressure wave flipped it end over end, windows exploding outward. It landed on its roof thirty meters from where it started, wheels still spinning uselessly.

Through the smoke and flame, Kenney could see surviving rebels abandoning everything—weapons, gold, wounded comrades. They streamed away from the plaza in every direction, some tearing off their uniforms as they ran, trying to blend in as civilians. One rebel stood in the bank's doorway, apparently in shock, still mechanically passing gold bars to no one.

"Boss, this is Deadeye," crackled through his comm. "That's some nice knife work. Want me to tag the runners?"

Kenney checked his displays—ammunition at twenty percent, knife inventory at five remaining, plasma blade fuel at sixty percent. "Negative. Let them spread the word about what happens when you tango with uprights."

The staff car—a black luxury sedan commandeered from some government official—burst from behind an overturned supply truck, tires shrieking as the driver floored it. Kenney's sensors immediately tagged it as a high-value target, the vehicle's excessive speed and erratic movement pattern screaming "command element fleeing."

His hands moved without conscious thought. Left hand pulling up vehicle intercept protocols on his tactical display while his right adjusted his mech's stance for pursuit. The neural interface calculated intercept vectors—the car was doing maybe eighty kilometers per hour, heading for the main boulevard. At his mech's sprint speed, he had a six-second window before they'd reach cover in the government district's narrow streets.

The staff car was accelerating hard, engine screaming in protest, tires smoking as they fought for traction on the rain-slicked asphalt. The driver—visible through Kenney's magnified optics—was sawing at the wheel, trying to weave between abandoned vehicles and debris. He clipped a burning truck, sending up a shower of sparks, but kept going.

Kenney's legs drove into the control pedals, his mech launching into a sprint. Two strides—each one covering fifteen meters. His left hand managed the gyroscopes, keeping the mech balanced as he vaulted over a destroyed fountain. Through the neural link, he felt his mech's weight distribution shifting, felt the precise moment when both feet left the ground. The landing sent tremors through the plaza, cracking the ornate tilework that had survived three centuries of hurricanes only to die under mechanized warfare.

His right hand was already reaching down as his targeting computer predicted the car's path. The massive metal hand—each finger as thick as a tree trunk—slammed down exactly where the vehicle would be in 0.7 seconds. The timing was perfect. The sedan crashed into his palm with a crunch of breaking glass and bending metal, the front end crumpling like aluminum foil. The engine block pushed back into the cabin, steam erupting from the ruptured radiator.

Through the cracked windshield, magnified on his primary display, he could see the occupants clearly. A rebel general in the passenger seat, his uniform torn and bloody, frantically waving something white—looked like a torn piece of rag, maybe from his shirt. The back seat held three women in various states of undress, evening gowns torn and makeup smeared. Whether they were escorts or "comfort staff" was hard to tell in places like this—the distinction mattered little when powerful men fell.

The driver was frozen, hands death-gripped on the wheel, eyes wide with the terror of someone whose world had just ended. His foot was still pressing the accelerator, the ruined engine whining uselessly against Kenney's immovable grip.

"Pilot Jaeger," Foxtrot chimed in with its crisp British accent. "Facial recognition confirms General Eduardo Ramirez. Primary instigator of rebel forces. Standing bounty: 2.5 million credits, dead or alive. Note: Bonus for live capture expires in six hours."

Kenney's left hand pulled up the bounty details on a secondary screen while his right maintained the mech's grip on the vehicle. The file photo showed Ramirez in better days—clean-shaven, medals gleaming, giving a speech about "liberation from oppression." The man cowering in the sedan looked twenty years older, three days of stubble and terror having aged him rapidly.

"Also detecting significant thermal signatures in the vehicle's trunk," Foxtrot added. "Consistent with precious metals.

Approximately two hundred kilograms based on heat retention patterns."

"Gold bars in the trunk and prostitutes in the back," Kenney muttered. "Really living up to those revolutionary ideals, General."

Through his external cameras, he could see rebel infantry in the distance, watching but not interfering. They knew better than to engage a mech over one general who'd probably been planning to abandon them anyway. Some were already stripping off their uniforms, preparing to disappear into the civilian population.

"Fox, external speakers."

"Speakers active."

The general was already pleading, his words tumbling out in a mix of English and Spanish. Inside the mech's cockpit, Kenney watched the man through his targeting display, the crosshairs automatically tracking center mass even though he had no intention of firing. His hands rested on the control sticks, forty tons of war machine responding to the slightest twitch of his fingers.

He toggled external speakers with his thumb. His voice boomed through the mech's external system, drowning the general out. "Well, General, looks like we caught you with your pants down."

"Please, you must understand!" Ramirez switched to accented but clear English, sweat pouring down his face. The man was gesticulating wildly, hands moving like he was conducting an orchestra of desperation. "The revolution—it is for the people! The workers must have their day! Cortez, he bleeds the country dry while children starve in the streets! We fight for justice, for freedom, for—"

The words became background noise, revolutionary rhetoric Kenney had heard a hundred times on a hundred different worlds. Through his neural link, he could feel the mech's weight shift slightly as he leaned back in his pilot's seat, the motion translating to tons of metal adjusting position. The general flinched at even that small movement, probably thinking he was about to be crushed.

They all thought their cause was special. They all had starving children and oppressed workers. They all thought it mattered. Kenney's fingers drummed against the control stick, each tap sending minute tremors through the mech's massive hand still pinning the staff car.

His attention drifted to the three women in the back. They couldn't have been older than twenty, dressed in what looked like expensive cocktail dresses modified for the tropical heat—silk and sequins cut high on bronze thighs, designer heels impractical for a war zone. Athletic builds, professional hair and makeup even now. Their faces showed the careful neutrality of people who'd learned to survive by being whatever powerful men needed them to be. The woman in the middle made eye contact with the robot. She offered a slight smile.

"—the corporatists and their mercenary dogs cannot stop the will of the—"

Kenney cut him off, gesturing with his mech's rifle at the women. "What's their deal?"

Ramirez fumbled with his door handle, finally managing to push it open. He stumbled out of the staff car, his dress uniform disheveled, medals jangling as he fell to his knees in front of the towering mech. His hands came up in a pleading gesture, looking up at forty feet of armored death.

"They... they are my daughters!" He shouted up at the sensor cluster that served as the mech's head. "My beautiful daughters. I was evacuating them from—"

Inside the cockpit, Kenney watched the general's performance through multiple displays. His external cameras showed every angle—the man's trembling hands, the sweat staining his collar, the way he kept glancing between the mech's weapons and its feet, probably calculating which death would be quicker.

"Your daughters." Kenney's voice was flat through the speakers. "All three of them. You bring your daughters to warzones in those outfits?"

One of the girls rolled her eyes. The middle one, shifted slightly in her seat, adjusting her posture and her hemline, offering the forty-foot mech a subtle view—the same calculated view she'd probably used on a hundred powerful men. Another muttered something in Portuguese that definitely wasn't familial.

Ramirez's face crumbled. He pushed himself to his feet, swaying slightly, hands still raised in supplication. "Okay, okay! They're not my daughters! They're... they're escorts. High-end companions."

He glanced back at the car desperately, then up at the mech. "You can have them! All three! They're very skilled, very beautiful. Just let me go! Please, I'm begging you—"

Ramirez took a step backward, nearly tripping over debris. "You don't understand! The burden of command, the isolation! These girls, they understand their place, they provide comfort—"

"Interesting offer," Kenney said flatly.

"The women then—take them! They'll do anything you want!" The general was bargaining with everything he had, which wasn't much. "A man like you must have needs—"

The general trying to trade human beings for his life was predictable. They always offered the same things in the same order—women, money, power. As if any of it mattered when you had a gun to their head.

Inside the cockpit, Kenney shifted his control stick slightly. The mech's massive head tilted, forty tons of metal conveying disgust with a simple gesture.

Kenney triggered the top hatch release. Inside the cockpit, his neural link cables disconnected with soft pneumatic hisses, the control tethers popping free from connection points along his spine and helmet. The feedback systems in his pilot suit powered down, leaving him suddenly aware of his own body weight after hours of feeling forty tons of mech as an extension of himself.

He pulled off his helmet, setting it in its cradle, then hauled himself up through the hatch. The mech continued to stand perfectly still, but its systems remained active—the rifle tracking smoothly from potential threat to potential threat, the sensor cluster sweeping left and right in predetermined patterns. Foxtrot's AI had switched to autonomous mode, maintaining overwatch. From the outside, you'd never know the pilot had left. The mechanical giant looked just as alert, just as deadly.

Foxtrot's mechanical arms grabbed him, lowering him the twelve meters to street level with practiced precision. His boots hit pavement with a satisfying thud, pilot armor flexing as he stretched muscles cramped from combat. He pulled off his helmet, running a hand through sweat-soaked sandy hair that had grown too long for regulations he no longer followed.

The general got his first look at the man who'd ended his revolution—younger than expected, maybe thirty-five, with the kind of face that would have been handsome if it wasn't so clearly exhausted. Sharp jawline covered in three days of stubble, blue eyes that had the thousand-yard stare of someone who'd seen too much and stopped caring about most of it. A scar ran through his left eyebrow, leaving a gap in the hair, probably shrapnel from some forgotten battle.

"General, here's the thing," Kenney said, his actual voice quieter but somehow more menacing than the booming speakers. "I don't care about your politics. Unless you can make me a better offer than 2.5 million credits."

"I can give you all the gold!" Ramirez gestured frantically toward the bank. "All of it! Tons of gold bars!"

Kenney glanced back at the bank, nodding sardonically. He caught the eyes of the three women and gave them a flirtatious wave. They grinned back, waving shyly, recognizing a different kind of power when they saw it.

"Well, General, that gold's already mine."

As if on cue, Streaks and Racer's mechs emerged from behind the bank, having made their way from the sports complex through half the city.

Streaks had his hull painted in urban camo—grays and blacks broken up with angular patterns. A grinning skull was painted across the cockpit that looked like it was eating the sensor cluster, and tally marks ran down the left arm—one for each mech kill. The words "CASH ONLY" were stenciled across the chest in military font.

Racer's mech was impossible to miss—painted bright orange with a white racing stripe running from head to toe, and a massive "01" emblazoned on both shoulders. An ancient flag design decorated the torso—stars and bars from some Earth nation that hadn't existed for centuries. The whole thing looked like a race car had mated with a war machine. "GENERAL MAYHEM" was scripted across the chest in stylized letters, and he'd added chrome exhaust stacks that served no purpose except looking fast.

They'd been securing the loading bay while Kenney dealt with the general, making sure none of the rebels decided to make off with the national reserves during the chaos.

"So if that's all you can offer, I'm afraid you'll have to pay the old-fashioned way."

The general's eyes darted between Kenney, the massive mechs flanking the bank, and his crashed staff car. The reality hit him like a physical blow—no escape routes, no backup coming, no cards left to play. His shoulders sagged for just a moment before desperation gave him one last surge of adrenaline.

"You mercenary bastard!" Ramirez's hand went for his gold-plated sidearm, a gaudy .45 with pearl grips that probably cost more than most soldiers made in a year.

Kenney was faster. The tranq gun—a military-issue Pacifier, designed for taking high-value targets alive—seemed to materialize in his hand from the concealed holster at the small of his back. The weapon was all business, matte black composite with a dual-barrel configuration. Two pneumatic puffs, barely audible over the distant gunfire. The darts hit center mass before the general even cleared leather, micro-needles punching through his dress uniform to deliver a cocktail of sedatives that would drop a charging rhino.

Ramirez's hand went slack, the gold-plated pistol slipping from nerveless fingers. His legs buckled like someone had cut his strings. He managed one confused "Wha—" before his eyes rolled back and he crumpled to the asphalt in a heap of medals and failed revolution.

The girls screamed—half fear, half excitement, that adrenaline shriek of people who'd just watched violence up close and survived it.

"Pilot Jaeger," Fox's voice crackled in his earpiece, "that was an unnecessary risk. You were pointlessly putting yourself in danger. Again."

Kenney spun the tranq gun on his finger, a smooth flourish that had no business working with a dual-barrel weapon but somehow did. He mimed fanning a non-existent hammer with his other hand—pure showmanship, the kind of gunslinger theatrics from old holovids that had no place in modern combat. Then he slipped the weapon back into its concealed holster with practiced ease, the whole display taking less than three seconds.

"You don't get it, Fox." Kenney stared at the unconscious general. "I gave him every opportunity to kill me. Perfect shot. And I'm still standing. Must be cursed."

"Your wife's death wasn't your fault, Kenney. You need to move on."

"Shut up, Fox."

The girl who'd smiled earlier stepped out of the car, one hand on the door frame for balance as she emerged. With her free hand, she smoothed her dress down over her thighs in that practiced way models do when exiting vehicles—barely maintaining modesty while making it look effortless. She adjusted the hem once more as she stood, then sauntered closer while maintaining a safe distance—smart girl, knew how to approach dangerous men without appearing threatening.

When she spoke, her voice was accented, sweet, carefully modulated.

"Thank you for... for stopping him," she said, gesturing vaguely at the unconscious general.

Kenney pointed at the gold-plated pistol on the ground. "Darling, can you bring me that pistol over there?"

She tilted her head, playing confused—testing whether he was setting her up.

He pointed again, slower, like talking to a child or someone who didn't speak the language well. "The gun. Bring. It. Here."

She nodded, understanding perfectly—she'd been testing his patience. The girl walked over, bent to pick up the pistol with deliberate grace, her dress riding up just enough to show. Her body was firm, and young. Her breasts were barely covered, the thin silk of her gown not hiding the stiffness of her dark nipples. She looked at him over her shoulder and smiled, a little flirtatious grin that said she was interested.

It was all he could do not to bark like a dog.

The woman turned around, a small smile still playing about her mouth, as if she could read his mind. As if she could see that the very sight of her was making him hard. Fox whispered in his earpiece: "Unnecessary risks, Kenney. She's armed now."

The girl walked back, the general's pistol held loosely, barrel down. She could have shot him, could have tried to run. Instead, she offered it to him handle-first, professional.

Kenney took it gently, then caught her hand and kissed it like some pre-war gentleman. "What's your name?"

"Magdalena," she said, a hint of surprise in her voice at the gesture.

"Beautiful. I collect showpieces like this," he said, holding up the gaudy pistol. Then he looked directly at her. "And like you and your friends, if you're interested."

Her eyes sharpened—business she understood. "What do you want?"

"Simple. First, help me drag the general back to the car. Then, wait here. When my people come back to collect him, you three go with them. It'll be safer than hanging around here."

She nodded, understanding the transaction. Together they hauled the unconscious general back to the staff car, his medals dragging across the pavement. The other two girls watched from inside, uncertain but following Magdalena's lead.

"Sir," Fox's voice chimed in his earpiece as they propped Ramirez against the wheel. "I've taken the liberty of editing our combat footage for the bounty package. I've enhanced the quick-draw sequence and your response time—really highlights the dramatic confrontation. The general's attempts at bargaining have been cut to maintain the narrative flow."

"The narrative flow?"

"The client wants to see a clean takedown of a dangerous rebel leader, not twenty minutes of a man trying to trade everything he owns for his life. I've crafted it as a proper showdown—the general going for his weapon, you outdrawing him. Very cinematic. Should add at least ten percent to the bounty for style points."

"Since when do bounties have style points?"

"Since I started editing the footage, sir. You're welcome."

President-General Eduardo Cortez emerged from his command bunker, stepping over chunks of concrete and twisted rebar. The palace corridors were a maze of destruction—blast marks scarring the walls, windows blown out, the marble floors cracked and stained with blood.

Republic Guard soldiers moved through the halls with purpose now that victory was assured. A squad dragged rebel bodies to a growing pile in the courtyard, while another sorted through the wounded. Those in government uniforms were rushed to medical stations. Rebels got a different kind of treatment—quick pistol shots echoed through the palace as the wounded were "processed."

Work crews were already arriving, sweeping glass, patching holes, trying to restore some semblance of order. A maintenance team struggled to remove a rebel who'd been impaled on the ornamental fence, his body serving as an unwanted decoration.

Cortez climbed the grand staircase, ignoring the blood trail some wounded loyalist had left on his way to medical. His private chambers had survived mostly intact—reinforced walls had their advantages. He stepped onto his balcony, fishing a cigar from his jacket.

In the distance, he could see two of the suppression mechs moving through the industrial district, their massive forms distinctive even from kilometers away. One was painted flat black with white skull imagery across its torso—death incarnate in forty feet of metal. The other bore jungle camouflage despite the urban environment, with what looked like kill tallies running down its arms like a prison sentence. They moved with casual efficiency, occasionally firing at something he couldn't see, probably rebels too stupid to surrender.

He lit his cigar, savoring the imported tobacco as smoke from the burning city mixed with smoke from his victory. The last-minute hiring of Kilkenney Solutions had been worth every credit. They'd come highly recommended from several of his fellow autocrats—those still breathing, anyway—and they hadn't disappointed.

He'd dragged his feet for three days on authorizing payment, hoping his Republic Guard could handle what he'd initially dismissed as "minor civil unrest." But revolutions were bad for business, and tourism was Nueva Kalloo's lifeblood. Empty beaches meant empty coffers, and empty coffers meant no money for the lifestyle to which he'd grown accustomed.

The rebels were in full retreat now, streaming into the jungle in whatever vehicles still ran, abandoning heavy weapons and wounded alike. The mech teams were pulling back to the spaceport for rest and rearmament, which suited Cortez fine—additional government battalions had finally arrived from the mainland, eager to show loyalty now that the outcome was certain.

The thought of how close he'd come to ending—not in some glorious last stand or honorable defeat, but dragged from his bunker and shot against a wall like a common criminal—made his stomach turn. He whispered prayers of gratitude to the only god he'd ever believed in: himself. After all, who else would a dictator pray to? He'd had the wisdom to pay when it mattered, the foresight to know when local solutions weren't enough.

"Your Excellency," his aide appeared at the doorway, carefully stepping around a bullet hole in the floor, "Kilkenney Solutions is requesting permission to pull back to Angel's Cove for R&R."

Angel's Cove—the crown jewel of Nueva Kalloo's tourist industry. A sprawling resort complex with crystal blue lagoons, zero-g pools, and casinos that ran all night. The kind of place where CEOs and crime lords vacationed side by side, no questions asked.

"Grant them full access. Presidential suite package, my compliments. And wire them a bonus—twenty percent on top of the contract."

"Twenty percent, sir?"

"Insurance, Colonel. For the next time someone decides paradise needs new management." Cortez turned to his aide. "And send them a case of that '89 rum reserve from my private collection. The one with the gold flakes. Warriors appreciate good liquor."

"Yes, Your Excellency. Anything else?"

"The ambassador's daughters—the twins studying dance at the academy. Invite them to join our heroes at Angel's Cove. Make it clear it's voluntary but... encouraged. Heroes deserve companionship after battle."

The aide nodded, understanding perfectly. Gifts, bonuses, and beautiful company—the currency of continued loyalty in their line of work.

CHAPTER TWO

The landing pad at Angel's Cove wasn't built for warships.

Constructed from compressed coral sand and reinforced with a lattice of carbon fiber mesh, the pristine white platform jutted into turquoise waters like an artificial peninsula. Palm trees lined the approach in perfect rows, their fronds manicured to frame the view of multimillion-credit yachts bobbing at private moorings. The pad itself was a marvel of engineering vanity—its surface embedded with micro-LEDs that could display landing guidelines or, during parties, synchronized light shows that turned arriving vessels into theatrical entrances.

Tiki torches burned at regular intervals despite the noon sun, their flames fed by aromatic oils that cost more per liter than combat fuel. The beach stretched for kilometers in both directions, the natural white sand formed from centuries of crushed coral and volcanic minerals unique to Nueva Kalloo's geology. The combination made it sparkle like diamond dust in the sunlight—one of the reasons the resort had been built here in the first place. Beachside cabanas in pastel blues and pinks dotted the shoreline, each one worth more than a colonial worker's lifetime earnings.

Inside the Purgatory's hangar bay, the launch sequence had already begun.

"Racer, Priest, you're up," Derg's voice crackled through the hangar's PA system. "Magnetic clamps releasing in thirty seconds."

In his cockpit, Racer's hands flew across his controls, fingers dancing between physical switches and holographic interfaces. His left hand gripped the throttle, feeling the rumble of his mech's reactor through the haptic feedback. His right worked the control stick, testing the range of motion while his feet pressed against the pedal controls, feeling the resistance that would translate to his mech's movement.

"Systems check," he muttered, eyes scanning three different displays simultaneously. "Hydraulics green, weapons locked for landing protocol, jump jets primed." He reached up to adjust his helmet's neural interface cable, making sure the connection was solid. "Ready to make an entrance, boss."

Two bays over, Priest was running through his own pre-launch ritual. His gloved fingers traced the small crucifix welded to his control panel—a personal modification the techs had learned not to question. His mech's cockpit was cramped but organized, religious iconography sharing space with military hardware. A rosary hung from the ejection handle, swaying with the ship's movement.

"Lord, grant us a landing that doesn't kill any tourists," he murmured, toggling his mech into active mode. The displays around him bloomed to life, painting his face in the green glow of operational status indicators. His left hand found the grip controls while his right settled on the primary stick. "But if we must kill tourists, Lord, let them be the annoying ones."

The hangar bay's massive doors groaned open beneath them, revealing the drop to paradise below. Through the opening, they could see Angel's Cove in all its manufactured perfection—infinity pools that seemed to blend with the ocean, a golf course so green it looked painted, and crowds of wealthy civilians who were about to get the shock of their lives.

"Launching in ten," Derg announced. "Nine, eight..."

Racer leaned forward in his harness, feeling the five-point restraint system hold him secure. Through his mech's sensors, he could already feel the tropical heat rising from below, so different from the hangar's recycled air.

"Three, two, one—"

The magnetic clamps released simultaneously. For a heartbeat, both mechs hung in space, forty tons of metal suspended by nothing but potential energy. Then gravity took hold.

"YEEHAW!" Racer screamed over comms as his mech plummeted toward the beach. His hands worked the controls frantically, firing stabilizing thrusters in micro-bursts to control his descent. His stomach lifted into his throat despite the inertial dampeners, that familiar drop sensation that never got old.

Priest's descent was more controlled, his thrusters firing in measured pulses. Inside his cockpit, warning lights flashed as altitude decreased rapidly—500 meters, 400, 300. His left hand pulled back on the thrust control while his right kept the mech oriented feet-down. "Incoming on the left," he called out, spotting a parasailing tourist about to intersect their drop path.

Both pilots fired emergency thrust simultaneously, mechs sliding sideways through the air. The parasailer passed between them, the tourist's scream doppplered past their external audio sensors.

They hit the shallows with thunderous impacts that sent walls of water cascading across the beach. Racer's mech sank knee-deep into the sand before the stabilizers compensated, his hands fighting the controls as warnings flashed about structural stress. Priest landed more solidly, his heavier frame crushing a decorative pier that had extended into the water, sending teak planks flying like matchsticks.

"Easy, easy!" Racer's voice crackled through the comm as his mech stood knee-deep in the surf, one arm raised to guide the Purgatory's descent. Inside his cockpit, his left hand worked the emergency override panel, shutting down alerts about sand in the knee actuators while his right hand gestured the mech's arm frantically at a cluster of beach umbrellas and cabanas that hadn't been cleared from the landing zone. "Priest, we got civilians at two o'clock!"

Through his enhanced optics, Racer could see tourists in various states of undress—a yoga class frozen mid-pose, their instructor still holding warrior position despite a forty-foot mech standing twenty meters away. A beach bar where patrons clutched their cocktails, unsure whether to run or finish their drinks. A wedding photo shoot, the bride's dress billowing as the photographer kept shooting, apparently deciding this would make the album unique.

Priest's heavier assault variant stomped through the shallows, each footfall sending up geysers of spray that caught the afternoon sun. Inside his cockpit, Priest worked his controls with practiced precision, his hands moving across the haptic interfaces while murmuring a quiet prayer through his helmet comm.

"Lord, grant me the serenity to relocate civilians gently," he muttered, toggling his mech's grip pressure to minimum, "and the wisdom not to accidentally squish them."

His mech was a walking cathedral of death—matte black base coat covered in hand-painted white crosses, each one representing a confirmed kill. They started small at the extremities, growing larger as they approached the torso where a massive Jerusalem cross dominated the chest plate. The right shoulder bore 48 crosses in neat rows—vehicle kills. The left shoulder held 23 larger crosses—enemy mechs he'd sent to meet their maker. Smaller crosses ran down both arms like rosary beads, marking infantry squads that had learned too late that God's mercy didn't extend to combat zones.

Biblical verses in Gothic script wrapped around the joints: "I will execute great vengeance upon them" (Ezekiel 25:17) curved along the right elbow. "The Lord is a warrior" (Exodus 15:3) adorned the left knee joint. The cockpit's exterior was framed by an elaborate painting of the Archangel Michael casting down Satan—if Satan had been a mech, and Michael had been armed with 30mm autocannons.

His targeting reticle settled on the frozen couple at the beachside massage table. Through his enhanced optics, he could see their eyes tracking between his mech and the descending carrier—pure deer-in-headlights paralysis. His left hand adjusted the servo controls while his right carefully maneuvered the control stick, bringing his mech's massive hand down with the delicacy of a watchmaker.

"Easy does it," he whispered, the hydraulics responding to his neural link's micro-adjustments. The fingers closed around both tourists, lifting them complete with their massage table. His grip pressure readout showed 0.3%—just enough to hold without crushing.

He reached down with surprising gentleness, plucking the frozen couple from their beachside massage table and depositing them fifty meters down the beach like action figures. The masseuse, still clutching her bottle of oil, stared up at the mech's sensor cluster before fainting dead away. Through his external audio pickups, Priest heard her whisper "Santa María" before she collapsed.

"The Lord moves in mysterious ways," Priest rumbled over external speakers, his voice processed through the mech's systems to sound like thunder from on high, "but today He suggests you find another beach."

The Purgatory's shadow fell across Angel's Cove like an eclipse, her ventral thrusters turning the lagoon into a boiling cauldron. Steam billowed up in great clouds, temporarily obscuring the tiki bars and infinity pools. Even at quarter thrust, the backwash was hurricane-force, sending lounge chairs cartwheeling across manicured lawns and turning carefully maintained sand sculptures into dust.

Scott Blake looked at the numbers glowing on his terminal in the CIC and bit back the string of expletives threatening to escape. The Command Information Center was nearly empty—its usual complement of twenty crew members had already departed for shore leave, leaving only the duty skeleton crew at essential stations. During operations, this place hummed with activity: tactical officers tracking targets, communications specialists managing encrypted channels, electronic warfare techs jamming enemy sensors. Now, with liberty granted, only three stations remained active—his own, plus navigation and basic communications, manned by the unlucky few who'd drawn the short straw.

Blake had claimed the logistics station by choice, needing the quad-monitor setup to properly track their tangled finances. At forty-two, he still maintained the military bearing—shoulders square, posture straight even after hours hunched over spreadsheets. He'd kept himself in fighting shape through daily PT, a habit from his days running convoy logistics through contested zones. His brown hair was regulation short, though he'd stopped caring about regulations years ago—it was just easier to maintain in the field.

The brass spittoon mag-locked to his console caught another stream of tobacco juice. It was his one vice, something to do with his hands while calculating ammunition costs and fuel expenditures.

As Kilkenney Solutions' de facto business manager—a title he'd inherited by virtue of being the only one who could do math without using his fingers—he had the unenviable job of making sure everyone got paid and the company stayed solvent.

The contract payment from Cortez blinked in pleasant green: 50,000,000 credits, plus the twenty percent bonus. The "tactical acquisitions" tallied below it in amber—still theoretical until they found buyers: estimated forty-three million for the gold if they could move it through the right channels, maybe eight million for the luxury goods from the brewery assuming they didn't drink it all first, bounties that might total twelve million if the authorities actually paid out.

It should have looked good. It didn't.

Operating expenses for the next quarter glowed an angry red beneath the income. Fuel for the Purgatory alone ran two million a month. Mech maintenance, parts, and repairs: another three million. Salaries, medical, food, bribes to dock authorities who looked the other way when a military carrier needed berthing—it added up fast.

But the real killer was ammunition.

A single 140mm sabot round cost eight thousand credits. They'd fired forty-nine of them today. The 30mm autocannon rounds ran five hundred credits per hundred—they'd burned through twelve thousand rounds across all units. Missiles? Forget it. Twenty-five thousand credits each for the good stuff, the kind with smart warheads that could think their way around countermeasures.

With the Core Worlds and ARMSEA implementing their "stability protocols"—corporate speak for arms embargos on anyone who might disturb their profitable peace—even finding military-grade ammunition was becoming a challenge. The premium distributors wouldn't touch mercenary units anymore, afraid of losing their licenses. That left the gray market, where prices doubled and quality was a dice roll.

Scott pulled up the ammunition expenditure from today's six-minute engagement: 14.7 million credits.

They'd literally shot their profit margin to pieces.

He'd spent eight years with the Galactic Relief Initiative, moving medicine and food through war zones with the efficiency of a master chess player. Every customs official who needed convincing, every "inspection fee" that needed paying, every manifest that needed creative restructuring—he'd handled it all with pride. Scott Blake, the man who could get antibiotics past warlords and grain through blockades. He'd bragged about it at conferences, wrote papers on "Dynamic Logistics in Hostile Territories" that got him speaking engagements at humanitarian summits.

The bile rose in his throat just thinking about those days, that naive fool who never questioned why GRI had so many "special shipments" leaving those same war-torn worlds. Containers that required delicate handling, specific temperature controls, careful documentation that he—in his infinite wisdom—had perfected to slip past any scrutiny.

He couldn't even remember which tragedy of the week had brought him to that backwater planet. They all blurred together—genocide, ethnic cleansing, religious purges, territorial disputes, mineral rights wrapped in ideological rhetoric. The planet's name was lost in the haze of a hundred similar catastrophes, each one an opportunity for the GRI to "provide critical humanitarian aid."

He'd been doing a site inspection. Routine stuff, checking the supply chain, making sure the local staff weren't skimming too much. Why he'd decided to check that specific refrigerated container, he still didn't know. Maybe it was the way the guards had looked nervous. Maybe it was how the numbers didn't quite add up. Maybe some part of him had always known but needed to see.

The lock had been easy to bypass—he knew all the codes, had designed half the security protocols himself. Inside, the temperature controls humming, keeping the cargo at exactly 39.5 degrees Fahrenheit. Optimal for organ preservation. For keeping sedated human beings at the edge of hypothermia. For storing merchandise.

Twenty-three of them, ages eight to sixteen, drugged and intubated, stacked in medical suspension units he'd personally requisitioned as "critical care equipment."

His genius at moving numbers, at making the impossible happen when everyone said no—it hadn't been saving lives. It had been stealing them.

Scott Blake reached into his shirt pocket and pulled out his tin of Copenhagen, the metal worn smooth from years of habit. He fished out the old wad from his cheek—three hours old and long past its flavor—and flicked it into the brass spittoon mag-locked to his console. The wet splat echoed in the mostly empty CIC as he packed a fresh pinch, the tobacco's earthy smell briefly cutting through the recycled air.

The landing struts deployed with a hydraulic scream that resonated through the entire ship's frame. Blake gripped the console as the deck suddenly lurched—they were coming in too hot. Through the main viewing screen, he watched the ground rush up, Conway fighting to bleed off velocity while keeping them level.

Impact.

The starboard strut hit first, crushing through what had been a beachside tiki bar. Blake watched the bamboo structure explode outward in slow motion through the screen's high-speed capture, bottles of premium rum becoming glittering projectiles. The whole ship tilted hard to port, throwing him against his restraints. His fresh dip nearly launched from his mouth as his teeth clenched.

The port strut slammed down a heartbeat later, sending a shockwave through the deck that made every loose object jump. Through the screen, a geyser of sand erupted forty meters high, the compressed coral platform cracking in spider web patterns from the point of impact. The stern struts followed in quick succession—WHAM, WHAM—each impact making the ship groan like a wounded beast.

The Purgatory bounced—actually lifted back off the pad for a terrifying second—before settling with a final, bone-rattling crash that made every screen in the CIC flicker. Blake's spittoon broke free from its magnetic lock, clanging across the deck and spraying tobacco juice in a brown arc across the navigation console.

Through the viewing screen, he could see the devastation in real-time. The landing pad itself had partially collapsed, one corner dropping two meters where the substrate had failed. Cracks ran from their landing zone to the marina, where several million-credit yachts were now taking on water through suddenly-breached hulls. A shock wave of sand and debris was still expanding outward, turning the crystal-clear resort waters into churning mud.

"Holy hell," Blake muttered, retrieving his spittoon as the ship finally stopped moving. Through the polarized glass, Angel's Cove sprawled before them—white sand beaches, swaying palms, those ridiculous tiki torches that burned even in daylight. Paradise for people who could afford to forget the universe was burning.

At least, it had been paradise five seconds ago. Now it looked like someone had dropped a war crime on a postcard.

He sighed, the paradise was making him think of other beautiful lies.

The memory just wouldn't let go. That boardroom in the GRI's headquarters, all chrome and glass overlooking New Geneva's spotless skyline. He'd stormed in, still shaking, his shirt soaked with sweat from running fourteen blocks because he couldn't wait for transport. The conference room door had crashed against the wall, leaving a dent in the imported wood paneling.

The board members sat around their polished table like carrion birds—twelve figures in suits that cost more than refugee camps spent on food in a year. The CEO—Charlie Ellis, who should have been sixty but looked barely twenty, her skin taut and glowing with the kind of youth money could buy—had barely looked up from her quarterly projections. It had never occurred to him to wonder why someone running a humanitarian organization looked like she'd stepped out of a Core World rejuvenation clinic. Her fingers, manicured and adorned with conflict-free diamonds, continued tapping at her tablet as if his entrance was merely a scheduling inconvenience.

"Scott, you're upset. That's understandable. But you need to see the bigger picture."

"The bigger picture?" He'd slammed his hands on the conference table hard enough to spill the CFO's coffee, a thin man with nervous hands who immediately started dabbing at the spreading brown stain with his monogrammed handkerchief. The impact had made Ellis's water glass jump, sending ripples through the imported spring water. "We're trafficking children!"

His voice had cracked on the last word, the image still burning behind his eyes—those kids in the container, tubes down their throats, monitors showing heartbeats kept deliberately slow.

"We're saving lives," Ellis had replied, her voice maddeningly calm, as if explaining expense reports to a junior accountant. She'd finally looked up then, her gray eyes as cold as the recycled air, set in a face that belonged on a university student, not a woman who'd spent decades in supposed humanitarian work. "Those medical supplies you move so brilliantly? They save thousands. The infrastructure we build? It prevents famines. Yes, there are... uncomfortable compromises. But those assets you observed? They were war orphans, Scott. No families, no futures. They would have died in refugee camps or worse."

"So we sell them instead?"

"We place them," another board member had corrected, as if semantics mattered. "With families in the Core Worlds who can provide opportunities. Education. Safety."

"For the pretty ones maybe," Scott had snarled. "What about the others? The ones that go to 'medical research facilities'? The ones listed as 'domestic inventory'?"

Ellis's expression had finally cracked, showing a flicker of something—annoyance, not guilt. "You're being paid eight hundred thousand credits a year, Scott. You live in a penthouse. Your daughter goes to the finest schools. That's the price of civilization. We do distasteful things so billions can live in peace."

She'd stood then, her movements fluid and graceful in a way that should have been impossible for someone her actual age. "Where do you think the Core Worlds get their compounds for rejuvenation treatments, Scott?" She'd gestured at her own face, that perfect twenty-year-old skin that had never occurred to him to question. "For the greater good, someone has to pay. Those children's stem cells, their growth hormones, their pristine organs—they serve a purpose. They keep civilization's leaders young and vital enough to continue their work."

"They would have died anyway," the CFO had added, like that justified everything. "At least this way, their loss serves a purpose."

Ellis had walked to the window then, looking out at New Geneva's spotless streets. "I'm one hundred and twelve years old, Scott. I've been running humanitarian operations for eight decades. The good I've done, the lives I've saved, the infrastructure I've built—all possible because someone, somewhere, paid the price to keep me functional. Those twenty-three children in that container? Their sacrifice will keep dozens of Core World leaders alive and productive for another century. Leaders who prevent wars, who manage resources, who keep billions from starving."

She'd turned back to him, her young face wearing an ancient expression. "So yes, we traffic in human resources. Because the alternative is chaos, collapse, and far more death than what we prevent."

Scott had broken in that moment, something fundamental snapping like an overstressed support beam. The knowledge of it all—thousands of containers, dozens of planets, years of shipments—crashed down on him at once. His vision tunneled, the edges going red. His hands started shaking, not from fear but from rage so pure it felt like electricity running through his veins.

His hand moved without conscious thought, reaching into his long coat for the Groesbeck 830 he'd started carrying after too many dock inspections went sideways. The quad-barrel pump shotgun came out in one smooth motion—four 12-gauge barrels arranged in a square pattern, the pump action allowing him to cycle through all four before reloading. The weapon was pure Fringe World brutality, designed for clearing trenches and boarding actions where reload time meant death.

"Security—" The CIO started to say, his hand reaching for the panic button under the table.

The first two barrels fired simultaneously with the Groesbeck's distinctive double-thump. At this range, the concentrated buckshot turned the CIO’s torso into a cavern you could see through. He hit the wall hard enough to crack the wood paneling, leaving a crimson silhouette as he slid down.

The boardroom erupted in noise and motion, but time seemed to slow. Scott worked the pump—ka-chunk—rotating the next two barrels into position. Ellis's humanitarian awards exploded off the wall in a shower of glass and wood as he fired again, catching Dr. Parker as she tried to stand. The double blast nearly cut her in half, her upper body spinning one way while her legs collapsed the other.

The Groesbeck's pump-action snapped back and forth in rapid succession with practiced ease, four spent shells ejecting in a brass rainbow. His left hand was already pulling loose shells from his coat. The action slammed open and the action snapped shut in under two seconds.

The CFO tried to duck under the table, whimpering something about his children. The HR director made it three steps toward the door before Scott cycled the pump. The double-blast caught they/them between the shoulder blades, turning it’s spine into memory and it’s chest into an exit wound the size of a dinner plate.

Ellis hadn't moved. She stood at the window, hands clasped behind her back, watching him work with those young eyes that held centuries of calculation. "You're proving my point, Scott. This is what humans are. This is what we do without proper management."

He pumped the Groesbeck one more time, bringing the last two loaded barrels to bear. At point-blank range, her perfect young face simply ceased to exist. The window behind her became a spider web of cracks painted in red and gray, her headless body standing for a surreal moment before toppling out of the broken window.

The others scrambled for exits that were too far away. Board members who'd signed off on turning children into cuts of meat tripped over each other, their dignity abandoned. Scott worked methodically, the Groesbeck's quad-barrel design letting him maintain almost continuous fire. Break, reload, snap shut, pump, fire. The rhythm of it was almost meditative.

When the smoke cleared and his ears stopped ringing, Scott stood alone among the executive suite's new decor. Twelve bodies arranged like a shareholder meeting in hell. He'd been methodical, professional—the same attention to detail that made him exceptional at logistics. His hands hadn't even shaken.

The Groesbeck was hot enough to burn through his gloves, all four barrels trailing smoke. Spent shells covered the floor like bloody brass confetti. The imported carpet was already soaking through, turning the GRI logo into an unrecognizable smear.

He'd walked to Ellis's terminal, still logged in with her executive credentials. Every file, every transaction record, every carefully doctored manifest showing the real cargo—he'd packaged it all and fired it off to three hundred news outlets across the Core Worlds. Reuters-Galactic, The New Geneva Tribune, even those sensationalist rags that usually covered celebrity scandals. Someone would run it. Someone had to.

Scott had straightened his jacket, noting the blood spatter across his face in the conference room's mirror. He'd slicked back his hair with a steady hand, then used every skill he'd learned moving contraband to simply vanish. New identity, new career, new life. Left his wife and daughter behind with nothing but a trust fund he'd established years earlier and a note saying he was sorry.

The only story that ever ran was a forty-second segment on Core News Network: "Disgruntled Employee Commits Workplace Violence at Charity Headquarters. Twelve Dead."

They'd called him mentally unstable. Said he'd been embezzling funds and snapped when caught. Six months later, Alake Zietsman had stepped in as the new CEO. Zietsman Industries' golden boy, the thirty-year-old wunderkind who'd turned his father's mining company into a Core World powerhouse, declaring he wouldn't let "one madman's violence destroy humanity's best hope."

The media had eaten it up. Young billionaire dedicates fortune to charity. A redemption story for the ages.

Within a year, under Zietsman's leadership, the GRI had tripled its operations. He brought in "efficiency experts" and "logistical innovators," franchising the operation across a hundred worlds. The Initiative became too big to fail, too integrated into the Core Worlds' infrastructure. Politicians praised Zietsman at galas. Ellis got a state funeral and Zietsman got her humanitarian awards plus dozens more.

The GRI was still out there, still operating. Zietsman had even improved their public image—better PR firms, cleaner messaging, more sophisticated media management. Now you couldn't find a journalist willing to even investigate the organization, let alone suggest anything was wrong. The man genuinely believed he was saving civilization, that the "displaced resources" were a necessary lubricant for the greater good. He'd written a book about it: "The Calculus of Compassion: Hard Choices in Humanitarian Work." It was required reading at three Core World universities.

Every major news outlet ran puff pieces about the GRI's latest humanitarian triumphs. Critics who asked uncomfortable questions found their careers mysteriously stalled, their sources drying up, their editors suddenly uninterested. The few independent journalists who tried to dig deeper hit walls of lawyers and libel suits that bled them dry before they could publish a word.

Scott's daughter would be twenty-three now. He wondered if she believed the news stories. Probably had to read Zietsman's book for her ethics class.

"At least with Kilkenney Solutions," Scott muttered to himself, "when we fuck someone, we don't make them thank us for it."

The Purgatory's landing struts finally locked into position with a pneumatic hiss that resonated through the deck plating. The ship gave one final shudder, like a beast settling after a fight, then went still. Through the CIC's displays, Scott could see hydraulic fluid leaking from the starboard strut where they'd overstressed the seals. Smoke still rose from the scorched landing pad, the compressed coral turned to glass in places from the thruster heat.

He stood, joints popping from sitting too long, and made his way to the weapons locker bolted to the CIC's wall. His fingers worked the combination lock from memory—not that anyone would steal from the company's accountant, but old habits died hard. Inside, his sidearm waited: a 2078 Bogen .45 that had seen better decades but still put holes where holes needed to be. He checked the magazine, racked the slide to chamber a round, and holstered it at the small of his back.

The spittoon got mag-locked back to its proper place after he wiped the tobacco juice off the navigation console with an old rag. No point leaving a mess for the skeleton crew.

The CIC's armored door hissed open, and Deadeye ducked through. At six-foot-four, he filled the doorway, moving with the careful precision of someone who'd learned that relaxation got you killed. The left side of his face told its own story—skin grafts had saved it from being a horror show, but the texture was wrong, too smooth in places, too rough in others, like a topographical map of trauma. A jagged scar ran from eyebrow to cheekbone through his left eye, now white and clouded. The other eye, sharp brown, constantly moved, cataloging exits and threats even here among friendlies.

He wore green digital camo military fatigue pants and a black long-sleeved with the sleeves pushed up that covered most of the burn scars running down his left arm. His hair was buzzed regulation short, more out of habit than requirement—a leftover from a landmine during a "routine peacekeeping operation" on Thessalonica, back when he'd still believed in things like peace and keeping it.

"Where's the boss?" Deadeye asked, his voice carrying that distinctive Confederate drawl that no amount of military service had beaten out of him.

Scott looked up from his terminal. "He was in the hangar going over damage reports with—"

"Captain Jaeger is currently in his quarters preparing for tonight's festivities," Tango's synthesized voice cut in from the overhead speakers, the ship's AI always eager to be helpful.

"Thanks, Tango." Deadeye reached into his chest pocket, pulling out a small bottle of medical drops. He tilted his head back, applying them to his damaged eye. The prosthetic beneath the damaged tissue could still feed data to his neural link, but the biological parts were beyond saving.

"Boss celebrating already?" Deadeye asked, blinking the drops through.

"You know Kenney. He's probably staring at the wall, running combat scenarios in his head and calling it 'preparation.'"

"You joking right?" Deadeye said, pocketing the eye drops. "If he's not doom and gloom about that dead wife of his, he's plowing through more tail and booze than is legal in most sectors that have morality laws. The man needs to see a therapist. I mean, hell, I know we all have issues but..."

Scott snorted. "A therapist? In this outfit? Doc Haywire can patch bullet holes and reattach limbs, but I don't think 'processing survivor's guilt' is in his skill set."

"I'm serious. Last week on Meridian, he drank an entire bottle of brandy then tried to pick a fight with three marines at once. When they wouldn't bite, he found some colonel's wife and her sister and... well, Tango had to cut the security feeds."

"The Captain's coping mechanisms are his own business," Tango interjected primly.

"His 'coping mechanisms' are gonna get him killed," Deadeye countered. "Either from alcohol poisoning, an angry husband, or standing still in combat hoping someone gets lucky. You see how he fought today? Walking through fire zones like he's invincible?"

Scott shifted uncomfortably. He'd noticed it too—Kenney taking unnecessary risks, exposing himself to enemy fire, always volunteering for the most dangerous positions. It wasn't bravery; it was something darker.

"Kira's death messed him up bad," Scott said quietly. "But what are we gonna do? Stage an intervention? 'Hey boss, stop trying to die and maybe cut back on the self-destructive sex and drinking?' That'll go over well."

"Someone needs to. Before he gets himself killed and takes half of us with him."

Kenney's command quarters were one of the largest berths on the ship, encompassing his office, living room, master bath, and bedroom all in that open-concept layout that had been trendy in Core World penthouses before the war. Rank had its privileges. Also helped that he'd taken this ship single-handedly—well, the previous owners had been there to argue, but they weren't alive anymore to press the point.

Behind his desk—a monstrosity of mahogany and gold leaf looted from some imperial despot on Caracalla—hung his Wall of Solutions. Quite possibly the largest collection of ornate firearms in the galaxy. Gold-plated pistols, gem-encrusted revolvers, platinum-inlaid submachine guns, silver-worked rifles. The kind of gaudy weapons that tinpot dictators and crime lords loved to wave around, thinking it made them look powerful instead of like jewelry stores that could kill people. Every job seemed to add another piece to the collection. Seemed a shame to leave them behind when their previous owners didn't need them anymore.

The shower was running across the room, filling the open space with steam. It was a walk-in affair, all black marble and chrome, big enough to hold ten people if you really packed them in. He knew because he had, though the details of that evening on Babylon were fuzzy around the edges.

Through the fogged glass doors, three feminine silhouettes moved in the steam. The escorts from the General's car—Magdalena and her friends—had taken his invitation. He sat at his desk in a towel, ostensibly examining a bottle from President Cortez's gift: a bottle of '89 rum reserve, the kind with flakes of gold suspended in amber liquid. The bottle itself was a work of art, crystal carved to look like a conquistador's helmet, sealed with wax and ribbon that probably cost more than most people made in a month.

The bottle opener in his hand—a simple military-issue multi-tool—seemed inadequate for the task. Like trying to defuse a bomb with a hammer.

"Kenney, why you don't come?" Magdalena's voice carried over the sound of running water, her accent thicker when relaxed. Playful with just a hint of professional calculation. “The water feels so nice, baby."

"Un momento," he called back, poorly accented, still wrestling with the wax seal. The multi-tool's knife blade finally found purchase, and the conquistador helmet's top popped free with a satisfying crack.

The smell hit him first—vanilla, caramel, and something darker, like burnt sugar and history. He poured two fingers into a crystal tumbler liberated from the same despot who'd donated the desk. The gold flakes swirled like a snowglobe of wealth.

The first sip was revelation. Smooth heat that had nothing to do with alcohol content and everything to do with craftsmanship. It tasted like what money would taste like if money was delicious—complex, slightly sweet, with notes of tobacco and leather and time itself. Easily in the top fifty bottles he'd ever had, maybe top twenty.

He took another sip, then thought about Kira and how she'd always made fun of his expensive tastes, and suddenly the measured appreciation turned into a long pull straight from the bottle. The gold flakes tickled his throat. The burn felt appropriate.

Kenney?" One of the other girls—he hadn't caught her name yet—called out with concern, her voice echoing off the polished bulkheads of the luxury cabin. "Everything good, papi? You coming or no?"

"Perfect," he lied, his voice rough like gravel under combat boots. He took another long chug from the bottle, the expensive rum burning down his throat like liquid fire. It deserved to be savored, sipped like a lover's whisper, but right now, he deserved nothing but the raw punishment of gulping it like cheap rotgut whiskey from a frontier outpost.

The bottle was already a quarter empty, the gold flakes swirling in the amber liquid like stars in a nebula. At this rate, he'd kill it before the shower was over—or before he could drown out the ghosts rattling in his skull.

His exposed chest was a brutal map of violence, every inch telling a story he wished he could forget. Jagged shrapnel scars from the hellfire of Thessalonica crisscrossed his pecs like lightning strikes, puckered and raised. A bullet wound from Maddox Prime sat low on his ribs, a dark, indented crater where the round had punched through armor and flesh. And the long, surgical line snaking down his sternum—where a field medic had cracked him open like a ration pack to dig out flechette rounds that had shredded his insides. They all converged on the globe and anchor tattoo dominating his left pec, the emblem of the Rogue Marine Corps. The ink had faded over the years, edges blurring like old memories, but the motto beneath it remained sharp and accusing: "Semper Fidelis."

Always Faithful. The Rogue Marines went anywhere, did anything, for the Force Commanders' Senate. He'd served with distinction for twelve years, clawed his way to Captain, believed in the mission with every fiber of his being. Then Kira died in that convoy ambush—blown to pieces by insurgent plasma charges—and the Senate's response had been a form letter, cold as deep space: "Regret for civilian casualties during stabilization operations."

He'd submitted his resignation the next morning—"for the good of the service," citing personal reasons that no one dared question. The colonel had processed it without a word, just a nod. Officers could resign after fulfilling their obligated service time, and Kenney had been months away from punching out anyway.

"Where will you go, Captain?" the colonel had asked during the exit interview, his eyes scanning the forms like they were after-action reports.

"Private sector."

"That's what they all say." The colonel had signed off, making it official. "Your DD-214 will show honorable discharge. Full benefits. You've earned that much."

Most Marines who got out struggled with the transition—the statistics were brutal, a litany of broken souls. Half ate their sidearms within the first year, unable to adjust to a universe without orders, without purpose, without the adrenaline rush of knowing death was one wrong step away. The other half found work that used their skills—private security gigs on corporate freighters, mercenary outfits raiding pirate strongholds, enforcement teams cracking skulls for megacorps. At least keeping the skillset sharp, if not the honor intact.

But most of them didn't have eight million credits sitting in their accounts from their dead wife's estate, a fortune in old Core World money she'd never touched, now transferred to him like some cosmic joke. Blood money, fueling his new career of professional violence—stacking bodies on a galactic scale until the scales balanced out for Kira.

Another pull from the bottle, longer this time. The gold flakes were starting to accumulate at the bottom like sediment of excess, mocking his restraint.

"We're getting lonely in here," Magdalena called out, her voice carrying that universal working-girl tone of manufactured desire—professional, transactional, but alluring as hell, like a siren's call from the void.

He stood, leaving the bottle on the desk next to his service pistol—not one of the gaudy trophies from fallen enemies, just simple military steel, matte black and reliable, the kind that had saved his life more times than he deserved. The towel dropped to the floor as he walked toward the shower, revealing more scars on his thick, muscled legs—burn marks from plasma grazes, knife wounds from close-quarters brawls—and across his broad back, a lattice of whip-like lashes from some forgotten interrogation gone wrong. A roadmap of survival without purpose, every mark a testament to his unyielding body.

The steam embraced him like a lover's arms as he pulled open the glass door, thick clouds billowing out. Three sets of eyes turned his way—appraising, professional, scanning him like targets in a kill zone. They were looking for cues about what type of client they'd be dealing with tonight. The grieving widower drowning his sorrows in flesh? The combat commander needing to reclaim power through dominance? The wealthy contractor who'd pay extra for discretion and wouldn't leave permanent marks?

They'd worked embassy parties on glittering Core Worlds, served generals and governors in opulent suites, been arm candy for arms dealers and intelligence officers trading secrets in shadowed backrooms. Men with real money, real power, real secrets. The kind who had specific tastes—rough, tender, twisted—and trusted these women to fulfill them without questions, without recordings, without judgment.

They giggled and said something in Spanish that he didn't catch, though the tone was universal—three women assessing new territory, their laughter like a promise of oblivion.

Magdalena stood in the middle, water cascading over her flawless bronze skin, rivulets tracing the curves of her body like liquid gold. Her hands worked soap into a rich lather across her perfect, round breasts—full and heavy, capped with dark, hardened nipples that begged to be sucked, pinched, claimed. Her stomach was flat and toned, leading down to wide hips that flared out invitingly, her ass a firm, heart-shaped masterpiece that jiggled slightly with every movement. She had the build of someone who'd grown up working hard—lean muscle rippling beneath soft, feminine curves, the kind of practical beauty that came from raw genetics rather than surgical enhancements or pampered spa treatments. Her long, black hair clung wetly to her shoulders, framing a face with full lips painted red, and eyes that smoldered with calculated heat. Between her thighs, her pussy was shaved smooth, lips plump and inviting, already glistening from more than just the water.

To her left, the one who'd smiled at him earlier—Durazna, they called her, because her pussy looked like a tight, round peach, ripe and juicy—had the kind of innocent look that came with youth, her dark eyes still holding a spark of genuine hope amid the profession. She was petite but shapely, her body a compact hourglass with perky breasts that bounced as she moved, nipples small and pink like fresh berries. Her ass was her crowning glory—deliciously fuckable, round and firm, the kind that made a man want to grab handfuls and spread her wide. She stood under the water, her brown eyes closed and her full lips parted in a soft moan as she tilted her head back to the stream, letting the hot spray cascade over her smooth, olive skin. Her pussy peeked out between her thighs, those peach-like lips tight and puffy, begging to be parted and filled.

The other woman, Yesenia, was a voluptuous red-skinned beauty who could've been a holo-mag model, her curves exaggerated and intoxicating—massive breasts that swayed heavily with every breath, wide hips that screamed fertility, and an ass so thick and plush it could swallow a man's cock whole. Her skin was an unnatural crimson, like polished ruby, enhanced by some exotic gene-mod that made her glow under the lights. Ancient Aztec symbols decorated her face in bold black ink: geometric patterns representing Quetzalcoatl scales across her high cheekbones, crossing the bridge of her nose in a stylized sun design, like fierce war paint that contrasted sharply with her sultry smile. Her lips were full and painted a deep scarlet, her eyes a piercing green that locked onto him with predatory hunger. She rubbed soap across her body slowly, her hands lingering on her swollen breasts, tweaking her thick nipples, then sliding down to her shaved mound, where her clit peeked out, already swollen and eager.

The shower was all black marble and chrome, a decadent enclosure built for sin. Multiple showerheads lined the walls and ceiling at different heights, each with independent temperature controls, spraying hot water from every angle like a tropical storm. Teak benches ran along two sides, the wood treated to handle constant moisture without warping. In the corner sat one of those curved loungers designed for "relaxation"—its ergonomic shape, with raised contours and strategic dips, suggesting uses that had nothing to do with washing, perfect for bending someone over or pinning them down. Water recyclers hummed quietly behind the walls, making conservation irrelevant in a space engineered for pure indulgence.

The hot water hit his scarred skin from three directions at once, like a baptism in fire or a punishment from the gods—he couldn't decide which, and didn't care. Magdalena moved closer, her wet body pressing against his, running a manicured finger along one of the longer scars across his ribs, tracing it like a lover's caress.

"Does it hurt?" she asked, her accent thicker now, husky with feigned concern, her breath hot against his ear.

"Not anymore," he said, reaching past her for the soap, his arm brushing her heavy breasts. "Nothing does."

He didn't remember her being this short—standing on her toes, she barely reached his chin, giving him a perfect view down her body, the curve of her hips flaring out, her dark nipples pointing right at him like invitations, taut and begging for his mouth. She leaned into him, her breath tickling his neck, sending shivers down his spine despite the heat. He felt her tongue dart out, warm and wet, running along the curve of his jaw up to his ear. She bit it gently, then whispered, "I was getting lonely, and so were my friends."

The two others joined in seamlessly, their hands all over him like a coordinated assault—soft palms gliding over his broad chest, fingers tracing his scars, lips pressing hot kisses to the faded tattoo. They scrubbed off the battlefield grime—dried sweat from hours in armor, grease from weapon maintenance, flecks of other people's blood that he'd carried like badges. Their bodies pressed close, breasts squishing against his sides, asses brushing his thighs.

"We don't have to talk," Magdalena said, her hand finding his cock, already thick and hardening under her touch, stroking him slowly from base to tip, her fingers wrapping around his girth with expert pressure.

"That's the only rule I have," he agreed, his voice a low rumble. "No talking." He looked at the three girls, their young bodies glistening under the water—dark, beautiful eyes locked on him, soft curves pressed together in a tangle of limbs. Their smiles grew wider as they ran their fingers over his chest, nails lightly scratching, lips kissing his scars like they were worshiping a war god.

"You like to get fucked," Yesenia whispered, her voice a sultry purr, her red skin flushing darker as she eyed his throbbing length. "We make you happy. We fuck you good." Her massive breasts heaved with each breath, nipples like cherries begging to be devoured.

"You know what I want," he growled, the voice coming from somewhere primal, deep in the recesses of his soul, where grief and rage mixed with raw lust.

Magdalena smiled, her full lips curving wickedly. "Of course, papi."

She slid down to her knees gracefully, the water pooling around her, and took him into her mouth without hesitation. Her lips stretched wide around his thick shaft, her tongue swirling along the underside as she bobbed her head. He put his hands on the top of her head, fingers tangling in her wet hair, and pushed her forward, making her take more—deeper, until he felt the back of her throat. She gagged slightly but didn't pull back, her eyes watering as she looked up at him, submissive and eager.

The other girls continued their assault, Durazna's petite hands rubbing soap over his abs, her perky tits pressing against his thigh as she kissed his hip. Yesenia dropped to her knees beside Magdalena, her voluptuous body jiggling, and started licking him lower—her tongue sliding between his thighs, hot and insistent, before moving up to suck on his heavy balls, drawing one into her mouth and humming around it.

He moaned, thrusting himself further into Magdalena's throat, her nose pressing against his pelvis. His body tensed, that familiar tightness building in his core, his cock twitching in her wet heat.

"That's it, baby," Magdalena pulled back just enough to gasp, her voice muffled around him. "Let me swallow your cum. Let me swallow your whole cock. Fuck my mouth. Fuck my face."

She sucked him harder, her cheeks hollowing, hand pumping the base while her tongue worked miracles. He was getting close—so fucking close—his whole body trembling, muscles rippling under his scars.

"Oh God!"

He pulled her off abruptly, his cock slick and throbbing, and yanked Durazna toward him by her hair. Her mouth opened in a shocked gasp, her innocent eyes widening. He forced his tongue inside, biting her plump lower lip hard enough to draw a whimper, tasting her sweetness.

In one fluid motion, he shoved her onto her back on the teak bench, the wood warm and slick under her. He was on top of her in a second, pinning her slender arms above her head with one hand, his scarred body dwarfing her petite frame. He pushed himself inside her without preamble, her tight peach-like pussy stretching around his girth, wet and clutching like a vice.

Her legs wrapped around his hips, drawing him deeper, her heels digging into his ass. She was so fucking tight, her walls rippling around him as he bottomed out.

"Oh yes! Fuck me!" Durazna screamed, her voice echoing off the marble, her perky breasts bouncing with each thrust.

He pumped his hips furiously, thrusting deep and hard, pounding her lithe body into the bench, the slap of skin on skin mixing with the water's roar. Her pussy lips gripped him, her clit grinding against his pelvis.

"You like that? You like me fucking you?" he growled, his free hand squeezing one of her tits, thumb flicking her nipple.

"Yes, please don't stop," Durazna begged, her eyes rolling back, her body arching up to meet him.

"Take my cum, you dirty whore. Take my cum. Take all of it."

Durazna let out a piercing scream as her orgasm hit, her body spasming uncontrollably, nails digging into his forearms, her tight pussy clamping down on him like a fist. It sent him over the edge, and he came deep inside her, flooding her with hot spurts, his cock pulsing as he ground against her.

He rolled off her, leaning against the wall, breathing hard, his chest heaving. The water continued to cascade down over them, washing away the evidence. Magdalena smiled wickedly and nodded to the others, her breasts still lathered in soap.

"My turn," Yesenia purred, straddling him where he sat, her voluptuous red body looming like a goddess. She took his cock in her hand—still hard from the combat stims coursing through his veins—and stroked it firmly, guiding it between her thick thighs to her dripping pussy.

"Mmm," she moaned, sinking down slowly, her hot, tight walls enveloping him inch by inch. "So thick. So hard. Stretching me so good."

He put his hands on her wide hips, fingers sinking into her soft flesh, and pulled her down hard, burying himself to the hilt. She groaned, her massive breasts bouncing as she began moving her hips, grinding against him in slow circles, her clit rubbing his base.

"You like this? You like me fucking you?" he said, mimicking her earlier words, his voice rough.

"Yes," she gasped, her Aztec-tattooed face flushing, eyes half-lidded in ecstasy.

"Show me. Show me how much you like it."

She leaned forward, her heavy tits brushing his chest, nipples dragging across his scars. He took one in his mouth and sucked hard, biting down just enough to make her yelp, her pussy clenching around him. She threw her head back, arching her back, her long red hair cascading like fire. He reached down and grabbed her massive ass, squeezing the plush cheeks roughly, spreading them as he thrust up into her.

"Mmm...you like my big ass," she moaned, her voice breathy, bouncing faster now.

"Yeah, I love your ass," he grunted, slapping one cheek hard, watching it jiggle. "I'm gonna fuck your ass."

"Oh God, yes," she cried, her green eyes blazing with lust.

He flipped her over effortlessly, lifting her thick legs onto his shoulders, her ankles by his ears. Her ass was presented like a gift—round, red, and inviting, her tight hole winking at him. He pushed himself into her slowly at first, feeling the resistance give way as her ass swallowed his cock, hot and impossibly tight.

"Fuck yes! Give it to me!" she screamed, her hands gripping the bench.

He started thrusting, slamming into her hard, his balls slapping against her pussy lips. Her voluptuous body shook with each impact, breasts heaving wildly.

"Take it! Take it!" he growled, his fingers digging into her thighs.

"Oh God! Oh yes!" she screamed, her face contorted in pleasure-pain.

Her orgasm built quickly—he could feel her muscles contracting around him, squeezing his cock like a velvet glove. "I'm gonna come!" she shouted.

"Come for me, bitch," he said through clenched teeth, pounding relentlessly.

Her whole body shuddered and shook, eyes rolling back, mouth falling open in a silent scream as waves of pleasure crashed through her. He felt his own release building and thrust one last time, shooting his load deep inside her ass, filling her with heat.

Yesenia slumped against him, breathing heavily, her red skin slick with sweat and water. He pulled her close and kissed her roughly, his tongue probing her mouth, tasting her submission.

"Thank you," he said, his voice softening for a moment. "That was amazing."

"My turn," Magdalena whispered, standing over him now, her bronze body glistening, breasts heaving with anticipation. Her eyes were dark and hungry, her pussy lips swollen from watching.

He grabbed her by the waist—her curves fitting perfectly in his large hands—and lifted her off the ground like she weighed nothing, spinning her around and pinning her against the cool marble wall. She wrapped her toned legs around his waist, pulling him toward her, her heels pressing into his back. He kissed her deeply, his tongue exploring her sweet mouth, battling for dominance.

"Oh God," she moaned into his lips. "I need you inside me. Fill this tight pussy."

"I'm going to fuck you so hard," he growled, lining up and pushing himself into her in one brutal thrust, her tight walls swallowing him completely, hot and slick.

"Oh yes!" she gasped, her nails raking his shoulders. "Give it to me. Fuck me. Fuck me hard."

He started thrusting, driving himself deeper and harder with every stroke, the wall shaking slightly behind her. Her round breasts bounced against his chest, nipples scraping his skin.

"Yes! Oh God! Yes! Fuck me! Fuck me!" she screamed, her accent thick with lust.

Her legs tightened around him, pulling him impossibly deeper, her pussy contracting like it was milking him. He could feel every ridge, every flutter.

"Oh God! I'm coming!" she screamed, her body trembling.

Her orgasm hit like a shockwave, nails raking down his back hard enough to draw blood, her pussy squeezing his cock so tight it bordered on pain. He couldn't hold back and came hard, filling her with his seed, thrusting through the aftershocks.

They stood there for a few moments, bodies pressed together, water raining down. Finally, Magdalena spoke, her voice hoarse.

"How are you coming this much?" she asked, her accent thicker now, words slurred with exhaustion.

"Combat stims," he replied, smirking. "They have recreational uses too. Keeps me hard, keeps me going."

"You're hurting me," she said, but her eyes sparkled with wicked delight.

"Good," he joked, thrusting again, harder, making her gasp. "I want to fill your womb. Breed you like you deserve."

She cried out in a mix of pain and pleasure. "Oh God, stop," she moaned, but her hips bucked against him.

He pulled out reluctantly and let her down, her legs wobbling. She stumbled and fell to her knees, looking up at him with those smoldering eyes. He grabbed her by the hair and yanked her head back, exposing her throat.

"Get on your hands and knees," he ordered, his cock still throbbing, slick with their juices.

She obeyed instantly, presenting her perfect ass to him—firm cheeks spread slightly, her pussy and ass on full display, dripping. He knelt behind her, slapping her ass hard, watching the bronze skin redden.

"You like that?" he said, spanking her again.

"Yes," she whispered, pushing back.

"Louder," he commanded, landing another smack.

"Yes!" she shouted, her voice echoing.

He lined himself up with her ass this time, pushing his cock into her tight hole, forcing it deep. She cried out, body trembling, but she took him, her walls stretching around his girth.

"Yes, yes, yes," she whimpered, rocking back to meet him.

He began pumping his hips, driving deeper with every thrust, his hands gripping her hips hard enough to bruise.

"Oh God! I'm coming," she gasped, her body quaking.

Her orgasm hit, her ass spasming around him, squeezing tight. It was too much—he came again, filling her with another load, groaning as he emptied himself.

They stayed locked like that for a while, bodies entwined, until the water started to cool. When it was over, they led him back to the bed, a massive emperor-sized expanse of high-thread-count silk sheets that came with the ship. They cuddled together, naked and sticky, bodies tangled in a heap of limbs and curves.

He lay on his back, his arm around Magdalena, her head on his chest, her full breasts squished against him. She nuzzled against his shoulder, sighing contentedly. Taking the opportunity, he slid his hand down Durazna's body, fingers exploring her petite frame, tracing her perky tits before dipping between her legs to finger her asshole—still tight and slick from earlier, clenching around his digit as he probed deeper.

"You were a virgin there, weren't you?" he murmured, twisting his finger.

"Yes, daddy," Durazna cooed, her innocent eyes fluttering, body arching into his touch. "But I'm not anymore. You claimed it."

He was getting hard again, the stims fueling his insatiable hunger. He rolled on top of her, pinning her slender wrists above her head with one hand. She giggled, her perky breasts heaving.

"Thirsty for more?"

"Yeah."

"Okay."

She lifted her legs and spread them wide, giving him full access to that deliciously fuckable asshole, her peach pussy still leaking his cum. He pushed himself inside her ass slowly, savoring the stretch, the way her walls gripped him like a glove.

She gasped, then moaned softly. "Yes... oh yes."

Her hands gripped the sheets tightly as he pushed deeper, feeling every inch. He picked up the pace, pumping his hips, slamming into her.

"Oh my god," she whimpered. "Oh fuck."

She wrapped her legs around his waist and squeezed, pulling him in. "Fuck me, daddy."

He slammed his cock into her ass, filling her completely, the bed creaking under them.

"I want you to cum inside me," she begged. "Please, daddy."

He did, thrusting deep as he unloaded again. "Yes!" she cried. "I'm cumming too!"

Her body shuddered violently, ass clenching in waves. Not wanting to be left out, Yesenia dove between Magdalena's thighs, her tongue probing the bronze beauty's slit, lapping up the mixed juices with hungry slurps. Magdalena moaned and writhed, bucking her hips, her round breasts bouncing.

"Oh God," she breathed, hands tangling in Yesenia's hair.

Yesenia sucked and licked with fervor, her own voluptuous body grinding against the sheets, until Magdalena cried out and convulsed, her pussy gushing. She pulled Yesenia up, pressing their breasts together—Magdalena's full and round against Yesenia's massive, heaving orbs.

"You're the only girl who's made me come twice," Magdalena sighed, her voice husky.

"I aim to please," Yesenia said, kissing her deeply, their tongues dancing in a wet, passionate tangle. They were both panting and sweating, bodies glistening.

"Yes!" Durazna shouted from under him. "Fuuuuuuuuck!"

Yesenia and Magdalena giggled, continuing to kiss each other, their hands roaming over curves and dips.

"What about you, daddy?" Magdalena said hoarsely, breaking away to look at him.

He smiled and pulled out of Durazna, rolling onto his back, his cock still semi-hard and glistening. The girls gathered around him eagerly, their hands stroking his length—Durazna's petite fingers, Yesenia's firm grip, Magdalena's expert twists. They were so eager to please, lips and tongues joining in, sucking and licking until he came again, spurting across their faces and tits.

Afterwards, the girls lay sprawled across the emperor-sized bed, completely worn out from the marathon. Magdalena had one arm thrown across Durazna's perky breasts, her own body limp and exhausted, bronze skin marked with faint bruises and bite marks. Yesenia was curled under the sheets, her voluptuous red form nestled between his legs, her hand still cupping his balls possessively, claiming the spot for herself. The sheets—high-thread-count silk that had come with the ship—were twisted into abstract art, stained and rumpled from their excesses.

The door buzzed.

Kenney carefully extracted himself from the pile of women, running his tongue across as many parts as he could in one fluid motion. Magdalena murmured something in Spanish but didn't stir. He grabbed his fatigues from the floor, pulling them on as he padded barefoot to the door.

The security monitor showed Deadeye waiting in the corridor, his scarred face impassive.

Kenney hit the intercom. "Report."

"Boss, I got those supplies you requested from the resort concierge." Deadeye held up several boutique shopping bags. "Women's clothes, like you asked."

"Oh." Kenney glanced back at the sleeping women, then at the bags. "Why didn't you say so? Come in."

Deadeye stepped inside, carefully averting his good eye from the bed. "Figured they might want something clean to wear when they wake up. The concierge was very helpful once I mentioned who it was for. Got a variety of sizes around your recommendations."

"Good thinking." Kenney took the bags, setting them on the coffee table. Through the thin boutique tissue paper, he could see evening wear—a black cocktail dress with beaded detailing, something emerald green and slinky, a deep burgundy number with a plunging neckline. There were shoes too, strappy heels that looked expensive, and smaller bags that had to be makeup and accessories. Everything three women would need to fit into a high-class event.

"Bill it to the company?"

"To the presidential suite package. Figured Cortez owes us that much."

Deadeye fought a losing battle to keep his gaze from the tangle of bare bodies draped across the rumpled sheets. His sharp eye, ever keen, traced the voluptuous curves of their forms, lingering on the soft swell of hips and the teasing shadows of skin before he forced it back to the wall. A slow, burning flush crept up his neck, betraying the heat stirring beneath his collar.

Durazna stirred with a languid stretch, her body unfolding like a forbidden promise. With brazen ease, she slipped from the bed, her naked form gliding across the room in a display of unapologetic allure. No sheet, no towel—just the sway of her hips and the confident rhythm of her steps toward the bathroom. Deadeye's resolve crumbled, his eyes helplessly drawn to the mesmerizing dance of her silhouette, each movement a silent siren's call he couldn't ignore.

The sound of running water and rustling bags woke the other two. Magdalena sat up, breasts bouncing with the motion, immediately alert, then broke into a genuine smile when she saw the shopping bags.

"¿Para nosotras?" she asked, then switched to English. "For us?"

"Figured you might want something nice for tonight," Kenney said. "There's supposed to be some kind of event at the casino."

Yesenia was already reaching for the bags, pulling out the green dress with obvious delight. "This is designer."

"We don't do knock-offs," Deadeye muttered, still studying their breasts.

The naked women laughed, waving at him as they started examining their new wardrobes. Durazna emerged from behind the bathroom door and squealed at the sight of the clothes.

Kenney caught his eye and gave him a look—that command glare that said "get the fuck out" without words. The kind of look that had sent subordinates scurrying and ended briefings.

"I should... I have... things," Deadeye stammered, backing toward the door. "Bye ladies."

They waved goodbye, already focused on dividing the outfits, and Deadeye escaped into the corridor like a man fleeing a firefight.

"Captain Jaeger," Tango's synthesized voice filled the room from hidden speakers. "I'm pleased to report that our off-duty crew complement has departed for shore leave at the resort facilities. Predetermined duty detail of fifty remains aboard under Commander Blake's supervision."

"Good." Kenney watched the women sorting through makeup palettes with the intensity of soldiers checking ammunition. "Security status?"

"Racer and Priest are maintaining exterior patrol in their uprights. Perimeter patrol. No threats detected. The victory celebration is scheduled to commence in forty-three minutes."

Magdalena held the black dress up against herself, looking at Kenney in the mirror. "Victory celebration?"

"Cortez is throwing a party. It's to celebrate 'the preservation of democratic values.'"

"And we're invited?" Durazna asked, already applying foundation with practiced strokes.

"We're the guests of honor. We saved his government."

"A resort vehicle is currently waiting at the main hangar," Tango continued. "Luxury ground transport suitable for your party of four. Shall I inform them of an expected departure time?"

"Twenty minutes," Kenney said, then looked at the women who were now in full preparation mode. "Make it thirty." He gave Yesenia a playful swat on her fat ass as he passed.

"Acknowledged. I'll inform the driver. Also, Captain, Commander Blake wishes to discuss potential contracts when you have a moment. He says the pipeline is looking dry and we're burning through credits faster than we're making them."

"After the party, Tango."

"Understood. Enjoy your evening, Captain."

Magdalena was helping Durazna with her hair, pinning it up in something elaborate. Yesenia had claimed the bathroom mirror, applying eye shadow that made her tribal tattoo stand out even more dramatically.

While the women finished their preparations, Kenney dressed in his formal wear—black slacks and a white shirt. Over it, he slipped on the shoulder holster, the leather rig crafted from the hide of an alpha predator from Crorth. The scales had an oil-slick sheen that seemed to shift colors in the light, from deep purple to green to black. The twin gold-plated .50 caliber pistols—lifted from a cartel boss on Nuevo Laredo—settled into place with familiar weight.

A ceramic knife went into his boot, thin enough to pass most scans. A garrote wire threaded through his belt, looking like decorative braiding. A single-shot derringer tucked behind his belt buckle. With these tyrant types, you never knew when they'd decide you knew too much, cost too much, or simply out-stayed your welcome. The party invitation could be genuine gratitude or an elaborate execution. Best to be prepared for both.

"Ready?" he asked the women.

They were. Magdalena wore the black dress like a second skin, Durazna had chosen the burgundy that made her look even younger, and Yesenia had claimed the green that brought out her eyes. They looked expensive, professional, perfect for a victory celebration.

The walk through the Purgatory displayed the ship's honest purpose—built to carry machines that killed for money. The corridors were wide enough to rush casualties to medical or ammunition to gun positions, their walls bare metal marked only by damage control stations and fire suppression systems. Kenney's boots rang against the non-skid deck coating, the sound absorbed by foam-steel bulkheads designed to contain blast damage. Every twenty meters, blast doors stood open on massive hydraulic pistons, ready to seal sections in case of hull breach.

They passed through officer country first—doors closed and locked, each cabin's occupant already on shore leave. The crew quarters deck came next, a vast open berthing area that could house two hundred. Triple-stacked racks ran in long rows, each bunk barely wide enough for a person to roll over. Even on shore leave, the bunks were squared away—thin mattresses aligned, wool blankets tucked with hospital corners, pillows centered. Personal gear lived in narrow lockers between the rack stacks—barely enough room for uniforms and basic necessities. Mesh laundry bags hung from each bunk's frame, names stenciled in black marker.

The overhead fluorescents stayed on even when empty, casting harsh shadows between the rack rows. Someone had left a paperback novel on their pillow—probably marking their spot for when they returned drunk in twelve hours. The faint smell of industrial detergent mixed with the underlying funk that no amount of cleaning could fully remove from a space where two hundred people slept in proximity.

A steep stairwell connected the decks, its metal steps grooved for traction. The angle was unforgiving—designed to save space, not accommodate comfort. The women gripped the rails, their heels ringing against each step in a descending rhythm. The medical bay's hatch stood open halfway down, revealing Doc Haywire slumped at his desk between racks of surgical supplies and sealed trauma kits. A bottle of medicinal alcohol sat at his elbow, its level suggesting it had been serving double duty since noon.

The main lift was pure function—a cargo platform with safety railings, designed to move ammunition and equipment between decks. It descended through the ship's guts with mechanical precision, passing deck markings stenciled in military yellow: MAGAZINE-3, ENGINEERING-2, REACTOR-1. The smell of lubricants and ozone grew stronger as they descended, the comfortable stink of a working warship.

The hangar deck opened before them like a cathedral of controlled violence—sixty meters of open space dominated by the silent mechs in their maintenance cradles. The hangar was mostly empty, the mechs secured in their maintenance bays. A few technicians were welding armor patches, the blue-white sparks casting strange shadows. The main ramp was down, humid night air mixing with the smell of hydraulic fluid and scorched metal.

Near the main ramp, two PMCs had drawn guard duty—volunteers who'd stayed sober while everyone else went ashore. They wore standard combat kit: plate carriers over fatigues, full-face tactical helmets with integrated HUDs glowing soft blue behind the visors.

The taller one carried an R-77 pulse rifle, its compact bullpup design perfect for shipboard use. The weapon's charge indicator glowed green along the stock—full magazine, 200 rounds of hypervelocity flechettes. His partner had an M-90 plasma shotgun, the shorter variant with enhanced heat dissipation for sustained fire in confined spaces.

"Captain Jaeger," they acknowledged through their helmet speakers, the voice modulation giving them an identical electronic tone.

"Pulling security tonight?" Kenney asked.

"Someone's gotta watch the ship while everyone's out getting stupid," the taller one said, adjusting his rifle's sling where it crossed his chest plate. "Besides, seen one liberty port, seen them all."

His partner's helmet turned slightly—tracking movement on the dock visible through the ramp. "Plus we're getting hazard pay to stand here while everyone else is paying to get drunk. We're the smart ones."

The taller one shrugged, his armor vest creaking with the movement. "Besides—" he tilted his helmet toward the women, "—view's not bad from here."

The women smiled back, used to the attention.

"I'll have someone relieve you later if you want to get your dicks wet," Kenney offered.

"Appreciate it, sir, but we're good. Half the crew's gonna stumble back here in about six hours, puking and broke. Someone needs to make sure they don't bring trouble with them."

At the bottom waited a hover limo, all cream leather and tinted glass, the resort's logo etched in gold on the doors. The driver, dressed better than most military officers, stood at attention.

"Captain Jaeger? Your chariot awaits."

The driver opened the door with a practiced flourish. The girls piled in, excited, already chatting about the resort's opulence. Kenney climbed in behind them, the limo's interior spacious enough that nobody had to squeeze.

"Oh, I need champagne," Durazna said, already reaching for the crystal decanters in the built-in bar. "Look at this selection!"

"They really stocked this place," Yesenia said, pouring herself something amber.

Magdalena had found the temperature controls, adjusting the climate until the air felt cooler. They were all laughing, helping themselves to drinks, the excitement of the evening infectious.

That's when Kenney noticed him.

Sitting in the opposite corner, so still he might have been part of the furniture. Tropical linen shirt, unbuttoned just enough to look casual, sunglasses on even in the dark limo. The kind of ccasual resort wear while the eyes said "intelligence operative." Middle-aged, forgettable face with a tan that was just a shade too perfect, like he'd been born with it.

The girls noticed him at the same moment, their laughter cutting off like someone had thrown a switch.

"Commander Jaeger," the man said, his voice carrying an accent-less quality that meant expensive education and careful training. "I apologize for the surprise. I represent interested parties who've been observing today's operation."

"Hopefully, not observing too closely, I sleep in the nude." Kenney's hand drifted toward his shoulder holster.

"Far enough to be impressed. Close enough to see the details." He produced a silver case from his shirt pocket, extracting a business card that somehow managed to say nothing while looking official. "Your efficiency caught attention in certain circles. Circles that pay well for that kind of precision."

The girls had gone quiet, instinctively moving away from Kenney. Professional escorts knew trouble when they saw it.

"We're off the clock," Kenney said.

"Of course. This is merely a social introduction. Tomorrow, perhaps, we could discuss opportunities. For now, enjoy your celebration. You've earned it."

The man leaned forward slightly, his eyes burned with predatory focus. "There's a situation developing on the Fringe. Multiple situations, actually. The kind that require... unofficial solutions."

"Still off the clock," Kenney growled.

"Of course. But consider this—if your team could solve certain problems for the people I represent, we could open doors in the Core Worlds. The kind of doors that would make your procurement issues disappear. Military-grade, no questions asked. Legal landing permits. Banking without scrutiny."

"Everyone promises to make things easier," Kenney said. "Usually right before they make them complicated."

The spook smiled—a thin, professional expression. "Fair enough. I'm not asking for commitment, Commander. Just... receptiveness. The Fringe is unstable. Revolution is profitable for men like you, but chaos? Chaos is bad for everyone's business."

"Tomorrow," the man said, tapping the window. The limo immediately pulled over, smooth as silk. "I'll call on you after you've had time to enjoy tonight. The presidential suite, I believe?"

He opened the door himself, stepping out into the humid night. Before closing it, he turned back. "Oh, and Captain? Your acquisition of the gold reserves was subtly impressive. My employers appreciate initiative."

The door closed with a soft click, and the limo pulled back into traffic.

"Who was that?" Durazna asked, her earlier excitement dimmed.

"Trouble," Kenney said, reaching for the champagne. "The expensive kind."

Angel's Cove at night transformed into something out of a fever dream—all neon and sin wrapped in tropical paradise. The main promenade glowed with bioluminescent palms, their gene-modified fronds pulsing blue and green in rhythm with the music drifting from a dozen venues. Beautiful women in designer nothing strolled between the casinos and clubs, their laughter mixing with the sound of waves against the artificial reef.

Kilkenney Solutions had made their presence known.

At the Platinum Lounge, thirty mercenaries had commandeered the entire top floor, running up a tab that would fund a small revolution. Someone had brought a karaoke machine, and the sound of drunk soldiers butchering classic ballads echoed across the water. Two more had started an arm-wrestling tournament that had drawn a crowd of tourists eager to bet on authentic killers.

Inside the main casino, McKnight was on fire at the craps table, his tropical print shirt unbuttoned drawing almost as much attention as his streak. The dice loved him tonight—seven straight passes, the chips piling up like combat honors. Big Country stood behind him, murmuring what might have been prayers or might have been probability calculations. Killjoy was at the blackjack table, his scarred hands steady despite the three bottles of whiskey he'd killed since landing.

Kenney watched it all from the VIP balcony, nursing a rum that tasted like power. He had a complicated relationship with gambling—he'd killed and stolen for his money fair and square, no reason to let the house take their cut. The risk wasn't the problem; it was the randomness. Combat had variables you could control. Cards and dice were just chaos dressed up in statistics.

Below, heads of state mingled with crime lords, all pretending they weren't the same thing with different business cards. President Cortez held court near the baccarat tables, his new wife—twenty years younger and bought from some Core World finishing school—draped on his arm like jewelry. The President of Zeanov was there too, the one who'd survived three coup attempts this year alone, his girlfriend's dress so revealing it was basically a suggestion.

The girls had drifted to one of Angel's Cove's notorious VIP hot tubs, where clothing was a mere afterthought, the air thick with steam and temptation. Through the swirling mist, Kenney's gaze was drawn to a decadent scene: a cluster of working companions, their slick, bronzed bodies glistening under the soft glow of lantern light. Full, rounded curves and taut, sculpted limbs intertwined with effortless sensuality—bare shoulders brushing against each other, thighs grazing in the warm water, every movement a study in provocative grace.

Magdalena, her raven hair slicked back and clinging to her neck, arched slightly as a stranger's lips traced the delicate curve of her collarbone, her olive skin flushed with heat. Her low, husky laugh rang out, blending with Durazna's whispered mischief, the younger woman's lithe frame leaning close, her pert breasts catching the light as she moved with feline confidence. Yesenia, all bold angles and smoldering intensity, had a curvaceous blonde perched in her lap, their bodies pressed close—Yesenia's toned arms encircling the woman's narrow waist, their slow, rhythmic movements sending ripples through the water that hinted at something far more intimate than casual chatter.

A polished silver tray sat poolside, brimming with elite party favors—designer vices that promised to blur the edges of restraint and ignite every nerve. The scene pulsed with a performative allure, each woman acutely aware of the eyes on them, their movements deliberate, inviting. They thrived on it, their confidence radiating like a current, pulling Kenney's attention with magnetic force. Magdalena leaned back, her voluptuous figure half-submerged, water beading on her smooth, caramel skin as it traced the swell of her chest. Her full lips parted in a lazy, uninhibited laugh, her dark eyes glinting with starlight and something dangerously inviting.

Every detail—their glistening bodies, the subtle flex of muscle, the teasing brush of skin—wove a spell of raw, hedonistic escape. At least they were having fun. That's what this was all about, right? Fun. Forgetting. Pretending tomorrow wouldn't come with its own bill.

"Captain Jaeger?" An attendant in the resort's gold-trimmed uniform appeared at his elbow, professionally ignoring the chaos around them. "President Cortez requests your company in the private salon. Would you accompany me?"

Kenney nodded, setting down his glass. Gold flecks from the ceremonial rum still stuck in his teeth, making everything taste like money and power. "Lead the way."

He left without a word to the girls. They wouldn't notice anyway, too lost in whatever chemical paradise they'd found. Magdalena was telling some story between kisses with another escort, their hands exploring beneath the water while she laughed at her own punchline. Durazna was draped over the edge of the tub, her head tilted back as someone worked between her thighs, her soft moans mixing with the bubbling water. Yesenia had paired off with two others, the three of them creating a tangle of limbs that made it hard to tell where one ended and another began.

The whole scene had that exhibitionist quality—professional companions putting on a show for whoever cared to watch, high enough not to care who that might be.

The attendant led him through the casino's back passages, away from the noise and neon, into the sections reserved for people who owned countries or wished they did. The carpet got thicker, the lighting more subtle, the security more obvious—men in suits who watched everything and tried to conceal the weapon bulges under their jackets.

"Right through here, sir."

The security detail stood at their posts—two by the door, one operating a handheld scanner. The lead guard, a thick-necked professional with prison tattoos creeping above his collar, held up his hand.

"Stop there. Arms out for scanning."

Kenney raised his arms to shoulder height, the movement making his white shirt pull tight across his chest. The shoulder holster rig was completely visible—dark leather straps crossing his torso, the twin gold-plated .50s catching the salon's ambient lighting.

The guard with the scanner ran it over Kenney's body, the device immediately shrieking its alert. The lead guard's hand moved to his own weapon.

"Sir, you'll need to remove those weapons before—"

"Stop," Cortez commanded from his position near the floor-to-ceiling windows. "This man saved my country today. Let him through."

The guards stepped back reluctantly, and Kenney entered the private salon. The private salon was all mahogany panels and crystal decanters, every surface polished to mirror brightness. Floor-to-ceiling windows dominated one wall, offering a view of the resort's artificial lagoon where bioluminescent algae had been introduced to make the water glow blue at night. Leather furniture sat arranged for intimate conversations, the chairs deep enough to swallow a person whole. A humidor built into the wall displayed cigars like artifacts in a museum, each band representing a different conquered world or extinct tradition. The carpet was thick enough to muffle footsteps completely, creating an unnatural quiet that made even breathing seem loud.

Cortez turned from the window, a fresh cigar smoldering between his fingers. "Kenney, my friend. Cigar? Drink?"

"Actually, yes. And thank you for that bottle you sent. The '89 reserve. That's a hell of a rum."

Cortez's face lit up with genuine pleasure. "You opened it already? Most people save bottles like that, put them on shelves like trophies."

"Seemed a shame to let it sit. Good liquors meant to be drunk."

"A man after my own heart." Cortez poured two glasses of something amber from a crystal decanter. "This is from the same distillery, the '76. Even better, if you can believe it."

They clinked glasses, and Kenney had to admit, the man knew his liquor.

"Now then," Cortez said, settling into a chair carved from a single piece of super-sequoia, its deep green/purple grain polished to liquid smoothness. "I have a proposition. Your men, your ship, your mechs—join me permanently. With that kind of firepower under my direct command, we would be unstoppable. I could extend my influence across the entire Caribbean sector."

There it was. The offer. It came like clockwork with these types, something about absolute power needing to acquire more power, like an addiction that could never be satisfied.

Kenney had seen how this movie ended too many times. The first few months would be paradise—parties, women, luxury beyond measure. Then someone would make a joke Cortez didn't like, and they'd disappear. Then Kilkenney's people would be training local forces as "backup." Then one morning, they'd wake up facing a firing squad because Cortez decided foreign mercenaries knew too many secrets.

"That's a generous offer," Kenney said carefully. He'd practiced this in the mirror, knowing the refusal had to be delivered with surgical precision. "The thing is, President Cortez, our effectiveness comes from our independence. We're valuable because we're outside your power structure. Make us insiders, and we become just another military unit. Another potential threat to manage."

Cortez's eyes narrowed slightly.

"Besides," Kenney continued, keeping his tone light, "you don't want mercenaries who'd abandon their business model for a better offer. That's how you get contract breakers. You want mercs who honor contracts and leave when the job's done. That's how you stay in power."

Cortez laughed, a genuine sound that seemed to surprise even his guards. "Ah, you are right, my friend. Better to have wolves who leave than mutts who stay and bite." He swirled his rum, studying the amber liquid. "Tell me, what was it like facing down that rebel general? Like something out of the old holo-westerns, no? The space cowboy strikes again!"

"He had his chance," Kenney said simply. "Went for his gun. Made his choice."

"And got his reward against a wall this evening," Cortez chuckled darkly. "Revolutionary justice, they called it. The same walls where he had my supporters shot last week. Poetic, no?"

"If you say so."

Cortez launched into a story about a hunting expedition on his private reserve, something about genetically modified tigers that could camouflage like chameleons. Kenney nodded at the right moments while Cortez described stalking invisible predators through tropical jungles.

"—and then my new yacht arrived last week," Cortez continued, barely pausing for breath. "Three hundred meters, submarine capability, defensive shields that could stop an orbital strike. The master suite has a transparency mode—the entire hull becomes clear steel. You can watch the ocean floor while you sleep."

"Sounds expensive."

"Everything worthwhile is. Speaking of which—" Cortez stood suddenly. "I'm famished. This revolution interrupted my lunch. Would you join me? The resort has a sushi master, trained in the old traditions. Exotic fish from our reserves, not that cultured space protein garbage you're probably used to."

They stepped into the private dining room, where a breathtaking tableau awaited, steeped in the provocative elegance of nyotaimori. The ambassador's twin daughters reclined on parallel ebony tables, their flawless bodies transformed into living platters. They were mirror images of each other—porcelain-pale skin glowing under the soft chandelier light, their lithe, sculpted forms stretched out in perfect symmetry. Midnight-black hair cascaded in intricate braids, adorned with vibrant tropical fruits and delicate orchid petals that teased the eye, drawing attention to the gentle curves of their necks and shoulders. Artfully arranged sushi and sashimi adorned their bodies, each piece strategically placed to accentuate the swell of their breasts, the taut plane of their stomachs, and the subtle dip of their hips, turning the presentation into a tantalizing dance of art and allure.

“The ambassador was very generous,” Cortez murmured, settling into his seat, his voice tinged with appreciation. “His daughters volunteered when they heard you'd be joining me. They're masters of the old traditions—absolute stillness, exquisite control, even their body temperature perfectly tuned to the moment.”

The twins remained utterly motionless, their breathing so subtle it was nearly imperceptible, their almond-shaped eyes fixed on some distant point, exuding an aura of serene seduction. Their skin, smooth and unblemished, shimmered faintly with a sheen of warmth, each piece of sashimi nestled against their curves seeming to invite closer inspection. Their disciplined stillness only heightened the effect, their bodies radiating a quiet, magnetic sensuality that made the air feel charged. They were more than mere presentation pieces; they were living sculptures of desire, as integral to the dinner's decadence as the finely honed chef's knives or the rare, imported sake chilling nearby.

Every detail—their silken skin, the delicate arch of their collarbones, the way the tropical blooms in their hair framed their ethereal beauty—pulled the gaze irresistibly. The room thrummed with an undercurrent of forbidden allure, each moment a calculated invitation to savor not just the meal, but the intoxicating vision before them.

Kenney had seen displays like this a dozen times before—Core World parties, crime lord celebrations, anywhere power and money intersected with a desire to show off. He selected a piece of tuna without hesitation, his movements casual. The fish was exceptional—buttery texture that dissolved on his tongue.

"Nice spread," he said to Cortez, earning a bark of laughter from the president. He took another piece, this time salmon from between the nearer twin's breasts, making sure his fingers were cold from the sake cup as he reached for it. She suppressed the tiniest shiver—barely visible, but there. Human after all.

After what he'd done today, after what he'd been doing for years, even this baroque display barely registered.

"Magnificent, aren't they?" Cortez selected a piece from one twin's stomach. "Gene-crafted for perfect symmetry. Their father had them made to order on Gemini Station. Cost him a fortune, but look at the result."

"Good return on investment," Kenney said, taking another piece. The fish was exceptional, though he barely tasted it through the rum haze. "He loans them out often?"

"When it serves diplomatic purposes. He's very strategic about his assets." Cortez smiled.

The chef continued his work in silence, placing new pieces with mathematical precision. The twins remained motionless, their breathing so controlled that the carefully balanced food never shifted.

"To strategic assets," Kenney raised his sake cup, and Cortez laughed, clinking his own against it.

As the night wore on, the booze and food kept flowing—sake giving way to whiskey, sushi replaced by grilled meats and exotic fruits. The twins eventually rose from their positions with practiced grace, excusing themselves briefly before returning in flowing silk costumes adorned with chains of coins and jewels that caught the light with every movement. They began to dance, their movements perfectly synchronized, trained since childhood for moments like these.

Kenney lit up one of Cortez's offered cigars—a hand-rolled masterpiece from Havana-7, the tobacco genetically modified to burn slower and smoother than anything nature had intended. The smoke curled up toward the ceiling, mixing with the incense the twins had lit.

"You know," Cortez said, his words slightly slurred from the evening's indulgences, "I keep thinking about my offer. Imagine what we could accomplish together. Your tactical genius, my resources..."

"You honor me with the thought," Kenney said diplomatically, watching the twins spin in perfect unison. "But we're specialists, President Cortez. We're good at what we do because it's all we do. Short engagements, clear objectives, then we move on."

"But the stability you could provide—"

"Would make us different people." Kenney took a long pull from the cigar. "You need us to be outsiders. That's our value. The moment we become part of your structure, we lose what makes us effective."

Cortez studied him through the smoke. "You really won't reconsider?"

"My men trust me to keep them moving, keep them sharp. Park us in one place too long, we get soft. Soft mercs are dead mercs."

"And loyalty? That means nothing?"

"Our loyalty is to the contract. That's what you're buying—the certainty that we'll complete the job and leave. No political ambitions, no palace intrigue. Just professional service."

Cortez sighed, raising his glass. "To professional service then. And to knowing when not to push."

"It really is a generous offer," Kenney said, setting down his glass. "Just not what we're looking for. But if you ever need help in the future, call us. Even if you don't need mechs—we've got connections with premier outfits in ground and air sectors too. Sometimes a problem needs a scalpel, not a hammer."

"Useful to know." Cortez pushed himself up from the bloodwood chair, his hands gripping the armrests for stability. He stood slowly, the evening's indulgences making him sway like a ship in rough seas. His medals jangled softly as he found his balance, one hand briefly touching the table to steady himself.

From somewhere outside, the distinctive chatter of automatic weapons fire erupted—celebration rounds, common at these victory parties. Someone had probably liberated a case of ammunition and decided fireworks weren't enough.

"Thank you again, my friend, for pulling my ass out of the fire today." The president extended his hand, his movement slightly exaggerated from the alcohol.

Kenney rose from his own chair in one fluid motion—the controlled movement of someone still sober, still alert despite the evening's hospitality. He clasped Cortez's hand firmly, feeling the slight tremor in the president's grip. "Just business, President Cortez."

"Without you, I'd be decorating a wall right now."

As Cortez moved toward the door, he suddenly spun, fingers pointed like pistols, mimicking a quick draw. "Bang!" He laughed at his own joke, the sound echoing off the walls. "Still not fast enough to beat a space cowboy, eh?"

His guards followed him toward the exit, professionally ignoring their president's drunken antics. At the threshold, Cortez paused, gesturing back at the twins who were still dancing.

"Girls, keep our hero happy tonight. He saved us all today. Show him proper appreciation."

Then he was gone, his entourage trailing behind, leaving Kenney alone with the twins, the smoke, and the weight of another successful contract. The automatic weapons fire outside intensified—someone had found a second case of ammunition.

The twins moved closer, their dancing shifting from performance to invitation.

Kenney's gaze shifted, seeing them properly for the first time all evening. Not as decorations or diplomatic assets, but as women—beautiful, trained, and currently very interested in showing their appreciation. The alcohol had burned through most of his better judgment, leaving only base needs and the familiar ache of trying to forget.

The twins moved with practiced synchronization, one taking his cigar to set it aside, the other refilling his glass. They knew their trade.

"The president said to thank you properly," one said, her accent musical.

"We're very good at showing gratitude," the other added, their movements suggesting exactly what form that gratitude might take.

Kenney stood, the room spinning slightly from the combination of rum, whiskey, and sake. Tomorrow there would be contracts to review, ammunition to source, and the endless logistics of keeping a mercenary company running. Tomorrow he'd have to be Commander Jaeger again, making decisions that kept five hundred people alive and profitable.

But tonight he was just a damaged man with too much blood on his hands and not enough reasons to wash them clean. The twins seemed to understand that—they'd probably seen it before in other soldiers, other killers who used pleasure like morphine for wounds that wouldn't heal.

The twins moved closer, their dance a hypnotic blend of grace and seduction, their bodies swaying in perfect sync. One slid behind Kenney, her delicate hands gliding up to his shoulders, fingers kneading the taut, combat-hardened muscles with a touch that was both firm and tantalizingly soft. Her breath was warm against his neck, sending shivers down his spine. The other twin faced him, her eyes smoldering with intent as her nimble fingers worked the buckles of his shoulder holster with startling expertise, her touch brushing his chest in a way that set his nerves alight.

“You don’t need to be armed here,” she murmured, her voice a sultry caress as she lifted the rig away, placing it on a side table—close enough to reach, far enough to promise safety. Her sister’s hands moved to his shirt, unbuttoning it with slow, deliberate precision, each undone button revealing more of his skin to the smoky air. The coins on their sheer costumes chimed softly, a seductive melody that pulsed through the haze-filled room, matching the rhythm of their swaying hips.

“The president says you’re a hero,” one whispered, her lips grazing his ear, her voice dripping with admiration.

“The president’s a friend,” Kenney replied, his voice rough from cigars and exhaustion, though his pulse quickened under their touch.

They laughed, a sound that wasn’t the practiced titter of working girls but something raw, almost genuine, vibrating with promise. Outside, another burst of celebratory gunfire rattled the night, but it was drowned out by the heat of their bodies closing in.

The twin in front knelt before him, her eyes gleaming with hunger, her movements swift yet deliberate. Her fingers found his belt, undoing it with a deftness that made his breath hitch. Her sister pressed herself against his back, her body warm and yielding, the heat of her skin seeping through her flimsy costume. “Just relax,” she purred, her lips brushing his neck, her voice a velvet command that sent a jolt straight to his core.

His pulse pounded as the kneeling twin slid his trousers open, her fingers trailing lightly down his abdomen, teasing the sensitive skin just above his groin before dipping lower. Her touch was electric, igniting a fire that spread through him. She smiled, her lips full and glistening, and Kenney groaned, his eyes fluttering shut as the world narrowed to the sensation of her hands. Her sister's breasts pressed against his bare shoulders, the sharp peaks of her nipples evident even through the thin fabric, grazing his skin with every subtle movement.

The kneeling twin's mouth found him, her lips hot and insistent, her tongue swirling with a skill that made his hips jerk involuntarily. She giggled—a soft, girlish sound that contrasted the raw intensity of her actions—her tongue tracing a slow, deliberate path along his length, her fingers curling into his hips as he moaned, his body taut with need. The twin behind him slid her hands down his chest, her nails grazing the ridges of his abdomen before tangling in her sister's hair, guiding her into a faster, more urgent rhythm.

"Oh, fuck," Kenney muttered, his voice a desperate rasp, his body a coiled spring of desire.

The kneeling twin's hand tightened on his hip, anchoring him as her lips slid further, taking him deeper, her tongue teasing the sensitive tip with maddening precision. Her eyes locked onto his, half-lidded and burning with lust, her breath hot against his skin. Her sister's hands roamed lower, fingers brushing the base of his shaft, her thumb pressing firmly into the sensitive spot just below the head, sending a shockwave through him.

Kenney's hands fisted in the silk of the kneeling twin's dress, pulling her closer as his hips bucked. "More," he growled, his voice raw with need. The twin behind him murmured soft encouragements, her hands stroking his neck and shoulders, but his focus was wholly on the twin before him, her lips gliding effortlessly along his erection, her tongue flicking with a rhythm that bordered on torturous.

Her teeth grazed him lightly, a delicate sting that made his hips jerk harder, each bob of her head driving him closer to the edge. The twin behind him moaned softly, her body rocking against his back, her breasts pressed tight against him, nipples hard and teasing through the fabric. The room filled with the wet, slick sounds of the kneeling twin's lips and fingers, mingling with Kenney's ragged breaths and her soft whimpers.

"Close," he hissed, his hands tightening in her dress, his body straining toward release.

The kneeling twin moaned, the sound vibrating through him, amplifying the intensity until it was almost painful. Her sister's hand slid lower, cupping him, her fingers tightening with perfect pressure. The kneeling twin's lips took him deeper, her throat constricting around him in a way that shattered his control.

"Fuck!" he shouted, the word torn from him as his hips surged forward. His hands pulled her closer, his body shuddering with an agonizing release that left him trembling. She pulled back, coughing softly, his release glistening on her lips and chin. Her sister leaned in, her tongue tracing slow, deliberate paths across her twin's face, lapping up the evidence of his pleasure with a sensual grace that made his head spin.

"Good boy," the kneeling twin purred, her voice a sultry promise as she licked her lips.

Kenney's head swam, the haze of alcohol and adrenaline making his legs weak. The twins giggled, their faces flushed, their eyes still alight with mischief. They pushed him gently back into his chair, and he sank into it, chest heaving. But they weren't done. Turning to each other, their hands moved with practiced ease, peeling away the sheer fabric of their costumes. Their breasts spilled free—full, pale, and perfect, with small, pink nipples that stood erect in the flickering candlelight, begging to be touched.

One twin leaned forward, capturing her sister's lips in a deep, hungry kiss, her hand cupping a breast, fingers teasing a nipple until it hardened further. The other arched into her touch, moaning softly, her body quivering. Kenney watched, transfixed, as the twins' hands roamed lower, fingers brushing the soft, neatly trimmed patches between their thighs. Their pussies were a vision—silken, glistening, and perfectly groomed, each adorned with a delicate strip of dark hair that framed their swollen, inviting folds.

He couldn't resist. Pulling one twin closer, he drew her onto his lap, his face buried against her, his tongue tracing the slick, sensitive lips of her pussy, savoring the sweet, musky taste as she gasped. Her sister straddled his hips, her own pussy—tight, wet, and pulsing—sliding down onto his still-hard cock. Her breasts bounced with each movement, full and jiggling, as she rode him, her lips locked with her twin's in a passionate kiss.

The first twin moaned, her pussy clenching against his tongue as he licked her clit with relentless precision, her juices coating his face. The second twin's movements grew frantic, her breasts swaying as she bounced, her pussy gripping him tightly. The twins' moans filled the room, their bodies pressed together, breasts brushing as they kissed, their tongues entwined. The first twin's orgasm hit hard, her scream muffled by her sister's mouth, her pussy pulsing against Kenney's lips as her body shook. Moments later, the second twin followed, her pussy contracting around his cock as she came, her juices mixing with his as he filled her.

Gasping, the twins collapsed beside each other, their pussies still glistening, their bodies trembling with aftershocks. Kenney, still hard and hungry, moved between them, kissing each in turn. He lifted the second twin onto his lap, her moan vibrating through him as his cock slid into her tight, dripping pussy. "God... you're so big," she gasped, rocking against him, her pussy clenching with every thrust.

The twins resumed their kiss, their hands roaming—one squeezing her sister's breasts, the other rubbing her clit as Kenney fucked her. He gripped their hips, pumping deeper, his cock hitting her core with each thrust. The first twin's fingers worked her sister's pussy, amplifying her pleasure, while Kenney's hands roamed to the other's ass, squeezing the firm curves. The second twin shuddered, her pussy tightening as another orgasm ripped through her, her juices coating him. Kenney turned to the first twin, pushing into her with a growl, her pussy hot and tight around him. She moaned, her body arching as he thrust deep, her pussy clenching with every stroke.

"Yes, yes, I'm gonna cum!" she cried, her pussy pulsing as she came, her juices mixing with his as he released inside her. "Fuck, you feel so good," he groaned, his cock sliding out, still slick with her. She begged for more, and he obliged, driving into her again, her pussy quivering around him as he fucked her hard, their bodies slick with sweat and desire, the twins' pussies the center of his world as they moaned and writhed in perfect, intoxicating unison.

He dressed quickly in the pre-dawn darkness, his movements efficient despite the lingering alcohol haze. The twins were tangled together on the salon's silk sheets, exhausted from their performance. He grabbed his pants, boots, shirt, and the shoulder holster, balling the shirt up in his fist rather than putting it on.

On his way out, he snagged a slice of gene-modified pineapple from the fruit display—bright blue flesh that tasted like the original but with twice the sugar content. The juice ran down his chin as he walked through the resort's quiet corridors, the first hints of sunrise turning the sky from black to deep purple.

The shoulder rig sat against his bare chest, the alien leather cool against his skin. A few early-rising staff members averted their eyes as he passed—a shirtless mercenary with visible weapons wasn't unusual after a victory celebration. They'd probably seen worse.

The walk back to the Purgatory was almost peaceful. The beach was littered with passed-out mercenaries and empty bottles, evidence of the night's excess. Someone had driven a stolen golf cart into the lagoon where it sat half-submerged. Two of his men were asleep in a decorative fountain, still clutching their naked companions.

The morning air was thick with humidity and ocean salt. For a moment, with the pineapple's sweetness on his tongue and the sunrise painting everything gold, he could almost forget what he was walking back to—the contracts, the killing, the endless cycle of violence that paid for nights like these.

Almost.

He stopped at the beach's edge, where the manicured resort sand met the natural shoreline. The sunrise painted the water gold and orange, the kind of view that travel brochures promised but rarely delivered.

Kira would have loved this place.

The thought hit him like a round to the chest. She would have mocked the resort's pretensions while secretly enjoying the luxury. Would have made friends with the staff, learned their names, heard their stories. She'd have pulled him into the water at midnight, laughing at his protests about wet clothes.

They'd been unstoppable together. Two rifles covering overlapping fields of fire. She'd been the better shot, though he'd never admitted it out loud. Could put a round through a playing card at three hundred meters in a crosswind. But more than that—she'd made him believe they could build something beyond the next contract, beyond the next battle.

The tear came without warning, salt mixing with the lingering sweetness of pineapple. Not from the beauty of the sunrise, but from the crushing weight of experiencing it alone. Another day starting without her. Another twenty-four hours of pushing through, self-medicating with whatever was at hand, pretending the hole in his chest was just another scar.

Three years now. Three years of mornings like this, where the world's beauty felt like mockery. The universe kept spinning, suns kept rising, and Kira stayed dead because he'd been too slow, too stupid, too focused on his career to see the ambush coming.

The sound of splashing pulled him from his thoughts. Joker emerged from the surf like some ancient war deity, wearing nothing but a diving knife on a belt and snorkel gear, a mesh bag in one hand and spear gun in the other. The morning sun illuminated every inch of her breathtaking form, casting a glow over the intricate tattoo work covering her body—a complete canvas of Neo-Slavic criminal hierarchy. Orthodox churches climbed her ribs, their spires curling just beneath the full, voluptuous curve of her breasts, each one a perfect, heavy teardrop that swayed slightly with her movements, drawing the eye with their lush, rounded allure. Eight-pointed stars spread across her shoulders, Cyrillic text wound around her arms and thighs, each mark a story she'd never share. Few in the company talked about their pasts, and Joker least of all.

She pushed the goggles onto her forehead as she jogged up the beach toward him, completely unbothered by her lack of clothing, her confidence amplifying the raw magnetism of her body. Her ass, a masterpiece of taut, rounded perfection, flexed with each step, the sunlight catching the smooth, bronzed skin and highlighting the intricate ink—a tangle of roses and skulls—that framed its heart-stopping curves like a work of art. She grinned as she hefted the bag, her breasts bouncing lightly, their firmness accentuated by the way her chest rose and fell with each breath. “Two grouper and something I’ve never seen before—purple fins, supposed to taste like butter though.” She dropped the gear in the sand, stretching in the morning sun, her body arching to showcase the generous swell of her chest and the tight, sculpted curve of her backside. “God, I love this place. Haven’t been diving in ages. We should’ve taken shore leave here years ago.”

Her enthusiasm felt jarring against his self imposed mood, but that was Joker—always finding light in the darkness, even when the darkness had teeth. He found himself cataloging the tattoos despite himself, his tactical mind automatically reading the criminal resume written on her otherwise perfect skin, filing images away for later.

He pushed the grief down, locking it away where it couldn't touch anyone else. No point dragging her into his darkness. He forced a smile, his eyes unavoidably drawn to the tantalizing sight of Joker's body as she stood there, unapologetically bare under the morning sun. The intricate Neo-Slavic tattoos adorned her form, but it was the meticulously shaved patch between her thighs that caught his breath—a perfect, sculpted landing strip, dark and neatly trimmed, accentuating the alluring contours of her pussy. The sunlight played across her skin, highlighting the smooth, inviting lines of her lower body, a provocative contrast to the dangerous edge of the diving knife strapped to her hip. He nodded at the bag of fish, forcing his gaze upward. "That purple one does sound interesting. You bringing me a plate when you cook them up?"

"Maybe," she said with a playful shrug, water still dripping from her hair and breasts. "Depends on what you're offering in trade."

He had a strict rule about not sleeping with employees—it caused too many issues, mixing business and pleasure. Command structures got muddy, people made stupid decisions, and when things inevitably went south, it compromised the whole team. He'd seen it happen too many times to other crews.

But that didn't stop them from trying. Joker saw him as that sort of forbidden fruit she was intent on getting one way or another. She was patient about it though, never pushing too hard, just maintaining this constant low-level flirtation that danced right along the edge of professional. Standing there now, making no move to cover herself or grab a towel, was just another move in her long game. She knew exactly what she was doing.

"I've got that bottle of vodka from Odessa," he offered, keeping his tone neutral. "Fair trade?"

Her grin widened. "Now you're talking."

He wiped his face with his balled-up shirt and kept walking. The Purgatory waited, ugly and functional, everything Kira hadn't been. At least there he could lose himself in paperwork and violence, the only honest things left in his world.

CHAPTER THREE

The hangar bay of the Purgatory had been hastily converted into a meeting space. They'd dragged a tactical planning table from storage; its holographic projectors still caked with dust from the last time anyone bothered with formal briefings. Kenney sat at the head, nursing black coffee that could strip paint. To his right, Scott Blake worked through ammunition costs on his datapad, occasionally spitting tobacco juice into his disposable cup filled with wadded napkins.

Chief Mechanic Derg slouched opposite them, grease permanently embedded under his fingernails despite the sonic shower he'd taken twice daily. The man was built like a brick—short, wide, and dense, with arms like hydraulic pistons from years of wrestling mech parts into submission. His coveralls bore the logo of three different militaries, all of them defunct.

Jenson Wilson, their chief of security, stood rather than sat. Six-foot-six of augmented muscle and barely contained violence, covered in prison tattoos that told the story of a misspent youth before military service gave him a legal outlet for his tendencies. His white hair was buzzed in a high-and-tight military cut, the precise lines speaking to old habits that decades of mercenary work hadn't broken. At fifty-three, Wilson was older than most of the crew by at least a decade, his weathered face carrying the kind of scars that came from surviving wars younger men hadn't even heard of.

The sidearms at his hips weren't standard issue—a matched pair of Krueger-Dynamics KD-50 Penetrators, custom jobs with extended barrels and integrated muzzle brakes. The weapons fired 12.7mm tungsten-core rounds designed to punch through power armor at close range. Each gun weighed nearly three kilos unloaded, the kind of hand cannons that would break a normal person's wrist. Wilson had added aftermarket grip stippling and ambidextrous mag releases, turning already lethal weapons into personalized instruments of violence.

Doc Haywire completed their leadership council, though "leadership" was generous. He was already three drinks in despite it being 0900 hours, his medical credentials from some fringe world that probably didn't exist anymore. But he could stitch a man back together with fishing line and prayers, reattach limbs with battlefield expedience, and had saved more of their people than anyone wanted to count.

The man who called himself Mr. Smith sat across from them all, still in his resort casual wear, looking like a tourist who'd wandered into the wrong meeting.

"Gentlemen," Smith began, activating a secure holo-projector. "The planet is Regalia. You may have heard of it—currently experiencing what the media calls a 'territorial dispute.'"

The projection showed a world torn in half, battle lines drawn across continents like infected wounds.

"Two factions, both claiming legitimacy, both committing enough war crimes to keep tribunals busy for decades." Smith manipulated the display, zooming in on a coastal city. Gray concrete blocks and industrial sprawl, the kind of Eastern Bloc architecture that prioritized function over form. "Sevastopol City. There's a facility here that needs to cease existing. Its purpose isn't your concern—what matters is that no evidence of it ever surfaces."

"Black site?" Kenney asked.

"The kind of black that absorbs light," Smith replied. "It needs to be thoroughly destroyed. We're talking tactical nuclear thoroughly."

Derg whistled low. "That's a lot of thoroughly."

"The complication," Smith continued, "is that the city sits in the contested zone. Both factions patrol it heavily. You'll be fighting through both sides to reach it."

The display shifted to show a subsea pipeline emerging from the harbor. "This pumping station services the entire eastern grid. Destroying it would create enough chaos—and draw enough military response—to give a small team of mechs a window to penetrate the facility's perimeter, plant the device, and evacuate."

"Rules of engagement?" Wilson asked, his voice like gravel in a cement mixer.

"Both sides are legitimate military targets. Collateral damage is... expected."

Scott looked up from his calculations. "Payment?"

"Fifty million up front for taking the job. Another hundred on completion."

"And if we find out what's in this facility?" Kenney asked.

Smith's expression didn't change. "Then you'll understand why it needs to not exist, and why you'll never speak of it again. Ever."

Smith leaned back in his chair, spreading his hands in a gesture of simplicity. "Don't overthink this, Mr. Jaeger. I want you to drop a package off and get out. I'll even be supplying the nuke on site—it's already on-planet, awaiting pickup. Get in, get out, don't ask questions, and profit."

He paused, letting that sink in before continuing. "If we can establish a working relationship here, my clients can offer you a Class 4 munitions license through our Core World wardog brokerages."

Scott's head snapped up from his datapad. A Class 4 license meant legal access to ARMSEA military-grade tech, no questions asked. No more gray market dealings, no more paying triple for surplus rounds.

"That means your logistics issues are over," Smith continued. "Legitimate suppliers, Core World prices, delivered anywhere in civilized space."

"There's always a catch," Kenney said.

"The catch is Regalia." Smith pulled up tactical overlays of the city. "For a Neo-Slavic Fringe world, they're remarkably well-armed. Both factions have been importing hardware for years. You'll be facing other mechs in that city, possibly even other merc units. This isn't some colonial brushfire with farmers in technicals. These people have high end equipment and know how to use it."

Wilson grunted. "Which mercs?"

"Unknown. Both sides have been hiring anyone willing to take their money. Could be corporate teams, could be independent operators like yourselves. The city's become a proving ground for every outfit looking to make their reputation in the region."

"Or lose it," Derg muttered.

"Precisely. But that's why the pay is commensurate with the risk. Fifty million just to show up, another hundred when that facility becomes a radioactive crater."

Doc Haywire looked up from his flask. "What about radiation exposure for our people?"

"Minimal. You'll be long gone before detonation. Remote trigger, thirty-minute delay once armed."

"Why can't we source our own nuke?" Scott asked, setting down his datapad. "I don't feel comfortable having someone else's finger on the button."

Smith's smile was thin. "Well, that's a layer of misdirection in and of itself. The device has certain... signatures that will push things politically in certain directions. Games of state and all that."

"You're framing someone," Kenney said flatly.

"I'm providing a narrative that serves multiple purposes. The nuclear material's origin, the specific yield, the detonation signature—all of it tells a story. The right story, for the right people."

"So when this goes off, it points to someone specific," Scott continued. "Someone who had nothing to do with it but makes a convenient villain."

"Or perhaps someone who needs to be reminded they're not untouchable," Smith replied. "The device is already configured, already in place. You simply need to deliver and arm it. The thirty-minute timer is mechanical, unhackable. Once you start it, nothing stops it."

"And if we decide we don't want to be part of your political theater?" Derg asked.

"Then you forfeit a Class 4 licenses and continue paying black market rates for long dead surplus that may or may not work when you need it. Your choice, gentlemen. But the device comes from us, or there's no deal."

Wilson shifted his weight, hands drifting toward his sidearms—an unconscious tell when he didn't trust someone. "What happens when whoever you're framing figures out it wasn't them?"

"By then, the facility won't exist, the evidence will be vapor, and the political machinery will already be in motion. These things take on a life of their own. Truth becomes remarkably flexible when enough people need it to be."

"Fifty million to be patsies," Doc Haywire observed, taking another pull from his flask.

"Fifty million to be delivery boys," Smith corrected. "Highly skilled, heavily armed delivery boys who happen to be very good at shooting their way in and out of places."

Kenney knocked back the rest of his coffee like it was a shot of whiskey and rolled his eyes. "When do you need it done by?"

"Immediately upon your departure from here. Tonight, ideally. The window of opportunity is narrow."

Scott turned in his chair, staring at Kenney. "You're taking him up on this?"

Kenney's jaw clenched, the exhaustion and annoyance clear on his face. "Look, guys, I know these black ops jobs suck, but it's not like we have a choice."

The temperature in the hangar seemed to drop. Everyone understood what he meant. Smith knew they knew about the facility now. They'd seen the coordinates, heard about the nuke. That made them loose ends.

"We're dead if we turn it down," Kenney continued, not breaking eye contact with Smith.

Smith's expression didn't change, but something in his posture confirmed it. "You don't trust me?"

"Not even a little bit."

"Smart. That'll help you survive this." Smith stood, straightening his linen shirt. "I've sent the complete tactical package to your AI, along with retrieval coordinates. The device is in a waterproof container on the seabed, twelve kilometers off Sevastopol's coast. Sunk there two weeks ago during a 'maritime accident.'"

"No orbital insertion?" Scott asked.

"No reason for you to be in-system. No flight plans, no humanitarian clearances, no paper trail at all. As far as anyone knows, Kilkenney Solutions is still drinking themselves stupid at Angel's Cove." Smith moved toward the hangar exit. "You'll jump in at the edge of the system, run silent to Regalia, and deploy directly to the ocean. Retrieve the package, hit the pumping station, deliver the device, and disappear. Ghost in, ghost out."

"And the locals?" Wilson asked.

"Won't know you're there until you want them to. The pumping station explosion will be their first indication that something's wrong. By then, you'll already be moving on the facility."

"This operation doesn't exist. You were never there. That facility was destroyed by local forces in the fighting, tragic collateral damage in a senseless war. The nuclear signature will tell a different story to those who need to hear it, but officially? Just another casualty of the Regalia conflict."

He paused at the hangar door. "Oh, and gentlemen? Once you arm that device, don't go back. No matter what you see, hear, or think you've left behind. Thirty minutes, then two square kilometers of city becomes glass."

"The hangar suddenly filled with the roar of engines from above. Through the open bay doors, something descended—at first just a shimmer in the air, like heat distortion, then solidifying as its stealth systems disengaged. The aircraft materialized piece by piece: sleek angular hull, weapons pods, vertical thrust arrays. Part strike fighter, part dropship, all predator.

Its stealth coating seemed to drink in light even when visible, the surface constantly shifting between matte black and deep gray depending on the angle. The vertical thrusters fired in sequence, sending hurricane-force winds through the hangar. Sand and debris whipped across the deck, unsecured equipment sliding into walls, Doc Haywire quickly covering his whiskey glass with his hand."

"Son of a—"

The craft touched down with barely a sound despite its size, landing gear extending with hydraulic precision. A ramp dropped from its belly, revealing an interior that looked more like a luxury transport than military hardware.

Smith turned back to them with that same thin smile, having to raise his voice over the dying turbines. "Gentlemen, the clock starts now. You have to complete the operation before other interested parties notice that facility still exists."

He walked up the ramp without looking back, his resort wear incongruous against the military craft's interior. The ramp sealed behind him with a pneumatic hiss.

The aircraft's engines spooled up again, and it lifted off as smoothly as it had arrived. At thirty feet, the stealth systems engaged, and it simply... wasn't there anymore. Just empty air where death had been hovering.

"Well," Derg said into the sudden silence, "that wasn't ominous at all."

Wilson finally took his hand off his sidearm. "Seventy-two hours. We can be in Regalia's system in twenty-four if we push the drives."

"Then we push the drives," Kenney said, already walking toward the CIC. "Scott, get everyone back from shore leave. We launch in four hours."

"Four hours? Half the crew's probably still drunk."

"Then they'll sober up in transit. Move."

The next several hours turned the Purgatory into barely controlled chaos.

Jensen Wilson became a one-man recovery operation, using every sober mercenary he could find—all twelve of them—to systematically sweep Angel's Cove for their scattered crew. He'd commandeered three resort shuttles and a delivery truck, turning the collection effort into something between a military operation and a riot control exercise.

At the Platinum Lounge, they found mercenaries who'd barricaded themselves in the VIP section and declared it "sovereign territory." Jensen had to load beanbag rounds into his shotgun, the less-lethal ammunition thumping into drunk mercenaries who thought they were still invincible.

"We're winning!" one slurred as a beanbag knocked him off his chair.

"We're leaving in ninety minutes," Jensen growled, racking another round. "Move or get shot again."

The beach was worse. Two pilots were found passed out in a half-buried landing craft they'd "borrowed" and tried to turn into a party boat. Another group had to be extracted from the resort's security office after attempting to liberate a statue they claimed looked like their old commanding officer.

Back at the ship, Doc Haywire had set up a medical station at the top of the ramp. As mercenaries stumbled or were carried in, he jabbed them with his "cure-all"—a cocktail that handled everything from alcohol poisoning to poor decisions made with questionable company. He didn't comment on their state, just administered the shot and waved them through.

"Next," was all he said, over and over, like the world's most jaded pharmacist.

One of the real problems was the uninvited guests already aboard. Prostitutes emerged from quarters, arguing about payment. A group of tourists who'd thought they were at a "real mercenary party" had to be escorted off at gunpoint when they wouldn't leave voluntarily. Someone had even brought a resort DJ who'd set up equipment in the mess hall.

"This isn't a pleasure ship!" Scott shouted at two women in bikinis who'd been found in the armory taking selfies with the heavy weapons.

Magdalena and her friends had vanished sometime during the festivities. Never came back for their payment, never said goodbye. Probably found richer targets at the casino. Oh well. Their absence from his quarters marked only by empty packaging and the lingering stains.

Derg was running through the hangar like a madman, trying to secure equipment while sobering load masters stumbled through pre-flight checks.

"No, no, NO!" he screamed at one tech. "The plasma lance needs to be locked into the transit rack first! You leave that thing unsecured during jump and it'll tear through the hull like tissue paper!"

McKnight arrived with a black eye, carrying an unconscious Killjoy over his shoulder. "Found him at the Chapel of Love," McKnight reported, touching his swollen eye gingerly. "He and some pleasure girl were halfway through their vows. He'd bought rings from a vending machine. When I tried to intervene, she hit me with her heel. Had to knock Killjoy out when he pulled a knife to 'defend his bride's honor.' The chapel's ruined."

With fifteen minutes to launch, they were still missing eight people. Jensen made the call. "Give them the warning siren. They can find their own way home or enjoy permanent vacation."

The Purgatory's departure siren blared three times across Angel's Cove—the universal signal for "get your ass aboard or get left behind." The sound echoed off the resort buildings, sending flocks of tropical birds into the air and causing several hungover mercenaries on the beach to look up in panic.

Out on the perimeter, Deadeye and Streaks stood in their mechs, maintaining overwatch as the chaos unfolded. They'd pulled the short straw at last night's duty roster—someone always had to stay operational during shore leave.

Inside his cockpit, Deadeye's hands worked the controls with practiced ease, scanning the approach roads through thermal imaging.

"That's three," Deadeye's voice crackled over the comm as the departure siren wailed across the resort. "You see anyone else coming?"

Streaks' mech pivoted, his sensors sweeping the area. "Dude, got two kooks booking it about half a klick out, totally harshing to make the ride." On his display, two red dots moved desperately toward them. Through his magnified optics, he could see them clearly—two mercenaries in yesterday's fatigues, one still clutching a bottle.

"Grab them," Deadeye ordered, already moving his mech forward. "Jensen will bitch if we're short-handed."

"Righteous, bro. Can't leave the crew hanging."

Both mechs jogged toward the stragglers, their footfalls leaving deep impressions in the resort's lawn. Deadeye reached his target first, scooping up the mercenary who yelped but held onto his bottle. Streaks grabbed the second runner, who immediately threw up from the sudden elevation change.

"Gnarly, dude," Streaks muttered. "That's gonna be totally rank when it bakes onto my ride."

They walked back toward the Purgatory at a steady pace, carrying their human cargo. The hangar doors were beginning their closing sequence, standard procedure once all mechs were accounted for.

"Deadeye, Streaks, you're clear to enter," Derg's voice came over comm. "Watch your clearance."

Both mechs ducked through the narrowing gap in sequence, their practiced movements making it look routine despite the tight fit. Streaks' paint scraped slightly on the doorframe.

"Bogus, man. Gonna need some touch-up on the paint job," Streaks commented.

The doors sealed behind them with a pneumatic hiss as both mechs moved to their maintenance cradles. They lowered the rescued mercenaries to the deck, where the one with the bottle stumbled away on shaking legs while the other needed help getting to medical.

"Cutting it close there," Derg shouted from the hangar floor.

"Someone had to make sure we didn't leave half the company behind," Deadeye replied through his external speakers, his mech moving toward its maintenance berth.

"All mechs secured," Streaks reported, powering down his systems. "We're totally ready to cruise, boss man."

"Finally," Kenney muttered from the CIC. "Conway, take us up. Best speed to the jump point." The Purgatory's engines roared, VTOL thrusters scorching the resort's carefully maintained landing pad as five hundred tons of carrier began its ascent.

The paradise of Angel's Cove fell away beneath them, becoming just another bright spot in the darkness, another place they'd been and left in various states of destruction.

As the ship lifted off, leaving the paradise behind, Kenney looked at his assembled leadership team.

"Tango," he said to the AI, "plot a course for Regalia. Maximum burn."

"Captain, shall I engage the sobriety protocol in the environmental systems?"

"God yes."

"Implementing aerosolized detox compounds now. The crew will be combat-ready in twelve hours. They will also be very unhappy."

"They're mercenaries," Kenney replied. "They're always unhappy."

Kenney left the CIC through the forward hatch, stepping into the main corridor that ran the length of the Purgatory like a spine. The ship's artificial gravity made walking feel normal, but the subtle vibration through the deck plates reminded him they were accelerating hard toward the jump point.

The corridor stretched ahead, its walls lined with conduits, emergency equipment stations, and the occasional viewport showing stars wheeling past. He moved with purpose, sidestepping a maintenance tech pushing a cart full of replacement filters. Twenty meters forward, he passed through the crew quarters section where mercenaries stumbled toward their bunks, faces green from Doc Haywire's cure-all. One had collapsed against a wall, dry heaving into a waste bag while his squadmate held him steady.

Kenney stepped around them without comment, continuing forward through another pressure bulkhead into officer country. This section was quieter, the corridor wider and better lit. The doors here had nameplates—department heads, senior pilots, the few mercenaries who'd earned private quarters through seniority or exceptional service. Most were still sealed, their occupants either on the bridge already or sleeping off the shore leave.

He passed his own quarters without stopping, the door still showing the security seal from when he'd left. Through another bulkhead, the corridor began to widen as it approached the nose of the ship. Here the viewports were larger, offering glimpses of Angel's Cove falling away below them.

The final pressure door to the bridge was heavier than the others, reinforced against potential breaches. It recognized his biometrics and cycled open with a deep mechanical hum.

The bridge opened before him, a reinforced command center with a panoramic view through armored transparisteel. Eight flight crew members in blue coveralls worked their stations with practiced efficiency, their sobriety having been mandatory. The pilot or Chief Flight Officer and co-pilot sat in the primary control seats, hands dancing over holographic controls as they managed the ascent. Navigation, communications, weapons systems, environmental controls—each station manned by someone who knew their job and did it without complaint.

"Captain on the bridge," the communications officer announced without looking up from her screens.

"As you were," Kenney said, moving to stand behind Chief Flight Officer Conway's chair.

Through the viewport, Angel's Cove was falling away rapidly. The resort's lights grew smaller, the beaches becoming thin white lines, then nothing but a bright spot on a dark landmass. The Purgatory climbed through the atmosphere, her hull beginning to glow with friction heat as they pushed toward escape velocity.

"Jump point in seventeen hours, forty-three minutes at current burn rate," the navigator reported.

"Regalia system entry eighteen hours after that," Conway added, keeping the controls steady as the ship vibrated around him.

Kenney watched the stars begin to appear as they broke through the upper atmosphere, the black of space replacing the blue of sky. Somewhere out there was a world torn by war

He settled into the captain's chair, the worn leather conforming to his body like an old friend. The chair sat elevated above the flight crew stations, giving him oversight of all operations while maintaining clear view through the forward viewport.

The Purgatory shuddered as she pushed through the upper atmosphere, hull temperature readings climbing into the yellow as friction heated their ablative armor. Outside, the sky transformed from deep blue to purple to black, stars emerging like diamonds against velvet. The ship's massive frame wasn't built for graceful atmospheric exits—she bulldozed through rather than sliced, every ton of her bulk fighting gravity's grip.

"Passing forty kilometers," Conway announced, keeping the controls steady through the violent ascent. "Aerodynamic control surfaces retracting."

"Switching to reaction thrusters," the co-pilot confirmed.

Kenney pulled up the navigation display on his chair's armrest console, the holographic star map blooming before him in three dimensions. The direct route to Regalia would take them through a dozen systems—half of them problematic.

Red zones marked Confederate territory where they had outstanding warrants. The Rogue Marine systems glowed amber—technically they weren't banned, but showing up in a stolen carrier with Kenney's service record would raise questions. The Core Worlds were outlined in blue, their automated defense platforms programmed to vaporize unlicensed military vessels on sight.

He manipulated the display, plotting alternative routes through the network of jump points that connected systems like an invisible highway. The direct route would take them through the Dusk Junction—currently a contested battleground between Confederate and Rogue Marine forces. The tactical display showed it in pulsing red, ship debris from a series of naval engagements those jump points impassible until cleared.

The main commercial route through Amarae's Gate was equally impossible. Core World regulations prohibited armed vessels over 10,000 tons from using their jump points—the Purgatory exceeded that by a factor of five. Their automated defense platforms wouldn't even warn them, just open fire.

Instead, he traced a path through unregulated systems and mining territories. First to the Buccaneer Nebula via the old Bandersnatch Point—the radiation made it useless for colonization but the jump point still functioned. From there, they could use the Majestic's Grief point to reach a brown dwarf system where there was no standing naval presence, no questions. Three more jumps through resource-poor systems that hosted small colonies but no strategic assets currently worth fighting over.

"Navigation," he called out, "I'm sending you a modified jump sequence."

The navigator, a thin flat chested woman who'd been plotting courses through war zones for fifteen years, studied the path. "That's... creative, sir. The Majestic's Grief point hasn't been a main stream nav point in eight years. Could have drifted."

"But it's unpatrolled?"

"Completely. Mining unions run those systems. We'll need to drop out early and recalculate, but it keeps us away from the fighting. These jump points connect backwater colonies and mining ops—biggest threats just going to be pirates."

"Do it."

The Purgatory finally broke free of the planet's gravity well, engines throttling back as they entered the calm of open space. Through the viewport, Angel's Cove was just a blue-green marble now, its resort paradise invisible from this distance.

"Course laid in," the navigator reported. "Seven jumps total. Estimated time to Regalia: thirty-six hours including recalculation stops."

"All stations report ready for jump," the communications officer announced after polling the ship.

Kenney watched the jump coordinates lock in on his display—a crooked path through space's back alleys, the kind of route only smugglers and pirates used. Perfect for arriving somewhere uninvited and unannounced.

"Execute when ready," he ordered.

The jump drive spooled up with a rising whine that could be felt in their bones. Space twisted, reality bent, and the Purgatory punched through into the void between stars, carrying them toward whatever waited in Regalia's cold waters.

Scott Blake and Jensen Wilson stepped onto the bridge, their boots clanging against the deck plating.

"Captain," Blake said, moving to the holographic projection table. "Here's what we were able to pull from the net while you were plotting our route."

He activated the display, and Regalia bloomed into existence—a world of browns and grays, its continents scarred by impact craters and radiation zones visible even from orbit. Cities appeared as red dots, contested zones outlined in yellow, active combat areas pulsing orange.

"Regalia entered a civil war shortly after the 3rd ARMSEA concluded peacekeeping operations and pulled out," Blake began, manipulating the display to zoom in on the eastern continent. "Classic power vacuum. The moment ARMSEA's transports broke atmosphere, every pre-occupation faction that had been playing nice started grabbing territory."

Wilson grunted. "ARMSEA. Peacekeeping my ass. They strip-mined half the planet's resources before declaring the situation 'stabilized.'"

"That's the Core Worlds for you," Blake spat tobacco juice into his cup. "But here's where it gets interesting. Both major factions managed to loot abandoned ARMSEA bases during the withdrawal. We're looking at lower-grade mechs—probably Sentinel-class, maybe some older Gladiators. Heavy infantry units with powered armor. The exact numbers are unclear because both sides might have contractors supplementing strike capability."

The display shifted to show Sevastopol's coastline. The city sprawled along a natural harbor, its eastern districts extending into industrial zones that had seen better days. Blast craters dotted the urban landscape like acne scars.

"The package is here," Blake indicated a point twelve kilometers offshore. "We'll need a sea drop to retrieve it. Water depth is about three hundred meters—well within our mechs' operational parameters."

Wilson leaned over the display, his scarred fingers tracing potential approach routes. "Here's the problem—we can't risk bringing Purgatory into atmosphere. Too easy for someone manning an orbital railgun to plug an unknown in their airspace. We'd be a sitting duck."

"So how do we insert?" Conway asked without turning from his controls.

Blake pulled up inventory manifests on his datapad. "We've got four flight packs in storage. The heavy-duty ones designed for orbital mech deployment."

"Four packs, ten mechs," Wilson said, doing the math. "That's not going to work."

"No, but four mechs might be enough," Kenney said, studying the tactical display. "Two teams of two. Small, fast, less likely to be detected."

Blake nodded, manipulating the holographic display to show Regalia's orbital space. "We drop the mechs from orbit with flight packs. They'll look like space debris or satellites losing orbit on anyone's scopes. Natural decay, maybe some old ARMSEA hardware finally coming down. By the time anyone realizes they're mechs, they'll already be in the water."

"Who goes?" Wilson asked.

"Me and Racer for the package and facility," Kenney said without hesitation. "We grab the nuke from the seabed, then work our way inland to the black site."

"That leaves Deadeye and Killjoy for the pumping station," Wilson nodded. "They'll need to make enough noise to pull every unit in the area."

"Can two mechs take that station?" the Scott asked, gesturing at the massive industrial complex on the display.

"They don't need to hold it," Kenney replied. "Just blow it to hell and keep everyone's attention while Racer and I deliver the package. Hit and run. Maximum chaos."

Blake was already running calculations. "Flight packs have enough fuel for atmospheric entry and maybe ten minutes of powered flight once they're down. That's your extraction too—once the nuke's planted, everyone burns hard for minimum safe distance and then dust off."

"What about Purgatory?" Conway asked.

"You stay in high orbit on the far side of the planet," Wilson said. "We'll rendezvous after extraction. If things go sideways, you jump out and we find our own way home."

"Comforting," Conway muttered.

The navigator looked up from her calculations. "First jump in two minutes. We're finalizing the entry vectors now."

Blake pulled up the orbital mechanics on the main display. "Entry here, thirty degrees north of Sevastopol. You'll be coming in over water the whole way. Terminal velocity until forty thousand feet, then flight packs engage for controlled descent. Hit the water about fifteen kilometers offshore."

"All four mechs enter here," Wilson indicated a point thirty degrees north of Sevastopol.

Blake pulled up the seafloor topology. "The package is here—" he marked a point on the ocean floor "—twelve kilometers from shore. All four mechs retrieve it together, then proceed underwater to this ridge at the eight-kilometer mark."

"That's where we split," Wilson continued, tracing the paths with his finger. "Deadeye and Killjoy follow the ridge south, staying submerged until they're at the pumping station. Then they surface first and hit it hard."

"Kenney and Racer continue underwater with the package," Blake added, "surfacing directly at the beach once the fireworks start, about two kilometers from the target facility. The whole approach is underwater until the final infiltration."

Wilson zoomed in on the retrieval point. "Total time underwater: maybe forty minutes."

"Communications?" Kenney asked.

"Line of sight burst transmissions only," the communications officer said. "Encrypted, frequency hopping. Anyone listening will think it's background radiation."

Blake saved the tactical plan to secured storage. "Once you're in the water, you're on your own for optics, visibility will be slim to none. No deep penetration satellite support, no overwatch. Just compass headings and whatever your sensors can pick up."

"Just like the old days," Killjoy's voice came over the intercom—he'd been listening from the hangar. "Except with nuclear weapons."

"Speaking of which," Wilson said, "who carries the package once you retrieve it?"

"I will," Kenney decided. "Racer can run interference if we hit resistance. He's fast enough to punch through if I get bogged down."

"Get those flight packs prepped," Kenney ordered Wilson. "I want full diagnostics, fuel checks, and backup systems verified. We only get one shot at this."

"Already on it," Wilson replied, heading for the door. "I'll have the tech crew start mounting them as soon as we drop out for recalculation."

Blake remained at the tactical display, studying the target city. "You know this is insane, right? Four mechs against potentially thousands of hostiles, with a nuke that we can't even control."

"Thursday," Kenney replied, settling back into his captain's chair.

"We won't be completely blind down there. We're deploying surveillance assets from orbit before the mech drop." Blake said, pulling up another display.

The tactical display shifted to show a constellation of small icons above Regalia. "Stealth reconnaissance drones—basically flying cameras with minimal heat signatures. We'll release a spread of six from high orbit about six hours before you go in."

Wilson, who'd paused at the door, turned back. "Those things are twenty feet across. Size of a large bird, solar-powered, almost invisible to radar. "

"How many will survive enemy ack-ack?" Kenney asked.

"Maybe half if we're lucky," Blake admitted, manipulating the display to show descent trajectories. "But even one or two will give us decent coverage of Sevastopol. Real-time intel on troop movements, patrol patterns, which buildings are occupied."

The communications officer pulled up technical specifications. "I can establish quantum-encrypted links with the drones. Data burst every thirty seconds to minimize detection. You'll have updated tactical maps on your HUDs throughout the operation."

"Until someone shoots them down," Wilson pointed out.

"The militias don't usually waste ammunition on surveillance drones," Blake said, spitting into his cup. "Too common in urban warfare. Both sides probably have their own up there already. Ours will just blend into the cloud."

Kenney studied the drone deployment pattern. "Priority coverage zones?"

"The pumping station obviously," Blake highlighted the industrial complex. "The route from the beach to your target facility. And we'll keep two in reserve circling high—backup eyes in case the primary drones get swatted."

"What about the retrieval point?"

"The drones can't penetrate water effectively, but they'll monitor surface activity." Blake pulled up the drone specifications. "Each one has about seventy-two hours of operational time before the batteries die. More than enough for this operation."

Wilson was already doing tactical math. "If we get real-time intel, Deadeye can start picking targets before he even surfaces. Know exactly where to hit for maximum chaos."

"And Racer and I can plot the cleanest route to the facility," Kenney added. "Avoid the worst of the fighting."

The navigator called out, "Jump transition in thirty seconds."

Blake saved all the tactical planning to his datapad. "I'll have the drone package prepped for deployment. We release them during our final approach; they'll reach Regalia's atmosphere about two hours before you do."

"Make it happen," Kenney ordered.

"Already on it. These Switchblades are basically flying cameras with solar panels and wings—about as sophisticated as a hobby drone. They're cheap enough that losing half won't matter."

The Purgatory lurched slightly as they transitioned through hyperspace, reality bending around them. Through the viewport, the twisted non-colors of the void streamed past—a reminder that they were racing through spaces human minds weren't meant to comprehend.

The jump drive's whine suddenly shifted pitch, dropping from a shriek to a grinding growl. The Purgatory shuddered as it prepared to transition back to normal space.

"Dropping out in ten seconds," the navigator announced. "First jump point recalculation."

Blake and Wilson grabbed nearby handholds as space outside the viewport began to distort. The flowing colors of hyperspace started to fragment, reality reasserting itself in jarring waves.

"All stations, prepare for transition," Kenney announced.

Reality snapped back like a rubber band. The stars stopped streaking, becoming fixed points of light again. They'd emerged in the middle of nowhere—empty space between systems. The navigator immediately began working her calculations for the next jump point.

"Position confirmed," she reported. "Majestic's Grief point is... two degrees off expected coordinates. Compensating. Next jump in fifteen minutes."

"All stations, prepare for jump two of seven," Kenney announced.

Reality folded again, the stars stretched into lines, and the Purgatory punched through into hyperspace for the second leg of their journey. Blake and Wilson left the bridge to oversee preparations. In the hangar, technicians would already be hauling the massive flight packs from storage, checking every bolt and seal that would keep their mechs from becoming very expensive meteors. The surveillance drones would need programming, their sensor packages calibrated for Regalia's atmosphere and magnetic field.

Kenney remained in the captain's chair, studying the tactical display. He looked to Conway at the pilot's station. "Helmsman, you have the bridge."

Kenney left the bridge. The hangover from Angel's Cove was mostly gone thanks to Doc's cure-all, but exhaustion went deeper than chemicals could reach. He'd need every ounce of readiness he could scrape together for what was coming.

The corridor to officer quarters was quieter than the rest of the ship, insulated from the constant hum of engines and life support. As he rounded the corner, Joker emerged from the communal officer showers wearing only a towel, water still beading down the tattoos covering her chest.

"You are needing company before mission?" she asked, leaning against the bulkhead with practiced casualness. "Ancient peoples, they believed was important for man to leave much seed behind, da? For making sure bloodline survives." She winked, the gesture somehow both playful and serious. "Is good tradition, no?"

"Just need some actual sleep, Joker."

Her smile didn't falter, but something in her eyes showed she'd expected the rejection. "Your loss, Captain. The offer stands if you change your mind."

"It always does," he said, continuing past her toward his quarters.

"One day," she called after him, "you will get tired of being alone with your ghosts."

He didn't respond, just palmed the lock on his door and stepped inside.

The quarters were dark. He kicked off his boots, letting them fall wherever they landed, and flopped onto the bed fully clothed. The sheets still smelled faintly of expensive perfume and sweat from the escorts. He should have had them changed, but exhaustion won over hygiene.

He slipped under the covers and rolled onto his back, staring at the ceiling. The familiar weight of being alone settled over him like a burial shroud.

The holo-projector activated automatically, triggered by his presence and the room's darkness. The recording materialized above him—Kira on their anniversary trip to Thessalonica, before it became a war zone, when it was still known for its gardens and museums.

She was laughing in the video, spinning in front of some fountain, her red hair catching the sunlight like copper fire. They'd spent the whole day playing tourist—overpriced coffee at sidewalk cafés, getting lost in the art district, buying terrible souvenirs they'd throw away a week later.

"Come on, soldier boy," her recorded voice teased as she beckoned to him from three years ago. "The museum closes in an hour."

His past self appeared in frame, grabbing her around the waist, both of them grinning like idiots. She turned to the camera—he'd propped his phone against a statue to record them.

"I'll always love you, Kenney," she said, her green eyes bright with life that had been extinguished six months later. "Even when you're being a grumpy bastard who won't dance with me at that embassy party."

The video looped, starting again with her laugh, that same spin, the same fountain. He'd watched it so many times he could recite every word, predict every gesture. But he couldn't stop watching, couldn't delete it, couldn't move on.

Sleep came eventually, but it brought no peace.

In his dreams, she was alive but always just out of reach. Running ahead of him through Thessalonica's gardens while he tried to warn her about the ambush. Sitting across from him at that sidewalk café, but when he tried to speak, to tell her to stay away from the convoy, no sound came out. Dancing at the embassy party they never made it to, her dress the same color as the blood that would pool beneath her when the IED tore their vehicle apart.

Sometimes in the dreams, he saved her. Pulled her from the wreckage, stopped the bleeding, carried her to safety. But even in dreams, she always died just as he thought she'd made it. Her last words changing each time—sometimes accusatory, sometimes forgiving, always final.

The worst dreams were the ones where she was simply gone, and he spent hours searching empty rooms and abandoned buildings, knowing she was somewhere close but never finding her. Those were the ones that left him waking with his throat raw from calling her name.

The Purgatory raced through hyperspace, while it's commander chased ghosts through his subconscious, fighting battles that had ended three years ago but would never truly be over.

CHAPTER FOUR

The Purgatory punched through the membrane between hyperspace and reality with a bone-rattling shudder that sent unsecured equipment sliding across decks. Reality reasserted itself with vengeance.

"Transition complete," Conway announced from the pilot's station, his hands already working to stabilize their trajectory. "Regalia system. We're approximately eight hundred thousand kilometers from the planet."

"Single ping only," Kenney ordered from the captain's chair. He'd managed four hours of broken sleep, enough to function but not enough to stop the persistent ache behind his eyes. "Let's see who else is playing in this sandbox."

The tactical display populated with contacts as their sensors swept the system. Two carriers in high orbit on opposite sides of Regalia—one broadcasting Eastern Coalition IFF codes, the other Western Republic. Three dozen smaller vessels, mostly converted freighters running supplies to their respective factions. A debris field where something large had died recently, probably within the last week based on the dispersal pattern.

"No one's painted us yet," the sensor operator reported. "We're just another piece of noise in the clutter."

"Keep it that way. Helm, take us in slow. Make it look like we're a cargo hauler with engine problems."

Conway throttled back, letting the Purgatory drift along a lazy arc that would bring them to Regalia in six hours. To anyone watching, they'd look like another civilian hauler trying to slip in unnoticed.

Blake radioed from the CIC. "Surveillance package is ready. Switchblade drones loaded."

"Fire when ready."

The ship trembled slightly as the torpedo tubes discharged. On the tactical display, six contacts separated from the Purgatory, accelerating toward Regalia on ballistic trajectories.

"Torpedoes away," the weapons officer confirmed. "Programmed to separate at forty thousand meters altitude."

They watched the projectiles race toward the planet, their heat signatures barely visible against the cosmic background. At the prescribed altitude, each torpedo split apart like a seed pod, releasing their drone package. The cheap, light gliders deployed their wings and scattered, their solar cells drinking in radiation as they began their long descent toward Sevastopol.

Twenty minutes later, the first drone reached operational altitude.

"Receiving telemetry," the communications officer announced. "Switchblade One is transmitting... now."

The main tactical display flickered, then resolved into a bird's eye view of hell.

Sevastopol burned in a dozen places. The urban landscape was carved into territories by trenches, tank traps, and rubble barricades. Artillery positions on both sides of the city traded fire in lazy arcs, their shells turning buildings into rubble with mechanical regularity.

"Jesus," someone whispered.

The drone's camera swept across the eastern district, where the morning's battle was already underway. Eastern Coalition forces—identifiable by their gray-green uniforms—were throwing another wave against Western Republic positions. Bodies littered the street from previous attempts, some still moving, most not. A mech, one of the older ARMSEA Gladiator models painted in Coalition colors, provided covering fire with its autocannons, walking rounds across a fortified apartment complex.

"Switchblade Three online," the operator reported. Another feed appeared, this one showing the pumping station. The massive industrial complex squatted at the harbor's edge like a mechanical spider, pipes running in every direction. Infantry and light armor units were dug in throughout the complex, using the industrial infrastructure as cover.

More drones came online, each adding another layer to the nightmare below. The city had been home to thirteen million people before the war. Now it looked like a mouth with half its teeth knocked out, entire districts reduced to blackened stumps.

"Mark that," Blake said, pointing at a feed showing the industrial district. "Republic armor column, eight tanks, moving toward the pumping station."

"Coalition battery here," Wilson added, having arrived to watch the feeds. "Six guns, dug in on this ridgeline. They've got clear lines of sight on the AO."

The drones continued their lazy circles, unless someone noticed and swatted them. Their cameras captured the systematic destruction of a civilized world—water treatment plants burning, hospitals with walls blown out, schools converted to strong points.

"There," Kenney pointed at a feed showing their target zone. Several blocks of commercial district filled the screen—warehouses and shipping facilities that had somehow avoided the fighting so far. No craters, no burned vehicles, the buildings intact while war raged just streets away. But the drone feeds showed the signs: Republic checkpoints being established on the eastern approaches, Coalition scouts probing from the west. The war was closing in on this pocket of calm.

"Zoom in on those warehouses," Kenney ordered.

The cluster of unmarked buildings came into focus. They showed that telltale sensor shimmer, their metal construction scattering electromagnetic signals. Steel and aluminum construction played hell with modern sensors. But their location and the fact that both factions seemed to be suddenly interested in this previously ignored district was telling.

"Zoom in on that intersection," he ordered.

The drone's camera focused, revealing a Republic checkpoint. Two squads of light infantry in urban camo, a technical—a civilian pickup truck with a pintle-mounted railgun, its bed reinforced with armor plates and capacitor banks feeding the electromagnetic weapon—and then the real threat.

"Mech," Wilson identified. "Sentinel-class, doesn’t look like militia equipment."

The Sentinel stood twelve feet tall, a far cry from their forty-foot assault mechs but dangerous in urban environments. It was essentially an armored exoskeleton scaled up—humanoid in shape with a pilot visible through the armored canopy that served as its "head." The arms ended in manipulator hands that could wield oversized weapons or tear through walls. This one carried a 30mm autocannon like a rifle, the weapon connected to an ammunition backpack via a reinforced feed system.

The mech's paint job made Wilson whistle—blue and white in a distinctive pattern, with a stylized "M" on the shoulder pauldron.

"Mithril," Blake said, recognizing the colors. "Professional outfit out of the Dragon sector. They don't work cheap."

"Republics hired some gunslingers," Wilson nodded. "And that technical's sporting a Mjolnir-6 railgun—that'll punch through tank armor at eight hundred meters. Mithril's got a reputation. Their Sentinel pilots are all ex-military, and those mechs might be smaller but they're agile as hell in tight spaces."

More feeds revealed the full scope of the battle. The resource extractors—massive industrial complexes that processed Regalia's mineral wealth—had become fortresses. Bodies carpeted the approaches where both sides had thrown waves of conscripts at hardened positions. Artillery had turned the surrounding neighborhoods into moonscapes.

"Current estimate on combatants?" Kenney asked.

Blake consulted his datapad. "Based on the drone coverage... maybe thirty thousand Coalition troops in the city, forty thousand Republic. That's just regular forces. Add in militia, conscripts, mercenaries, and irregular units—could be double that. But in a city of thirteen million, even a hundred thousand fighters can disappear."

"Lot of city to hide in," Wilson added. "Both sides are concentrated around strategic points—the extractors, the pumping station, major intersections. Everything else is either contested territory or changes hands daily. Civilians are trapped wherever they happen to be when the fighting reaches them."

"All fighting over ruins," Wilson muttered.

"Ruins with resources," Blake corrected. "Those extractors are worth billions. Whoever holds them when the dust settles owns a good chunk of Regalia's economy."

Conway called out from the helm, "Four hours to orbit, Captain."

Kenney studied the feeds, watching an artillery strike delete a city block in real-time. Somewhere down there, four mechs were about to drop into this meat grinder carrying a nuclear device that would add one more crater to a city that already looked like the surface of a hostile moon.

The City of Sevastopol continued to die on the screens above them, unaware that its executioner was approaching through the dark.

Kenney stood from his captain's chair and reached behind it to the equipment rack, grabbing his helmet and gloves. The seal clicked into place with a pneumatic hiss as he pulled the helmet on. The full-seal combat gloves followed, reinforced knuckles and haptic feedback systems coming online. When running orbital drops, they depressurized the hangar bay to prevent explosive decompression—one less variable to worry about when launching mechs from orbit.

He left the bridge without another word, heading for the hangar where the other pilots would already be preparing their mechs.

The hangar was a symphony of swears and auto-wrench noise as the techs made final preparations. The massive flight packs were already mounted, technicians running final calibration sequences on the thruster arrays and checking the wing deployment mechanisms. Each flight pack was the size of a small building—fuel tanks, vectored thrusters, heat shields, and retractable wings that would deploy during atmospheric entry to provide stability and limited maneuverability. The rocket pods from their earlier ground operations had been stripped and stowed hours ago.

Maintenance teams swarmed the mechs, testing the wing actuators—watching the massive surfaces extend and retract smoothly, checking for any binding in the joints. One tech was laser-scanning the heat shield tiles, ensuring none had cracked during storage.

The bay still had gravity thanks to the grav plates, letting the techs work without having to wrestle equipment in zero-g. Kenney activated his comm system, the helmet's speakers crackling to life.

"Derg, I want the 30mm with all the ammo she'll carry. Full blade loadout too if the power systems can manage it."

"Copy that, Boss," Derg's voice came back, already distorted by his own sealed suit. "We're maxing out your ammunition stores. The flight pack's gonna be sluggish with all that extra weight, but once you dump it, you'll be loaded for war."

Around the hangar, the other three pilots made similar preparations. Deadeye in his bulky combat suit was already climbing the catwalk to his mech's cockpit. Killjoy and Racer were reviewing targeting data on a shared tactical pad, their helmets reflecting the hangar's work lights.

Maintenance teams swarmed each mech like ants on a carcass. They checked every connection, tested every seal, verified that the flight packs were properly mated to the mechs' dorsal hardpoints. One mistake here meant a pilot would burn up on entry or crater on impact.

To the side, Joker and Hammer were loading their dropships with combat engineers—what Kenney called his ANTs (Armored Salvage & Technical). Each engineer wore sealed combat armor with integrated jump jets for rapid deployment and non-horizontal movement, their equipment loadouts bristling with plasma cutters, hydraulic spreaders, and shaped charges. They could cut a trapped mech free from collapsed buildings or strip a captured enemy mech to its frame in minutes, swarming over the metal like army ants on a carcass.

With the current arms embargos making replacement assault mechs nearly impossible to source, the ANTs had become essential. Every operation, they launched ready to carve their machines free from whatever urban grave they might fall into. The same teams that could reduce enemy hardware to spare parts in minutes would work twice as hard to save their own.

Joker caught Kenney's eye across the hanger. She blew him a kiss through her helmet's faceplate and gave an exaggerated bow before boarding her ship, her flight suit doing nothing to hide her figure even through the armor.

"Boss, you ever gonna stop runnin' from that filly?" Racer's voice crackled over the private comm channel. "That girl's sweeter on you than honey on cornbread, I tell you what."

"That's the problem," Kenney replied, watching Joker disappear into her cockpit. "The chase is half the fun for her. The moment she gets what she wants, she'll lose interest."

"Could be. Or could be you're more skittish than a june bug at a chicken convention when it comes to lettin' folks past that fence you built."

"Focus on the mission, Racer."

"Roger that, Boss. You're the one conducting this holo-soap."

Kenney climbed his own catwalk, each step clanging against the metal grating. His mech stood like a sleeping giant, the flight pack making it look even more massive than usual. The pack added another fifteen meters to the mech's height, all of it fuel and thrust.

He reached his cockpit and settled into the pilot's seat. Connections snapped into place—neural link, hydraulic assists, life support. The cockpit pressurized with a soft hiss, and his displays came alive with pre-flight data.

The squad tracker showed on his left display panel, four mech silhouettes appearing in a diamond formation. Each icon glowed red—systems not ready. His fingers danced across the interface, programming the readiness indicators to show real-time status.

Deadeye's icon flickered from red to amber, then solid green. Systems online, weapons hot, pilot ready.

A moment later, Killjoy's indicator shifted—red to amber as his systems spun up, then green as everything checked out.

Racer's icon stayed amber longer than the others, probably running his pre-flight checks twice like always. Finally it flashed green, his Confederate perfectionism satisfied.

All four green lights. His squad was ready to drop.

Through his tactical display, Kenney could see the hangar bay beginning its final transformation. Warning lights flashed amber, then red. The massive doors at the far end began to crack open, revealing the star field beyond. Atmosphere vented in a controlled rush, ice crystals glittering as they dispersed into vacuum.

"Purgatory control, this is Boss Actual," Kenney said. "Request permission to launch."

"Boss Actual, Purgatory control," The combat controller from the CIC's voice came back from the bridge. "You are cleared for launch. Good hunting."

The hangar floor began to reconfigure, panels sliding back to reveal the launch rail—a magnetic acceleration system running the full sixty-meter length of the hangar bay. The rail glowed with electromagnetic energy, designed to hurl forty-ton mechs into space like bullets from a gun.

Deadeye's mech moved first, its massive feet clanging against the deck as it walked to the rail's starting position. The mech's feet locked into the launch cradle with heavy mechanical chunks, electromagnetic clamps securing it to the acceleration sled. His mech crouched slightly, adopting a launch position to minimize stress on the frame.

"Deadeye locked and ready," came his voice over comms.

The rail hummed to life, building charge. Then the catapult fired. Deadeye's mech accelerated from zero to two hundred meters per second in three seconds, the G-forces that would liquify an unprotected human barely registering through his suit's dampeners. His mech shot out of the hangar like a missile, already beginning its long fall toward Regalia.

Killjoy was already moving forward as Deadeye cleared the rail, the launch cradle racing back to starting position on its return track. His mech stepped into position, feet finding the locking points with practiced ease.

"Launching," was all he said before the rail fired again, sending him hurtling into the void.

Racer taxied up next, his orange-striped mech almost bouncing with eagerness. "Y'all save some fun for me down there, ya hear?" The rail grabbed him and fired before anyone could respond.

Kenney moved last. The rail cradle locked around his feet, the electromagnetic systems reading the weight distribution and adjusting acceleration accordingly. Through his viewports, he could see the three points of light that were his squad, already falling toward the planet below.

The catapult engaged, and forty tons of death launched into the void, following his men toward Regalia's cold waters. It had once been a first-world planet with all the technological conveniences that implied—satellite networks, orbital defense platforms, global communications. Then ARMSEA had arrived for their "peacekeeping" operation.

The first thing the Armed Forces Space Expeditionary Army did in any theater was establish information dominance. That meant wiping out every satellite, every orbital platform, every piece of hardware that could observe their operations. They called it "operational security for public safety"—can't have locals broadcasting images of ARMSEA troops doing what ARMSEA troops did best.

In three days, they'd reduced Regalia from a connected, modern world to something resembling old Earth's Mogadishu. Ground commanders who'd relied on satellite reconnaissance suddenly found themselves blind. Radar systems designed to integrate with orbital networks became standalone units with limited range. Communications that had bounced off satellites now had to rely on line-of-sight radio towers, easily jammed or destroyed.

It was like watching civilization get its eyes plucked out.

Now, two years after ARMSEA's withdrawal, Regalia still operated in that enforced dark age. Neither faction had the resources to launch new satellites—any money that might have gone to space infrastructure went to bullets and bombs instead. Ground commanders relied on aerial reconnaissance aircraft that rarely lasted more than a few sorties before someone shot them down. Vehicle-mounted radar provided what little early warning they had.

On a Core World, the Purgatory would have been tagged the moment they entered the system. Defense satellites would have painted them with targeting lasers, orbital railguns would have tracked their approach, and they'd have been vaporized before hitting atmosphere.

But Regalia was blind.

The four mechs fell through the void like medieval soldiers attacking a castle whose watchtowers had been burned. Below them, armies fought with advanced weapons but stone-age intelligence, unable to see beyond the next hill or around the next corner. The Switchblade drones circling above were probably the best reconnaissance anyone had over Sevastopol right now.

"Two minutes to atmosphere," Deadeye's voice crackled over the secured channel.

Kenney checked his displays. They were coming in on the night side, their heat signatures masked by the planet's shadow. Even if someone on the ground happened to be looking up with thermal imaging, they'd appear as nothing more than meteorites—common enough in a system where orbital debris rained down regularly from destroyed satellites.

The first wisps of atmosphere kissed his mech's hull, barely noticeable through the flight pack's bulk. In minutes, those wisps would become a furnace, the friction of entry turning them into falling stars.

"Going dark," Kenney announced. "See you in the water."

The comm channel clicked off. Each pilot was now alone with their thoughts, their mechs, and the long fall through fire toward cold ocean below.

During the descent, Kenney's mind drifted to that day, pulled there by the familiar sensation of falling through darkness.

Back then he'd still had hope. He'd been a Captain in the Rogue Marines, a rank he'd earned the hard way—starting as a boot private and climbing every rung through competence, stubbornness, and an unhealthy disregard for personal safety. No academy commission, no family connections, just twelve years of proving himself in every shit detail and firefight the Corps could throw at him. Captain Jaeger—he'd been proud of those railroad tracks on his collar, proud of what they represented. Making officer from enlisted was rare enough, but making O-3 meant the brass actually trusted him with lives and decisions that mattered.

He'd met Kira at an embassy party on Halifax. She'd been arguing with some Core World diplomat about the rules of engagement, how Marines were handcuffed by bureaucrats who'd never seen combat. Her passion made her green eyes flash like emeralds in firelight. He'd been nursing a whiskey in the corner, trying to avoid the politics, when she'd cornered him and demanded to know what a Marine thought about fighting with one hand tied behind their backs by politicians who cared more about optics than soldiers' lives.

They'd fallen madly in love. The kind that made other couples look like they were playacting. The sex had been... transcendent. Not just physical but something deeper, like their bodies had been designed as matching pieces of the same machine. Every touch electric, every moment together worth whatever hell came next.

She could've done better. Core World education, the money that went with it, connections that opened doors he didn't even know existed. But she'd chosen him, said his love was worth more than all the political polish in the galaxy.

She'd been working to broker a stay of the embargo the Confederacy was enforcing on Halifax. The restrictions were causing undue hardship on the civilian population—medicine couldn't get through, food prices had tripled, children were dying of treatable diseases. Civil unrest was building. They just hadn't realized how much.

The convoy had been routine. Three armored vehicles, local security, taking her to meet with opposition leaders who might help negotiate. She'd kissed him goodbye that morning, told him she'd be back for dinner. They were going to try that new seafood place near the embassy.

The IED had flipped the lead vehicle completely over. The second—hers—had taken the blast directly underneath. By the time the mob descended, the survivors were too stunned to defend themselves. They'd beaten them with pipes, stones, their bare hands. Rage at the embargo, at the Marines, at anyone who represented the boot on their necks.

He'd shown up with his platoon eight minutes later. Eight minutes. The time it took to gear up and roll out. Eight minutes that might as well have been eight years.

The rioters tried to scatter when the Marines arrived, but Kenney's platoon opened fire immediately—standard ROE for hostile mobs. The M440s on the vehicles cut down runners in sweeping arcs. Riflemen picked off anyone still standing. The crowd that had numbered in the hundreds became dozens in seconds, then none.

Bodies littered the street—rioters piled on top of the convoy's defenders, blood mixing in the gutters without distinction. Some still moved, crawling or twitching, until precise shots ended that too. The Marines moved through systematically, checking bodies, searching for survivors from the convoy.

He'd found her by the ID chip and the remnants of the dress she'd worn that morning—the blue one with small flowers he'd said made her look like spring.

Her body was so badly mangled he couldn't identify her face. Couldn't find her eyes. Couldn't hold her hand because they couldn't find it. Just meat and fabric and the electronic chip saying this had been his wife.

Something in him died that day. The part that believed in justice, in protection, in the possibility that love could survive in a universe built on violence. He'd stood there in the street, his Marines forming a perimeter finishing off enemy survivors, staring at what remained while Halifax burned around them.

The after-action report blamed inadequate intelligence. The embassy expressed regret. The Confederacy lifted the embargo two months later—too late for Kira, too late for the hundreds who'd died in the riots, too late for anything but the next tragedy.

He'd resigned his commission the day after her funeral. Took his severance, his training, and his rage, and went mercenary. At least then the violence was indiscriminate. No pretending it served some higher purpose. Just killing for money, which was all it had ever been anyway.

The mech shuddered as it hit thicker atmosphere, heat shields beginning their work. The flames outside his cockpit looked like the embassy district burning. Like the convoy wreckage. Like the crematorium where they'd burned what was left of her because there wasn't enough to bury.

The flames grew brighter, and Kenney fell through them toward the cold, dark ocean below, carrying his ghosts with him like cargo that would never deliver.

The afterburners fired in sequence, four controlled explosions against the planet's gravitational pull. Kenney felt the deceleration crushing him into his seat, the g-forces making his vision tunnel despite the suit's compression systems. His mech's frame groaned under the stress, but held.

"Altitude three thousand meters," his AI announced with mechanical calm. "Two thousand. One thousand. Brace for impact."

The ocean rushed up to meet them like a wall of black glass. The stubby wings that had provided atmospheric control retracted immediately into ground mode, armored panels sliding over them with pneumatic hisses. Without the wings' resistance, the mechs would sink like stones. The mechs hit the water in a neat pattern, each impact sending up geysers a hundred meters high.

Kenney's world went from fire to darkness in seconds. The ocean closed over his mech's head, pressure readings climbing steadily on his displays. Emergency lights activated automatically, cutting through the murky water with sharp white beams that revealed nothing but more water and occasional debris from past battles—a sunken patrol boat here, aircraft wreckage there.

His feet hit the ocean floor with a muffled thump that sent sediment swirling. Depth gauge read 287 meters. The pressure outside would crush an unprotected human in seconds, but the mech's frame barely noticed.

"Systems check," he commanded over the tactical net, the LOS signal degraded but functional through the water.

His displays lit up with diagnostic data. Hydraulics: green. Weapons: green. Life support: green.

On his tactical display, green indicators flashed on each of the four mechs. They'd landed in a rough diamond formation, about two hundred meters apart. The ocean floor here was relatively flat—sand and silt over bedrock, dotted with rocks covered in some kind of growth that pulsed with dim blue light.

A holographic waypoint materialized on his HUD, marking the nuke container's location 3.7 kilometers to the northeast. The beacon's signal was weak but steady, waiting for the right activation codes to surface its deadly cargo.

The four mechs split into their pairs, mechanical giants walking along the ocean floor like myths from ancient sailors' nightmares. Their lights carved through the darkness, illuminating a graveyard of war—burned-out tanks from crashed transports, bodies that the ocean hadn't finished claiming.

The waypoint pulsed on his display, counting down the distance. 3.5 kilometers. 3.4. Through the murky water, he could see Racer keeping pace to his right, the other mech's orange racing stripes barely visible even with lights on full.

At 3.2 kilometers, Deadeye and Killjoy's lights became visible ahead, their beams sweeping across the seafloor like searchlights. The four mechs converged on the container's location, moving through a graveyard of past amphibious assaults. Spent shell casings the size of trash cans littered the ocean floor. Fragments of armor plating jutted from the silt like metal tombstones. Their lights created overlapping cones of illumination, revealing the occasional unexploded ordnance half-buried in the muck—sleeping death waiting for the wrong disturbance.

Kenney was glad for the space suit maintaining his temperature because the mech's cockpit was freezing this deep. Without the suit's heating elements, he'd be hypothermic in minutes. Ice crystals were already forming on the inside of his viewports where the heaters weren't keeping up.

"There," Racer's voice crackled through the water-degraded comm. His mech's light swept across an innocuous shipping container, rusted and covered in marine growth but intact.

Killjoy moved forward, the bayonet blade attached to his 30mm extending with a mechanical click. Together with Racer, they worked the blade into the container's seal, prying and cutting. The metal groaned and split, releasing a cloud of trapped air that rushed toward the surface in a silver stream of bubbles.

Inside, secured with military-grade clamps, sat their package.

Racer reached in with his mech's massive hands, carefully extracting the device. It wasn't much bigger than a vending machine—a matte black cylinder with minimal markings, just serial numbers and handling warnings in three languages. The kind of anonymous death that could end a city without anyone knowing where it came from.

Kenney turned to let Racer mag-lock it to his mech's back. The magnetic clamps engaged with solid thunks that Kenney felt through the neural feedback.

"Hope this thing's radiation shielding doesn't fry my swimmers," Kenney said, trying to lighten the moment.

"There's enough biological material in your sheets to clone a thousand of you," Deadeye shot back. "Don't be worried about your legacy, Boss."

"That's disgusting."

"That's what the laundry crew says too."

They began moving toward the separation point, their mechs' footfalls stirring up clouds of sediment. The ocean floor began to slope upward gradually—they were approaching the continental shelf.

Static burst through the comm channel, followed by Scott's voice from orbit, heavily distorted by distance and water. "Don't know if you can read me, Boss, but we're getting some weird thermal signatures ahead of you. Multiple objects, moving as a group about five hundred meters from your position."

Kenney held up a closed fist—the universal signal for halt. All four mechs stopped immediately, their lights clicking off in unison. The darkness swallowed them completely except for the dim glow of bioluminescent organisms.

A whole company of heavy infantry materialized out of the underwater gloom, moving in textbook formation. Each soldier wore a sealed exoskeleton—seven feet of articulated armor that looked like someone had built a tank around a human. The suits were bulky, first-generation military hardware with none of the sleek efficiency of newer models. Thick ceramic plates covered every surface, the joints protected by overlapping segments that gave them a segmented, almost insectoid appearance.

The helmets were completely sealed, no visors—just clusters of sensors where eyes should be, feeding data directly to internal displays. Life support packs bulged from their backs like turtle shells, containing air recyclers and power cells. The suits' arms ended in three-fingered manipulator claws that could still handle weapons but could also crush steel if needed.

Through the murky water, at least eighty of these armored figures bounded across the seafloor in synchronized leaps, their suit thrusters firing in short bursts to extend each jump. The power assistance let them move with surprising grace despite the bulk—each soldier carrying nearly three hundred pounds of armor plus weapons, yet moving like they weighed nothing.

Behind them came the real problem.

Four Arachne-class assault walkers, their eight legs each moving with hydraulic grace across the ocean floor. Walking main battle tanks on articulated limbs—low-slung hulls built for minimal water resistance, dual 90mm smoothbores in fully rotating turrets, rocket pods clustered along their flanks in hexagonal launch arrays. Each leg ended in a splayed foot designed to distribute weight across soft surfaces, with retractable spikes for purchase on rock. The turrets sat centerline, capable of 360-degree traverse without affecting the legs' movement pattern. Active camouflage panels flickered between gray-green ocean tones, trying to match the murky environment. The Coalition had deployed serious hardware to protect their approach to the pumping station.

"Nobody fucking move," Kenney whispered over the comm, his voice barely above subvocal.

The lead spider mech passed within fifty meters of their position, its legs stirring up sediment clouds that drifted across Kenney's viewports. Probably what saved them from being ambushed. Through the murk, he could see the rocket pods more clearly—at least twenty tubes per side. Enough firepower to turn his mech into scattered fragments across the ocean floor.

"Boss," Deadeye's voice was tight with tension. "If they're heading to the pumping station..."

"I know." Kenney watched another spider mech pass, its sensor suite sweeping active sonar pulses that made his teeth ache through the neural link. "They must think were subsea junk."

The formation continued past, the ground trembling under the weight of the Arachne assault walkers. Through gaps in the sediment clouds, Kenney could see unit markings—Coalition 13th Morskaya Pekhota Battalion. These weren't conscripts or militia. This was an elite amphibious assault unit.

They waited five minutes after the last Coalition soldier disappeared into the murky darkness ahead. Five minutes that felt like hours, the nuke on Kenney's back a constant weight reminder of their timeline ticking away.

"Well," Killjoy finally said. "That complicates things."

"The pumping station's going to be friggin warzone," Deadeye added. "A full company plus armor support? That's not a patrol, that's an invasion."

Kenney ran quick calculations. The Coalition force would reach the pumping station in twenty minutes at their current pace. Deadeye and Killjoy would arrive maybe five minutes after that. Instead of hitting a lightly defended industrial target, they'd be walking into a major engagement zone with nearly a hundred power-armored soldiers and four spider mechs that they knew of.

"We fixin' to tuck tail and run?" Racer asked, though his tone suggested he already knew that wasn't happening. "Boss, that's more hornets than a stick usually stirs up."

"No." Kenney checked his chronometer. "But we adjust. Deadeye, Killjoy—give them thirty minutes to settle in. Let them think they own that station. Then hit them in the water, shoot and scoot. Use their numbers against them—that many troops in tight spaces means confusion, panic."

"Two mechs against a reinforced company," Killjoy mused. "I've had worse odds."

They began moving again, but more carefully now. The separation point arrived too quickly. Deadeye and Killjoy peeled off toward the pumping station, their mechs disappearing into the murk like myths returning to the deep.

Kenney and Racer continued toward the beach. Through his mech's passive sensors, Kenney could feel the vibrations of the assault beginning—the distinctive thump of spider mech cannons firing in sequence, the higher-pitched crack of rocket salvos. The Coalition was moving in to take the pumping station, and they weren't being subtle about it.

"Sounds like the party started without us," Racer commented.

Moving up on the rear of the invasion force, Deadeye and Killjoy extended their plasma blades with barely audible hisses, the superheated edges casting eerie blue glows through the murky water. The Coalition force was focused entirely forward, their attention on the pumping station assault.

The assault force ahead was churning up massive sediment clouds, eighty suits and four walkers turning the clear water into an impenetrable murk. Deadeye and Killjoy moved fast, using the billowing silt as cover, their plasma blades already extended and glowing faintly blue through the haze.

They surged forward into the cloud, their mechs' movements hidden in the brown-gray haze that the Coalition force was creating. The heavy infantry at the rear of the formation were the stragglers—comms operators, ammunition carriers, and those with suit malfunctions from the underwater transit. One soldier's left leg actuator was misfiring, making him hop-swim in lurching movements. Another's helmet lights flickered on and off, the seals holding but the electronics failing in the salt water.

In the churned-up water, thermal signatures became useless, sonar just bounced off the particulate matter, and visual was down to maybe three meters. The Coalition soldiers were navigating by inertial guidance and formation discipline, trusting the man ahead to lead them right.

Deadeye reached the first straggler, his plasma blade sliding through the power armor's neck joint like it wasn't there. The superheated edge vaporized water on contact, creating a brief bubble of steam that was immediately swallowed by the murk. The suit's systems died instantly, the occupant with them, body drifting down into the silt.

Two more large shapes moving through the sediment cloud didn't register as threats—everything was shadows and ghosts in the murk. By the time the rear guard realized those shapes were getting closer rather than falling behind, the plasma blades were already at work.

Killjoy mirrored the action twenty meters away, his blade punching through a soldier's back plate and into the power core. The armor went dead, sinking into the silt.

Everything underwater moved with that strange, dreamlike quality—like fighting through jelly. The heavy infantry, for all their powered assistance, were still fundamentally ground troops. Their suits could survive underwater, get them from point A to point B, but they weren't designed for aquatic combat. Every movement was sluggish, delayed, fighting against water resistance. No one with half a brain wanted to fight underwater.

The mechs, meanwhile, had been built with amphibious operations in mind. Their movements were still slow, but purposeful, calculated. They moved like predators evolved for this environment.

Six more soldiers went down in silence, their suits' death registrations lost in the electronic noise of the ongoing assault. Then eight. Then ten. A dozen Coalition Morskaya Pekhota dead before anyone noticed something was wrong.

A sergeant finally turned, perhaps to check on a unresponsive subordinate. His helmet lights swept across Killjoy's mech standing over a pile of dead power armor, plasma blade still glowing.

The soldier's scream over the comms was cut short as Deadeye's blade took his head off, but the damage was done.

"Contact rear! CONTACT REAR!"

One of the spider mechs began its turn, all that armor and firepower rotating with mechanical precision. Its dual 90mm barrels swung toward them like the eyes of an angry god. The turret was halfway through its rotation when Killjoy surged forward, moving faster than anything that size should move underwater.

He slapped one of the demolition charges he'd liberated from a dead Coalition marine onto the spider mech's commander hatch. The magnetic clamp engaged with a solid thunk that the tank crew probably felt through their whole hull.

"MOVE!" Killjoy roared over comms, already diving away.

The spider mech's guns finally came to bear, both barrels depressing to track Killjoy's movement. But underwater, even hypervelocity rounds moved slower, their trajectories visible as cavitation bubbles.

The demolition charge detonated.

The explosion was muffled by water but devastating in effect. The commander's hatch, designed to withstand artillery strikes from above, wasn't rated for point-blank shaped explosives. The blast punched through, water hammer effect multiplying the force as it flooded the crew compartment in milliseconds.

The spider mech lurched, its legs spasming as dying crew members' neural links sent random signals. One 90mm gun fired wild, the shell screaming past Deadeye's head to impact somewhere in the distance. Then the war machine collapsed, eight legs folding under it like a dying insect.

But the spider mech was already turning, and the remaining heavy infantry still underwater were trying to reverse their formation. Half their force had already surfaced and engaged the Republic positions, leaving the underwater element undermanned and suddenly vulnerable. The marines still submerged moved in slow motion through the water, trying to pivot toward a threat they couldn't see through the murk.

"Well," Deadeye said, raising his autocannon as the first rockets started streaming toward them, "this is about to get loud."

The underwater battle erupted in earnest, the careful infiltration becoming a point-blank melee where the only rule was survival.

They engaged their thrusters simultaneously, but not before finishing their grisly underwater work. The sediment cloud had become a killing field—visibility down to arm's length, bodies drifting in the murk. The surviving Coalition marines abandoned all pretense of formation and bolted for the surface.

It became a desperate scramble. Power-armored soldiers fired their suit thrusters at maximum burn, not caring about formation or tactical spacing—just up, up, get out of the death trap the ocean had become. The remaining Arachne walker started an emergency ascent, its eight legs pumping frantically as it tried to protect what was left of its infantry support.

Deadeye and Killjoy burst through the surface in the middle of this chaos. Coalition marines were still erupting from the water around them like panicked dolphins, some immediately getting cut down by Republic fire from the pumping station, others stumbling onto the beach only to realize they'd surfaced between two hostile forces.

The Republic defenders, already engaged with the first Coalition wave, saw more enemies emerging from the surf in complete disorder. They opened fire on everything coming out of the water—Coalition marines fleeing the underwater massacre and the two mechs that had caused it.

Ahead, the massive industrial complex was already a battlefield. Republic defenders had fortified the pumping station—machine gun nests in the pipe galleries, snipers in the cooling towers, anti-tank teams behind concrete barriers. They were putting up fierce resistance against the Coalition assault force.

Deadeye pulled out one of his mech's grenades—scaled up for forty-ton warriors, a 1000-pound bomb shaped like a regular hand grenade. He hurled it into the densest pack of Coalition infantry still emerging from the surf.

The explosion turned thirty meters of beach into a crater. Bodies cartwheeled through the air, the pressure wave knocking over power-armored marines hundreds of meters away.

The Republic defenders saw the explosion and the two mechs cutting through Coalition forces from behind. Confusion rippled through both lines—whose side were these mechs on?

A Republic IFV, positioned behind sandbags near the station's main gate, swiveled its turret between targets—the Coalition forces in front, the unknown mechs behind them. Its 30mm autocannon opened fire on the Coalition infantry caught in the open, tracers streaming into the confused marines.

"They think we're with them!" Killjoy laughed, his plasma blade bisecting a Coalition marine who'd turned to face the wrong threat.

More Republic vehicles were taking defensive positions—three M-557 Badger Armored Personnel Carriers (APC) had backed into the pump house loading bays, their 25mm chain guns chattering from the cover of reinforced concrete. A pair of technicals—had taken elevated positions on the maintenance catwalks. One carried a Rheinmetall L-55 railgun, its capacitor banks whining as it charged between shots. The other mounted a quad-barrel Hydra anti-personnel system, spraying 7.62mm rounds at 3,000 rounds per minute.

Two Republic Wolverine Infantry Fighting Vehicles (IFV) had hull-down positions behind the massive storage tanks, only their turrets visible as their 30mm autocannons tracked targets. Their coaxial plasma repeaters glowed hot, the cooling vents steaming in the ocean spray.

They were all focused on the Coalition assault, treating the two mechs as reinforcements.

The two remaining spider mechs had finally made it to shore, their eight legs finding better purchase on solid ground. Their commanders had a choice—engage the Republic defenses as planned, or deal with the two hostile mechs carving through their rear.

"Boss, we've got everyone shooting at everyone!" Killjoy reported, ducking as both Coalition and Republic fire crisscrossed the battlefield. "This is beautiful chaos!"

A Republic tank, hull-down behind a concrete revetment, put a 120mm shell into one of the spider mechs. The Coalition war machine staggered, one leg blown off at the joint, but its dual 90mm cannons swiveled and returned fire, turning the Republic position into rubble.

The pumping station itself was taking hits from all sides—Coalition rockets, Republic mortars, stray rounds from the escalating battle. Storage tanks ruptured, sending burning fuel flowing toward the ocean. Secondary explosions rippled through the complex.

"Half the city's heading our way!" Deadeye called out, watching his tactical display populate with more contacts—both factions sending reinforcements to what was turning into a major assault.

The incline was getting steeper now, the ocean floor rising to meet the land. Depth gauge read 150 meters and falling. Another series of explosions rippled through the water—heavier this time. The Coalition wasn't just taking the pumping station; they were flattening any Republic forces that might have been holding it.

"Boss, we're at fifty meters depth," Racer announced. "We break surface in about two hundred meters."

Ahead, Kenney could see the faint glow of sunlight filtering through the water. His tactical display updated with data from the Switchblade drones—the beach ahead was empty of defenders but littered with obstacles. Massive tetrapods—four-pronged concrete breakwater blocks each the size of a house—formed an irregular maze extending from the waterline up to the coastal highway. Between them, the rusted hulks of civilian pleasure craft and fishing trawlers had been dragged up and abandoned, creating additional cover and obstacles.

"Thirty meters," Racer called out. "Twenty."

Their heads broke the surface simultaneously, water cascading off their armor as they rose from the depths. The beach was eerily quiet—no alarms, no scrambling defenders. Just the maze of concrete tetrapods and wrecked boats they'd have to navigate.

They picked their way carefully through the obstacles, each footstep calculated. The tetrapods were slick with algae, and the spaces between them were filled with twisted metal from the boat wrecks. One wrong step could send a forty-ton mech tumbling.

That's when they heard the engines.

A Coalition convoy came rumbling down the coastal highway—two Lynx-3 scout cars leading, eight-wheeled vehicles with thin angular hulls designed for speed over protection. Each mounted a remote-operated 12.7mm heavy machine gun and a 40mm automatic grenade launcher in a light turret. The armor was just thick enough to stop small arms fire.

Behind them followed three Bearcat II APCs, descendants of the old BMP design but optimized for counter-insurgency work. Six-wheeled with light composite armor. Each carried a small unmanned turret with a 7.62mm minigun for suppressing infantry and smoke grenade launchers for breaking contact. The rear compartments could carry a squad each, with firing ports along the sides so infantry could shoot from inside.

These weren't tank hunters—they were designed to move troops fast and deal with irregular forces. The kind of vehicles that excelled at patrol work and urban pacification but would evaporate under real armor engagement.

The convoy was moving fast, probably heading to assist in unit shuffle from the pumping station.

The lead Lynx driver saw the mechs at the same moment Kenney saw him. The convoy screeched to a halt, weapons traversing toward the two mechanical giants picking their way through the tetrapods.

Nobody fired.

The moment stretched like taffy. The Coalition forces knew that at this range, the mechs would annihilate them before they could even scratch the paint. Their anti-infantry weapons would be like throwing pebbles at battleships. The 12.7mm might spark off the armor. The 40mm grenades wouldn't even dent it. They were equipped to fight rebels with rifles, not forty-ton war machines.

The convoy's guns tracked them as the mechs continued moving through the obstacles, neither side willing to break the tense détente.

A Coalition soldier was visible in the lead Lynx's cupola, his hands shaking on the 12.7mm gun but not firing, just watching.

Kenney's mech stepped over a capsized yacht, his foot finding purchase on a pile of tetrapods. The convoy rolled forward slowly, maintaining the same speed as the mechs' careful progress. They were parallel now, maybe fifty meters apart—the convoy on the highway, the mechs in the obstacle field.

"Well ain't this awkward as a long-tailed cat at a dog show," Racer muttered over private comms, his drawl thicker with tension.

The strange procession continued for another hundred meters. Then the highway curved inland while the mechs' path led toward the city. The convoy accelerated away, and both sides let out collective breaths they didn't know they'd been holding.

"Think they'll report us?" Racer asked.

"Probably. But we'll be in Republic turf by the time anyone comes to look."

They cleared the last of the tetrapods and moved into the industrial district beyond, leaving the bizarre standoff behind.

CHAPTER FIVE

The glass walls of the holding cell were three inches thick, reinforced with wire mesh that turned everything beyond into a fractured mosaic. Valeria pressed her palm against the cold surface, watching her breath fog the glass before fading. She'd stopped counting the days after sixty. Or was it seventy? Time blurred when every hour looked the same—white walls, white floors, the endless hum of ventilation systems recycling the same stale air.

She was eighteen, maybe nineteen now. Her birthday had probably passed unmarked while she rotted in this medical nightmare. The smock they'd given her was thin, industrial-washed so many times it was translucent in places. No shoes, no undergarments, nothing that could be fashioned into a weapon or noose. They'd learned that lesson with the boy 5 cells down.

Through the wire-reinforced glass, she could see dozens of other cells stretching down the corridor. Each one held another kid from her frontier settlement, all wearing the same defeated expression, the same thinning frames from whatever they were doing to them. The youngest was maybe eight. The oldest, twenty at most.

A Viper automated infantry unit patrolled past her cell, its mechanical legs clicking against the polished floor in perfect rhythm. The combat android stood almost seven feet tall, humanoid in proportion but clearly mechanical. Its chassis was painted military black, the armor plating angular and functional. The head was the most distinctive feature: a pointed, wedge-shaped sensor housing that tapered forward like a blade, red optical sensors glowing where eyes would be.

It carried a standard M-47 assault rifle—the same mass-produced weapon that had equipped infantry for the past thirty years. Reliable 7.62mm rounds, iron sights, and a fire selector worn smooth from use. The rifle was held at port arms, angled across its chest in a non-threatening but ready position.

The tactical vest strapped over its chest was standard military surplus painted medical white—pouches for magazines, restraint cuffs in what would be a first aid pouch, even a flashlight it didn't need with its enhanced optics. Everything about it suggested control, order, routine.

The Viper paused at cell 47B, three down from Valeria. The locks disengaged with pneumatic hisses, and a boy—Chase, she remembered, he'd talked about becoming a shuttle pilot—stepped out without being asked. He knew the routine. They all did by now. Walk calmly, don't run, don't resist. Those who fought back didn't come back at all.

Chase walked past her cell, his eyes meeting hers for just a moment. She saw resignation there, the same look they all had after the first few weeks. He disappeared around the corner with the Viper, heading toward the testing area.

A gunshot echoed from that direction. Sharp, final.

Nobody flinched anymore.

"That's four today," whispered the girl in the cell next to hers. Sasha, eight years old, taken from the same settlement as Valeria. Her parents had run the general store, always gave kids free candy on holidays.

"Don't count them," Valeria said softly, moving to the shared wall between their cells. The glass muffled voices but didn't block them completely—they could hear each other if they spoke clearly and stayed close to the wall. "It just makes it worse."

"What do you think they're doing to us?" Sasha asked, her voice small. She'd lost weight, her cheekbones too sharp for a child's face. "The needles, the scans, all those tests?"

Valeria didn't answer because she didn't know. Blood draws every morning. Neural scans twice a week. Injections of things that made some kids scream for hours, others go silent and vacant-eyed. Physical stress tests that pushed bodies until they broke. Psychological evaluations that probed every fear, every memory, every dream.

"Tell me about home again," Sasha said. "About the flower festival."

Valeria closed her eyes, summoning memories that felt like they belonged to someone else. "Every spring, the whole settlement would gather in the main square. Mrs. Brigsby would set up her flower stalls, hundreds of varieties she'd been growing all winter in her greenhouses. Roses, lilies, those blue things that smelled like vanilla..."

"Prosperity flowers," Sasha supplied. "My mom loved those."

"Right. And there'd be music, and dancing, and Mr. Dunkle would make that fruit punch that was definitely spiked but all the parents pretended not to notice." Valeria smiled despite herself. "You and the other kids would run around with flower crowns, getting into everything."

"I had a puppy," Sasha said suddenly. "A little brown thing with one white ear. I called him Captain. Do you think... do you think someone's feeding him?"

Valeria's throat tightened. Their settlement had been emptied when the Vipers came in the night. No resistance, no warning, just families pulled from their beds and sorted. Adults to one transport, children to another. She'd heard her mother screaming her name until the transport doors sealed.

"I'm sure someone is," she lied.

Another Viper approached, this one's chassis scarred from combat, a melted patch on its torso where someone had hit it with a plasma cutter. It stopped at Sasha's cell.

"No," Valeria said, pressing against the glass. "She went yesterday. Check your logs, she already went yesterday!"

The Viper's sensor dome swiveled toward her, scanning, evaluating. Then it turned back to Sasha's cell. The locks disengaged.

Sasha stood slowly, her tiny frame shaking. She pressed her hand against the glass between their cells, matching where Valeria's palm pressed from the other side.

"If I don't come back," Sasha whispered, "feed my puppy for me?"

"You're coming back," Valeria said fiercely. "You're going to come back and we're going to get out of here and find Captain and go to next year's festival."

Sasha managed a smile that broke Valeria's heart. "The testing area's not so bad. Sometimes they give you juice afterward. Apple, if you're lucky."

The Viper waited with mechanical patience as Sasha walked out of her cell. She looked so small next to the combat android, barely coming up to its chest. She turned back once, waved with fingers that trembled, then followed the Viper down the corridor.

Valeria stayed pressed against the glass, watching until they turned the corner. She kept watching, waiting.

Five minutes passed. Ten. Twenty.

A single shot echoed from the testing area. Sharp, final.

Sasha didn't come back.

Three cells down, another kid—Tommy—was rocking back and forth, humming something tuneless. He'd bragged about being here longest, almost four months. Whatever they'd done to him in the testing area had left him like this, present but not really there anymore.

Valeria slid down the glass wall until she was sitting on the cold floor. Her reflection stared back from the polished surface across the corridor—hollow cheeks, dark circles, hair that had been thick and black now hanging limp. She looked like a ghost of the girl who'd been planning to study electrical engineering at the colonial university. The girl who'd stayed up late messaging friends, who'd snuck out to dance at the settlement's underground clubs, who'd had a life and a future and parents who loved her.

They'd taken two hundred kids from her settlement alone. She'd recognized most of them when they'd first arrived—classmates, neighbors, the boy who'd worked at the charging station and always flirted badly when she bought snacks. Now maybe forty were left in this wing. She didn't know if the others had been moved or...

Another Viper approached. Then another. And another.

Six Vipers arranged themselves along the corridor, each stopping at a different cell. Valeria's stomach dropped as one positioned itself at her door.

This was different. They never took this many at once.

The locks disengaged simultaneously, a chorus of pneumatic hisses. All six cell doors swung open.

"Please proceed to testing area," the Vipers announced in unison, their synthesized voices creating an unsettling echo. "Compliance is mandatory. Resistance will be met with termination."

Valeria stood on legs that felt like water. Around her, five other kids emerged from their cells—Tommy still humming, a girl named River who never spoke anymore, three boys whose names she'd never learned.

They formed a line, Vipers flanking them. Valeria tried to catch someone's eye, to share a moment of human connection, but they all stared straight ahead. Maybe it was better that way. Easier.

The corridor seemed endless, their bare feet slapping against the cold floor. They passed other wings, other cells, hundreds of them all mostly empty.

The testing area was different from the usual medical bays. Larger. The walls were lined with observation windows, darkened from the inside. Equipment she didn't recognize filled the space—massive scanners, surgical tables with too many restraints, tanks filled with murky fluid.

In the center of the room stood someone who wasn't a Viper. A human, wearing a lab coat over a medical jumpsuit. Female, middle-aged, with perfectly styled hair that seemed obscene in this place of suffering. She held a tablet, scrolling through data with manicured nails.

"Excellent," she said, not looking up. "Subject batch 47 through 52. We're ready to begin Phase Three trials."

"Phase Three of what?" Valeria asked, surprising herself with the words.

The woman looked up, mild surprise on her face. "You're still verbal. Interesting. Most subjects have entered selective mutism by this stage." She made a note on her tablet. "To answer your question—Phase Three of compatibility testing. You should be honored. Your genetic markers indicate potential for integration with the artifact."

"What artifact?"

The woman smiled, the expression not reaching her eyes. "You'll see soon enough. We discovered it during deep space mining operations. It's... unique. And it seems to have an affinity for certain neural patterns."

"What does it do?"

"That's what we're determining." The woman turned to the Vipers. "Begin preparation. Load all subjects onto the exposure platforms."

The Vipers moved with mechanical precision, guiding each of them to medical tables arranged in a circle. The restraints were different here—not just wrists and ankles, but a full harness system including a head restraint that kept them facing inward toward an empty central platform.

Valeria was strapped down between Tommy and River. She could see the others around the circle—six kids, all facing the center like spokes on a wheel. Above them, observation windows remained dark, but she could sense people watching.

"Phase Three trial commencing," the woman announced, her voice now coming through speakers. She'd retreated to somewhere safe. "Subjects in position. Initiating mass exposure event."

The lights dimmed. The Vipers filed out through a heavy door that sealed with multiple locks engaging. For a moment, they were alone in near-darkness, just the sound of frightened breathing.

Then the central platform began to rise.

It emerged from the floor with a low hum, and as emergency lighting flickered on, Valeria saw it clearly. The artifact was wrong—that was the only word for it. A twisted spire of something that might have been metal or crystal or organic tissue, about three meters tall, covered in geometries that hurt to follow with your eyes. Symbols or patterns covered its surface, shifting and writhing like living things. It pulsed with a sick greenish light that made her stomach turn.

"Beginning exposure," the woman's voice announced. "Monitoring all subjects."

The artifact's glow intensified.

Tommy started screaming first. Not pain, well not at first, but terror—pure, mindless terror as something invaded his consciousness. His back arched against the restraints, muscles straining until Valeria heard something pop.

River followed seconds later, her quiet demeanor shattered as she thrashed against the restraints, words tumbling from her mouth in languages that shouldn't exist.

Around the circle, the others joined the chorus of agony. One boy's eyes rolled back, blood trickling from his nose. Another went rigid, every muscle locked in a full-body seizure.

Valeria felt it then—a presence, alien and ancient, pressing against her mind. It whispered without words, showed her things that couldn't be, shouldn't be. Star systems being born and dying in seconds. Mathematics that folded in on themselves. Technologies that violated every law of physics she knew.

Her mouth opened, but what came out wasn't a scream.

"Primary fusion containment requires magnetic field strength of 15 Tesla minimum with superconducting coils maintaining temperature below 4.2 Kelvin," she heard herself say, the words flowing without conscious thought. "Plasma density must reach 10^20 particles per cubic meter for ignition. Lawson criterion satisfied at triple product of 3×10^21 keV seconds per cubic meter."

"Interesting," the woman's voice crackled through speakers. "Subject 47 is exhibiting technical glossolalia. Continue exposure."

The visions intensified. Valeria saw weapons that could crack planets, ships that moved through folded space, energy sources that pulled power from the quantum foam itself. Her mouth kept moving, spilling specifications and formulas.

"Particle beam convergence at 0.7c requires gravitational lensing compensation. Primary accelerator ring diameter 500 meters minimum. Synchrotron radiation peaks at 511 keV indicating positron-electron annihilation efficiency of 97.3 percent."

Her eyes had rolled back, she realized distantly. She couldn't see the room anymore, just the endless stream of advanced knowledge the artifact was forcing into her brain. It felt like drowning in mathematics, suffocating on equations.

"Rail gun projectile velocity achievable at 200 kilometers per second using room-temperature superconductor rails. Lorentz force equation

F equals I times L times B where current reaches 2 million amperes. Capacitor bank requirement 50 megajoules minimum."

Around her, the screaming continued. Tommy had gone silent—passed out or dead, she couldn't tell. River was speaking in tongues, guttural sounds that predated human language. One of the boys was laughing, high and broken, tears streaming down his face.

"Neural interface bandwidth requires 10 terabit per second minimum for full sensory integration. Quantum entanglement protocols enable instantaneous communication across 1000 light-year range. Heisenberg compensators necessary to maintain coherence."

The artifact pulsed brighter, and Valeria felt something tear inside her mind. Not breaking, but opening—pathways that shouldn't exist, connections that violated everything she understood about human consciousness.

"Initiating emergency protocol," the woman's voice came urgently. "Exposure exceeding safe parameters."

The artifact's glow suddenly cut out, plunging them into darkness. The absence of its presence was almost worse than its touch—like suddenly losing a sense she didn't know she had.

Emergency lighting flickered on. The Vipers had returned, forming a circle around the tables. The woman entered behind them, studying her tablet.

"Results are conclusive," she announced. "Only Subject 47 showed desirable compatibility and precognitive tendencies. Terminate the others."

Valeria's blood turned to ice. "What? No, you can't—"

The Vipers moved with mechanical efficiency. The one nearest to Tommy raised its arm, the integrated pulse rifle extending. A single shot, point-blank to the temple. The table beneath him opened—a disposal hatch she hadn't noticed before—and his body slipped through with a wet sound.

"NO!" Valeria screamed, straining against her restraints.

River was next. The girl was still whimpering, curled up as much as the restraints allowed. The Viper didn't hesitate. Shot. Hatch. Gone.

Around the circle, it continued. The boy who'd been laughing—shot. The one who'd seized—shot. Clinical, efficient, like putting down livestock.

"Stop! Please stop!" Valeria thrashed against the restraints, the metal cutting into her wrists. "They're just kids! They're just—"

"They're failed test subjects," the woman said calmly. "Resource allocation demands we focus on viable specimens."

The last shot rang out. Five bodies, five hatches, five children who would never see home again. The Vipers stood at attention, weapons still deployed, waiting for orders.

"Release Subject 47," the woman commanded.

The restraints around Valeria's arms clicked open. She slumped forward immediately, exhausted from the strain and grief. The nearest Viper moved to catch her, its mechanical hands reaching for her shoulders.

The moment it made contact, everything changed.

Valeria's body went completely rigid, her eyes rolling back until only the whites showed. She didn't fall—the Viper held her upright—but she wasn't there anymore. Something else was.

The woman stepped forward, intrigued. "Subject 47? Can you—"

The Viper holding Valeria suddenly jerked, its grip tightening. Through its speakers came a sound that wasn't quite Valeria's voice—deeper, distorted, wrong. Not words, just a low growl that built into something like laughter.

"Fascinating," the woman began, raising her tablet to record. "Some kind of defensive—"

She never finished the sentence.

The Viper's free hand shot out faster than human eyes could track, fingers wrapping around the woman's throat. But it wasn't just one Viper moving. All six turned as one, their movements perfectly synchronized, no longer the measured mechanical precision of before but something fluid, predatory.

The woman had half a second to see her reflection in the Viper's sensor dome—her eyes wide with realization—before it pulled. Her head separated from her body with a wet tear, blood painting the white walls in arterial spray.

The medical technicians tried to run. The Vipers were faster.

One tech made it three steps before a Viper's blade extended through his chest. Another was caught at the door, two Vipers gripping his arms and legs, pulling in opposite directions until he came apart at the joints. The screaming lasted only seconds.

Through it all, Valeria's body remained catatonic, held by the first Viper like a broken doll. Her mouth hung open, drool running down her chin, but something lived behind those rolled-back eyes. Something the artifact had awakened or created. A passenger that had been waiting for the right moment, the right trigger.

The Vipers moved through the facility like a plague, still in perfect synchronization. They didn't use their pulse rifles—too quick, too clean. They used their hands, their blades, their mechanical strength. Door locks meant nothing. Security barriers crumpled like paper.

In the observation room above, technicians frantically tried to trigger emergency protocols, to shut down the Vipers remotely. But the connection went both ways. Whatever was riding Valeria's consciousness had access to their systems now, spreading through the facility's network like a virus.

Vipers throughout the facility stopped mid-patrol, their sensors flickering, then joined the synchronous movement. Twenty units. Fifty. Every android in the facility turned toward the nearest human and began the methodical work of taking them apart.

The facility's human security forces responded quickly. Squads in tactical armor poured into the corridors, pulse rifles chattering, trying to establish defensive positions. The Vipers met them with inhuman coordination, moving like a single organism with dozens of bodies.

A security team set up behind overturned tables in the main corridor, laying down suppressing fire. The Vipers didn't seek cover—they just walked through the fusillade, armor sparking where rounds hit but barely slowing. When they reached the barricade, the killing was methodical.

By the time Valeria's consciousness crashed back into her own body, the facility was a charnel house of human remains mixed with wrecked Vipers. She gasped, finding herself on her hands and knees in a pool of blood, unsure how she'd gotten there.

"What..." Her voice was raw, throat burning like she'd been screaming. She couldn't remember screaming. Couldn't remember anything after the Viper had touched her.

She stood on shaking legs, trying not to look at the bodies—or parts of bodies—scattered around her. Alarms wailed through the facility. Emergency lights painted everything in hellish red. She could hear distant explosions—Vipers fighting still, or maybe just systems failing catastrophically. She had to get out.

Valeria picked her way through the carnage, bare feet slipping on blood and hydraulic fluid. Every few meters she passed another tableau of horror—security forces torn apart, Vipers riddled with bullet holes, the walls painted with arterial spray.

A doorway ahead promised escape, but she had to step over a security officer's torso to reach it. His eyes were still open, staring at nothing. His tactical vest read "Schmidt, P."

She recognized him. The rage hit her so suddenly she staggered. Schmidt—the one who'd come to the cells at night during the first weeks. Who'd picked the older girls, sometimes two at a time. Who'd smiled while doing it.

Without thinking, she kicked his corpse hard in the face. Then again. And again.

"You deserved worse," she spat, her voice breaking. The memories she'd tried to bury came flooding back—his hands, his breath, the helplessness. The other girls crying in their cells afterward.

She kicked him one more time, feeling a rib crack under her bare foot, then forced herself to step over him and continue. He was dead. That had to be enough. But a dark part of her, maybe the same thing that had controlled the Vipers, whispered that she was glad he'd died badly. That she hoped he'd been conscious when they tore him apart.

The corridor beyond was worse. Bodies stacked like cordwood where a squad had tried to make a stand. Viper parts scattered like a child's discarded toys. The overhead lights had failed here, leaving only emergency strips along the floor to guide her through the darkness.

She tried not to think about what had happened during her blackout. The memories felt like trying to grasp smoke—there but not there, leaving only the sensation of something vast and hungry that had moved through her, used her as its instrument. She couldn't remember controlling the Vipers, couldn't remember the killing, but the evidence was all around her.

Had she done this? The thought made her stomach lurch. All these people, torn apart while she was... what? Unconscious? Possessed? She didn't even have words for what had happened when the Viper touched her.

CHAPTER SIX

The intersection ahead was a kill box.

Kenney pressed his mech against the facade of what had been a luxury apartment complex, the building's glass and steel groaning under forty tons of metal. Through his displays, he could see the Republic armor column—five Hurricane IFVs in a staggered formation, each one packing a turret-mounted railgun, capacitor banks glowing along their hulls.

In front of the vehicles, conscript infantry platoons were moving up through the rubble, hauling portable rocket launchers and anti-tank missiles. They were trying to establish firing positions in the destroyed storefronts and collapsed building entrances—anywhere that would give them clear shots when the mechs tried to push through. At least two squads were already setting up, their AT-14 launchers being loaded with tandem-charge warheads designed to defeat reactive armor.

"Boss, those are Mjolnir-6 railguns," Racer's voice crackled through the comm, his mech pressed against the opposite building. "Them things'll punch through us like we're made of paper. Seen one core an upright at half a klick."

The street was too narrow for evasive maneuvers—maybe thirty meters across, lined with burned-out civilian vehicles and rubble from collapsed balconies. The kind of urban canyon where mechs lost all their advantages. No room to dodge, no space to flank. Just a straight shooting gallery where the first to expose themselves died.

"Deadeye, Killjoy, what's your status?" Kenney asked, checking his tactical display.

"Still dealing with the clusterfuck at the pumping station," Deadeye responded, the sound of explosions punctuating his transmission. "You know, the 'distraction' that was supposed to pull forces away? Yeah, it worked great—now half the city's hosting us as the guests of honor."

A Republic soldier with a megaphone was shouting from behind the APCs: "Unidentified mechs! You are surrounded! Power down and surrender immediately!"

"We were the moment we hit atmosphere," Kenney replied, his fingers finding the smoke launcher controls on his left arm panel. He checked the angle, calculating trajectories in his head. The buildings here were old concrete and steel, strong enough to handle a ricochet. The rail cannons needed direct line of sight to fire—their tungsten penetrators traveled too fast for any kind of guidance system.

"Racer, on my mark, full smoke deployment. Fill that whole stretch of road."

"Copy that, Boss. Ready when you are."

Kenney raised his mech's left arm, angling it at a forty-five-degree angle. His targeting computer showed the probable ricochet pattern.

"Mark."

Twelve smoke canisters launched simultaneously from both mechs, spiraling through the air on tiny rocket motors. They struck the building facades with metallic clangs, ricocheting into the intersection at wild angles. The canisters hit the ground and erupted, each one spewing thick orange smoke that expanded rapidly in the still air.

"Moving!" Kenney surged forward into the smoke, but not toward the intersection. His mech's hands found the apartment building's facade, fingers punching through glass and concrete to create handholds. He began climbing, using each floor like a ladder rung, his forty tons of metal and weapons ascending with surprising dexterity.

The building immediately protested. Concrete cracked and spalled around his grip points. Internal supports, never designed for this kind of lateral stress, began to buckle. Windows exploded outward in cascading showers of glass.

Across the intersection, Racer was doing the same thing, his orange-stars and bars mech hauling itself up the opposite building. "Boss, I'll tell you what—bet I can beat you to them fancy boys down yonder! Yeehaw!"

"Building's not gonna hold," Kenney grunted, feeling the structure sway beneath him as he reached the roof. The entire top floor was already beginning to separate from the supporting walls.

"Then we best skedaddle 'fore she drops!" Racer launched himself from his building's roof just as it began to implode, his mech's jump jets firing to extend the leap.

Kenney followed, both mechs now running across the rooftops as the buildings collapsed beneath them like dominoes. Each footfall punched through roof material, each landing caused another structure to fail catastrophically. They were surfing a wave of architectural destruction, staying just ahead of the collapse.

Below, the Republic forces were trying to react, but their railguns couldn't elevate enough to track targets eight stories up. The turrets whined, servos straining against their maximum elevation stops. The infantry scattered, trying to avoid the rain of debris—chunks of concrete, steel beams, entire sections of facade crashing down into the street.

Kenney's autocannon roared, firing straight down into the top armor of the lead IFV. Inside his cockpit, he felt each round discharge through the neural feedback—the rhythmic thump-thump-thump reverberating through his arms. His targeting display showed the impact points in real-time, each armor-piercing round glowing white-hot as it punched through.

The brass casings ejected from his mech's autocannon in a continuous stream—each one nearly a meter long and thick as a man's forearm, still glowing orange from the heat of firing. They tumbled through the air, spinning end over end, weighing forty pounds each.

The first casing struck a Republic soldier who'd been trying to set up a rocket launcher. The massive brass cylinder hit him square in the helmet, the impact crushing his skull instantly, driving his body into the pavement with such force it left an impression in the asphalt. His squad mate dove aside as another casing crashed where he'd been standing, the hot metal sizzling against the wet street.

Kenney pulled the trigger again, walking rounds across the IFV's engine compartment. Each pull sent more casings cascading down, turning the street below into a kill zone of falling brass. A medic trying to reach wounded soldiers had to abandon his patient as casings cratered the ground around him, each impact throwing up chips of concrete.

The IFV's turret finally sparked and died, smoke pouring from the crew hatches as electrical fires consumed the interior. But Kenney kept firing, making sure it would never move again, his cockpit filling with the acrid smell of cordite despite the filtered air system.

Racer landed on another rooftop, the building immediately beginning its death throes. He didn't stop moving, his mech's feet barely touching before he leaped again. Mid-jump, he hurled one of his combat knives downward like a javelin. The three-meter blade punched through an IFV's engine deck, pinning it to the street like an insect to a board.

"That's two down, three to go!" Racer whooped, landing on another structure that immediately began to pancake under his weight.

The Republic militia were in full panic now. They'd prepared for a ground assault, not mechs raining death from above while bringing down entire city blocks. Rocket teams tried to aim upward, but falling debris and dust clouds made targeting impossible.

More casings rained down—a deadly brass hailstorm. One punched through the canvas top of a supply truck, the driver looking up just in time to see death falling from the sky before the casing caved in his chest. Another struck an infantry sergeant in the shoulder, the impact spinning him around before the weight drove him to his knees, his arm hanging useless.

Another building went down, this one taking out power lines that draped across the street in showers of sparks. Kenney rode the collapsing structure like a giant surfboard, firing his autocannon in controlled bursts at the remaining IFVs below. One tried to reverse out of the kill zone but backed directly into a falling wall that buried its rear half.

Below, a Republic squad leader screamed at his men to find cover, but there was nowhere to hide from the brass rain. One soldier raised his rifle skyward in futile defiance before a casing struck him between the shoulder blades, dropping him face-first into the rubble.

"Watch it!" Racer called out. His building was tilting too far, threatening to throw him backward into the destruction.

Both mechs made final leaps as the last of the buildings gave way completely. They landed hard in the street beyond the intersection, the ground cracking under their combined weight. Behind them, an entire city block had been reduced to rubble, the Republic armor either destroyed or buried under tons of debris.

Through the dust cloud, they could see surviving infantry pulling wounded from the wreckage. The street they'd just "crossed" was now an impassable canyon of collapsed buildings and twisted metal.

They moved forward several blocks, the streets eerily quiet after the chaos of the intersection. Too quiet. Kenney's threat indicators stayed dark, but something felt wrong.

They emerged into a wide parking area, multi-level parking garages flanking both sides like concrete canyon walls. The space opened up—maybe a hundred meters across, littered with abandoned civilian vehicles.

The first railgun shot came from above without warning.

His instincts kicked in before his conscious mind registered the threat. He threw his mech sideways, slamming his shoulder into Racer's mech and knocking him clear. The tungsten penetrator screamed through the space where Racer's cockpit had been, punching through three parked cars before embedding in the asphalt.

Pain feedback flooded Kenney's neural link—his right arm had taken a glancing hit. The tungsten round had carved a groove along the shoulder joint, shearing away armor plates. Inside the cockpit, warning lights cascaded across his displays—hydraulic pressure dropping, myomer bundles damaged, structural integrity compromised.

"Right arm damage," Foxtrot announced. "Running diagnostics."

Kenney tested the arm, flexing his own right hand in the control glove. The mech's arm responded, but sluggishly. He could feel the delay through the neural link, the hesitation between thought and movement. His fingers worked the individual joint controls on his armrest panel—shoulder rotation sluggish but operational, elbow flexion at sixty percent efficiency, hand grip strength compromised but functional.

"Contact! Parking garage, roof level!" he shouted, rolling behind a delivery truck that immediately exploded as another railgun shot cored through it. "Can you still shoot?"

Kenney raised the damaged arm, trying to aim his secondary weapon mount. The targeting reticle wavered on his display, the damaged servos unable to hold zero.

"Barely," he admitted, switching primary control to his left arm. Inside the cockpit, he had to reconfigure his entire control scheme, his left hand now managing weapons while his damaged right tried to maintain movement control. Sweat ran down his back as his brain adjusted to the reversed setup.

On the garage roof, the Mithril Sentinel stood in a textbook firing position. Twelve feet of professional military hardware, painted in the company's signature blue and white. Unlike militia equipment, this mech moved with fluid precision, already displacing to avoid return fire. The pilot knew what they were doing.

"Son of a bitch nearly took my head clean off!" Racer snarled, his mech coming up from behind an overturned bus. "That tears it!"

He reached behind his back, pulling out what looked like an oversized football—a demolition charge designed for bunker busting, five hundred pounds of shaped explosive in an aerodynamic casing.

"Hut hut!" Racer shouted, his mech dropping into a quarterback's stance. He cocked his arm back, then hurled the charge in a perfect spiral.

The Mithril pilot saw it coming, tried to move, but the parking garage didn't allow for quick escapes. The charge hit the structure's support pillar and detonated on impact.

The explosion was devastating. The entire corner of the parking garage vanished in a ball of fire and concrete dust. Without that support, the structure began a catastrophic progressive collapse. Floor after floor pancaked down, thousands of tons of concrete and steel folding in on itself.

The Sentinel tried to jump clear, its smaller frame more agile than their assault mechs. It almost made it—cleared the collapsing edge, jump jets firing—but debris clipped its leg mid-flight. The mech tumbled, slamming into the ground hard. It tried to rise, servos whining, but its left leg was twisted at an unnatural angle.

"Got 'im!" Racer whooped, already moving to engage.

But the Mithril pilot wasn't done. Even damaged, prone, with one leg useless, the Sentinel's railgun swiveled toward them vectoring for a shot. These weren't weekend warriors or conscripts—Mithril hired veteran killers.

"Move!" Kenney barked, both mechs scattering as another hypervelocity round split the air between them.

Kenney's left hand went to his smoke launcher controls on instinct, muscle memory from a dozen urban engagements. His fingers found the switches but the indicators showed empty—all twelve canisters spent at the intersection.

"Shit," he muttered, diving behind a concrete barrier as another railgun shot carved through the air where he'd been standing.

The shots were coming fast but wild, desperation rather than precision. The Mithril pilot was hurt—maybe a concussion from the fall, maybe internal injuries from the impact. Professional or not, the human inside that metal shell had limits.

"He's firing scared!" Racer called out, his mech weaving between shots that went wide by meters. "Lost his cool!"

They moved in opposite directions, forcing the damaged Sentinel to choose a target. Its railgun swiveled toward Kenney, tracking but overshooting. Another round screamed past, punching through empty air.

Racer closed the distance in long strides. The Sentinel tried to traverse back toward him but its damaged leg made the whole frame shudder with each movement.

"Should've stayed on that roof, partner," Racer said, bringing his mech's foot down on the Sentinel's railgun arm. The kick connected with devastating force—the entire arm sheared off at the shoulder joint, the railgun spinning away across the asphalt, sparks flying from severed power cables.

The Mithril pilot tried to raise the Sentinel's remaining arm in defense, but Racer's bayonet was already extending with a mechanical click. He raised the three-meter blade overhead and drove it down through the Sentinel's chest armor, through the cockpit, and deep into the parking lot asphalt beneath. The smaller mech went limp instantly, all systems dying at once.

Racer wrenched his bayonet free, hydraulic fluid and other fluids spraying from the wound. "Well, that's that. Mithril's gonna want their deposit back."

Alarms suddenly screamed through Kenney's cockpit, red warnings cascading across his displays.

"Evasive maneuvers!" Foxtrot's British accent cut through sharply. "Missile barrage incoming—multiple launches detected!"

Both mechs moved in a split second. Inside his cockpit, Kenney slammed the jump jet controls forward with his palm while his other hand yanked the control stick hard left. The sudden acceleration crushed him back into his seat, the G-forces making his vision tunnel as his mech rocketed sideways.

"Evading!" he grunted through clenched teeth, fighting to maintain consciousness as his suit's compression systems struggled to compensate.

His mech's jets fired at maximum burn—four primary thrusters and eight maneuvering jets all screaming at once. The thrust indicators on his console redlined instantly, temperature warnings flashing as the engines consumed fuel at an unsustainable rate. Through the neural link, he felt the heat building in his mech's back, the thrust nozzles glowing white-hot.

Racer's response was even more violent. His entire mech rotated mid-leap, jets firing in a corkscrew pattern that sent him spinning through the air. Inside his cockpit, the world became a blur of motion, his inner ear screaming protests as up and down lost all meaning.

Above them, the sky lit up with exhaust trails—dozens of dumb-fire missiles arcing down like steel rain. Each missile was two meters long, packed with high explosive and shaped fragmentation charges. Their solid fuel boosters left thick white contrails that crisscrossed the sky like a deadly net. The rockets weren't smart—no guidance systems, no target lock—just pure ballistic trajectories calculated to saturate an area with death.

The first wave hit where they'd been standing 1.2 seconds earlier.

The parking lot erupted in a chain reaction of detonations. Each missile impact created a crater three meters wide, the shaped charges designed to penetrate bunker roofs before detonating. Concrete fountained upward in gray geysers, mixed with red-hot shrapnel that scythed through the air at supersonic speeds. Abandoned cars were lifted and tossed like toys—a sedan flipped end over end before crashing through a storefront, a delivery truck split in half lengthwise, its cargo of consumer goods transformed into deadly projectiles.

Inside Kenney's cockpit, proximity alarms shrieked as shrapnel pinged off his armor. His displays flickered from electromagnetic interference as each detonation created a localized EMP burst. The shock waves hit his mech in rapid succession, each one threatening to knock him off balance even thirty meters from the impact zone.

"Holy shit!" Racer's voice cracked over comms, his mech stumbling as it landed, servos whining in protest as the legs absorbed the impact.

Through the smoke and debris, something massive rounded the corner.

Kenney's threat indicators went haywire, every warning system in his cockpit screaming at once. The seismic sensors registered the ground vibrations first—rhythmic tremors that made his mech's stabilizers automatically adjust stance. Then the audio pickups caught it: the grinding shriek of tank treads crushing asphalt mixed with the hydraulic whine of mech servos.

It emerged from the smoke like something from a mechanized nightmare. The abomination of military engineering stood thirty feet tall even hunched on its tracks—someone had taken a main battle tank's hull and grafted a mech's torso onto it, creating a hybrid that violated every principle of elegant design. The tank treads were massive, each track link the size of a dinner table, designed to support the obscene weight of the merged systems. The torso rose from the hull like a mechanical centaur, arms ending in manipulator claws that could either wield weapons or tear through armor.

A Stout-class hybrid. Kenney's tactical computer immediately pulled up the specifications—120 tons of armor and firepower, designed for siege warfare and area denial. The kind of thing that turned urban battlefields into graveyards.

But it was the paint job that made his blood run cold. MITHRIL's blue and white colors were pristine despite the combat, that professional military contractor polish that said this wasn't militia equipment. The stylized "M" on its shoulder was three meters tall, impossible to miss. This wasn't some captured surplus—MITHRIL had deployed serious hardware.

The hybrid's back was the real threat. Massive rocket pods sprouted like mechanical wings, each one the size of a shipping container. Kenney's sensors counted the tubes—forty-eight per pod, two pods total. Ninety-six rockets, though smoke still streaming from dozens of empty tubes said it had already expended at least a third of its loadout. The individual missiles were visible through his magnification—MDFS-8 "Swarm" rockets, unguided but devastating in volume.

Inside his cockpit, Kenney's fingers flew across his weapons panel, trying to get a targeting solution. But the Stout was designed to defeat exactly that—its hybrid nature confused targeting computers that expected either a mech or a tank, not both. His lock-on indicators flickered between red and yellow, unable to maintain a steady fix.

"That thing's got enough ordnance to level six city blocks," Racer observed, his voice tight with barely controlled panic. His mech was already moving, trying to find cover in a parking lot that had been turned into a moonscape. "And we're standing in the open like idiots at a shooting gallery!"

The Stout's torso rotated with mechanical precision, its sensor array—a cluster of cameras and targeting lasers where a head should be—sweeping across them with the slow confidence of a predator that knew its prey had nowhere to run. Inside that hybrid monster, a MITHRIL pilot was likely running through the same calculations Kenney was: distance to targets, minimum safe range for rocket deployment, probability of kill.

The rocket pods began to angle upward with a hydraulic whine that Kenney could hear even through his sealed cockpit. Targeting lasers painted both mechs—thin red lines visible through the smoke and dust, marking them for death.

"Second barrage incoming!" Kenney shouted, his left hand already slamming the jump jet controls while his right tried to target something, anything, on the hybrid that might be vulnerable.

The rocket pods flared again, another wave of missiles spiraling into the air. The launches came in sequence—thoom-thoom-thoom-thoom—each rocket igniting a fraction of a second after the last, creating a rolling thunder that shook windows for kilometers around.

"What's the deal with the drone coverage, Scott?" Kenney snarled into the comm, his mech stumbling to its feet. "We should've had early warning of a Stout in the AO!"

Blake's voice crackled back from orbit, tight with frustration. "Switchblades are getting swatted. Tasking the back-ups to your AO. We're blind in your sector."

The Stout's torso rotated, tracking them with surprising speed for something that size. More missile pods were already angling upward, ready to unleash another barrage.

"That thing's got enough ordnance to level a city block," Racer observed, his mech already moving to find cover. "And we're standing in a dang parking lot with nowhere to hide!"

The rocket pods flared again, another wave of missiles spiraling into the air.

"I see what's hitting them," Deadeye cut in over the channel, his transmission crackling with static from the pumping station firefight. "There's a whole anti-air battalion sitting pretty on the seawall. Radar dishes, laser point defense, the works. Probably why the Coalition had to do their beach assault instead of coming in by air."

"Can you take it out?" Kenney asked, diving behind a collapsed wall as another missile barrage bracketed his position.

"Give me thirty seconds," Deadeye replied. "Then your sky should be clear."

Through the comm, they could hear Deadeye's 90mm rifle firing in rapid succession, the distinctive crack of hypervelocity rounds. In the background, secondary explosions started cascading—ammunition cooking off, radar arrays detonating.

"Beautiful fireworks over here," Deadeye reported. "Air defense grid is officially offline. Your drones should have clear airspace in about... now."

Kenney was too busy trying to close on the Stout to worry about the drone situation. He needed to get inside its minimum rocket range—those pods couldn't depress enough to hit anything closer than fifty meters. His jump jets fired in short bursts, zigzagging through the missile impacts that turned the parking lot into a moonscape.

Just as he thought he had a clear run at the hybrid, movement caught his peripheral sensors.

Glass exploded outward from two storefronts flanking the Stout. The buildings—a former electronics shop and what looked like a restaurant—had been concealing the Sentinels perfectly. They burst through in showers of debris, their twelve-foot frames moving with Mithril's signature precision. No hesitation, no startup sequence—they'd been powered up and waiting, probably watching through their thermals as Kenney approached.

Inside his cockpit, Kenney's threat display suddenly showed two new contacts at danger-close range. The left Sentinel emerged through the electronics shop's facade, its foot crushing display cases that sparked with residual power. The right one simply walked through the restaurant's wall, tables and chairs bouncing off its armor. Both mechs were pristine—no battle damage, full ammunition loads, their blue and white paint barely dusty.

Their 30mm autocannons were already spinning up, the six barrels on each weapon rotating with an ascending whine that Kenney knew meant two seconds until they reached firing speed. The weapons were chest-mounted on articulated arms, capable of tracking independently while the mechs maneuvered. At this range—less than fifty meters—they couldn't miss.

"Shit, ambush!" Kenney called out, trying to bring his damaged right arm's weapon to bear. The targeting reticle wavered drunkenly across his display, the damaged servos unable to hold steady.

Racer was a few strides behind, but his position gave him the perfect angle.

Inside his cockpit, Racer's hands moved with practiced speed. His left thumb flicked the ammunition selector to armor-piercing while his right hand swung the targeting stick smoothly across. The crosshairs in his display swept past the right Sentinel—too much cover from the building debris—and settled on the left one. The pilot had made a tactical error, stepping too far into the open to get a clear shot at Kenney.

"Got you, you bushwhacking bastard," Racer muttered, squeezing the trigger.

His autocannon roared to life. Inside the cockpit, he felt each round fire through the stick's feedback system—a steady hammering rhythm as the 30mm shells left the rotating barrels. His targeting display showed the impact points in real-time, the first three rounds sparking off the Sentinel's shoulder armor, walking up toward the head unit.

Racer adjusted his aim minutely, a tiny movement of his wrist that translated to a two-meter correction at target distance. The next burst found the cockpit area—a vulnerable spot where the armor was thinner to allow for the pilot's viewports and sensor clusters. His display showed the rounds penetrating, each one flashing white as it punched through.

Inside the Sentinel, the pilot had just enough time to see his displays crack before the rounds arrived. The 30mm armor-piercing shells, each one designed to penetrate battleship armor, punched through the cockpit's forward plating like it was aluminum foil. The pilot's compartment erupted from within—ammunition cooking off, control panels shorting in showers of sparks, hydraulic fluid igniting.

Through Racer's thermal imaging, the Sentinel's heat signature bloomed white-hot for an instant—internal fire consuming everything flammable. Then the mech simply stopped moving, its autocannon spinning down with a dying whine. It stood there for a moment, smoke pouring from the holes in its cockpit, before toppling backward with a crash that shook the ground. The pilot never had a chance to fire a single round.

"One down!" Racer shouted, already tracking toward the second Sentinel, but it had ducked back behind the restaurant's remaining wall, using the structure as cover while its autocannon finally reached firing speed.

The second Sentinel focused everything on Kenney—30mm rounds, small arms fire from infantry taking positions in the windows, even RPGs streaking from rooftops.

"Kinetic shield!" Foxtrot announced as Kenney's left hand found the activation stud.

The air in front of his mech shimmered, then solidified into a translucent orange barrier. Rounds sparked and deflected off the electromagnetic field, creating a light show of ricochets and deflected projectiles. The shield caught everything—heavy autocannon rounds spinning away harmlessly, small arms fire simply vaporizing against the energy field.

But the shield drained power fast. His displays showed the capacitors dropping—eighty percent, sixty, forty. It would only hold for seconds more.

"Racer, that Sentinel!" Kenney shouted, still pushing toward the Stout.

"On it, Boss!"

The Stout's commander saw Kenney closing and tried to traverse the rocket pods downward. Inside the hybrid's cockpit, the MITHRIL pilot's hands flew across the controls, attempting to override the mechanical limitations. Warning messages flashed across their displays—"ELEVATION LIMIT REACHED" and "MINIMUM SAFE DISTANCE EXCEEDED."

The pods groaned on their mounting servos, hydraulics straining to force them below their designed parameters. But the hybrid's design—that ungainly marriage of tank hull and mech torso—worked against it. The rocket pods had been mounted high on the back to clear the tank hull during traversal, which meant they physically couldn't depress below fifteen degrees. At close range, that created a massive dead zone directly in front of the machine.

The tank treads ground in reverse, the sound like grinding metal teeth as hundreds of tons tried to accelerate backward. The treads churned up asphalt, sending chunks flying, leaving deep gouges in the street. Inside his cockpit, the Stout's pilot was likely fighting between systems—the tank hull's driver controls competing with the mech torso's combat interface. The hybrid lurched, one tread moving faster than the other, causing it to veer slightly left.

Kenney was faster. His mech's legs pumped like pistons, each stride covering eight meters. Inside his cockpit, he leaned forward into the run, his neural link translating his body language into mechanical motion. His damaged right arm hung slightly loose, throwing off his balance, forcing constant micro-adjustments through the control sticks. The distance counter on his HUD ticked down rapidly—forty meters, thirty, twenty.

At twenty meters, the Stout tried one last desperate measure. Its mech arms swung toward Kenney, anti-personnel guns in the manipulator claws spraying 12.7mm rounds in a futile attempt to slow him down. The bullets sparked harmlessly off his armor, not even scratching the paint.

Ten meters. Kenney could see individual rivets on the Stout's hull through his viewscreen. His kinetic shield, which had been holding at five percent power, finally collapsed with a distinctive electronic shriek—the capacitors completely drained. His shield indicator went from amber to red to black, the generator automatically entering emergency cooling mode. Sparks flew from the emitter panels on his mech's left arm as they overloaded.

But he was inside the rocket envelope now.

The geometry was simple and unforgiving—the rockets needed at least fifty meters to arm their warheads after launch, a safety feature to prevent the operator from blowing themselves up. At ten meters, even if the Stout fired every remaining rocket, they'd just be sixty-kilogram metal tubes hitting without exploding. Dangerous to infantry, annoying to a mech, but not the city-leveling devastation they were designed for.

Inside the Stout's cockpit, the pilot was probably experiencing that unique sensation of watching your castle turn into your coffin—hundreds of tons of armor and weapons, completely useless. Like bringing a howitzer to a knife fight and realizing they're already inside min range.

Kenney vaulted onto the Stout's back, his mech's hands finding purchase on the rocket pods. The hybrid's arms flailed frantically, trying to reach backward to grab him, but the human torso on tank treads wasn't designed for this. Its joints couldn't rotate enough to defend its own back.

He deployed his plasma blade with a crack-hiss, the superheated edge glowing blue-white. He drove it into the gap between the Stout's head and neck—the weak point where armor plates met. Once, twice, three times, each thrust sending sparks and hydraulic fluid spraying. The hybrid bucked like a mechanical bull, trying to throw him off, but Kenney held on, stabbing repeatedly until the arms went limp and the torso slumped forward.

Behind him, Racer had problems of his own. His autocannon burst had caught the remaining Sentinel's arm, sending its 30mm spinning across the asphalt. But Mithril pilots were trained for everything. The Sentinel smoothly drew its combat knife with its remaining hand—three meters of monomolecular steel—and dropped into a fighting stance.

"Well butter my biscuit and call me a short stack," Racer drawled, pulling his own bayonet free. "You wanna dance? Let's do-si-do, partner!"

The two mechs circled each other like prizefighters. The Sentinel moved with textbook precision—weight balanced, knife held in a reverse grip, watching for openings. Racer was looser, almost casual, but his stance showed someone who'd been in plenty of knife fights.

The Sentinel struck first, a straight thrust aimed at Racer's cockpit. Racer parried with his bayonet, metal shrieking against metal, then used his mech's superior weight to shoulder-check the smaller machine. The Sentinel stumbled but recovered quickly, slashing at Racer's leg hydraulics.

"Nope!" Racer jumped back, then immediately pressed forward with an overhead chop that the Sentinel barely deflected.

They exchanged a flurry of strikes—thrust, parry, slash, dodge. The Sentinel was faster, more agile, but Racer had reach and mass. When the Sentinel tried a spinning strike, Racer caught its wrist with his free hand, twisted, and drove his bayonet up through its chest.

The Sentinel shuddered, tried one last weak strike, then went still. Racer yanked his blade free and let the smaller mech topple backward.

"And that's why children should never fight adults, I reckon," Racer said, wiping his bayonet on the dead Stout's hull. "Boss, you still breathing up there?"

Kenney climbed down from the smoking Stout, his damaged arm sparking. "Still functional. But we need to move. Our window of opportunity is closing."

Through the smoke, they could more street fighting breaking out across the city.

The pumping station had become hell on earth.

Deadeye caught a Coalition Hind dropship as it tried to deploy troops on the station's main platform.

The transport was still ten meters off the ground, its pilot fighting the thermal updrafts from the burning pumping station. Through his cockpit displays, Deadeye could see the Hind's rear ramp beginning to lower—Coalition marines visible inside, packed shoulder to shoulder, weapons ready. The dropship's twin turbines screamed as it tried to hover steady, the pilot probably thinking he was at a safe altitude for fast-rope deployment.

Inside his cockpit, Deadeye's hands moved to the override controls for his mech's grip strength. He'd need precise pressure—enough to hold sixty tons of aircraft, not enough to crush it prematurely. His targeting computer calculated intercept vectors as he moved, his mech's legs eating up the distance in massive strides.

The Hind's door gunner saw him coming, the mounted 12.7mm gun swiveling desperately. Rounds sparked off Deadeye's armor as he reached up with both massive hands. The mech's fingers, each one as thick as a tree trunk, clamped around the aircraft's tail boom—that narrow section connecting the main fuselage to the tail rotor.

The metal groaned immediately under the pressure. Inside the Hind, alarms would be screaming—"STRUCTURAL FAILURE IMMINENT" and "AIRCRAFT CAPTURED." The pilot tried to pull up, engines going to emergency power, but forty tons of mech anchored them as effectively as a chain.

"Special delivery!" Deadeye shouted over external speakers, his voice booming across the battlefield.

He began to spin, using his mech's torso rotation to build momentum. Inside his cockpit, Deadeye had to fight the disorientation as his viewpoint whirled—pump station, ocean, city, pump station, ocean, city. His inner ear protested, but he kept building speed. One rotation, two, three—like an Olympic hammer thrower, if the hammer was a fully loaded military transport.

The Hind's engines were still at full thrust, adding to the chaotic forces. The aircraft's frame was never designed for these stresses. Through his audio pickups, Deadeye could hear metal starting to tear, the screams of the marines inside as they were thrown against the walls by centrifugal force.

On the third rotation, he released.

The math was beautiful in its destruction. Sixty tons of aircraft, already traveling at rotational velocity, with its own engines adding thrust—the Hind cartwheeled through the air in a diagonal trajectory that defied its aerodynamic design. It tumbled end over end, the main rotor blades shearing off immediately, the tail boom finally separating completely. Marines were falling from the open rear ramp, some already unconscious from the G-forces, others firing their weapons uselessly as they fell.

The dropship slammed into a Coalition tank formation two hundred meters away. Three T-95 main battle tanks had been advancing in formation, their commanders probably watching the aerial acrobatics with disbelief through their periscopes. The Hind hit the middle tank turret-first, the impact crushing the armored vehicle's top armor like a sledgehammer hitting a tin can.

The fuel cells ruptured on impact—thousands of liters of aviation fuel atomizing instantly. The smallest spark—from crushed electronics, from scraped metal, from the tanks' own systems—was all it took. The explosion started white-hot at the point of impact, then expanded outward in a perfect sphere of destruction. The fireball consumed all three tanks and the dropship in a single expanding ball of orange and black.

Inside his cockpit, Deadeye's displays automatically dimmed to compensate for the brightness. His thermal imaging went completely white, overwhelmed by the heat bloom. The shock wave hit a second later, strong enough to make his mech sway slightly even at two hundred meters.

Infantry that had been using the tanks as cover—maybe two platoons—simply ceased to exist. They were inside the fireball's radius when it expanded, their bodies vaporized before their nervous systems could register pain. Others further out were thrown like dolls, their armor no protection against the overpressure that liquefied organs inside intact shells.

When the smoke began to clear, there was just a crater where the tank formation had been. Pieces of track and armor plating had been thrown hundreds of meters. The Hind's tail rotor landed in the ocean with a splash visible even from the pump station. One of the tank turrets had been launched skyward and came down through a warehouse roof three blocks away.

"That's gotta be a strike in bowling terms!" Killjoy laughed, his miniguns beginning their startup sequence.

Inside his cockpit, Killjoy's hands flew across the weapon controls. The arm-mounted M134G rotary miniguns didn't just "spin up"—they went through a complex initialization ritual. First came the electrical primer, capacitors charging with a rising whine. Then the barrel motors engaged, six barrels per arm beginning their rotation. The sound started low, almost like a turbine warming up, then climbed in pitch as they accelerated toward operational speed.

His displays showed the ammunition feed status—ten thousand rounds per gun, twenty thousand total, linked in continuous belts that ran from the massive drum magazines on his back. The feed mechanisms clacked as they aligned, mechanical fingers checking each link, ensuring smooth delivery at 6,000 rounds per minute.

Through his viewscreen, he could see them coming—a formation of Coalition TX-7 "Toxic" gunships approaching from the northeast. Five aircraft in a tactical V formation, each one bristling with weapons. The Toxics were ugly machines built for punishment—angular composite armor, redundant systems, stub wings loaded with HYDRA-88 rocket pods and a chin-mounted M230 chain gun. They were coming in low and fast, using the industrial complex's towers as cover, probably thinking they could catch the mechs focused on ground forces.

"Oh, you want to dance?" Killjoy muttered, his targeting computer already calculating lead angles and convergence zones. At their current speed and trajectory, the gunships would be in optimal range in twelve seconds.

The miniguns reached full speed, the barrels now just a blur, the sound changing from mechanical whine to that distinctive buzzsaw roar. Inside his cockpit, Killjoy felt the vibration through his seat, his entire mech humming with contained violence. The ammunition feeds were live, rounds chambered in all twelve barrels, firing pins armed.

His thumbs hovered over the triggers, watching the range counter tick down. The key to fighting aircraft with miniguns wasn't accuracy—it was volume. He wasn't going to shoot down the Toxics so much as create a wall of lead they'd have to fly through. At 200 rounds per second combined rate of fire, he could fill a cubic kilometer of airspace with lethal projectiles.

"Deadeye, Toxics inbound!" he called out. "I'm about to make it rain!"

The lead TX-7 fired first, rockets streaking from its pods. Killjoy's defensive systems tracked the incoming missiles, but he didn't move. Moving would throw off his firing solution, and he needed every round to count.

Eight seconds to optimal range. The miniguns' targeting systems were painting predictive paths, showing where to put rounds not where the gunships were, but where they'd be. The ammunition counters glowed green—full loads, ready to deliver.

Five seconds. The Toxics were close enough now that he could see the pilots through their armored canopies, probably wondering why the mech wasn't evading.

Three seconds. Killjoy's mech adopted a slight forward lean, compensating for the recoil that was about to hit.

One second.

"Let's make it rain," Killjoy said, and squeezed both triggers.

The world exploded into noise and light. Twenty thousand rounds per minute erupted from his mech's arms, the tracer rounds creating solid lines of fire through the air. Inside his cockpit, the recoil hammered through the neural feedback, his mech automatically leaning forward to compensate. His ammunition counters started spinning down like slot machines, numbers blurring as they decreased.

The wall of lead met the incoming missile barrage first. The HYDRA-88 rockets, designed to overwhelm point defense with sheer numbers, ran into something worse—a literal cloud of bullets. The 7.62mm rounds might not have been designed for missile interception, but when you put enough metal in the air, physics took over.

Rockets detonated prematurely as rounds found their warheads—bright orange flashes fifty meters out. Others had their propulsion systems shredded, sending them tumbling off course. A few simply disintegrated, turned into scattered debris by multiple hits. The missile barrage that should have deleted his mech became a fireworks display, harmless explosions painting the sky.

Then the bullet stream reached the Toxics.

The lead TX-7 flew straight into the convergence zone—that point in space where both miniguns' fire intersected. For one horrible second, it continued forward on momentum alone, its armor holding. Then the cumulative damage caught up. The armored canopy shattered inward, thousands of rounds turning the cockpit into a blender. The stub wings sheared off, rocket pods tumbling away. The engine compartment took hundreds of hits, turbines disintegrating, fuel lines severed.

The gunship came apart in midair. Not an explosion, but a disintegration—the aircraft literally shredded into increasingly smaller pieces. The largest intact section was the tail boom, which spun away like a thrown knife.

The second and third Toxics tried to break formation, banking hard left and right. But Killjoy was already tracking, his arms following their movement, the stream of tracers sweeping across like a scythe. The left gunship's pilot managed half an evasive roll before rounds found the fuel tanks. The TX-7 became a fireball, burning wreckage raining down on the pump station.

The right one lasted three seconds longer. Its pilot dove low, trying to get below the angle of fire. The miniguns followed, rounds chewing through the gunship's dorsal armor, walking forward toward the cockpit. The pilot ejected—the canopy blowing clear, rocket seat firing—just before the rounds arrived. He rocketed upward as his aircraft plowed into the ground, cartwheeling through industrial equipment in a spectacular crash.

The fourth TX-7 tried to return fire, its chin gun spraying 30mm rounds at Killjoy's mech. But firing while flying through a bullet storm was like trying to aim in a hurricane. The pilot's shots went wide as rounds starred his canopy, destroyed his targeting systems, shredded his control surfaces. The gunship went into an uncontrolled spin, the pilot fighting dead controls all the way down until it impacted the seawall in a geyser of concrete and fire.

The last Toxic's pilot made the only smart choice—he turned and ran. Full emergency power, climbing desperately for altitude. But he'd already entered the engagement envelope. Rounds found him anyway, climbing up the aircraft's belly, through the cargo compartment, into the engines. Black smoke poured from both turbines as they failed in sequence. The TX-7 managed another two hundred meters on momentum before it nosed over and dove into the harbor.

Total engagement time: eight seconds. Five aircraft destroyed. Approximately 6,000 rounds expended.

Inside his cockpit, Killjoy released the triggers, the sudden silence almost shocking after the continuous roar. His barrels glowed cherry-red, heat warnings flashing across his displays. The ammunition counters showed 14,000 rounds remaining—he'd burned through nearly a third of his load in eight seconds.

"Holy shit," Deadeye said over comms, having watched the entire thing. "You turned them into confetti."

Burning wreckage was still falling from the sky, pieces of the Toxics raining down across the industrial complex. The surviving Coalition forces were staring in shock—their air support had just been deleted from existence by one mech with miniguns.

"That's how you swat flies," Killjoy said, his miniguns beginning their cooling cycle, steam rising from the overheated barrels. "Big, expensive, military-grade flies."

"One's trying to get away," Deadeye said, gesturing with his mech's arm toward a Coalition dropship that was breaking off from its attack run. The pilot had seen what happened to the Toxics and wanted no part of it.

The dropship tried to abort its landing, pulling up hard. The transport's engines screamed as the pilot firewalled the throttles, trying to gain altitude and distance. The rear ramp was still half-open, Coalition militia visible inside, some already unbuckling, ready to jump rather than stay aboard what might become a flying coffin.

But Killjoy was already moving.

"Oh no you don't," he muttered, his hands slamming the jump jet controls to maximum.

Inside his cockpit, the acceleration crushed him into his seat as all four primary jets and eight maneuvering thrusters fired simultaneously. His altitude indicator spun upward—five meters, ten, fifteen, twenty. The jump jets were screaming, temperature warnings flashing as they exceeded designed parameters. This wasn't a combat jump—this was a barely-controlled rocket launch.

His mech intercepted the dropship twenty meters up. Through his viewscreen, he could see the door gunner's eyes go wide behind his helmet visor, the mounted gun trying to track but unable to depress enough. Killjoy's massive arms wrapped around the aircraft's fuselage like a bear hug, his mech's fingers finding purchase on armor plates and access panels.

The dropship's pilot felt the sudden weight—forty tons of mech now hanging from his aircraft. Inside the cockpit, every warning light would be illuminating: "EXCEEDING MAXIMUM CARGO WEIGHT," "ENGINE OVERTORQUE WARNING," "STRUCTURAL

STRESS CRITICAL." The transport lurched, nose dipping despite the pilot's desperate attempts to maintain altitude.

"Going down!" Killjoy announced over external speakers, his voice booming loud enough for the militia inside to hear.

They plummeted together, Killjoy riding the dropship toward the ground. He rolled clear at the last second, his mech's legs absorbing the impact with a ground-shaking thud while his jump jets fired in reverse to bleed off momentum.

Behind him, the transport pancaked into the industrial complex's parking area. The dropship hit nose-first, the cockpit section compressing into a space a third its original size. The main fuselage accordioned, crushing an entire mechanized infantry platoon that had been advancing through that section of garage. APCs were flattened like cans, infantry who'd been using them as cover simply disappeared under sixty tons of crashing aircraft.

The pumping station had become a meat grinder where two armies collided without clear lines, chaos of close-quarters warfare, a real knife and gun show.

Coalition militia advancing through the northern pipes met Republic infantry pushing from the south. They clashed in the maintenance tunnels beneath the station, fighting with knives and entrenching tools when the confined space made rifles useless. Bodies piled up at chokepoints, each side climbing over their own dead to get at the enemy.

Above ground, a Republic tank platoon punched through Coalition lines, only to find themselves surrounded as Coalition reserves counterattacked from three directions. The tanks formed a defensive circle, their guns firing continuously while Coalition AT teams tried to get close enough for kill shots. The battlefield became layered—Coalition forces holding buildings, Republic armor controlling the streets, infantry from both sides fighting room to room, floor to floor.

The two mechs in the middle turned this organized chaos into wholesale destruction. Deadeye grabbed a Coalition IFV and hurled it into a building where Republic snipers had dug in. The vehicle crashed through three floors before exploding, taking out the snipers but also the Coalition platoon that had been advancing up the stairwell to do the same thing.

"Push through! Push through!" Republic commanders screamed over their nets, trying to exploit gaps that appeared and disappeared in seconds.

Coalition forces responded with their own surge, two companies of mechanized infantry dismounting under fire, advancing through the vehicle graveyard the parking area had become. They met Republic troops doing exactly the same thing. The engagement range was so close that soldiers could see each other's eyes through their visors before pulling triggers.

A Coalition Vodnik pushed through burning wreckage, its roof gun chattering at Republic positions, only to take an RPG from behind—Republic forces had infiltrated past the front lines. As it burned, Coalition militia used its hull as cover to engage Republic troops who were using a destroyed Republic APC for the same purpose, twenty meters apart, both sides' dead mixing in the space between.

Killjoy's miniguns swept across this tangled battlefield, catching a Coalition squad assaulting a Republic strongpoint. Both attacker and defender were cut down in the same burst, their bodies falling together in the doorway they'd been fighting to control.

The industrial infrastructure everyone was supposedly fighting over was gradually disappearing. Cooling towers fell, crushing advancing units from both sides who'd been too focused on killing each other to notice the structural damage. Pipeline manifolds exploded, spraying burning fuel that created walls of fire that trapped Coalition and Republic units together, forcing them to fight to the death in flame-bordered arenas.

Reinforcements kept pouring into the meat grinder, the lines so intermingled that artillery support was impossible without destroying their own forces.

"Deadeye, another flight incoming!" Killjoy warned, pointing at three more dropships approaching from the east.

"I see 'em." Deadeye's 90mm rifle cracked, the hypervelocity round punching through the lead dropship's cockpit. It nosed over immediately, crashing into the seawall in a shower of sparks and flame. "These idiots keep flying straight lines. You'd think they'd learn."

"How many is that?" Killjoy asked, grabbing another approaching dropship by its landing skids.

"Lost count after thirty," Deadeye replied, using the dropship Killjoy was holding as a club to sweep aside a squad of power-armored heavy infantry. "Both sides keep feeding units into this meat grinder."

Killjoy paused mid-throw, a Coalition soldier still dangling from his mech's hand. "Hey, wait a minute. If both sides are able to deploy dropships, I suppose that means it's safe for ours, right?"

Deadeye stopped, his 90mm rifle lowering slightly. "I see what you're getting at. Yeah, let's finish up here."

To emphasize the point, he climbed onto the last standing structure—a concrete pump house that had somehow survived the battle. His mech's feet came down hard, stomping through the roof. The building groaned, walls cracking, then collapsed inward like a house of cards. The pumping station's primary infrastructure was officially demolished.

"Dust-off, this is Deadeye," he radioed, switching to the extraction frequency. "Looking for pickup, heading to extraction point alpha. The distraction's run its course."

"Copy that, Deadeye," Joker's voice came back, her accent thicker under combat stress. "Dust-off Two inbound, ETA three minutes. Try not to get shot up, da?"

"Good luck, Boss-Actual," Deadeye added on the tactical channel. "Don't get turned into a glowie on us."

Through the smoke and flames of the destroyed pumping station, they could see more forces arriving—both Coalition and Republic, drawn to the destruction like moths to a flame. But the two mechs were already moving, heading for the extraction point as the industrial complex burned behind them.

The distraction had worked perfectly. Half the city's military was here, fighting over nothing but rubble and twisted metal.

Valeria continued to make her way out of the facility, her legs trembling with each step. She hadn't realized they were so far underground—level after level of stairs and corridors, each one revealing new horrors. Rooms with surgical equipment she couldn't identify. Tanks filled with things that might have been human once. Walls covered in equations that made her head hurt to look at.

The facility was a bloodbath. Bodies and Viper components littered every corridor, blood painted on white walls like abstract art. Her bare feet had gone numb from the cold floors, leaving bloody footprints as glass and debris cut into them.

Another stairwell. Another climb. Her strength was waning, black spots dancing at the edges of her vision. When had she last eaten? Last had water? Time had become meaningless underground.

Then suddenly—daylight.

She stumbled through a blown-out emergency exit and fell to her knees outside. The overcast sky felt alien after months of fluorescent lights, but god, it was beautiful. She could have cried if she had any tears left.

The relief lasted exactly two seconds before the world exploded into noise.

Two massive war machines were demolishing buildings barely fifty meters away. Valeria pressed herself against the rubble, unable to look away despite the danger. Her ears immediately began bleeding from the percussion of their weapons—she could feel warm trickles running down her neck.

The orange mech fired its autocannon in a sustained burst, and she watched the muzzle flash through her fingers, each shot making her whole skeleton vibrate. The sound wasn't just loud—it was a physical thing that pressed against her chest, made breathing difficult.

Movement to her left—a squad of scout walkers emerging from a side street. Valeria had seen these before in her settlement, police units using them for crowd control. But these were militarized, the drivers exposed in their open cockpits, hands gripping the spade grips of their mounted machine guns. They looked so small, so fragile, like insects compared to the titans they were approaching.

The lead walker's driver opened fire, the belt-fed M2 chattering. She watched the tracers spark harmlessly off the black mech's leg armor, not even leaving scratches. The driver's face—she could see it from here—went from determination to terror in the space of a heartbeat.

The black mech's foot came down.

Valeria couldn't look away. The walker and its driver simply ceased, crushed into the asphalt with a sound she felt in her bones. Red spread from beneath the massive foot when it lifted. The second walker tried to reverse, the mechanical legs stumbling, almost comedic if it wasn't so horrible. The mech's hand swept out, catching it like a child grabbing a toy.

She watched the walker crumple in that massive fist, metal screaming, the driver's scream cut short. The wreckage flew through the air, crashing through a storefront where she'd seen soldiers hiding moments before.

The orange mech turned toward the remaining two walkers with cold intent. Through the smoke and dust, she could see inside its movements something almost dismissive—like these weren't even worth its full attention. Three shots from its rifle, perfectly placed. The third walker's legs disappeared, the platform toppling forward. She watched the driver try to crawl free, his legs pinned, reaching toward nothing, toward anyone.

The fourth driver ran. Just abandoned his walker and ran. Valeria found herself mentally willing him to escape, to make it to cover, but the abandoned walker exploded from a stray round, shrapnel catching the fleeing man in the back.

Then the warehouse wall exploded outward. A smaller mech—pristine blue and white paint, corporate precision in its movements. The same blue and white as the medical equipment in the facility. The same colors the doctors wore. Her heart lurched. It raised its rifle toward the black mech's back, the pilot inside probably thinking he had the perfect ambush.

The orange mech's bayonet was already moving. Valeria watched the blade punch through the Sentinel's armor like it was paper, entering the left side, exiting the right. Hydraulic fluid sprayed in an arc that looked almost like blood in the firelight. The Sentinel reached toward the wound, an oddly human gesture, before falling backward.

The orange mech's foot came down on the Sentinel's head unit. The crunch was definitive, final. No different from stepping on an insect.

Through all of this, Valeria couldn't move. She watched these giants deal death with casual efficiency, watched human bodies disappear under metal feet, watched millions of credits of military hardware become scrap in seconds. The violence was so absolute, so overwhelming, that her mind couldn't fully process it.

But something else was happening too. That part of her the artifact had changed, the part that could feel machines, was reading these mechs. Not like the Vipers—those had been empty, just programming and protocols. These had people inside. She could sense the pilots' intent, their training, their exhaustion. They weren't killing for pleasure or ideology. They were just... working.

And they were moving away from the facility. Away from where she'd been imprisoned.

These weren't her captors. These weren't her enemy.

These were her only chance.

The orange one reminded her of home somehow. The bright paint job was so incongruous with the violence—like someone had decided their instrument of death should be cheerful. It made her think of the racing posters her brother had hung in his room, the hot rods the older kids had worked on behind the settlement's garage.

She tried to stand, to call out, but her voice was gone. She had to get to them. Had to make them see her before they moved on or before someone else found her first.

Using a chunk of concrete for support, she pulled herself up and started stumbling toward them. Every step was agony, her body failing, but she pushed forward.

The darker mech—black with camo striping—set something down from its back. A large device, about the size of a vending machine, matte black with minimal markings. Even from this distance, she could feel something wrong about it. This device screamed of endings.

She tried to run, managed three steps before falling. The impact knocked what little air she had from her lungs. But she had to reach them. They were leaving—she could see them preparing to move on.

With the last of her strength, she crawled forward, leaving bloody handprints on the rubble. The orange mech was turning away.

"Please," she whispered, though she knew they couldn't hear her over the combat. "Please don't leave me here."

"Nuke deployed, exiting mech for activation," Kenney radioed, his left hand finding the canopy release sequence on his armrest panel. "Racer, keep overwatch."

"Copy that, Boss. Make it snappy—we're burning daylight and ammunition."

Inside his cockpit, Kenney's fingers worked through the control procedure for dismounted operations. Neural link disconnect—a soft pop as the cable disengaged from his helmet port. Weapons to auto mode—the switches clicking as he safed each system.

"Transferring master control to autonomous mode," he announced, flipping the final switch. The displays around him shifted from blue to amber—Foxtrot taking over.

"Control transferred," Foxtrot's British accent confirmed through the speakers. "I have the helm, sir. Initiating defensive overwatch protocols."

The front hatch locks disengaged with a series of mechanical chunks. Kenney hit the final release, and the armored canopy swung open with a pneumatic hiss. Hot air rushed in, thick with smoke and cordite, replacing the filtered atmosphere of the cockpit. His first breath outside almost made him cough—the air tasted of burning meat.

He unbuckled his five-point harness, the restraints retracting automatically. Standing from the pilot's couch required effort after hours in combat—his legs had gone partially numb from the constant neural feedback. He grabbed his rifle from its mount beside his seat, checking the magazine, then hauled himself up through the hatch.

Foxtrot's control was immediately apparent. The mech's movements became more mechanical, precise but lacking the human fluidity. The AI's massive hands closed around Kenney's torso.

The descent was perfectly smooth—Foxtrot minimized both time and jarring motion. Once Kenney's boots touched rubble, the hands retracted and the mech shifted into a defensive stance—weapons tracking in slow arcs, sensors sweeping for threats.

"I'll maintain overwatch while you're dismounted," Foxtrot said through Kenney's earpiece. "Do try not to get shot, sir. The paperwork for pilot replacement is tedious."

Inside Racer's cockpit twenty meters away, the Confederate pilot had switched to overwatch mode. His hands moved across his sensor panels, cycling through thermal, electromagnetic, and motion detection.

"Got movement, two blocks east," Racer reported, his thumb hovering over the weapons release. "Looks like stragglers, not heading our way."

"Copy," Kenney replied through his helmet comm, walking toward the nuclear device.

Behind him, his mech stood perfectly still except for the subtle movements of its sensor array—Foxtrot running thousands of threat calculations per second, ready to engage anything that threatened its pilot. The AI might lack imagination, but it never missed a target.

He knelt beside it, fingers working the activation panel. The mechanical timer was simple—no electronics that could be hacked or jammed, just springs and gears that would count down exactly thirty minutes once started. He input the activation code, heard the distinctive click as the timer engaged.

"Timer running," he announced, standing to leave.

That's when he saw her.

A teenage girl, so slight and still he'd almost mistaken her for a corpse among the debris. She crawled from behind the device, her medical smock torn and bloodstained, feet leaving red prints on the concrete.

"Pl...please," she managed, her voice barely a whisper. "Help me."

Then she collapsed, face-first into the dirt.

"Boss, what's taking so long?" Racer's voice boomed from above, his mech looking down at them. "It's go time!"

"There's a girl," Kenney said, already moving toward her. "She needs help."

"There's no time for picking up strays! That nuke's gonna turn this place into glass in twenty-nine minutes!"

Kenney checked her pulse—weak but there. She was breathing, barely. Through the tears in her smock, he could see she was malnourished, covered in cuts and bruises. But she was alive, and she was here.

"I don't care," Kenney said, scooping her into his arms. She weighed almost nothing. "She needs our help."

"Boss, this is a bad idea," Racer protested, his mech shifting nervously.

"She's a kid who needs help," Kenney cut him off, carrying her back to his mech. Foxtrot's arms reached down, taking her gently and lifting them both into the cockpit.

"Whatever," Racer sighed, his mech already turning to leave. "Let's just get out of here before we become shadows on the walls."

Kenney settled into his pilot's seat with Valeria unconscious in his lap. She was so small, curled against his chest, her breathing shallow but steady. The cockpit wasn't designed for two people, but they'd make it work.

"Foxtrot, get us out of here," he ordered, sealing the hatch.

"Sir, I must point out that bringing an unknown civilian into a secured cockpit is highly inadvisable—"

"Noted. Now shut up and move."

Both mechs began running, their massive strides eating up distance as the timer continued its countdown. Behind them, the facility—and all its secrets—waited to be erased from existence.

Twenty-eight minutes and counting.

The flight packs engaged with a roar that shook the ground beneath them.

Inside Kenney's cockpit, his hands flew across the ignition sequence. Primary boosters—armed. Fuel flow—seventy percent. Thrust vectoring—forty-five degrees. He had to balance speed with survivability—the girl wasn't wearing a G-suit, and too much acceleration would kill her.

"Launching controlled ascent," he announced, his left arm securing her against his chest while his right handled the controls. "Keep it smooth, Racer."

The ignition was still violent, but manageable. The mechs launched at an angle, heading inland—trading vertical distance for horizontal separation from ground zero. The acceleration pressed them into the seat, but the cockpit's inertial dampeners kicked in, reducing the G-forces from crushing to merely uncomfortable.

Kenney felt the girl's weight shift against him as they climbed. She was so light he barely noticed her through his suit, but Foxtrot's medical sensors were tracking her vitals constantly—heart rate elevated but stable, breathing shallow but regular.

They climbed at a diagonal, heading northwest away from the coast. Below them, Sevastopol shrank rapidly, but they were also putting lateral distance between themselves and the pending nuclear detonation. Each second took them further inland—away from the facility, away from the blast zone, away from two square kilometers that would soon cease to exist.

"Flight pack fuel at sixty percent," Racer called out, his mech keeping pace alongside. "We're making good distance, Boss. Already eight klicks inland and climbing."

Inside Kenney's cockpit, the temperature was rising despite the cooling systems. The controlled burn was hard on the engines—they were designed for maximum thrust, not sustained medium output. Heat bled through the armor, making the cockpit feel like a sauna. The girl stirred slightly against him, her head rolling against his chest.

At two kilometers altitude and twelve kilometers inland, they began to level off slightly, maintaining a steady climb but prioritizing distance over height. The g-forces eased to almost normal as they transitioned to more horizontal flight.

"Twenty minutes to detonation," Foxtrot announced. "Current distance from ground zero: fifteen kilometers and increasing. We should achieve minimum safe distance with four minutes to spare."

Through his rear cameras, Kenney watched Sevastopol shrinking behind them. The coast was now a distant line, the city a gray smudge against blue water. Mountains rose ahead—the inland ranges that would provide additional shielding from the blast.

The flight packs burned steadily, carrying them inland, each meter of distance a meter further from nuclear annihilation. Below them, the urban sprawl gave way to industrial districts, then suburbs, then farmland, as they raced against a countdown only they knew was happening.

He pulled the emergency med kit from the side panel, working carefully in the cramped cockpit. The girl was in bad shape—dozens of cuts on her feet from walking on debris, bruises covering most of her visible skin, signs of severe malnutrition. He cleaned the worst wounds with antiseptic, wrapping her feet in gauze.

Her eyes fluttered open as he pulled the emergency blanket around her shoulders.

She looked past him, out through the viewscreen at the city spread below them. From this height, Sevastopol looked almost peaceful—you couldn't see the bodies or hear the gunfire, just buildings and streets laid out in orderly grids.

"So this is where they've been keeping me," she said weakly, her voice hoarse. "I don't recognize it. I don't even know what planet this is."

"Regalia," Kenney said, securing the blanket. "Sevastopol City."

"Regalia," she repeated, as if tasting the word. "It's an ugly city."

Before he could think of a response, the horizon lit up.

The nuclear detonation started sooner than expected, as a pinpoint of light brighter than the sun, then expanded into a perfect sphere of destruction. Even from thirty kilometers away, the flash was blinding. The shockwave followed seconds later, a visible wall of compressed air racing outward, flattening everything in its path.

Where the facility had been a mushroom cloud began its slow climb toward the stratosphere. Two square kilometers of city simply ceased to exist, transformed into glass and vapor.

The girl watched it with an expression Kenney couldn't read. Horror? Relief? Both?

"It's gone," she whispered. "It's really gone. They're all gone."

The exhaustion hit her again, her body going limp against his chest. She curled into him instinctively, seeking warmth and safety she probably hadn't felt in months. Within seconds, she was asleep again, her breathing finally steady.

Kenney held her carefully as Foxtrot continued their flight path. Behind them, Sevastopol burned. The facility and all its secrets were now radioactive glass. And in his arms, a girl who'd somehow survived whatever personal horrors had been happening down there slept peacefully for perhaps the first time in months.

"Boss," Racer's voice came through the comm, "Dust-off's vectoring for pickup. ETA to extraction in fifteen."

"Copy," Kenney replied quietly, not wanting to wake her.

He didn't know who she was or what had happened to her, but she was alive, she was free, and for now, that was enough.

CHAPTER SEVEN

The Purgatory's hangar bay was still in vacuum when the two dropships arrived, each carrying a mech in their reinforced cargo clamps.

Dust-off Two descended through the massive doors first, Kenney's mech held beneath it in a compressed squat position—knees bent, arms tucked, head down, like a forty-ton metal gargoyle. The damaged right arm was folded awkwardly, hydraulic fluid still seeping from where the railgun had carved through the shoulder armor. The flight pack had been retracted tight against the back to minimize the profile. The dropship's belly clamps gripped the mech at reinforced hardpoints on the shoulders and hips, though the right shoulder clamp had to compensate for the missing armor plates.

Behind it, Dust-off One followed with Racer's mech in the same compressed position. Inside their cockpits, both pilots were essentially folded up with their mechs, the squatting position forcing them to lean forward, knees up near their chests.

"Coming in heavy," Hammer announced from Dust-off Two's cockpit, fighting the controls as forty tons of mech threw off the dropship's center of gravity. "This thing handles like a pregnant whale, and that busted arm ain't helping the balance."

The first dropship touched down hard, landing struts compressing to their limits. The deck plates actually deformed slightly under the concentrated weight. Through his cramped viewpoint, Kenney could see the hangar deck just meters below through his foot cameras.

"Releasing clamps," Hammer announced.

The electromagnetic clamps disengaged. Kenney's mech dropped the final two meters, his legs absorbing the impact as the mech automatically stood from its squat. The damaged right arm jerked unnaturally as it extended, servos whining in protest. Joints that had been compressed for the flight groaned as they extended. The girl in his lap shifted from the movement but remained unconscious.

Dust-off One performed the same maneuver, Racer's mech dropping and standing with slightly less grace due to his damaged stabilizer.

"Damn, feels good to stretch," Racer's voice came over comms, his mech working its arms to restore full range of motion. "Boss, that arm's looking rough. Derg's gonna have a field day with that."

Through his displays, Kenney could see hydraulic fluid dripping from his right arm onto the deck—a spreading puddle of amber liquid that maintenance would have to clean. The arm hung slightly lower than it should, the damaged shoulder actuator unable to hold proper position.

"Hangar secured," came the announcement. "Beginning pressurization."

Red lights switched to amber. Air began flooding in from vents. Finally, green lights—standard pressure. Kenney popped his cockpit hatch with his left hand—his right arm controls were too damaged to trust—ready to get the unnamed girl to medical, ready to find answers about who she was.

"Pressurizing hangar," came the announcement over comms. "Stand by for atmosphere restoration."

The girl was curled against his chest, the emergency blanket wrapped around her thin frame. She'd been unconscious for most of the flight, occasionally murmuring things he didn't understand. Her vitals were stable according to Foxtrot's monitoring, but she needed medical attention.

Air hissed into the hangar bay, pressure gauges climbing steadily. Kenney could hear it through the mech's audio pickups—the whistle of atmosphere flooding back in, the gradual return of normal sound conduction.

"Pressure nominal," the announcement came. "Hangar secure."

Kenney popped his cockpit hatch, the seal breaking with a pneumatic hiss. The hangar's recycled air flooded in—hot metal, hydraulic fluid, and that distinctive ozone smell from welding torches already at work. "I need medical down here," he called out, his voice echoing across the vast space.

The maintenance crews were already swarming the mechs like ants on fallen giants. Tech specialists with diagnostic tablets checking armor integrity, fuel teams dragging heavy hoses toward the empty thruster ports, weapons engineers cataloging expended ammunition. Sparks flew from Racer's mech where a welder was already patching a hull breach.

Derg looked up from his diagnostic tablet, squinting at the cascade of damage reports scrolling across his screen—hydraulic pressure loss in the right arm, armor integrity compromised at seventeen points, primary actuator efficiency down to sixty percent. His coveralls were already stained with grease from inspecting Racer's damaged stabilizer.

"Doc Haywire's already halfway to drunk, but I can—" He stopped mid-sentence as he climbed the maintenance ladder, getting his first look into Kenney's cockpit. His eyes went wide. "What the hell, boss?"

The girl was curled against Kenney's chest, still wrapped in the emergency blanket that was now stained with blood from her feet. In the harsh hangar lights, she looked even smaller, more fragile—pale skin marked with cuts and bruises, the medical smock torn and filthy.

"Found her near the target zone," Kenney said, carefully adjusting his hold on her. "She needs help."

Derg's expression shifted from surprise to concern as he took in her condition—the malnourishment visible in her hollow cheeks, the way her ribs showed through the thin smock, the bloody bandages on her feet. "Jesus, what happened to her? She looks like she's been through hell."

"I don't know. Just get medical."

Derg was already on his comm unit, his usual sarcasm replaced with urgency. "Medical team to Bay Three, immediate response." He paused, looking at the girl again. “Get Doc here now, drunk or not."

The hangar's activity slowed as word spread. Technicians looked up from their work. The welding torches went quiet. Even the fuel teams paused their operations. It wasn't unusual for Kenney to come back damaged, but bringing back an unconscious civilian—especially one in this condition—was something else entirely.

The hangar went quiet for a moment, then erupted in laughter.

"Only Kenney Jaeger!" someone shouted from the gantry.

"Leave it to the boss to find a girlfriend in a warzone!" another tech called out.

"Was she worth almost getting nuked?" Derg asked, grinning as he climbed the ladder back down.

"It's not like that," Kenney said, carefully lifting her unconscious form. "Found her in the warzone. She needs help."

The joking stopped as the crew saw Kenney emerge carrying the girl. She looked like a broken doll in his arms—too thin, too pale, feet wrapped in bloody bandages. The medical smock could have been from any hospital or aid station.

Doc Haywire appeared, weaving slightly but professional enough when he saw a real patient. "Lets get her to medical," he ordered, suddenly focused. "She's malnourished, dehydrated, probably been through hell."

As they transferred her to the stretcher, Kenney had to support most of her weight with his arms while Doc Haywire and Derg took her legs. She'd been so quiet in the cockpit, just occasional murmurs he couldn't make out over the engine noise and combat stress.

But now, in the relative quiet between them, Doc Haywire could actually hear her.

"...requires magnetic bottle containment at 10^8 Tesla..." she was saying, her voice soft and monotone, lips barely moving. "...antimatter catalyst injection at .0003c for optimal yield..."

Doc gently lifted her eyelids. Both eyes completely rolled back, showing only white, yet she continued murmuring.

" Boss, her eyes..." Doc leaned closer, then pulled back slightly. "Is she speaking?"

Kenney nodded. "Since I picked her up. Thought she was just delirious. Couldn't really hear it clearly with everything going on."

They laid her on the stretcher carefully. Now without the mech's background noise, her continuous stream of specifications was clearly audible to the three of them:

"Yield optimization requires seventeen-stage compression sequence... detonation velocity exceeds 0.4c at minimum configuration... casualty radius twelve kilometers assuming standard atmospheric density..."

"She's completely unconscious," Doc said quietly, checking her vitals. "But her eyes...It's like she's in some kind of trance."

"Gravitational lensing compensates for beam dispersal at ranges exceeding 10,000 kilometers," she continued peacefully. "Primary accelerator requires superconducting coils maintained at 2.7 Kelvin..."

Derg had moved closer, listening. "Poor kid's brain is stuck on her studies. Sounds like engineering coursework. You know how trauma makes people retreat to familiar things."

"The whole flight back she's been doing this?" Doc asked.

"The whole time," Kenney confirmed. "Figured it was shock."

Her fingers twitched gently on the stretcher, moving in small patterns. The specifications kept flowing: "Neural interface bandwidth 10 terabits per second minimum for full weapons system integration..."

"Let's get her to medical," Doc said, deeply concerned by patients condition. "Whatever's happened to her, she needs proper examination."

As they wheeled her toward medical, her soft voice continued: "Antimatter containment failure results in 2.4 gigaton yield minimum..."

"Lucky you found her when you did," Derg commented. "Thirty minutes later and she'd have been nuclear ash like everything else in that city. She must've been some kind of prodigy. Shame to find her in a warzone."

Racer climbed down from his own mech, pulling off his helmet. "Boss, you sure she was just a civilian? That technical stuff sounds pretty advanced."

"Where else would she be from?" Kenney asked. "The whole district was just urban warfare. Probably a war orphan or something, been hiding since ARMSEA pulled out."

Blake's voice came over the hangar PA: "All pilots to debrief in twenty minutes."

The hangar slowly returned to its normal combat turnaround.

Fuel teams dragged heavy hoses across the deck, the thick conduits designed to handle the high-flow rates needed to fill mech tanks quickly. Each mech required 8,000 liters of fuel, plus another 2,000 for the retracted flight packs. The fuel chief was already calculating burn rates, checking manifests against what they'd used escaping Regalia.

"Port side tank first!" he shouted to his team. "Kenney's right arm hydraulics are leaking—I don't want fuel mixing with that!"

At Kenney's mech, Derg supervised a complete right arm rebuild. Three techs had the damaged armor panels off, exposing the twisted internal structure. The railgun had done more damage than initially visible—primary actuators were cracked, myomer bundles torn, the entire shoulder joint needed replacement.

"We don't have a spare shoulder unit," one tech reported.

"Then we make one," Derg replied, already pulling up fabrication specs on his tablet. "Cannibalize parts from the damaged upright we recovered last month. Won't be pretty, but it'll work."

Weapons teams worked both mechs simultaneously. Empty ammunition drums were disconnected and rolled away on specialized carts—massive cylinders that took two men to move even with power assists. Fresh drums were brought up from the magazine, each one containing 2,000 rounds of 30mm ammunition, mixed armor-piercing and high-explosive in a 3:1 ratio.

"Check every third linkage," the weapons chief ordered. "We had two jams last operation—that's two too many."

At Racer's mech, the stabilizer was getting emergency repairs. A tech with a plasma cutter was removing the damaged unit entirely while another prepped a replacement—not new, but functional, pulled from their dwindling spare parts inventory.

"This is held together with prayers and spot welds," the tech muttered, examining the damaged stabilizer. "How was he even walking?"

"Racer could pilot a trash can if it had legs," Derg replied. "Just make sure the new one holds through jump. We can do proper repairs later."

The missile pods were being reattached, each missile requiring individual inspection before loading. The techs handled them carefully—one damaged warhead could turn the hangar into a crater. They'd expended sixty percent of their missile loadout on Regalia. At black market prices, that was nearly a million credits they'd have to replace.

"Load standard high-explosive," the weapons chief decided. "Save the special ordnance for when we know what we're facing."

Hydraulic systems were being flushed and refilled. Cooling systems checked and coolant topped off. Every joint lubricated, every servo tested. The hangar floor was slick with various fluids all mixing into the drainage systems.

Spare armor plates were being welded over the worst damage—not full repairs, just enough to maintain structural integrity through jump stress. The welding torches created a light show of sparks that reflected off the hangar's metal walls.

"Boss's mech needs a full diagnostic," Derg told his team. "Every system. That arm took damage, but the shock would've traveled through the whole frame. Check for stress fractures, especially around the joint connections."

Power systems were being tested, capacitors charged, batteries replaced where needed. The mechs would need full power for combat readiness, even if they were just jumping to a friendly port. In this business, friendly was always temporary.

Fresh combat knives were being mounted—three-meter blades of tungsten carbide, secured to magnetic hardpoints. The ones they'd used on Regalia were being sharpened and inspected for stress fractures.

"Two hours to fuel completion," the fuel chief reported. "Four hours to full ammunition load. Six hours to mobility capable."

"Make it happen," Derg replied, then quieter to himself, "Because something tells me we're going to need these machines ready sooner than anyone thinks."

The hangar continued its orchestrated chaos—hundreds of tasks being performed simultaneously, all focused on returning the war machines to killing readiness. Because in the end, that's what kept them alive in a universe that seemed determined to prove otherwise.

After a couple long hours of after-action work—filing reports, checking equipment, pretending everything was routine—Kenney's comm buzzed.

"Ken, need you in the infirmary," Blake's voice was quiet, serious. "Privately."

Kenney found Blake standing outside the medical bay, chewing tobacco and staring at his datapad with the expression of someone who'd found something they wished they hadn't.

"What's wrong? The girl okay?"

"She's stable. Sedated. But..." Blake spat into his cup, choosing his words carefully. "The things she's been saying while unconscious—I've been having Tango transcribe them. The AI was running audio capture in the hangar, picked up everything she's been muttering since you brought her into the mech."

He showed Kenney the datapad, lines of technical specifications that Tango had parsed and organized into categories.

"The Tango has been trying to make sense of it," Blake continued. "It ran it through every technical database we have access to. Even tried to cross-reference with known weapons systems, theoretical physics papers, engineering manuals."

The screen showed Tango's analysis:

TRANSCRIPT ANALYSIS - SUBJECT: UNKNOWN FEMALE

DURATION: 4 HOURS 23 MINUTES CONTINUOUS

LANGUAGE: TECHNICAL ENGLISH, 98.7% COMPREHENSION
CONTENT: WEAPONS SPECIFICATIONS, THEORETICAL PHYSICS
MATCH TO EXISTING SYSTEMS: 0%
THEORETICAL VIABILITY: CALCULATING...

Below that were pages of the actual transcription—formulas for antimatter containment, specifications for faster-than-light communication systems, weapons that could glass entire continents.

"Tango says the math checks out," Blake said, scrolling through the data. "It ran simulations on some of the simpler concepts. They work, at least theoretically. But this stuff is decades, maybe centuries ahead of current tech."

"So? You said it yourself, probably an engineering student."

"That's the thing, boss. This stuff doesn't exist." Blake scrolled through his research. "I looked up every concept she mentioned. Quantum entanglement communication arrays that work across thousand light-year distances. Fusion reactors the size of a shuttle engine with output that would power a city. Weapons that violate everything we know about physics."

"Maybe she's just delirious, mixing up sci-fi with—"

"I thought that too. But the math checks out. The formulas, the specifications—they're internally consistent. Whoever this girl is, she's either the greatest theoretical physicist of our generation, or..." Blake trailed off.

"Or what?"

"Or she learned this somewhere else. Somewhere that had access to knowledge we don't." Blake pulled up another screen. "There's more. I scanned her ID chip while Doc was working on her. Standard procedure for civilians, in case we need to notify next of kin."

The screen showed an error message: NO RECORD FOUND.

"Her chip's been scrubbed. Not just deleted—professionally wiped. The kind of job intelligence agencies do when they need someone to never have existed." Blake looked up from the datapad. "She's nobody, boss. No birth records, no education history, no medical records. According to every database I can access, that girl in there doesn't exist."

Kenney stared through the infirmary window at Valeria's sleeping form. She looked even smaller in the medical bed, surrounded by monitoring equipment.

"You think she's from the black site," Kenney said. It wasn't a question.

"I think she wasn't just at the facility. I think she was the facility. Or at least, what they were working on there." Blake lowered his voice, glancing around even though they were alone. "Boss, black sites don't just research weapons. Sometimes they research people. And sometimes those people know things they shouldn't."

He pulled up another screen on his datapad—Tango's risk assessment.

"The AI ran the numbers. If even ten percent of what she's been saying is achievable, we're talking about technology that would shift the balance of power in the galaxy."

Blake spat into his cup again, his hands actually trembling slightly. "Ken, do you understand what this means? Governments would kill entire colonies to get this information. Corporations would burn systems. ARMSEA would classify us so hard we'd cease to exist in any database, anywhere."

He scrolled through more of Tango's analysis. "The AI estimates the black market value of just the antimatter containment specs she recited at around 500 million credits. The FTL communication protocols? Incalculable. We're not talking about money anymore—we're talking about the kind of knowledge that starts wars or ends them."

"She's just a kid," Kenney said.

"A kid whose brain contains what might be the most dangerous information in human space." Blake's voice dropped to barely a whisper. "If anyone finds out what she knows—really knows, not just suspects—every intelligence agency, every military contractor, every terrorist organization will come for her. And they won't care if they have to go through us to get her."

Blake pulled up one final screen—a partial schematic Tango had reconstructed from her murmurings. Even incomplete, it showed something that looked like a weapon system beyond anything in service.

"This is just from four hours of unconscious rambling. Imagine what she could tell us if she was awake, if she could actually explain these concepts." Blake met Kenney's eyes. "Or imagine what someone could extract from her if they didn't care about keeping her functional afterward."

"What are you suggesting?"

"I'm suggesting we have a decision to make. Either she's the most valuable asset we've ever acquired, or she's the most dangerous liability imaginable. Because there's no middle ground with knowledge like this. You can't just know how to build doomsday weapons and live a quiet life."

Blake closed the datapad. "The facility we nuked—someone spent enormous resources experimenting on her, putting this information in her head. They're all dead now, but their work isn't. It's sleeping in our medical bay, and when she wakes up, we better have a plan for what we're going to do with her."

Through the window, Valeria stirred in her sleep, her lips moving. Even from here, Kenney could see her mouthing numbers, formulas, specifications for things that shouldn't exist.

"What do you recommend?" Kenney asked.

"Honestly? We should've left her there. But since we didn't..." Blake shrugged. "Keep her sedated until we're far from here. When she wakes up, we find out what she knows. Then we decide if she's an asset or a liability."

"She's a person, Blake. Not cargo."

"In this business, everyone's cargo. Question is whether they're profitable or dangerous." Blake turned to leave, then paused.

Kenney shook his head. "Blake, think about it. Everyone within two kilometers of that facility is dead. You said it yourself—nuclear glass. The job is complete. No witnesses, no evidence, no one left to come looking for her."

"Boss—"

"She's a nobody, literally. No records, no identity. As far as the universe is concerned, she doesn't exist." Kenney kept his voice level, reasonable. "And this mission? It never happened. Everyone knows that. They'd end up dead or worse if they talked."

Blake shifted uncomfortably, but Kenney continued.

"So what do we really have here? We rescued a girl—traumatized, sure. Maybe she overheard some technical discussions wherever she was hiding. Stress makes people's brains do weird things. Doc said it himself, could be some kind of trauma response."

"The surgical scars—"

"Could be from anything. Medical procedure, accident before the war. We don't know." Kenney turned away from the window. "Look, as long as we keep our mouths shut about this mission—which everyone will because they like being alive and free—we're fine. We rescued a civilian with some undiagnosed sleep disorder who talks in her sleep. That's all."

Blake studied him for a long moment. "You really believe that?"

"I believe she needed help and we gave it. Everything else is speculation."

"Dangerous speculation."

"Only if we make it dangerous. She's nobody, from nowhere, with no one looking for her. Sometimes the simplest explanation is the right one—we found a war refugee who needs medical attention and a fresh start."

Blake spat into his cup again, considering. "And if she starts talking about those weapons when she's awake?"

"Then she's a brilliant engineering student with an active imagination. Lots of those in the universe."

"You're taking a hell of a risk, boss."

"I took a risk the moment I picked her up. But leaving her to die would've been wrong, and you know it."

Blake sighed, pocketing his datapad. "Your call. But when this goes sideways—and it will—remember I warned you."

"Noted. Now, how about we focus on getting paid and getting out of this system before someone notices that new crater we left?"

Blake left, shaking his head. Through the window, Kenney watched Valeria sleep, still mouthing those strange formulas. Whatever she was, wherever she'd come from, she was their responsibility now.

For better or worse.

Over the next several days, as the Purgatory jumped through systems putting distance between them and Regalia, Kenney found himself in the infirmary whenever he wasn't on duty. He'd pull a chair next to Valeria's bed, watching her sleep through whatever deep recovery her body had entered.

At first, he just sat quietly. Then, feeling foolish but unable to help himself, he started talking.

"We're passing through the Terminus system today," he'd say, as if she could hear him. "Nothing special about it—couple gas giants, some mining stations. But the view's nice."

When that felt too awkward, he'd brought a reader, working through old fiction from the ship's digital library. Adventure stories, mostly. The kind where heroes saved people and everyone lived happily ever after. Nothing like reality, but maybe that was the point.

"You would've liked Kira," he told her unconscious form one evening. "She had this way of seeing good in everything, even in places like Nueva Kalloo. Even in people like me."

Valeria slept through it all, occasionally muttering those weird specifications, her eyes moving rapidly beneath closed lids.

On the fourth day, Doc Haywire called him aside. The doctor was more sober than usual—never a good sign.

"I need to tell you what I've found," Doc said quietly, pulling up medical scans on his tablet. "Her brain... someone's been in there. Surgically. Multiple times."

The scans showed areas of scarring, unusual neural pathways, sections that looked different from normal brain tissue.

"They removed parts—sections of her hippocampus, some of her amygdala. But they also added things. Implants maybe, or grafted tissue. I can't tell without opening her up, which I'm not qualified to do." Doc scrolled through more images. "Whatever they did, it changed her brain's architecture. She's processing information in ways that shouldn't be possible."

"Will she recover?"

Doc hesitated. "Physically? She's healing remarkably fast. But mentally..." He pulled up another set of scans. "There's more. Evidence of repeated sexual trauma. Dozens of incidents based on the scarring. She was systematically abused."

Kenney's jaw clenched, thinking of her collapsed at the facility, begging for help.

"When she wakes up—if she wakes up normally—she might not be entirely sane," Doc continued. "The trauma, the brain modifications, whatever they did to her... people don't come back from that unchanged. She might have episodes, dissociation, violent reactions to triggers we won't see coming."

"We'll deal with it."

"Boss, I'm not talking about some PTSD you can therapy away. Her brain has been fundamentally altered. She could be dangerous."

"She asked for my help," Kenney said simply.

Doc sighed. "Just... be careful. When someone's been broken that badly, sometimes the pieces don't fit back together right. Sometimes they form something else entirely."

That night, Kenney sat by her bed again, reading another chapter from a book about ancient Earth pirates. Valeria's hand twitched, her fingers moving like she was typing on an invisible keyboard.

"Railgun velocity achievable at Mach 7 with proper capacitor discharge," she murmured, then fell silent again.

Whatever she'd become in that facility, whatever they'd turned her into, she was safe now. He'd make sure of that.

Even if Blake was right, even if Doc's warnings came true, he couldn't bring himself to regret pulling her from that nuclear ground zero. She'd asked for help, and that was enough.

The universe had taken Kira from him. Maybe saving this broken girl was some kind of balance. Or maybe he was just adding another ghost to his collection.

Either way, he'd stay by her bed until she woke up.

In a lot of ways, he wasn't just trying to save Valeria—he was trying to save himself.

The routine of it helped. Having someone who needed him, someone whose survival depended on his presence. It gave structure to days that had been blurring together in an endless cycle of contracts and killing. He'd wake up thinking about checking on her instead of reaching for the bottle. He'd end his shifts eager to get back to the infirmary instead of losing himself in another meaningless distraction.

She wasn't the only one healing.

Sitting by her bed, reading those stories aloud, he found himself remembering why people fought to protect things instead of just destroy them. When he talked to her sleeping form about Kira, it was the first time he'd said his wife's name without feeling like he was drowning. The words came easier each time, like a wound finally starting to close.

"Kira would have liked you," he told Valeria one evening, watching her breathe steadily. "She had a thing about strays too. Always bringing home broken things and fixing them. Guess I learned that from her."

The nightmares hadn't stopped, but they'd changed. Sometimes now, instead of failing to save Kira, he'd dream about pulling Valeria from the nuclear fire. About making it in time. About saving someone.

For three years, he'd been looking for a way to die that wouldn't look like suicide. Now, he had a reason to live—at least until she woke up. Until he knew she'd be okay.

Late at night, when the infirmary was quiet except for the soft beeping of monitors, he'd sometimes find himself talking to both of them—Valeria sleeping in the bed, Kira somewhere beyond.

"I couldn't save you," he'd whisper to his ghosts. "But maybe I can save her. Maybe that counts for something."

Valeria would murmur in response—more specifications, more impossible mathematics—but sometimes her hand would move toward his, fingers stretching, reaching like someone drowning.

Kenney recognized the movement, the desperate seeking. He'd seen it in combat casualties, that primal need for human contact when the mind was lost in trauma. The way her fingers would curl slightly, grasping at empty air, reminded him of soldiers he'd held as they died—that final reach for connection, for something solid in a world coming apart.

One evening, he finally took her hand.

The moment their fingers interlocked, her muttering stopped. The endless stream of weapons specifications cut off mid-sentence. Her breathing, which had been shallow and rapid, deepened. She was still unconscious, eyes still moving beneath closed lids, but something changed. The drowning person had found something to hold onto.

"It's okay," he said quietly, not knowing if she could hear him. "You're safe now."

Her grip tightened—not much, she was too weak for that, but enough that he could feel it. Like she was using his hand as an anchor, pulling herself back from wherever her mind had gone. The technical specifications stayed silent as long as he held on.

When he eventually had to let go—duties called, meetings needed attending—the muttering would return within minutes. But each time he came back and took her hand again, she would quiet, that drowning reach would calm, and she would surface just a little bit more.

In those moments, holding this stranger's hand in the medical bay, he felt something he hadn't experienced since Kira died: the simple human act of keeping someone from slipping away. Not through violence or tactics or nuclear weapons, but just by being there, being solid, being real.

Hope.

CHAPTER EIGHT

"And with that, payment cleared," Blake announced from his station in the CIC, smiling as he looked at his screens. "Mr. Smith was good on his word. We're sitting far into the green for the first time in months."

He pulled up the financial display on the main screen. Their accounts showed numbers that made everyone in the room stop what they were doing. The fifty million upfront plus the hundred million completion bonus, all there in clean, untraceable credits.

"Hot damn," someone whistled from across the room. "That's more than we made all last year."

"Enough to finally fix everything that's held together with prayer and duct tape," Derg added from his engineering console. His workspace was a disaster zone—cigarette butts overflowing from three different makeshift ashtrays (one an actual ashtray, two repurposed coffee mugs), and at least six empty coffee cups in various states of mold cultivation. Burn marks on the console showed where he'd set down hot cups or forgotten cigarettes. Despite regulations against smoking near sensitive equipment, nobody said anything—Derg kept the ship running, and if he needed nicotine and caffeine to do it, that was a small price to pay. "Maybe even upgrade some systems that haven't been touched since this boat was commissioned."

Kenney looked up from the tactical planning table. "We need a port that won't ask questions about battle damage. Somewhere unregulated."

"Wait," Derg interrupted, looking up from his disaster zone of a console. "What about that Class 4 license Smith promised? I thought we'd finally be able to avoid cesspits and resupply through legitimate military contractors."

Blake shook his head, spitting tobacco juice into his cup. "That's going to take a couple weeks minimum to process. Paperwork needs to go through ARMSEA bureaucracy, establish our vendor codes, get us into the supply chain systems. For now, we're still roughing it in the gray market."

"Figures," Derg muttered. "Promise you the galaxy, deliver it on geological time."

Kenney looked up from the tactical planning table. "Then we need a port with military-grade resupply and a proper dry dock. Those mechs need more than patch jobs, and we're running on fumes for ammunition."

"Our 30mm stores are at twenty percent," Blake confirmed, checking his inventory. "Missiles at thirty. And that's not counting what we'll need to replace small arms calibers, larger calibers, and the weapon and mech parts."

"Plus, the hull stress from that combat landing a couple months back," Derg added. "We need a shipyard that can handle a carrier this size."

"Which brings us back to immediate needs," Blake continued, pulling up a star chart on his terminal. "I've evaluated the options and think I know just the place—Hammerhead Station. It's in the Tortuga system—no government, no regulations, just commerce and whoever has the biggest guns. Used to be a mining hub before the ore ran out. Now it's a free port for anyone who can pay docking fees."

Wilson leaned over the display. "They have full dry dock facilities there. Can handle anything up to battlecruiser displacement. The yards are run by ex-military engineers who don't ask the wrong kind of questions."

"They also have the best black market armament suppliers in the sector," Blake added. "We can get military-grade ammunition, replacement parts, maybe even those new shield generators everyone's talking about. At markup, sure, but available now."

"How far?" Kenney asked.

Blake ran the calculations. "Four jumps through mostly uncontrolled space. Maybe eighteen hours if we push it. I'll send the coordinates to Conway on the bridge."

"Do it. Have him set course for Hammerhead Station."

"The crew's going to want to blow off steam," Wilson warned. "Hammerhead's got everything—bars, brothels, fighting pits. After what we just pulled off, they'll want to celebrate."

"Let them. They've earned it." Kenney turned to Blake. "Make sure everyone gets their full share—combat pay, hazard differential, completion bonus. I want accounts settled before we dock."

Blake nodded, already pulling up the crew roster on his datapad. "Full payout comes to about 150K per head for the mech pilots, 75K for support crew, 50K for everyone else. That's serious money."

"Hammerhead's a crossroads," Wilson added, understanding where this was going. "Lot of outfits recruit there. With that kind of payout, some of our people might be thinking about moving on."

"Then let's not give them a reason to sneak off," Kenney said. "Anyone wants to leave; they can walk with our blessing and their full share. No hard feelings, no burned bridges. We're professionals, not a press gang."

"You sure about that, boss?" Derg asked, looking up from his console. "We lose too many techs, we'll be hurting."

"Better to lose them honest than have them jump ship in the middle of the night or, worse, stay bitter and half-ass their work." Kenney looked around the CIC. "We just pulled off a rough deployment cycle and everyone walked away rich. If someone wants to cash out and retire, or join another outfit, that's their choice."

Blake was already drafting the announcement. "I'll make it clear—anyone wanting to leave should notify us before shore leave. Full pay, no questions asked, clean separation. Hell, we'll even give them recommendation letters if they want."

"Smart," Wilson admitted. "Nothing breeds resentment like feeling trapped. This way, whoever stays actually wants to be here."

"Exactly. And Hammerhead's the perfect place for it. Enough traffic that people can find new berths, enough money flowing that our crew can celebrate properly if they're staying." Kenney stood. "Have Conway set course. And Blake? Make sure those payments clear before anyone sets foot on that station. I want everyone walking off this ship knowing exactly where they stand."

Blake nodded, already working his datapad. "I'll make sure everyone understands." Blake hit the intercom to the bridge. "Conway, coordinates coming your way. Hammerhead Station, best speed."

"Copy that," Conway's voice came back. "First jump in thirty minutes."

The briefing broke up, and as Kenney walked toward the infirmary, a thought occurred to him. Hammerhead Station—a black market port where nobody asked questions and everything had a price. If Valeria woke up, she'd need more than medical care. She'd need an identity, documents, a past that existed in databases.

And in a place like Hammerhead, where forgers and data-sculptors operated openly, creating a person who'd never existed was just another transaction. Birth certificates, education records, travel documents—all of it could be manufactured for the right price.

He'd have to be careful about it. Find someone trustworthy, if such a thing existed in that den of thieves. But it was possible. Give her a clean slate, a chance to be someone new without whatever horror she'd escaped following her.

First, though, she had to wake up.

Kenney made his way to medical, but stopped short of the doorway. He could hear voices—young voices, whispering and giggling. Peering in, he saw an unexpected scene.

A group of children, ranging from maybe six to fourteen, had gathered around Valeria's bed. McKnight's kids—all twelve of them. The mercenary pilot kept his bastards aboard, unwilling to leave his blood scattered across foreign worlds. It wasn't clear if they all came from the same mother, though the variety in their features suggested otherwise. Some had McKnight's sharp nose, others his stubborn chin, but all had that same watchful intelligence.

The oldest, a girl named Sara who'd inherited her father's steady hands, was holding a book. The younger ones sat cross-legged on the floor or perched on nearby equipment, all watching the unconscious girl with curious eyes.

"She still sleeping?" the youngest, a boy maybe six, whispered.

"Yeah, dummy," his older brother replied. "That's why we're reading to her."

Word had spread about Kenney's visits, about him reading stories to the comatose girl. The kids had taken it upon themselves to continue the tradition when he wasn't there.

It was a dangerous life aboard a military ship, but the kids earned their keep. They pulled shifts in the kitchen, helped with cleaning, ran messages between decks, did basic maintenance chores. The crew had practically raised them collectively—teaching them to strip weapons, patch hull breaches, navigate by star charts. They were probably the most well-rounded bunch of military brats in the sector.

"Captain Kenney!" Sara spotted him first, starting to stand.

"At ease," he said automatically, then caught himself and smiled. "Sorry. Old habits. Don't let me interrupt."

"We were reading her the one about the pirates," the youngest boy said proudly. "Sara does different voices!"

Truth be told, Kenney had always had a soft spot for kids. Maybe because they hadn't learned to be afraid of him yet, or maybe because they reminded him of possibilities beyond warfare. Having them aboard added something human to the cold metal corridors.

"She like the story?" Kenney asked, moving closer to the bed.

"Her hand moved," one of the middle children reported seriously. "When Sara did the parrot voice."

Kenney looked down at the girl. She was still pale, still muttering occasionally, but the children's presence had brought something different to the sterile medical bay. Their innocent chatter, their simple unquestioning acceptance that she would wake up—it all created a bubble of normalcy in the chaos.

"Room for one more?" he asked, pulling up a chair.

The kids immediately scooted to make space, the youngest climbing into his lap without invitation. Sara handed him the book.

"We're at the part where they find the treasure," she informed him.

As Kenney began to read, he noticed Valeria's hand moving slightly, fingers curling as if reaching. One of the children, without prompting, gently took her hand. The muttering stopped.

"See?" the child said matter-of-factly. "She likes company."

The kids had grasped what the adults overlooked—healing wasn't always about medical procedures or advanced technology. It could be as simple as not being alone, as basic as voices reading stories, as fundamental as small hands holding bigger ones and promising without words that someone would be there when you woke up.

As Kenney read about pirates dividing their treasure on a remote island, something changed in the room. The smallest child, still in his lap, whispered, "Captain, her eyes..."

Valeria's eyes fluttered open—not the rolled-back white, but clear and blue, blinking in the medical bay's harsh lights. She looked disoriented but not frightened, her gaze moving slowly across the circle of young faces surrounding her bed.

"Oh," she said softly, and her voice took on an almost maternal warmth despite her own youth. "Hello there, little ones. Where... where am I?"

"You're safe," Kenney said, carefully setting the book on the side table. He kept his movements slow, non-threatening, his voice low and steady—the same tone he'd used with panicked civilians in warzones. "You're on a ship called the Purgatory. My ship. I pulled you out of Sevastopol before... before things got bad there." He gestured to the circle of young faces watching her with curious concern. "These are some friends—they've been taking turns sitting with you, reading stories. They were worried you'd wake up alone."

Valeria's eyes found his, studying his face with an intensity that seemed older than her years. "I don't want to go back," she said, and though her voice stayed calm, her free hand clutched the blanket. "Please, I can't go back there."

"You'll never go back," Kenney said firmly. "The people who hurt you—they'll never do it again. I'll never let anyone hurt you again."

She studied him for another moment, her gaze moving from his eyes to the scars visible on his hands, then back to his face. Something in her expression shifted—recognition maybe, or perhaps just the decision to trust. Her face softened into something that wasn't quite a smile but held warmth nonetheless.

"You have nice eyes," she said, the words coming out with surprising directness, as if she'd never learned to filter her thoughts. "Kind eyes. Sad, but kind. Like someone who's seen too much but hasn't let it make them cruel." She paused, seeming to realize how that sounded, and a faint blush colored her pale cheeks. "I'm sorry, that was... I tend to say exactly what I'm thinking. Mother always said I had no proper sense of discretion."

She shifted slightly in the bed, wincing at some hidden pain, then focused on the book in his hands. "Would you... would you read the part about the treasure again? I think I missed it the first time. I remember voices, children's voices, but the words kept slipping away like water."

The youngest girl, maybe eight with braids McKnight had done himself, piped up: "What's your name?"

Valeria turned to her with an expression of gentle surprise. "Oh, how frightfully rude of me! Here you all are, watching over me like guardian angels, and I haven't even introduced myself properly." She tried to sit up a bit straighter, though she was clearly still weak. "I'm Valeria. Valeria Magleby. And I'm terribly pleased to make all of your acquaintances, though I do wish it were under better circumstances."

"I'm Lily," the little girl said, beaming. "And that's Tommy, and Sara, and James, and—"

As the children rattled off their names, Valeria nodded to each one with serious attention, as if memorizing them was the most important thing she could do. When they finished, she said, "What a delightful collection of names! Each one perfectly suited to its owner, I'm sure."

"You talk funny," Tommy observed with six-year-old honesty.

"Tommy!" Sara scolded.

But Valeria laughed—a real laugh, though tired. "I suppose I do. My mother always said I talked like I'd swallowed a dictionary and was determined to use every word before it expired." Her expression flickered with something sad before returning to warmth. "Now then, about that treasure? I have a particular fondness for stories about pirates, you know. They're so deliciously dramatic."

Kenney found himself smiling as he picked up the book again. Valeria was awake, she was coherent, and despite everything she'd been through, she was being kind to the children. Whatever had been done to her, whoever she'd been before, she was here now. Safe.

As he began reading again, he noticed her hand had found the child's who'd been holding it, giving it a gentle squeeze of thanks.

Over the next several hours, Doc Haywire ran Valeria through a battery of tests, his normally rum-hazed demeanor sharpening into professional focus.

"Follow my finger," he instructed, moving it slowly across her field of vision. "Good. Now touch your nose, then my finger, then your nose again."

Valeria complied, her movements still slightly shaky but coordinated. "Am I passing, Doctor?"

"You're doing better than my normal run of patients, and they haven't been through what you have." He checked her reflexes with a small hammer, nodding at the responses. "The metabolic boosters I've been giving you are working overtime. You've gained fourteen pounds in three days—mostly muscle mass and organ recovery."

She looked down at herself, noting how the borrowed clothes—someone had found her a set of gym clothes instead of the worn medical smocks—no longer hung quite so loosely. While still thin, she was beginning to resemble a healthy young woman rather than a starvation victim.

"Now, about these scars," Doc said carefully, examining the surgical marks on her scalp. "Do you remember—"

Valeria's hand instinctively went to her head, fingers tracing the thin lines hidden beneath her hair. "I remember..." she started, then paused, her eyes going distant. "It's like trying to recall a nightmare after waking. There are flashes—bright lights, cold metal tables, voices discussing things I couldn't understand. They did something to me, opened me up, put things inside my head."

She blinked, focusing on Doc again. "Sometimes I hear myself saying things—technical specifications, formulas, weapons designs. The words just spill out, especially when I'm sleeping or scared. I don't know where they come from. It's like someone else's knowledge was poured into my brain and sometimes it overflows."

Doc exchanged a glance with Kenney. "You were muttering constantly while unconscious. Advanced physics, weapons systems that don't exist yet."

"I was?" Valeria looked genuinely surprised. "I don't... I mean, sometimes I have dreams about numbers and equations, but when I wake up, they scatter like smoke. The facility is the same way—I know terrible things happened there, I can feel it in my bones, but the specifics keep slipping away. Like my mind is protecting me from remembering."

She shook her head, frustrated. "There were other children. Tests. Machines that looked at our brains. Something about compatibility, about integration. But it's all fragments, and honestly?" She looked between them, her voice dropping. "I'm not sure I want to remember more clearly. The pieces I have are horrific enough."

Then, as if flipping a switch, she brightened deliberately, that forced cheer a clear defense mechanism. "But I'd rather not dwell on unpleasantness when there's a whole future to explore, wouldn't you agree?"

Before Doc could respond, the medical bay door burst open and Tommy rushed in, followed by his siblings.

"Valeria! You're cleared for walking?" Sara asked, shooting a questioning look at Doc.

"Light activity," Doc warned. "No running, no heavy lifting, and if she gets dizzy, you bring her straight back."

"We'll take excellent care of her," Lily promised solemnly, already taking Valeria's hand.

Valeria stood carefully, testing her balance. "Well then, my dear guides, where shall we begin our grand tour?"

"The mess hall!" Tommy declared. "Cookie's making chocolate pudding today, my favorite!"

As they walked through the corridors, Valeria marveled at everything with genuine curiosity. "These passages are so efficiently designed! Like a metal labyrinth."

"That's a funny way to say 'ugly corridor,'" James laughed.

"Oh, but it's not ugly at all," Valeria protested. "Look at how the support beams create a rhythm, and how the lighting panels follow the natural flow of movement. It's quite ingenious really."

They reached the mess hall, where Cookie—a gruff ex-Navy cook—was ladling out what passed for stew.

"New face," he grunted at Valeria.

"Valeria," she said, extending her hand as if they were at a formal dinner. "I'm delighted to make your acquaintance. The aroma of your stew is absolutely transportive."

Cookie stared at her hand, then at her face, then barked out a laugh. "You're the politest person to ever board this rust bucket." He shook her hand with his flour-dusted one. "Cookie. Don't expect fancy, but you'll never go hungry."

"That sounds perfectly wonderful," Valeria said sincerely.

The tour continued through the ship. The children showed her the observation deck ("You can see the stars during jump if you don't throw up," Tommy explained), the recreation room ("Don't play cards with Joker, she cheats," Sara warned), and the lower mechanical decks.

"This is where we help sometimes," Lily explained, showing Valeria how to sort bolts by size. "Everyone has jobs on the ship."

"How marvelously democratic," Valeria said, genuinely interested. "Like a floating community where everyone contributes. I'd very much like to help too, once I'm steadier on my feet."

"You could help us in the kitchen," Sara suggested. "Or maybe with the inventory. You seem smart."

"You're tremendously kind to say so. I'd be honored to assist wherever I'm needed."

As they passed the hangar, Valeria stopped, staring at the mechs being serviced.

"Are those the giants that saved me?" she asked softly.

"That's my dad's," James pointed to McKnight's mech. "And that's Captain Kenney's—he's the one who rescued you."

Valeria studied the massive machines, and for a moment, her eyes went distant. "They're beautiful and terrible all at once, aren't they? Like sleeping dragons made of metal and fury."

"You okay?" Sara asked, noticing the change in her demeanor.

Valeria shook herself slightly. "Yes, dear one. Just remembering... but that's behind us now, isn't it? Onward to new adventures?"

The children agreed enthusiastically, pulling her along to show her more of their floating world, their chatter and warmth slowly drawing the shadows from her eyes.

They spent the next hour exploring every corner the children deemed important—the engineering deck where pipes ran like metal veins along the ceiling and Lily demonstrated how she could identify different systems by their hum, the lower cargo holds where Tommy swore he'd once found an old Earth coin (though he could never produce it as evidence), and even the backup life support room where someone had scratched years of graffiti into the walls—mostly complaints about food and duty rotations from crews past.

"We're not supposed to be down here," Sara admitted, running her finger along a particularly creative piece of profanity that had been turned into a flower by some other artist, "but the adults never check."

By the time they reached the mess hall, Valeria had learned all their names, their favorite foods, and which siblings couldn't be trusted in card games (apparently James cheated, but Sara cheated better). Cookie took one look at the group and groaned.

"Don't tell me you're all here to 'help,'" he said, making air quotes with flour-covered fingers.

"Valeria's never seen ship's kitchen!" Tommy announced, which wasn't entirely true but Valeria didn't correct him.

"Fine, fine. But if you're in my kitchen, you work," Cookie grumbled, tossing an apron at Valeria. "You kids know the drill."

The rest of the day had been filled with scrubbing dishes for Cookie, Valeria working alongside the children with her sleeves rolled up, humming softly as she cleaned. She'd insisted on doing her share, despite Cookie grumbling that she was "still too skinny to be useful."

"Now for the best part," Lily announced after they'd finished, grabbing Valeria's still-damp hand. "Our secret spot!"

"It's not really secret," Sara corrected as they led her deeper into the ship. "Everyone knows about it."

They stopped at what looked like an ordinary cargo container, but Tommy produced a keycard with obvious pride. "We all have one," he explained, swiping it. The heavy door unsealed with a hiss.

Inside, Valeria gasped. "Oh my stars!"

The container had been retrofitted to be a children's paradise. Special child-sized jump seats were arranged in neat rows facing a wall-mounted screen that could have graced any theater. The seats had full harness systems, but decorated with colorful fabric to make them less military.

"Dad had it built," James explained, flopping into one of the seats. "If there's ever boarders or an attack, we come here and lock down."

Sara pointed to the control panel by the door. "It's got independent life support, can seal against hull breach, even has its own emergency beacon. But mostly we use it to watch movies."

One corner held bins of toys and games, another had shelves stocked with snacks and water bottles—enough supplies for days if needed. The walls were covered in drawings and posters the children had put up, making it feel like a real playroom despite its defensive purpose.

"We've got all the classic movies," Tommy said, pulling up the media library on the screen. "Even some from Old Earth!"

"This is absolutely marvelous," Valeria said, genuinely delighted. "Your own private sanctuary! Like a secret clubhouse that could survive a direct hit."

"Wait, there's more!" Tommy said excitedly, grabbing the remote. "Show her the cool stuff!"

Sara took the controller and pulled up a different menu. "It's not just for movies. Watch this."

The screen split into multiple feeds—suddenly Valeria was looking at the ship's corridor cameras, the hangar bay, even the bridge.

"We can see everything," James said proudly. "And when Dad goes on missions..."

He switched to another feed, and Valeria saw the inside of a mech cockpit, currently powered down.

"That's the direct feed from my dad's mech," Sara explained. "When he's in combat, we can watch. He doesn't know we figured out how to access it."

"He totally knows," James corrected. "He just pretends not to because he'd rather we watch from here where it's safe than sneak around trying to see."

"It's scary sometimes," Lily admitted quietly. "When things explode really close."

Valeria studied the children with new understanding. They'd grown up watching their father fight through his own eyes, seeing war from the safest seat possible but unable to look away.

"That must be very difficult," she said gently.

"It's better than not knowing," Sara said firmly, sounding older than her years. "At least this way, we know if he's okay."

Tommy quickly switched back to the entertainment menu. "But mostly we watch movies! Wanna see 'Star Pirates of New Zion'? It's about these pirates who steal starships and fight the evil Corporation!"

"With laser swords!" Lily added.

"And space krakens," James contributed.

Valeria settled into her seat, touched by how quickly they'd shifted from the harsh reality of watching their father's combat feeds to the fantasy of space pirates. "That sounds absolutely perfect. I do hope the pirates win."

"They always do," Tommy said confidently, starting the movie. "That's why it's fun."

As the opening credits rolled—dramatic music over starfields and pirate ships that looked suspiciously like toy models—Valeria noticed how the children automatically checked their harnesses were secure. Even in play, safety came first. The screen that could show their father fighting for his life now showed cartoon pirates stealing treasure from corporate villains.

"The best part's coming up," Lily whispered. "The pirate captain has a pet space parrot that can breathe in vacuum!"

Valeria smiled, letting herself be drawn into their world. It was their normal, and they were sharing it with her.

Kenney decided to get some shut-eye before they reached Hammerhead Station. The eighteen-hour journey through hyperspace had everyone on edge, and he'd need to be sharp for whatever came next.

He'd just finished two hours in the ship's gym—nothing fancy, just a converted storage room with salvaged equipment bolted to the deck. The bench press bar was bent slightly from when Trollibee had loaded too much weight and dropped it, and the pull-up station squeaked with every rep, but it served its purpose. His shirt was soaked through with sweat, muscles burning from pushing himself harder than usual. The physical exhaustion helped quiet the mental noise, made sleep seem less of a concept.

He toweled off briefly, not bothering to hit the showers—they'd be docking soon enough and water conservation was always a concern during jumps. The corridors were quieter than usual, most of the crew either at their stations or grabbing rest while they could. His boots echoed on the metal decking as he made his way through the ship, still cooling down from the workout, endorphins making everything feel slightly distant and manageable.

The medical bay was on his route back to quarters anyway, so he ducked inside for a quick check. Valeria was asleep in the hospital bed, curled on her side with one hand tucked under her cheek. The harsh medical lighting had been dimmed, and someone—probably one of the kids—had left a stuffed animal near her pillow. She looked peaceful, younger in sleep, without that careful composure she maintained while awake.

He watched her for a moment, sweat still cooling on his skin, then continued toward his quarters. The familiar space felt different somehow, less like a tomb he returned to each night.

He peeled off his clothes, leaving them in a heap, and climbed into bed. For the first time in months, he didn't feel the compulsion to activate the holo-projector, to watch Kira's recording on repeat. The absence of that need was both relieving and unsettling.

He was just drifting off when he heard his door cycle. The mechanism disengaged and the door opened and closed. A small form slipped into his room, moving carefully in the darkness.

He knew it was Valeria before she even reached the bed—something about the way she moved, careful but determined. She climbed in beside him, and he caught the scent of her hair, clean with a hint of the ship's standard soap. She was wearing those company gym shorts and a tank top, probably borrowed from the ship's stores.

She pressed her back against his chest, curling into him, fitting herself into the curve of his body like she was seeking shelter.

"Valeria, what are you doing?" he asked quietly, not moving, acutely aware of her warmth against him.

"I can't sleep in that hospital bed," she whispered, her voice tight with something like fear. "I don't want to sleep in a hospital ever again. The smell, the sounds, the lights—it's too much like... before."

She shifted, turning to face him in the darkness. Even without light, he could sense her studying his face. Then she wrapped her arms around his neck, not romantically but desperately, like someone clinging to driftwood in a storm.

"Please don't send me back there," she said against his shoulder. "I know this is improper, I know I shouldn't be here, but I... I need to not be alone. And you're the only one who feels safe."

Kenney remained still, processing the situation—a traumatized young woman in his bed, seeking comfort. "Valeria, this isn't—"

"I'm not trying to... I don't want anything from you," she said quickly. "I just need to sleep somewhere that doesn't smell like antiseptic and suffering. Where I can hear another person breathing. Where I know I'm not going to wake up back there."

Her body was trembling slightly, and he realized she was on the edge of panic.

"Okay," he said carefully. "You can stay. But we need boundaries. You sleep on your side; I sleep on mine."

"Yes, of course," she said, relief flooding her voice. But she didn't let go, her arms clung around his neck. "Thank you. You don't know what it means to not be alone."

Actually, he thought, he knew exactly what that meant. The weight of her against him was different from the emptiness he'd grown accustomed to—making the darkness less absolute.

"Get some sleep," he said. "I'm here and I'm not going anywhere."

She shifted slightly, pressing her back more firmly against his chest, as if trying to absorb his solidity. "Kenney?" she whispered into the darkness. "Your eyes aren't just kind. They're sad. Like you're carrying something heavy that you can't put down."

The observation hit closer than he expected. He stayed silent for a moment, feeling her wait for a response that wouldn't come. How could he explain three years of planned self-destruction to someone who'd just escaped her own nightmare?

"We all carry things," he finally said, his voice barely audible.

"Yes," she agreed softly. "But some people let it crush them, and others..." She trailed off, her hand finding his in the darkness, fingers interlacing. "Others keep going anyway. Even when they don't want to."

He didn't answer, but he didn't pull away either. Her thumb traced small circles on his hand, a gentle, repetitive motion that was somehow soothing. The silence stretched between them, but it wasn't uncomfortable—more like a shared understanding that some things didn't need words.

Eventually, her breathing began to deepen, the tension slowly leaving her body as exhaustion overtook fear. Her grip loosened but didn't release entirely, as if even in approaching sleep she needed that anchor. He lay awake much longer, processing this strange turn—the girl who shouldn't exist, seeking safety in his bed, both of them refugees from different kinds of trauma.

The ship hummed around them, metal settling with familiar groans as it hurtled through space. For the first time in years, the sound didn't feel lonely.

CHAPTER NINE

The Purgatory dropped out of hyperspace at the edge of the Tortuga system, her hull groaning from the stress of multiple jumps. The transition from the twisted non-space of hyperspace to normal reality sent ripples through the ship's superstructure—bulkheads flexing, deck plates shifting millimeters as physics reasserted itself.

Through the bridge viewports, Hammerhead Station sprawled before them like an industrial parasite feeding on the dead. The asteroid it had consumed was easily three kilometers across, its natural rock face now bristling with docking arms, sensor arrays, and the skeletal frameworks of ship gantries that reached out like grasping fingers into the void.

"Jesus Christ," Conway muttered from the pilot's station, his hands dancing across the holographic controls as proximity alarms began their symphony. "Look at all that wreckage."

The debris field was a three-dimensional maze of twisted metal and shattered dreams. A Confederate dreadnought tumbled past their starboard side in a lazy end-over-end rotation it had probably maintained for decades, its kilometer-long hull split open like a flowered seed pod, the internal decks visible through gaps wide enough to fly a shuttle through. Frozen bodies, preserved in the vacuum, drifted among clouds of crystallized atmosphere that caught the local star's light like deadly diamonds.

Conway's fingers worked the maneuvering thrusters, micro-bursts of reaction mass pushing them around a cluster of fighter craft still locked in their final dogfight formation—six interceptors frozen in an eternal spiral, their pilots' last seconds preserved in metal and ice. The navigation computer was screaming warnings, calculating collision probabilities as thousands of pieces of debris—from capital ship hull sections down to individual bolts—populated their flight path in a deadly cloud.

The station itself was built into a massive asteroid, its original mining structure expanded over decades into a sprawling complex of habitat rings, industrial modules, and defensive installations. The asteroid's rotation had been arrested and replaced with artificial gravity generators that created pockets of different orientations—visitors often found themselves walking on what had been someone else's ceiling moments before. Atmospheric processors jutted from the rock face like mechanical barnacles, venting excess heat in shimmering waves that distorted the starfield behind them.

But what made Hammerhead unique was the graveyard surrounding it—hundreds of derelict ships floating in the asteroid field, remnants of an ancient battle that had turned this sector into a scrapyard. Vessels from three different factions tumbled slowly through space in a complex gravitational ballet, their hulls torn open like metal flowers, their crews long dead. A Rogue Marine battlecruiser, its proud eagle and anchor insignia still visible beneath laser scarring, drifted past a Confederate carrier that had been sheared in half by some unimaginable weapon. The carrier's hangar bays were still lit by emergency power that had somehow survived the decades, casting ghostly orange light onto fighters that would never launch again.

The station had grown fat on this bounty. Salvage crews worked the field constantly in modified EVA frames—humanoid mechs designed for zero-gravity operations, their pilots visible through reinforced canopies as they carved valuable components free with plasma cutters. Conway watched one crew attaching magnetic grapples to what looked like an intact fusion reactor, probably worth millions if they could extract it without breaching the containment systems.

As they approached their designated vector, massive gantry cranes extended from Hammerhead's main structure like skeletal fingers, each one currently cradling a ship in various stages of dismemberment. These work platforms could accommodate anything from a scout ship to a dreadnought, systematically stripping them of anything valuable. One crane held a merchant vessel being peeled apart layer by layer—hull plating stacked neatly for recycling, electronics bundled for resale, even the crew quarters' furniture visible as it was catalogued and removed. The efficiency was both impressive and deeply morbid.

"Hammerhead Control, this is cargo vessel Purgatory requesting docking clearance," Conway transmitted, using their false registration. His fingers danced across the quantum encryption panel, ensuring their real identity stayed buried beneath layers of digital camouflage.

The response came through awash with static from the debris field's interference. "Purgatory, this is Hammerhead Control." The voice was bored, professional—someone who'd guided thousands of ships through this graveyard daily. In the background, Conway could hear the chatter of other controllers, the ping of proximity alarms, the constant noise of a station that never slept. "Transmit tonnage and purpose of visit."

Conway glanced at his displays where their fake manifest scrolled past—carefully crafted lies mixed with enough truth to pass casual inspection. "Fifty thousand tons, requiring dry dock repairs and resupply."

A longer pause this time. Conway could imagine the controller pulling up their specifications, running the numbers through the station's docking algorithms. Through the viewscreen, he watched a salvage crew's cutting laser slice through a destroyer's hull, the beam so bright his viewport automatically polarized to compensate.

"Fifty thousand tons puts you in capital ship classification." The controller's bored tone shifted slightly—bigger ships meant bigger fees, bigger problems, bigger profits. "That's Gantry Seven or Eight. Let me check availability."

Conway could hear fingers working haptic interfaces, the soft chime of data queries. In the background, another controller was arguing with someone about berthing fees, their voice rising and falling in the universal rhythm of commercial negotiation.

"Seven's occupied for another six hours—got a surplus Confederate heavy cruiser getting her spine realigned. Eight is... available, but it'll cost you. Fifteen thousand credits per day, minimum three-day booking. Non-negotiable, paid up front, and that doesn't include services—just the berth."

Blake winced from his station, fingers already calculating their burn rate on his datapad. The stylus tapped against the screen as he ran scenarios—even with their recent windfall, forty-five thousand credits just for parking was steep. His other hand adjusted the gain on his communication array, filtering out the cosmic background radiation that made everything sound like whispers from dead ships.

"Confirmed, Hammerhead. Gantry Eight."

"Copy that, Purgatory. Transmitting approach vector now." The controller's voice shifted to practiced warnings. "Follow beacon trajectory exactly—I'm serious about this. Do not deviate. We've got automated defense platforms hidden throughout the debris field that run on motion-prediction algorithms. They don't transmit warnings, don't recognize surrenders, and definitely don't ask questions. The wreck field isn't completely mapped either—we're still finding mines from the original battle. Stray too far from the beacon path and you might clip a dead dreadnought or trigger ordnance that's been waiting forty years for a target."

Conway's navigation display lit up with the prescribed route—a twisting path through the carnage marked by pulsing blue waypoints. He engaged the autopilot's precision mode, letting the computer handle the micro-adjustments needed to thread between hulks separated by mere meters.

As they descended into the debris field proper, the true scale of ancient slaughter became apparent. They passed through what had once been a battle line—capital ships arranged in textbook formation, now frozen in their moment of destruction. An LDS destroyer's bow section drifted past their viewports, the bridge still intact behind armored transparisteel. Conway could see command chairs with their occupants still strapped in, preserved by vacuum, their final moments an eternal tableau.

The Purgatory's collision warning systems were having a nervous breakdown. Conway had to manually override them every few seconds as they calculated impact probabilities with debris that the beacon path would narrowly avoid. Their sensor officer was calling out the biggest threats: "Unexploded ordinance cluster at two-seven-mark-four, distance three hundred meters and closing... clear. Debris cloud, metallic fragments, navigating around... clear."

The station proper housed tens of thousands—shipyard workers, salvage crews, merchants, criminals, and everyone in between. Built into and around the asteroid, habitat modules had been carved from rock or constructed in natural caverns, their architecture a chaotic blend of dozens of civilizations' engineering philosophies.

The main habitation drum spun at precisely 0.7G, generating artificial gravity through rotation that had been maintained for so long the asteroid's core showed stress fractures from the constant torque. Environmental systems pumped recycled air through kilometers of ventilation shafts, the atmosphere carrying traces of machine oil, ozone from welders, and the distinctive metallic tang that came from so many species breathing the same processed oxygen.

Lights flickered from thousands of windows cut directly into the rock face—some were proper transparisteel viewports, others just holes covered with whatever clear material the occupants could scavenge. Each window told a story: a family's laundry hanging in artificial sunlight from grow-lamps, a merchant's neon sign advertising "AUTHENTIC CORE GOODS" in seventeen languages, shadows moving behind privacy screens in what were clearly brothels or drug dens or both.

The industrial sectors never slept. Welding sparks cascaded from the gantries in fountains of molten metal, crews working in shifts that ignored any planet's day-night cycle. A massive cargo hauler was currently being rebuilt in Gantry Three—its entire engine assembly had been removed and workers in powered exoskeletons were installing something that definitely wasn't standard manufacturer specs. The sparks from their work created a constant meteor shower of cooling metal that drifted into space, adding to the debris field one droplet at a time.

"Look at that," the navigator pointed to where three destroyer-class wrecks were being processed. Salvage crews in EVA suits swarmed over them like ants, cutting away valuable components. "They're stripping them down to the frames."

"Probably from the Air Marshal deployments," Wilson said, having arrived on the bridge. "That battle left enough scrap metal to keep this place running for decades."

Gantry Eight loomed ahead—a massive framework of carbosteel beams and magnetic clamps designed to hold a warship steady while crews worked. The structure itself was a testament to brute-force engineering, each beam thick enough to walk through, painted with reactive coating that shimmered between black and deep blue as it absorbed and redistributed electromagnetic forces. Power conduits ran along the framework like exposed veins, pulsing with enough energy to hold a hundred-thousand-ton battleship motionless against its own momentum.

Currently, it held the half-stripped remains of a heavy cruiser, classification markers still barely visible on its hull: CNS Indomitable. The ship hung in the gantry's embrace like a carcass in a butcher's shop, its valuable components already harvested—the bridge module had been cut away entirely, leaving a hollow socket where command decisions had once been made. Salvage crews had tagged the remaining sections with holographic markers: "GRADE-3 ARMOR - RESALE," "STRUCTURAL SUPPORTS - RECYCLE," "CREW QUARTERS - STRIP AND DUMP."

"They'll move that hulk for us," Conway said, watching as a cluster of tug-drones began attaching magnetic grapples to the cruiser's corpse. The drones were barely visible against the wreck's bulk, like remoras on a dead whale. "For a fee, of course."

"Everything costs extra here," Blake muttered, already pulling up the station's fee structure on his terminal. The list scrolled past in depressing detail: "Hulk Removal - 5,000 credits," "Gantry Cleaning - 2,000 credits," "Environmental Hookup - 500 credits per day," "Waste Processing - 300 credits per cycle." He spat tobacco juice into his cup with venom. "They're charging us for our own shit. Literally."

The tug-drones fired their engines in unison, the dead cruiser beginning its final journey to the breaker yards deeper in the asteroid. It moved with agonizing slowness, every meter carefully calculated to avoid collision with the gantry's framework or the Purgatory herself. Conway watched their clearance readings, calling out distances as tons of dead metal drifted past their viewports close enough to see individual rivet heads.

Kenney arrived on the bridge, looking more rested than he had in months. The dark circles that had been permanent fixtures under his eyes had faded slightly, and he'd actually shaved—his jawline clean for the first time since Nueva Kalloo. He wore his standard ship fatigues, but they were fresh, pressed even, the fabric still carrying the sharp chemical smell of the automated laundry. His sidearm sat in its usual position, but his hand wasn't constantly checking it the way it had been for years—that nervous tic of someone expecting violence at any moment.

Behind him, trying to stay unnoticed, was Valeria in borrowed crew clothing that didn't quite fit right. The standard gray coveralls were too long in the legs, bunched up at her ankles where she'd tried to roll them, and too broad in the shoulders, making her look even smaller than she was. Someone had found her ship boots that were close to her size, but she walked in them carefully, like someone not used to the magnetic soles that could lock to deck plating in zero-g. Her hair had been pulled back in a simple ponytail, revealing the faint surgical scars at her hairline that she usually kept hidden.

"I thought you were going to stay in quarters and rest," Kenney said quietly, though there was no real reproach in his voice.

"I wanted to see," she replied, her eyes wide as she took in the bridge's panoramic view. The way she moved through the space was distinctive—careful, deliberate, like someone who'd learned that sudden movements attracted unwanted attention. But there was curiosity there too, her gaze drinking in every detail of the tactical displays, the crew stations, the organized chaos of a working warship's command center.

Her eyes widened as she took in the view, her hands unconsciously gripping the viewport's edge until her knuckles went white. The surgical scars on her fingers—thin lines where someone had once opened them up for reasons she couldn't remember—stood out against her pale skin. "It's like a graveyard in space. All those ships... how many people died here?"

"Thousands," Wilson answered, moving to stand beside her. His augmented arms crossed over his chest, the servos in his cybernetic joints whirring softly as they adjusted to the motion. The prison tattoos on his neck seemed to pulse in the bridge's lighting as he spoke. "The Battle of Tortuga was one of the bloodiest of the LDS Civil Wars. Three fleets met here thinking they each had the advantage. Intelligence failures all around. None of them really won—just varying degrees of losing."

She pressed closer to the viewport, her breath fogging the transparisteel slightly. Her reflection overlapped with the carnage outside—a ghost among ghosts. Through the view, a small salvage craft drifted past, its magnetic grapples towing what looked like a fighter's cockpit module. The canopy was cracked but intact, and inside, still strapped to the ejection seat, the pilot remained at their post—frozen for decades, their final moment preserved in ice and vacuum.

"They're picking the bones clean," she murmured, her modified mind making connections at unusual angles. Her fingers traced patterns on the viewport—equations maybe, or possibly memories trying to surface. "Making profit from tragedy. Taking apart the dead to keep the living flying."

"That's Hammerhead," Blake said, shifting his weight to lean against his console. He pulled out his tin of tobacco with practiced movements, the metal worn smooth from years of the same gesture. "They don't judge, don't take sides, don't ask where you got the holes in your hull or the blood on your deck plates. Just process the dead and service the living. Morality's a luxury they can't afford out here."

Valeria's hand found the viewport again, this time pressing flat against it as if she could somehow reach through to the frozen pilot. "Do they ever find anyone alive? In the wrecks?"

Wilson's expression darkened, his scarred face telling its own story. The cybernetic eye whirred as it refocused, its red lens contracting like a mechanical pupil remembering things better left forgotten. "Sometimes. Usually wish they hadn't. Vacuum does things to people when life support fails slow—blood boiling in the veins, moisture sublimating from every membrane, consciousness lasting just long enough to feel it all happen. Better to go quick."

His augmented hand moved unconsciously to his throat, where old decompression scars formed a necklace of white lines against dark skin. Everyone on the bridge knew the story—Wilson had survived a hull breach on Marcus Prime, spent forty seconds in hard vacuum before rescue arrived. The experience had cost him an eye, most of his throat, and any ability to see space as anything but hostile.

The docking sequence began with Conway's hands dancing across holographic controls that materialized above his console. Each gesture sent commands through the ship's neural network, adjusting thrust vectors by fractions of meters per second. They had to navigate through a designated corridor in the wreck field, passing between the hollow shells of dead ships that loomed like canyon walls on either side.

"Proximity alert starboard," the navigator called out, her fingers pulling up a magnified view. "Dead frigate, distance forty meters and closing."

Conway micro-fired the port thrusters, the whole ship groaning as it shifted laterally. Through the viewports, they could see directly into the frigate's blown-out bridge—command consoles dark, chairs still perfectly arranged, a coffee mug somehow still mag-locked to a dead captain's armrest.

The massive mechanical arms of Gantry Eight began their approach, each one the size of a city block, moving with surprising delicacy for something that could crush a destroyer. Electromagnetic clamps at their ends crackled with visible energy, purple lightning playing across contact surfaces as they sought the Purgatory's designated hardpoints. The first arm made contact with a reverberating clang that echoed through every deck, the ship actually shifting several meters as thousands of tons of mechanical force gently but firmly took hold.

"Hard dock confirmed," Conway reported, sweat beading on his forehead from the concentration required. His hands finally released the controls, fingers cramping from the sustained precision work. "We're stable. Gantry's got us."

The mechanical arms continued their work, more clamps engaging along the Purgatory's spine and wings. Through the hull, they could hear the magnetic locks engaging in sequence—chunk, chunk, chunk—each one capable of holding a hundred thousand tons against the pull of gravity.

Through the viewports, they could see work crews already moving with the practiced efficiency of people who'd done this thousands of times. The lead team wore heavy EVA suits with reinforced joints—not for vacuum protection here, but to handle the massive equipment without servo-assistance crushing their bones. Some carried scanning arrays that looked like geometric spiders, their sensor arms unfolding to crawl across the Purgatory's hull, mapping every stress fracture and micrometeor impact with millimeter precision.

The cargo umbilical began its approach—a segmented tunnel fifty meters long and ten meters in diameter, its sections articulating like a mechanical serpent. The structure was built from transparent aluminum, allowing visual confirmation of cargo movement, with pressure rings every five meters that could seal independently in case of breach. It moved on its own propulsion system, small thrusters firing in calculated bursts as it navigated from the station toward the Purgatory's main cargo airlock.

"Umbilical approaching," Conway announced, watching its progress on his displays. "Contact in thirty seconds."

The passenger bridge followed—a more elegant structure with actual windows and climate control, carpeted flooring visible through its transparent sections. This one was for people who paid premium rates, complete with gravity plating that would maintain orientation regardless of the ship's position. It extended from a different section of the station, its approach guided by a pilot in a small tug who made micro-adjustments with hand signals to the automated systems.

The first connection was anything but smooth. The cargo umbilical's magnetic collar met the Purgatory's airlock with a grinding screech that resonated through the hull. Pressure sensors immediately began their dance—red lights flickering to amber as the two atmospheres fought to equalize. Through the transparent sections, they could see debris from the imperfect seal being blown into space in small puffs of crystallizing atmosphere.

"Seal integrity at ninety-two percent," someone reported. "Within acceptable parameters."

Others brought fuel lines—massive flexible conduits as thick as tree trunks, their surfaces ribbed with cooling coils to handle the superheated reaction mass that would refill the Purgatory's depleted bunkers. The fuel team approached with respect—one leak of that concentrated propellant and half the gantry would be ionized gas. Parts pallets followed on magnetic sleds, each one tagged with holographic manifests that flickered and updated as they moved, showing real-time inventory synchronized with the station's logistics network.

"All department heads to the CIC," Kenney ordered, his voice carrying the weight of command that made even veteran mercs straighten unconsciously. "We need to discuss shore leave rotation and procurement priorities."

The bridge crew began their shutdown procedures, hands moving across controls in practiced sequences. The navigation officer secured her star charts, encrypting them with her personal key—navigation data was currency in places like Hammerhead. The weapons officer powered down the targeting systems, each one requiring a specific shutdown sequence to prevent the capacitors from holding dangerous charges. Conway ran through his post-flight checklist, fingers dancing across holographic displays as he transferred helm control to the station's docking computer.

As the crew filed out through the bridge's armored bulkhead door, Valeria remained at the viewport, studying the floating graveyard. Her reflection in the transparisteel overlapped with the carnage outside, creating a double image—the living girl and the dead fleet occupying the same space.

"All those ghosts," she said quietly, her breath misting the viewport slightly. "Floating forever in the dark. Do you think they know they're dead?"

Kenney paused at the door, looking back at her. The bridge lighting cast harsh shadows across his features, making the exhaustion lines seem deeper. "The dead don't care what happens to their ships," he said, his tone carrying the weight of too many battles, too many friends left drifting in the void. "And the living need parts to keep flying."

She nodded slowly, her fingers tracing invisible patterns on the viewport. "I suppose we're all just trying to keep flying, aren't we? Even if we're made of salvaged pieces."

Through the viewport, another wreck drifted past—a passenger liner, the "Celestial Dream" still visible on its hull in faded gold lettering. Its windows were dark, slowly spinning through space for decades in a waltz with gravity that would continue until the stars burned out. Hammerhead Station had grown rich on such death, and now the Purgatory would add its credits to that economy of survival.

The walk to the CIC was short—just down the main corridor from the bridge, passing the sealed doors of officer quarters. Each door bore a nameplate and status light: Blake's showing green for "aboard," Wilson's amber for "on duty," several others dark for officers already heading to the station. The corridor's walls were lined with conduits and emergency equipment stations, everything functional, nothing decorative. Their footsteps echoed on the non-skid deck plating, the sound absorbed by the foam-steel bulkheads.

The CIC's armored door recognized Kenney's biometrics and cycled open with a pneumatic hiss. Scott Blake was already there at his logistics station. His datapad was propped against his console, displaying operational costs, and his spittoon sat within easy reach. The dented brass mug had "FUCK AROUND AND FIND OUT" etched into the side—last year's Christmas gift exchange, when Deadeye had drawn Blake's name and decided the straight-laced accountant needed something with personality.

"Boss, I'm taking Wilson and four of the security team to meet with suppliers," Blake announced, spitting a stream of dark tobacco juice into his brass cup with practiced accuracy. The sound echoed slightly in the CIC's metal confines. "Got appointments prearranged with three arms dealers and two parts wholesalers. Want to get business out of the way before enjoying port."

Blake pulled up his datapad, the holographic display flickering to life above the device to show a three-dimensional map of Hammerhead Station's labyrinthine interior. The merchant sector sprawled across multiple levels, color-coded by legitimacy—green for licensed dealers, amber for gray market, red for the areas where credits and blood changed hands with equal frequency. His finger traced a route through the maze, highlighting stops with gestural commands that left glowing waypoints hanging in the air.

"We're starting at Bonvillian's Heavy Armament on Level 19," he said, zooming in on a section that showed surprising organization compared to the chaos around it. "Former ARMSEA quartermaster, runs a tight operation. Then working our way through the salvage dealers in the Reclamation Quarter. Kowalski's got those targeting arrays Derg wanted, and Hex-Nine claims they found an intact magazine from a Confederate destroyer—thirty thousand rounds of 30mm, still in the original packaging."

"Raise me on comms if you need authorization for anything over a hundred thousand," Kenney said, watching the credit projections Blake had annotated on the map. "Especially if they try to push junk. Last time we were in port, scrappers tried to sell us weapons systems that were obsolete when my grandfather was flying."

"Will do." Blake's gaze shifted to Valeria, who had moved to the CIC's external viewports and was watching salvage crews dissect a freighter with the same intense focus she'd shown on the bridge. "What about our guest?"

"I'm taking her to get proper clothes," Kenney replied. "Can't have her walking around in borrowed coveralls forever. She needs to blend in if she's going to be crew."

Blake nodded, already pulling up his procurement list on a secondary screen, the items scrolling past in order of priority—ammunition, spare parts, medical supplies, food stores, and at the bottom, optimistically, "crew morale items" which everyone knew meant alcohol and entertainment subscriptions.

Blake's expression suggested he had opinions about that, but he kept them to himself. "The market district's on Level 3 through 5. Avoid the lower levels—that's where the organ merchants and worse operate."

"Noted." Kenney turned to address the bridge crew. "Conway, you have the conn. Announce to all departments: thirty-six hour liberty rotation for anyone not on essential duties or watch. Standard rules apply—no fights you don't win, no debts you can't pay, don't create or kill anything on leave, and nobody goes anywhere alone."

Conway grinned, already reaching for the ship-wide comm panel—a restored piece of military hardware with actual physical switches that clicked satisfyingly under his fingers. "Aye, Captain. The crew's going to love you for this."

He toggled the main broadcast switch, the one that would reach every compartment from the reactor room to the forward observation blister. A brief squeal of feedback echoed through the CIC as the system initialized, then his voice boomed through the Purgatory's corridors, processed through speakers that ranged from pristine military-grade to jury-rigged tablet computers zip-tied to bulkheads:

"All hands, this is the bridge. Thirty-six hour shore leave is authorized for non-essential personnel. Liberty rotation begins at 1400 hours ship time." He paused, letting that sink in, already imagining the cheers echoing through crew berthing. "Standard rules apply—no fights you don't win, no debts you can't pay, no marriages without command approval. Remember, you're representing the ship—try not to embarrass us too badly. Bridge out."

The moment he released the comm switch, they could hear the response through the deck plating—boots thundering as crew members rushed to prepare, lockers slamming open, someone whooping loud enough to echo through ventilation shafts.

Blake was already heading for the CIC exit, his movements efficient as he secured his datapad in a shoulder holster and checked that his credit chip was properly encrypted. "Come on, Wilson. Let's go spend some of Mr. Smith's money before the arms dealers figure out we actually have it."

Wilson fell in step beside him, his augmented hand automatically checking the charge level on his sidearm. The weapon sat in a custom holster that compensated for his cybernetic arm's different draw angle. "Think they'll have those new Viper automated infantry units everyone's talking about?"

"If they do, we can't afford them. But we'll ask anyway." Blake paused at the CIC exit, his hand on the door control as he looked back at Kenney. The overhead lighting caught the worry lines around his eyes—the look of a man who'd calculated too many bad odds. "Boss, watch yourself out there. Hammerhead's neutral, but that just means everyone's equally ready to stab you in the back. Nobody's your friend, nobody's your enemy, everybody's looking for a payday."

The CIC door cycled shut behind them with a soft pneumatic sigh, leaving Kenney and Valeria alone with the skeleton duty crew—two technicians monitoring ship security feeds, their faces illuminated by the glow of their workstations, already calculating how they'd spend their shore leave when the next rotation came up.

Kenney turned to Valeria. "Ready to see the station?"

She pulled herself away from the viewport, a mix of excitement and apprehension on her face. "I haven't been shopping in... I honestly can't remember when. Before they took us."

"Then let's fix that," he said, offering his arm in an oddly formal gesture—something from a more civilized age when soldiers were gentlemen between battles. "Every gorgeous woman needs beautiful clothes that she can call her own."

Valeria took his arm with a small smile, her fingers light on his forearm. They left the CIC through its main exit, entering the central corridor that ran the length of the ship like a spinal column. The passage was already transforming from military efficiency to barely-controlled chaos as liberty preparations took over.

The route to the airlock took them through the main crew areas. They passed the mess hall where Cookie was posting his "CLOSED FOR SHORE LEAVE" sign with obvious relief—thirty-six hours without having to pretend protein paste was food. Through the open door, they could see him pulling out a bottle of something amber from behind the industrial freezer, his personal stash that everyone knew about but nobody mentioned.

The corridor widened as they approached the primary airlock—designed to handle mass crew movements during emergencies, now serving as a funnel for desperate shore leave. The walls here bore the scars of the Purgatory's history: blast marks from a boarding attempt near Corvus, hastily-welded patches from that hull breach at Meridian, and someone's artistic graffiti of a naked woman riding a missile that had survived three captains and nobody had the heart to paint over.

The airlock corridor was already filling with off-duty crew, all eager to escape the ship's recycled air and gray walls. The atmosphere was electric—that particular energy of people about to be free, even temporarily. Someone had a portable speaker blasting music that thumped through the deck plates, the bass competing with the hum of the ship's systems.

Joker was there with several of the flight crew, dressed in civilian clothes that somehow still looked militant—cargo pants with too many pockets, boots that could double as weapons, jackets that didn't quite hide the knife sheaths. Her Neo-Slavic tattoos were on full display, sleeves rolled up to show the orthodox churches climbing her arms. She was applying lipstick using the reflection in a wall panel, the color a violent red that matched her flight helmet's kill markers.

"Captain!" she called out in her Russian accent, thick with amusement. "You are taking little bird shopping? Good! She needs color, not these gray rags we give her. Make her pretty, da? Though she is already prettier than most of these spacer suka who think they are God's gift."

Derg pushed past them, already lighting a cigarette despite the prominent NO SMOKING signs every three meters. His coveralls had been replaced with civilian clothes that had seen better decades—jeans with more patches than original fabric and a shirt advertising a bar that had been destroyed in the LDS civil wars. "Thirty-six hours to get properly drunk and forget that nukework. Don't expect me back sober, Boss."

"Don't expect me to bail you out if you get arrested," Kenney replied.

"Fair enough!" Derg took a long drag, blowing smoke toward the life support vents in specific defiance of regulations. "Though if I'm not back in forty-eight, check the drunk tank on Level 33. That's where they usually find me."

The airlock itself was a massive chamber, designed to hold a full platoon in combat gear. Now it was processing the crew in groups of twenty, the inner door cycling with mechanical precision. Each cycle took about thirty seconds—the automated systems scanning for contraband going out, checking atmospheric composition differences between ship and station, and verifying identities. Hammerhead's atmosphere had a slightly different mix than the Purgatory's—more industrial pollutants, traces of exotic compounds from alien life support systems—and the airlock's scrubbers provided a buffer zone to prevent the ship's systems from contamination.

The crew had formed a rough queue, the kind that existed more in theory than practice, with people constantly pushing forward or holding spots for friends. A holographic display showed the current atmospheric conditions on both sides—Purgatory running military standard mix, Hammerhead showing elevated carbon dioxide and trace benzene compounds that wouldn't kill you immediately but weren't doing your lungs any favors.

"Next group!" the automated system announced, and another twenty crew members surged forward, pressing their hands against the biometric scanner that confirmed they were authorized for shore leave and not currently on duty rotation.

The airlock cycled, and they stepped onto Hammerhead Station proper. The transition was jarring—from the Purgatory's military-grade environmental systems to the station's cobbled-together life support that had been expanded and modified so many times nobody remembered the original specifications. The docking arm was industrial brutalism at its finest, all exposed pipes sweating condensation and harsh sodium lighting that turned everyone's skin a sickly yellow. Overhead, massive ventilation fans churned with a rhythm that suggested they'd been repaired more than replaced, each blade slightly off-balance, creating a subtle whub-whub-whub that veteran spacers learned to tune out.

The customs checkpoint was a joke—three guards who'd clearly drawn the short straw, slumped in chairs behind scratched plexi barriers. One was openly playing a handheld game, the digital sounds of explosions tinny through his device's speakers. Another was eating something from a foil container that might have been food at some point. The third barely glanced at their IDs, running them under a scanner that beeped approval without him looking at the results.

"Purpose of visit?" he asked, already stamping their entry permits with a device that looked held together with prayer and adhesive tape.

"Shopping and resupply," Kenney answered.

"Yeah, you and everyone else. Stay out of the Underguts unless you're looking to disappear. Next!"

Beyond customs, the station opened up like a cancerous flower. Level 3's market district had been carved from the asteroid itself over decades of haphazard expansion. The original mining tunnels were still visible—smooth bore holes that had once sought precious metals now converted into thoroughfares. But where those original tunnels ended, human ambition had continued with less precision. Some sections were rough-carved, the rock face still showing drill marks. Others had been melted smooth by industrial lasers, the stone transformed into a glass-like surface that reflected the neon in nauseating patterns.

Neon signs competed for attention in a visual assault that would have been illegal on any regulated world. "AUTHENTIC SILKS" flashed in English and Mandarin next to "□□□□□□□ □□□□□□□ - □□□ □□□□□□□□" in Cyrillic. A holographic dancer gyrated above a brothel entrance, her form flickering between human and something decidedly not. Gene-mod parlors advertised their services with before-and-after photos that made Valeria unconsciously touch her own surgical scars.

The air was a cocktail of competing environments—cooking food from a dozen worlds creating a smell that was simultaneously appetizing and nauseating. The sharp ozone of spot welders from a repair shop operating right on the main thoroughfare, sparks cascading onto passing pedestrians who didn't even flinch. The musty, organic smell of recycled atmosphere that had passed through too many lungs, been filtered through systems running on patches and goodwill, and still carried traces of every species that had breathed it.

Crowds pushed through corridors that had been designed for mining equipment, not foot traffic. Salvage workers stomped past in mag-boots that hadn't been cleaned in months, their cybernetic arms designed for zero-G work clicking and whirring with each movement—some had replaced entire limbs with tool arrays, becoming more machine than man in pursuit of efficiency.

A merchant captain in a uniform that had once been prestigious—gold braid now tarnished, insignia from a fleet that no longer existed—argued with a vendor over the price of reactor coolant, their voices rising above the crowd's noise in what sounded like three different languages.

Working girls in clothing that wasn't so much revealing as a suggestion of clothing leaned against walls, their skin showing the telltale shimmer of pheromone mods designed to make them irresistible to humans. One caught Kenney's eye and winked, her eyelids closing horizontally, her three breasts flagrantly on display.

Station security moved through in pairs, their black armor scarred from actual combat, not parade-ground pristine. Their helmets' visors were dark, but the way their heads moved suggested they were scanning everyone, recording faces, looking for trouble or opportunity. One had a collection of ears hanging from his belt—trophies or warnings, depending on your perspective.

Valeria pressed closer to Kenney as they navigated the chaos, her fingers tightening on his arm each time someone brushed past. A salvager with exposed neural ports along his skull accidentally bumped her shoulder, mumbling an apology in a dialect that sounded like grinding gears. "It's so alive," she said, her voice carrying wonder despite the sensory assault. "So many people just... existing. Building lives in the cracks between death and commerce."

"People adapt," Kenney said, steering her around a puddle of something viscous that glowed faintly purple—either industrial runoff or alien bodily fluids, neither worth investigating. His hand found the small of her back, guiding her toward a clothing shop with an actual fabric display in the window. "They always find a way to keep going."

"Like us," she said quietly, then her entire demeanor shifted as she saw the shop window. Her eyes widened, and she pressed her nose against the transparisteel like a child. "Oh, is that real wool? Not just printed synthetics?"

"Let's find out," he said, pushing open the door. Instead of an electronic chime, actual brass bells rang—an anachronism that probably cost more than most station dwellers made in a month. The sound was startling in its purity after the electronic chaos outside.

The shop's interior was a sanctuary of fabric and thread. Bolts of material lined the walls in a rainbow of textures—everything from rough spacer's canvas to what looked like genuine Terran silk. An elderly woman sat at an ancient sewing machine that might have been older than the station itself, her fingers guiding fabric through the mechanical feet with practiced precision. She looked up at the bell's chime, and her eyes—augmented with subtle magnification implants that gave them an insect-like quality when they focused—immediately began cataloging everything about them.

Her gaze swept over Kenney first: the military bearing that no amount of civilian clothes could hide, the way his hand never strayed far from his sidearm, the quality of the weapon itself—not standard issue but not flashy either, the choice of someone who valued function over form. Then to Valeria: the ill-fitting coveralls that bunched and gaped, the way she held herself like someone who'd learned to take up as little space as possible, and most tellingly, the complete absence of any personal belongings—no jewelry, no datapad, nothing that said she owned anything in the universe.

"New arrivals," the woman said, not a question but a statement of fact. Her accent was unplaceable—the kind that came from living in too many systems for too long. She set down her sewing, rising with the careful movements of someone whose bones had been replaced at least once. She moved closer, her augmented eyes focusing with tiny mechanical whirs. "And the young lady... hmm."

She circled Valeria like a predator, but not unkind—more like an artist studying a canvas. "No undergarments of her own—the ship's standard-issue is chafing here," she touched Valeria's shoulder where the fabric had rubbed raw. "No shoes that fit—those boots are at least two sizes too large. Hair that hasn't seen proper care in months." She clicked her tongue. "Someone's been through the ringer, haven't they, dear?"

Valeria flushed but lifted her chin. "I need... everything, I suppose."

"Everything," the woman repeated, and her weathered face split into a smile that revealed teeth replaced with ceramic implants. "Oh, it's been years since someone needed everything. Come, come. We'll build you a wardrobe from the skin out. Make you beautiful—no, make you feel human again. There's a difference."

She was already pulling Valeria toward the back of the shop, past racks of completed garments that looked like they belonged in different centuries and different worlds. "You," she pointed at Kenney without looking back, "sit there. This will take time. There's tea in the pot. And don't touch the merchandise with those gun-oil hands."

As Valeria was whisked away behind heavy velvet curtains that had probably once graced a luxury liner's first-class cabin, Kenney found a chair and settled in. The seat was surprisingly comfortable—salvaged from some captain's ready room, the leather worn soft by decades of use. Through the shop window, he could see the station continuing its commerce—deals being made, arguments being settled, people trying to survive another day in the shadow of a thousand dead ships.

"Stand still, dear," the shopkeeper's voice drifted from behind the curtain. "Arms up—yes, like that."

Kenney could hear the soft whir of measurement lasers, the shopkeeper recording Valeria's dimensions with precision tools that created a three-dimensional model for custom fitting.

"My goodness, you're tiny," the woman muttered. "But good proportions. We can work with this."

There was rustling, fabric moving, then Valeria's surprised laugh—the first genuine happiness he'd heard from her. "This is so soft!"

"Salvaged from the Starlight Princess," the shopkeeper said proudly. "Passenger liner that went down forty years ago. I bought three wardrobes from the first-class cabins—the vacuum preserved everything perfectly. Try this one."

More rustling. When the curtain parted slightly, Kenney caught a glimpse of Valeria in a deep blue dress that had probably cost someone's annual salary. The fabric shimmered with embedded fiber optics that created subtle constellation patterns. She was looking at herself in a mirror, her expression one of wonder.

"It fits perfectly," she said softly, running her hands down the fabric.

"The woman who owned it was about your size," the shopkeeper said, adjusting the hem with practiced movements. "A diplomat's wife, according to the ship manifest. She had excellent taste."

"It feels strange," Valeria admitted, "wearing a dead woman's dress."

"Everything here belonged to someone dead, dear. But fabric doesn't care about ghosts, and beauty deserves to be worn, not float in vacuum forever." The shopkeeper stood back, appraising. "Now, let's try something more practical."

Over the next hour, Kenney watched the curtain part periodically as Valeria modeled different finds. A flight suit from a courier service, modified with decorative stitching. Work clothes from an engineering crew, taken in to fit her small frame. A formal gown that made her look like she belonged at a Core World gala rather than a station carved from rock.

"This one's my own creation," the shopkeeper said proudly, and Valeria emerged in an outfit that was clearly custom work—pants that moved like liquid shadow, a top that seemed to shift color depending on the angle, both fitted perfectly to her form. "I've been working on this fabric blend for months. Thermally adaptive, self-cleaning, and practically indestructible."

"It's incredible," Valeria said, moving experimentally. The clothes moved with her, never binding or pulling. She looked at Kenney, a slight blush coloring her cheeks. "What do you think?"

"Beautiful," he said simply, and meant it. The clothes transformed her from a refugee in borrowed rags to someone who belonged wherever she chose to be.

The shopkeeper smiled knowingly. "Now for the underthings. A woman needs proper foundation garments, not whatever industrial nonsense the ship provided." She pulled Valeria back behind the curtain. "These are from my private collection—silk from actual worms, not the synthetic stuff. A freighter captain traded them for repairs years ago."

There were more soft sounds, fabric against skin, then Valeria's voice, slightly breathless: "Oh, these are... I'd forgotten clothes could feel like this."

When she finally emerged, dressed in a practical but flattering combination of the custom pants and a salvaged military jacket tailored to her size, she looked like a different person. The clothes fit properly, moved with her body instead of hanging off it. She stood straighter, moved with more confidence.

"Seven complete outfits," the shopkeeper announced, packaging everything in vacuum-sealed bags. "Undergarments, sleeping clothes, and two pairs of boots that actually fit. Everything you need to feel human again."

As Kenney paid—the price was steep but fair for custom work and salvage—the shopkeeper leaned close to Valeria. "You hold onto him, dear. Men who'll spend that much to see you properly clothed are rarer than honest station administrators."

"Come on," Kenney said after they'd collected the packages, Valeria still glowing from the transformation. "There's something you should see. The real Hammerhead experience."

He led her down through the station's levels, each descent marking a shift in the station's character. They took a freight elevator that had been converted for passenger use—badly. The walls were still bare metal marked with load ratings in a dozen languages, and something organic had died in the corner, leaving a stain no one had bothered to clean. The elevator shuddered and groaned as it descended, occasionally stopping between floors while its ancient systems decided whether to continue.

Level 5 was where the legitimate businesses began to thin out. The lighting here came from industrial panels jury-rigged to the ceiling, half of them flickering or dead.

Level 6 housed what the station euphemistically called "personal services"—brothels with windows displaying their workers like merchandise, gene-mod parlors where you could have your humanity surgically amended, and establishments offering experiences that required liability waivers written in languages most humans couldn't pronounce.

Level 7 was the buffer zone—abandoned mostly, the corridors dark except for emergency lighting that cast everything in hellish red. They passed through quickly, Kenney's hand on his sidearm, though the only life they saw was a maintenance bot that had been stripped for parts and left to twitch against a wall, its servos still trying to complete some long-forgotten task.

The fighting pits were on Level 8, carved from a natural cavern in the asteroid that pre-dated human settlement. The entrance was marked by a massive archway cut from the living rock, polished smooth by thousands of hands touching it for luck. Holographic displays flanked the entrance, showing previous fights in graphic detail—blood spraying in slow motion, violence frozen at the moment of impact, credits changing hands in streams of numbers that updated in real-time.

The sound hit them first—a roar of voices that seemed to come from the asteroid itself, echoing up through the entrance tunnel. The smell followed: sweat, blood, ozone from the barrier fields, and something primal that spoke directly to the hindbrain about violence and survival.

They descended carved steps worn smooth by decades of traffic. The walls here were covered in graffiti—names of fighters who'd died gloriously, odds for upcoming matches, propositions in various languages, and crude artwork depicting acts of violence that would be considered war crimes in civilized space.

The tunnel opened into the cavern proper, and Valeria gasped. The space was enormous—a natural hollow in the asteroid that stretched up into darkness, the ceiling lost in shadow. The architects had worked with the natural formation, carving seating directly from the rock in concentric circles that descended toward the pit itself. Thousands of people filled those seats, their combined voices creating that roar they'd heard above.

The arena itself was massive. The cavern had been hollowed out over decades to create a bowl shape, with seating tiers carved directly from the asteroid's iron-rich rock. The stone had been polished in places by countless bodies sliding across it, while other sections remained rough enough to tear skin. In the center, a cage made of reinforced titanium mesh could be raised or lowered through the floor on massive hydraulic pistons. Currently, it was down, enclosing two figures in a twenty-meter octagon. The mesh itself hummed with low-level electricity—not enough to kill, just enough to discourage fighters from using it to climb or escape.

"Kenney!" A woman's voice cut through the crowd noise. Vera waved from a section near the cage—McKnight's mistress, a woman in her late twenties with the kind of beauty that turned heads even in a place like this. She had the toned physique of someone who worked out religiously, her skin decorated with geometric tattoos that shifted color under the arena lights. She wore a tank top that showed off her midrift and cargo pants that suggested she could handle herself in a fight. Her hair was dyed electric blue, pulled back in series of braided ponytails. She'd been with McKnight for years now—longer than most—and had somehow managed to win over his kids, who were notoriously protective of their father. The children were all there, standing on their seats to see better, the younger ones on the older ones' shoulders.

They pushed through the crowd, a living organism of greed and bloodlust. Salvage workers clutched betting slips in grease-stained fingers, the papers already soft from sweaty palms. Off-duty mercs shouted odds in the harsh argot of a dozen militaries, their voices competing to be heard. Station prostitutes worked the audience with professional efficiency, their hands finding wallets while their marks watched the violence below.

Vendors moved through the throng with trays suspended from their necks on grav-repulsor units that kept the weight off but couldn't prevent the trays from swaying dangerously. "Grilled Kroone sticks!" one called, the smell suggesting the protein's origin was best left unquestioned. "Mountain beer! Guaranteed less than forty percent synthetic! Stim-tabs, three for twenty credits—keep you awake for the whole card!"

Kenney flagged down a vendor whose tray held various snacks in packets labeled in languages he didn't recognize. He bought a bag of something called "void corn"—kernels that had been flash-frozen in vacuum then rapidly heated, causing them to puff up into crunchy spheres that were somehow both freezing and hot. Valeria tried one tentatively, her expression shifting from suspicion to delight at the sweet coating that tasted vaguely of caramel and something fruity.

In the cage, McKnight was stretching, his scarred torso gleaming with sweat under the harsh lights. Killjoy and Priest stood in his corner. Killjoy was wrapping his hands while Priest—true to his name—appeared to be giving some kind of benediction.

"Who's he fighting?" Kenney asked Sylvianne.

"Some gene-modded thing from the outer Fringe," she said, not taking her eyes off her lover. "Calls itself Tarrind. Look at it."

McKnight's opponent was horrific. Seven feet tall, snake like features, muscles bulging unnaturally under skin that looked scaled and too tight. Its arms were longer than they should be, knuckles dragging near its knees. The genetic modifications were obvious—probably illegal military augmentation, the kind that killed most subjects but made the survivors into monsters.

"LADIES AND GENTLEMEN!" The announcer's voice boomed through speakers carved into the cavern walls. "TONIGHT'S MAIN EVENT! IN THE RED CORNER, THE SERPENT SUPREME, THE GENE-WARPED WARRIOR... TARRIND!"

The crowd roared. Betting slips changed hands frantically.

"AND IN THE BLUE CORNER, THE CONFEDERATE KILLER, THE FATHER OF TWELVE, THE MAN THE MYTH THE LEGEND... MCKNIGHT!"

"DAD! KILL HIM!" Tommy screamed, his small voice lost in the crowd's noise.

The bell rang—a ship's collision alarm repurposed for drama, its warbling electronic scream designed to trigger primal fear responses in spacers who knew that sound meant hull breach. The echo bounced off the cavern walls, multiplying until it seemed to come from everywhere at once.

Tarrind moved first, frighteningly fast for something so large. Its gene-modded muscles fired in sequence, the augmented fibers contracting with enough force to crack bone. Its elongated arm—a full meter longer than baseline human proportions—swept toward McKnight's head in a arc that displaced air with an audible whoosh. The knuckles had been surgically enhanced with subdermal carbon fiber plates, turning the fist into a biological hammer. At that velocity, connection would have separated McKnight's head from his shoulders, sending it spinning into the crowd like a grotesque souvenir.

McKnight ducked, his combat reflexes firing before conscious thought. He dropped so low his palms touched the cage floor, feeling the wind from Tarrind's swing ruffle his hair—that close to death. He rolled left, the textured metal of the cage floor scraping skin from his shoulder, and came up behind the creature in one fluid motion. His military training showed in every movement—no wasted energy, no telegraphing, just pure efficiency refined through hundreds of real combat engagements.

His counterattack was textbook close-quarters combat. Three strikes to the kidney area in rapid succession, each one delivered with his full body weight behind it. His fist impacted with meaty thuds that echoed through the arena—the kind of sounds that made audiences wince. The first strike landed perfectly on the floating rib, designed to rupture the organ beneath. The second drove deeper, targeting the cluster of nerves that should have dropped anything with a human nervous system. The third was insurance, delivered with enough force that McKnight's knuckles split against the creature's hide.

Against a normal human, any one of those strikes would have ended the fight. The kidney would have ruptured, flooding the abdominal cavity with blood. The nerve cluster would have sent the victim into shock. The pain alone should have dropped Tarrind to its knees.

The creature barely flinched. Whatever they'd done to transform it from human to this had included redundant organs, rerouted nervous systems, and pain inhibitors that turned agony into mere information.

"The modifications run deep," Valeria said quietly, watching with an analytical eye. "Look at the scales covering his skin. Like organic armor."

The creature spun with inhuman speed, its enhanced muscle groups firing in perfect sequence. The backhand caught McKnight across the jaw with the sound of a thunderclap. The impact lifted him off his feet, sending him flying across the cage like he'd been hit by a ground car. He hit the electrified mesh hard, the low-voltage current making his muscles spasm as he bounced off. Blue sparks danced where his skin had made contact, leaving electrical burns that would hurt for weeks if he survived the next few minutes.

The crowd's collective gasp created a pressure wave in the enclosed cavern. Blood ran from McKnight's nose in two steady streams, painting his chin and chest red. He shook his head, trying to clear the ringing that drowned out everything except his own heartbeat. Through blurred vision, he could see Tarrind advancing—not rushing, just walking forward with the confidence of an apex predator that knew its prey was wounded.

"Get up, Dad!" Sara yelled, her young voice cutting through the crowd noise with the pure desperation only a child watching their parent in mortal danger could produce. She was standing on her seat, hands cupped around her mouth, tears streaming down her face but her voice steady. "GET UP!"

McKnight heard her through the fog of near-unconsciousness. His hand found the cage floor, pushed. His legs felt like they belonged to someone else, responding seconds after he told them to move. Tarrind was five meters away. Four. Three. Each footfall shook the cage structure, the creature's weight warping the metal grid beneath its feet.

McKnight rolled away from Tarrind's stomp, the creature's foot denting the cage floor. He was in trouble—his normal techniques weren't working. The thing was too strong, too durable.

"Switch tactics!" Killjoy shouted from the corner. "It's not human anymore! Rip his dick off!"

McKnight understood. The next time Tarrind charged, he didn't dodge completely. Instead, he shifted his weight minutely, letting the creature's momentum work against it. Tarrind's massive hand clamped around McKnight's throat, lifting him off the cage floor. The creature's grip was like a hydraulic press, each finger capable of crushing bone. McKnight's feet dangled, kicking uselessly as his airway compressed.

But this was exactly where McKnight wanted to be. Close enough that Tarrind's reach advantage meant nothing. Close enough that the creature's own bulk blocked its vision. Close enough for what came next.

McKnight's hand came up fast, his thumb extended like a blade. He drove it into Tarrind's left eye with all the force his oxygen-starved muscles could generate. The eye was soft—no amount of genetic modification could armor jelly. His thumb sank in to the second knuckle with a wet pop that was audible even over the crowd's roar. He twisted, feeling the optical nerve tear, the lens rupture, the vitreous humor spurting out between his fingers.

Tarrind howled—a sound that started as human scream and descended into something primitive and bestial. The creature's enhanced vocal cords produced frequencies that made the crowd closest to the cage clutch their ears. It threw McKnight with such force that he actually dented the cage where he hit, the titanium mesh bending inward to cradle his body before springing back and dropping him to the floor.

But now it was half-blind, green fluid leaking from the ruined socket—not blood but something synthetic, probably a nutrient solution for the enhanced tissues. The fluid glowed faintly in the arena lights, leaving phosphorescent trails down Tarrind's face. The creature pawed at its destroyed eye, its movements suddenly less coordinated. Depth perception gone, balance compromised, it stumbled slightly as it turned to track McKnight.

"That's it!" Priest called from the corner, his deep voice carrying absolute conviction. "The Lord helps those who help themselves! David had his sling, you've got your thumb!"

The fight turned brutal. McKnight stopped trying to box and started trying to survive. He circled Tarrind carefully, keeping to the creature's blind side, but the cage was only twenty meters across—not much room to maneuver when your opponent had arms that could reach halfway across it.

"Dad needs an edge!" Tommy shouted from the crowd, his child's mind seeing the solution with clarity that escaped the onlookers. The six-year-old broke free from Sylvianne's grip and sprinted toward the cage, dodging through legs and around vendors.

"Tommy, no!" Sylvianne screamed, pushing through the crowd after him.

The boy reached the cage's edge where a maintenance worker had left a polymer push-broom—the kind used to sweep blood and teeth from the floor between fights. Tommy grabbed it and shoved the whole thing through the mesh with all his small strength.

"Dad! Here!"

McKnight dove for it, rolling as Tarrind's fist cratered the floor where he'd been. His hands closed around the broom, and in one motion he snapped it over his knee, the polymer handle breaking with a sharp crack. He now had two weapons—each piece about half a meter long with jagged, splintered ends where they'd separated.

When Tarrind charged again, McKnight didn't retreat. He swept low with his leg, catching the creature's ankle. Combined with its blind momentum, Tarrind went down hard, eight hundred pounds of gene-modded muscle hitting the deck with an impact that made the entire cage structure groan.

McKnight was on the creature instantly, driving one broken broom half deep into Tarrind's chest where the ribs met. The jagged polymer punched through the scaled skin with a wet crunch, finding the gap between modified bones. Green fluid spurted from the wound—that same synthetic blood that had leaked from its eyes. The creature's howl cut off into a gurgling wheeze as the makeshift stake found something vital.

But Tarrind wasn't done. Even with a polymer shard in its chest, it tried to rise, its enhanced physiology fighting through damage that would have killed anything baseline human.

McKnight was on its back instantly, arm around its throat.

"Choke's not gonna work!" someone in the crowd yelled. "Thing don't need air like we do!"

But McKnight wasn't trying to choke it. He was using leverage. His legs wrapped around Tarrind's torso, his arms locked around its head, and he began to twist.

"Oh god," Sylvianne whispered, covering the youngest child's eyes.

The crowd went silent, the collective intake of breath creating a vacuum in the cavern. McKnight wasn't taking chances. His hands found either side of Tarrind's massive head, fingers digging into the scaled flesh for purchase. The creature was still twitching, its enhanced nervous system trying to fire signals through severed pathways.

With a roar that came from somewhere primal, McKnight twisted and pulled simultaneously. The sound started as tearing—wet, organic, like fabric ripping underwater. Then came the crack of vertebrae separating, each one popping in sequence like firecrackers. Cartilage stretched, snapped. Blood vessels that had been reinforced with synthetic fibers fought against the separation before finally giving way with sounds like breaking guitar strings.

McKnight's muscles stood out in sharp relief, every vein visible as he continued pulling. The crowd watched in horrified fascination as the inevitable became reality. With a final, catastrophic separation of tissue and bone, Tarrind's head came free.

McKnight stood, holding the massive head by its hair-like appendages, green fluid dripping onto the cage floor in thick ropes. The body below him spasmed once more, then went completely still. He dropped the head, and it landed with a wet thud that echoed through the absolute silence of the arena.

For three heartbeats, nobody moved. Nobody breathed.

Then the arena exploded. Credits flew through the air like confetti. The cage began lowering into the floor, automated systems already preparing to dispose of Tarrind's remains.

"DAD!" All twelve kids rushed forward as the cage fully retracted, jumping on McKnight despite the blood and gore covering him. He caught them, laughing through his exhaustion, lifting the smallest onto his shoulders where they sat like victorious princes despite the carnage around them.

"Ice cream for everyone!" he announced to his children.

"You're insane," Sylvianne said, but she was smiling as she kissed him, not caring about the blood and sweat.

Valeria watched the family celebration, her hand unconsciously finding Kenney's as they stood at the crowd's edge. Her fingers interlaced with his naturally, like they'd been doing this for years instead of days. The gore and violence of moments before seemed to fade as she watched the children pile onto their blood-covered father, their joy unmarred by the carnage surrounding them.

"They're happy," she said softly, her thumb tracing small circles on Kenney's hand. The gesture was unconscious, intimate. "Even here, even after watching their father almost die, after seeing him tear a man's head off with his bare hands, they're happy."

"It's their normal," Kenney replied, drawing her slightly closer as the crowd jostled around them. The warmth of her against his side felt right, natural in a way that surprised him. "Kids adapt to whatever world they're born into."

She turned to face him then, the arena's harsh lights catching the gold flecks in her brown eyes he hadn't noticed before. The question came suddenly, but her voice was gentle, almost vulnerable: "Did you ever want children? Before?"

The question hit like a physical blow, but softer somehow with her looking at him like that. He thought of Kira, of the nursery they'd planned in their quarters, the names they'd playfully argued about during long hyperspace jumps. The future that had been atomized along with her in that convoy.

"Yeah," he said quietly, his voice rough. "We were going to try after my tour ended."

Valeria stepped closer, eliminating the small space between them. She reached up with her free hand, her palm resting against his chest, feeling his heartbeat. "I'm sorry," she said, and the words carried weight—not just sympathy, but understanding from someone who'd lost their own futures to violence.

Around them, the arena was starting to clear, crowds dispersing to collect winnings or drown losses. But in their small bubble of space, Valeria rose up on her toes and kissed his cheek, a gesture both tender and bold.

"Thank you," she whispered against his ear, "for giving me a chance at a different future."

The way she looked at him then—not with pity for his losses but with hope for what they might build together—made something shift in his chest. A loosening of the constant ache he'd carried for three years.

In the cage, McKnight was letting his kids ride on his back, playing monster despite having just killed an actual monster. The crowd was already clearing, moving on to the next fight, the next bet, the next chance to feel alive.

"Come on," Kenney said. "Let's go find that ice cream shop before McKnight's kids eat all their inventory."

They followed the celebrating family out, leaving Tarrind's modified corpse for the station's recycling crews. The corridors leading away from the arena were thick with dispersing crowds—winners clutching credit chips like religious talismans, losers already calculating what they could pawn to cover their debts. By tomorrow, even Tarrind's remains would be salvage—organs harvested for research despite their modifications, bones ground for calcium supplements that would end up in someone's morning nutrition paste, nothing wasted in Hammerhead's economy of efficiency.

The ice cream shop was four levels up, in what passed for Hammerhead's "family district"—a section where the brothels were required to keep their doors closed and the drug dealers at least pretended to be selling candy. The sign read "Cosmic Creamery" in flickering neon, half the letters struggling to maintain their glow. Through the transparent aluminum window, they could see McKnight already at the counter, his children bouncing with excitement as they pressed their faces against the display case.

Inside, the shop was a strange attempt at normalcy in the chaos of Hammerhead. The walls were painted with murals of Old Earth ice cream trucks floating through space, serving cones to aliens that probably violated several xenobiology accuracy standards. The freezer units hummed with the labored sound of equipment well past its warranty, held together by determination and creative engineering.

"What'll it be?" the proprietor asked—a heavy-set man with prosthetic taste buds on his tongue, visible when he talked. "Got fresh shipment yesterday. Real dairy from the agri-platforms, not that synthetic protein substitute."

The flavors were displayed in neat rows, each more improbable than the last. "Neutron Star Swirl"—black ice cream with silver sparkles that supposedly tingled on your tongue. "Quantum Mint"—which changed temperature as you ate it. "Void Vanilla"—classic flavor in unsettling pure white. "Supernova Strawberry"—pink with pop rocks that simulated stellar explosions in your mouth.

McKnight's kids were already demanding everything. "Four scoops of Asteroid Crunch!" Tommy shouted, pointing at a gray concoction studded with what looked like actual rocks but were probably just sugar crystals.

"Plasma Berry for me," Sara said more reasonably, though she still wanted three scoops.

Kenney looked at Valeria. "What sounds good?"

She studied the display with the same intensity she'd shown watching the fight, as if the choice of ice cream was a crucial decision. "The Cosmic Swirl," she decided, pointing at a flavor that seemed to shift between purple and blue. "It looks like hyperspace."

"Two small cones of Cosmic Swirl," Kenney told the proprietor, who began scooping with practiced efficiency.

They found a table in the corner while McKnight's family took over three tables, the kids already getting ice cream on everything despite Sylvianne's attempts at damage control. The contrast was surreal—minutes ago they'd watched their father decapitate a gene-modded monster, now they were arguing about who got to try whose flavor.

Valeria took a small bite of her ice cream, her eyes widening. "It tastes like... I don't even know. Like if starlight had a flavor."

"Marketing," Kenney said with a slight smile, though he had to admit the flavor was unlike anything he'd tried. "Probably just sugar and synthetic flavoring."

"Still," she said, taking another bite, "sometimes the lie is better than the truth."

They ate in comfortable silence for a moment, watching the McKnight clan melt down. Tommy had already dropped his cone once, and Sylvianne had ordered a replacement with the pragmatism of someone who'd factored ice cream disasters into the family budget.

Valeria turned to him, a small smear of purple-blue ice cream at the corner of her mouth. "Why is it called Kilkenney Solutions? Your name isn't Kilkenney, it's just Kenney."

He stopped mid-bite, the question catching him off-guard. The ice cream suddenly tasted too sweet, too artificial. Most people assumed it was a family name, a corporate identity, something that didn't need explaining.

"It's not a name," he said quietly, setting his cone in the holder and moving his chair closer to hers to avoid being overheard by the celebrating family. The shop's background noise—freezers humming, kids laughing, the distant echo of station life—seemed to fade. "It's... a statement of intent."

Valeria studied his face with those perceptive eyes, her own ice cream temporarily forgotten. A drop of melted Cosmic Swirl ran down the cone onto her fingers, but she didn't notice. "I don't understand."

Kenney leaned against the rough asteroid wall, trying to find the words. Around them, station life continued—vendors hawking wares, drunken sailors stumbling past, the constant background hum of recycled air.

"When Kira died, I wanted to die too," he said, the words coming out flat, matter-of-fact. "But I couldn't bring myself to do it. Couldn't just... eat a bullet. Felt like cowardice, somehow. Like giving up."

"So you found another way," Valeria said softly, understanding beginning to dawn on her face.

"I came up with a plan. Start a mercenary company. Take the worst contracts, the suicide missions, the jobs nobody else would touch. Fight and kill and keep putting myself in harm's way until eventually..." He shrugged. "Until someone did what I couldn't do myself."

"Kill Kenney," she whispered. "It's a solution to kill Kenney."

"Kilkenney Solutions," he confirmed, bitter smile on his face. "Been three years. Somehow I keep surviving. Keep walking away from things that should have killed me. That nuke on Regalia? Should have been it. The Mithril mechs? Should have been it. But here I am."

Valeria moved closer on the bench they shared, her leg pressing against his. The ice cream shop's other patrons created a bubble of noise around them—McKnight's kids arguing over flavors, the freezer units humming their mechanical lullaby, the proprietor haggling with a customer over the price of imported dairy. A drop of her Cosmic Swirl ice cream dripped onto their joined hands, cold and sticky-sweet.

"That's... that's one of the saddest things I've ever heard," she said, her voice barely audible over Tommy declaring that Asteroid Crunch was objectively the best flavor in the galaxy.

"It's practical," he said, watching the purple-blue ice cream melt between their fingers. "I get to go out fighting. The crew gets paid well for the dangerous work. Everyone wins."

"Do they know? Blake, Wilson, the others?"

"Blake probably figured it out. He's too smart not to. But we don't talk about it."

She was quiet for a moment, processing this revelation while her ice cream continued its slow melt. Through the shop window, they could see Hammerhead's eternal commerce—a salvage crew dragging reactor components past, their exoskeletons leaving gouges in the corridor floor. The contrast between the violence of their lives and this moment of sweetness wasn't lost on either of them.

"What about now?" she asked finally, turning to face him fully. Her free hand came up to wipe a drop of ice cream from his chin, the gesture intimate and natural. "Do you still want that? To have someone... complete your solution?"

Kenney looked at her—this strange girl who'd survived horrors he could only imagine, who'd sought comfort in his bed just to escape her nightmares. In the shop's flickering light, with ice cream on her lips and hope in her eyes, she looked like everything he'd thought he'd never want again.

"I don't know," he admitted. "Things feel... different around you."

"Different how?"

He struggled to articulate it, his thumb absently stroking her hand. "Like maybe there's a reason I kept surviving. Like maybe I was supposed to be there to pull you out of that hellhole."

"Fate?" she asked, a small smile playing at her lips as she leaned closer. "That's terribly romantic for a man with a death wish."

"Not fate. Just... timing. Coincidence. I don't know." He brought their joined hands up, sticky with melted ice cream, and kissed her knuckles despite the mess. "All I know is that for the first time in three years, I went to sleep without wanting it to be permanent."

She set down what was left of her cone and cupped his face with her free hand, forcing him to meet her eyes. "Perhaps we saved each other then. You from your solution, and me from my nightmare."

"Maybe," he said, leaning into her touch.

They sat there for a moment in the cosmic ice cream shop, two damaged people finding something worth keeping in each other. Around them, McKnight's family continued their celebration—Sylvianne had given up on keeping them clean, Sara was trying to steal bites of everyone's ice cream, and Tommy had somehow gotten Neutron Star Swirl in his hair.

"Would you consider changing it?" Valeria asked suddenly. "The company name?"

"To what?"

She smiled, real and warm. "I don't know. Something about second chances. Or just 'Kenney Solutions'—solving problems without the death wish."

He laughed—not bitter, but genuine. "I'll think about it."

"Good," she said, then picked up her cone again. "Because I rather like having you around, Kenney Jaeger. Death wish and all."

They finished their ice cream as McKnight's family began their exodus, the kids now sticky with various flavors despite Vera's efforts with napkins that seemed to just spread the mess around. Tommy had to be carried, already crashing from his sugar high, while Sara tried to convince her father to go back for seconds.

"Thanks for the show, McKnight," Kenney called out as they passed.

McKnight grinned, his face still swollen from the fight but his spirits high. "Next time I'm charging admission. These kids are expensive."

Outside the Cosmic Creamery, the station's artificial day cycle was shifting toward evening. The harsh white lighting was dimming to amber, supposedly to help maintain circadian rhythms though most station dwellers had given up on regular sleep cycles years ago. The corridors were less crowded now—the morning shift heading to bars, the evening shift trudging to their posts with the resigned expressions of people who'd drawn the short straw.

They descended through the levels via a cargo lift that shuddered with every floor. Two salvagers shared the space with them, their exoskeletons powered down but still reeking of cutting fluid and scorched metal. One had a fresh bandage wrapped around his head, blood already seeping through—occupational hazard of salvage ops.

"Level 27," one salvager said to his partner, his voice muffled by a half-melted respirator. "That's where Crross said the good stuff is. Intact military AI cores from that Confederate destroyer."

"Cross's full of shit. That wreck's been picked clean for decades."

They exited at Level 15, leaving Kenney and Valeria alone in the groaning lift. She moved closer to him; their hands still intertwined despite the lingering ice cream stickiness.

"This place never stops, does it?" she observed, watching the level indicators flash past. "Always someone working, someone fighting, someone trying to survive another day."

"That's life on the Fringe," Kenney replied. "No safety nets, no guarantees. Just what you can take or make for yourself."

The lift shuddered to a stop at Level 22, deeper than most legitimate businesses operated. Here the corridors were narrower, carved roughly from the asteroid's rock without much concern for aesthetics. They had to step around a man passed out against a wall, empty stim injectors scattered around him like spent shell casings.

"One more stop," Kenney said as they walked, still holding hands. The gesture felt natural now, her fingers fitting perfectly between his. "Need to get your ID chip updated. Can't have you scanning as nobody forever."

He led her down a side corridor, then another, each one seedier than the last. The lights here flickered, and the walls were stained with things best not examined closely. They stopped at a door marked only with a medical caduceus that had been modified—the snakes were eating each other.

"Try not to touch anything," he warned, pushing the door open.

The smell hit first—disinfectant failing to cover decay and ozone. Behind a scratched plexi barrier sat an old man, his fingers replaced with surgical manipulators that clicked against each other constantly. One eye was a cheap cybernetic that focused independently from the other.

"What you need?" the man asked, his voice like gravel in a disposal unit.

"New ID chip," Kenney said simply. "Clean install."

The man's good eye fixed on Valeria while the cybernetic continued scanning the room. "Female, approximately eighteen to twenty-two standard years, baseline human..." He pulled up a holographic display, text scrolling past. "I got options. Fresh harvests from the wreckage fields."

Valeria tensed, but Kenney squeezed her hand reassuringly.

The list appeared—dozens of names, each with a small photo and basic details. All young women who'd died in various battles, their bodies recovered by salvage crews who sold more than just ship parts.

"This one," the old man highlighted an entry. "Confederate Ensign, communications division. Very clean death—explosive decompression, no trauma to the chip. Tavo Manwill, age twenty-one, born on an agri world, educated at the Confederate War College."

"Let me see the full record," Kenney demanded.

More details appeared on the old man's display. Tavo had been a junior communications officer on the CNS Meridian, a destroyer that had been hulled six months ago during a routine patrol near the Thessalonica jump point. Pirates had hit them with an EMP mine that killed their systems, then carved through the hull with mining lasers. The entire crew vanished—no bodies officially recovered, no confirmation of death, just an empty hulk drifting in space.

The Meridian had been towed to Hammerhead by those same pirates, sold to the breakers for scrap value. The old man's records showed the transaction—seventeen bodies recovered and processed, their ID chips harvested before the corpses were recycled into protein base. Standard salvage economy. But officially, the Confederate Navy had no idea what happened to the crew.

"Good clean death, no official confirmation," the old man continued, his surgical fingers clicking faster as he pulled up more data. "Confederate Navy lists her as MIA—Missing In Action. No body, no confirmation, just gone. They'll keep her on the rolls for five years before declaring her dead. Perfect for you—she could theoretically still be alive somewhere."

The irony wasn't lost on Kenney—Valeria would be taking the identity of someone killed by pirates, sold for parts at the very station where they now stood, but officially just "missing." In the eyes of the law, Tavo Manwill might have escaped in a pod, might be a prisoner somewhere, might be anything. It gave Valeria's new identity flexibility that a confirmed death wouldn't.

"She was twenty-one," Valeria said softly, reading the display. "Had her whole life ahead of her."

"Still does, technically," the old man emphasized. "The Confederates think she might be floating in a life pod somewhere. Now that life is yours, if you want it. Better than letting a perfectly good identity rot in my storage."

"How much?" Kenney asked.

"Five thousand credits."

"Two thousand."

"You insult me," the man's surgical fingers clicked faster. "This is a premium identity. Clean harvest, full background, no security flags. Four thousand."

"Twenty-five hundred, and you extract her old chip."

The cybernetic eye swiveled to focus on him."Three thousand total, both procedures."

Kenney transferred the funds, his account barely registering the loss after their recent windfall. The old man smiled, revealing teeth replaced with titanium implants.

"Sit," he commanded, gesturing to a surgical chair that had seen better decades.

Valeria sat carefully, trying not to think about who else had been in this chair, what had been done to them. The old man wheeled over, producing an injector that looked military-grade.

"This contains Ensign Manwill's chip. Hold still."

He pressed the injector against Valeria's neck, just below her hairline. There was a soft hiss, then pressure as something pill-sized pushed under her skin. Valeria gasped but didn't move.

"Good, good," the man muttered, already preparing an extraction tool. "Now the old one."

He ran a scanner over her neck, then her arm, finally finding the dead chip near her shoulder. "Professionally wiped," he noted with interest. "Someone didn't want you to exist."

The extraction was quick—a small incision, surgical manipulators reaching in to grasp the dead chip, pulling it free. He dropped it in a specimen container and handed it to Kenney.

"You're now Tavo Manwill," he told Valeria. "Confederate citizen, clean record. Don't do anything to make people look too close."

As they left, Valeria rubbed the injection site. "That woman—Tavo—did she have any family? People who think she's dead?"

"She is dead," Kenney said gently. "You're just borrowing her name."

They emerged back into the main corridors, leaving the chop shop's decay behind. The transition was jarring—from the medical stench and flickering lights to the industrial chaos of Hammerhead's arterial passageways. Here, the station's true nature revealed itself: a massive organism of commerce and survival, its metal veins pumping with the lifeblood of desperate humanity.

Overhead, exposed conduits leaked condensation that had passed through so many recycling systems it probably contained trace DNA from half the sector's human population. A maintenance drone whirred past at head height, its anti-gravity repulsors creating a localized pressure wave that made Valeria's newly-purchased clothes ripple. The drone's optical array swiveled to scan them—routine security protocol or something more sinister, impossible to tell on Hammerhead.

Valeria had an identity again. She existed in the system, could travel, could start over. The weight of that—of suddenly being someone in the galactic databases—seemed to settle on her shoulders like armor.

"Thank you," she said, her fingers unconsciously touching the injection site where Tavo Manwill's life had been inserted into hers. "For giving me a chance to be someone again."

"Everyone deserves to exist," Kenney replied, guiding her around a gravity flux where two sections of the station met imperfectly—a remnant of haphazard expansion that created a pocket where up and down briefly disagreed. "Even if it's under borrowed names."

His comm unit buzzed against his ribs, the vibration cutting through the ambient station noise. The device was military-grade, its quantum encryption creating a brief halo of static on nearby displays as it established a secure channel. Blake's voice came through, carefully neutral but with an undertone that Kenney recognized—the sound of a man who'd found either an opportunity or a trap, possibly both.

"Boss, need your input on a supply contract. Got something interesting here."

"Where?" Kenney's hand moved instinctively to his sidearm, a gesture so automatic he didn't realize he'd done it.

"Sending coordinates." Blake's transmission included a data packet that made Kenney's comm grow warm as it processed the encryption. "Level 12, industrial sector. Crater Mining Group warehouse."

The coordinates appeared on his comm's display as a three-dimensional map, showing their current position as a blue dot and the destination as pulsing amber. The route wound through seven levels and three different atmospheric zones—Hammerhead's attempt at accommodating various industrial processes that required different air mixtures.

Kenney looked at Valeria. In the station's harsh industrial lighting, her new identity seemed to sit uneasily on her, like clothes that technically fit but weren't quite broken in yet. "Business. Want to come or head back to the ship?"

"I'll come," she said, that curious intensity returning to her eyes. "I'm curious about everything here."

The Crater Mining Group corporate offices—thirty floors of black glass and military-grade steel. The logo glowed in holographic cyan above the entrance, shifting to gold as Kenney and Valeria approached through the plaza. The black glass had been hauled in at enormous expense during the colony's boom years, a declaration that this rock would be more than just another mining outpost. At its base, a circular fountain sent water arcing twenty feet into the air, the spray catching the habitat dome's artificial light before crashing back into a pool lined with polished asteroid stone.

The fountain's mist drifted across the plaza, cutting through the recycled air's metallic tang with something that almost resembled Earth-normal humidity. Visitors would slow as they approached, breathing deeper, their lungs grateful for the reprieve from the station's perpetual dryness. The water's endless cascade almost drowned out the hum of the air recyclers and the magnetic clicks of boots on the plaza's metal decking, where miners coming off-shift mixed with corporate liaisons headed for the transit tubes.

Valeria paused at the fountain's edge, the mist settling on her face like a benediction. "Oh, Kenney, isn't it perfectly sublime how the water catches the light? Like diamonds being perpetually born and destroyed—such tragic beauty!" She rummaged in her pocket, producing a small credit chip. "One simply must make a wish in a fountain that tries so valiantly to bring grace to this carved-out rock we call home."

"That's a week's worth of food," Kenney said, but his voice held more amusement than protest.

"Some things," Valeria said, closing her eyes as she held the chip between her fingers, "are worth more than protein. I'm wishing for something magnificent—not just ordinary magnificent, but the kind that makes one's soul feel too large for one's body." She tossed the chip with a theatrical flourish, watching it disappear into the churning water. "There! I've cast my dreams into the fountain's keeping. Though I suppose it's dreadfully romantic of me to believe that water recycled through infinite cycles of station plumbing could carry wishes anywhere at all."

Kenney shook his head but reached for her hand, pulling her away from the spray before her uniform got soaked. "Come on, Anne of Green Asteroid. CMG management doesn't like to be kept waiting."

"Anne of Green Asteroid!" Valeria clutched his arm, delighted. "That's the loveliest thing you've called me all week. Though this place could use some green, don't you think? Just imagine—vines crawling up all that imposing black glass, turning corporate tyranny into a verdant paradise!"

The reception area continued the theme: polished floors, comfortable chairs, a wall display cycling through footage of mining operations across the system. The secretary looked up from her desk as they entered—her console pinged their ID chips the moment they crossed the threshold. Red hair caught in perfect waves, her CMG uniform tailored in ways the company definitely didn't pay for. The kind of curves that suggested someone upstairs understood that mining contracts often got negotiated by lonely frontier men.

"Captain Jaeger?" Her smile was practiced warmth with just enough suggestion. "They're expecting you. Can I offer you anything? Coffee? Tea? We just received a shipment of Confederate blend."

"Oh, do you happen to have any soda? Something deliciously, breathtakingly cold that might rescue me from this absolute desert that's taken residence in my throat?"

"Of course." The secretary opened a recessed cooler behind her desk, producing a can with frost still on it. "And for you, Captain?"

"I'm good."

"Right this way, then."

The secretary's heels clicked across the polished floor as she led them through a security door that required her biometric scan. The corridor beyond was lined with offices—middle managers behind glass walls, working at displays full of production quotas and shipping schedules. She moved with the confidence of someone who knew she was being watched, and knew exactly what that was worth.

"Your colleagues arrived about two hours ago," she said over her shoulder, keying another security door. "Our logistics director is briefing them now."

The door opened onto a cargo elevator. The polished corporate facade ended abruptly—industrial coating on the floors, exposed conduits on the ceiling. The secretary's expression didn't change as the elevator descended, as machine oil and ozone began filtering through the vents.

Valeria cracked the soda, the hiss loud in the confined space. The secretary's eyes flicked to it briefly, a micro-expression of distaste crossing her features before the professional smile returned.

"So," Kenney said, nudging Valeria's shoulder, "why does my perfectly normal girlfriend sometimes transform into a Victorian poetry enthusiast? The 'divine icy rapture' of soda? Really?"

Valeria took a long sip, then gave him a slightly embarrassed smile. "My mother used to read us these ancient stories from Earth—about this red-haired girl who saw everything as if it were magical and tragic and wonderful all at once. Anne something." She shrugged, rotating the can in her hands. "I suppose I found it a rather delightful way of looking at things, especially in a place like this. I try not to, honestly, but when I'm nervous it just... emerges. Like my brain decides ordinary words aren't quite enough for the situation."

"You're nervous now?"

"Aren't you? This is my first time anywhere so utterly devoid of life—back home we had crops and growth cycles and things that reached toward light. Here it's all carved rock and recycled air that tastes of forgotten things."

"Loading dock three," the secretary announced when the doors opened onto the warehouse proper. The cacophony hit them—pneumatic hisses, crane warnings, the constant hum of magnetic rails overhead. "Your party is at the logistics station. Just follow the yellow line."

She gestured into the organized chaos, then turned back toward the elevator. "If you need anything else, just call up to reception."

The warehouse thrummed with the constant motion of a supply hub that never slept. Overhead, magnetic rails carried container after container in crossing patterns—mining charges, atmospheric processors, drilling assemblies—all headed for the bellies of ships bound for mining sites across the sector. The crane operators worked their stations in glass booths suspended twenty meters up, orchestrating the mechanical ballet.

They followed the arrows painted on the composite floor, dodging a loader that whined past with a pallet of pressure suits. Another freighter had just locked in—umbilicals snaking out to feed it fuel and supplies while crews swarmed its cargo holds.

Machine oil hazed the air. Pneumatic hisses marked each container seal breaking, each manifest scanner confirming delivery. Workers in coveralls marked with CMG patches moved between the towers of crates, tablets in hand, checking serial numbers against shipping orders. Normal dock business. The kind that kept the frontier running.

The logistics station sat in a cleared section between the cargo racks—a fortress of scratched steel and embedded displays. A man in his fifties leaned against the desk, work pants and a red CMG polo shirt barely stretched over a gut earned from late nights and fast food, one hand resting on the desk's surface while shipping data flowed beneath his fingers in red and green streams.

Blake and Wilson stood studying the holographic manifests floating above the station, their body language suggesting they'd been there long enough to grow impatient. Two CMG security guards in tactical gear had positioned themselves with good sightlines of their guests. Professional contractors, from the way they held their weapons—slung but ready.

Another man—tropical shirt over cargo pants, drink sweating in his hand—observed from beside a stack of crates with military-grade locks.

Behind Blake and Wilson, four Kilkenny Solutions operators had spread out in a loose casual formation. They wore civilian clothes, hands never far from concealed weapons. Professional, but relaxed enough not to escalate tensions in what was supposed to be a friendly business meeting.

The logistics chief straightened as they approached. "Captain Jaeger?" He extended a calloused hand that told a different story than the manicured offices upstairs. "Lem Cleavon. I run the practical side of things down here."

His eyes moved to Valeria, took in the soda, eyes lingering a little too long. "Was just explaining to your boys that CMG finds itself with some excess inventory.

Kenney's attention stayed on the man in the tropical shirt. Something familiar nagged at him—the jawline, the way the eyes sat, the general proportions of the face. He knew those features, but they were... off. Like looking at someone's brother who'd had bad plastic surgery, or a wax sculpture made from photographs rather than life. The face was wrong in every small detail that mattered. Too smooth here, too sharp there, as if someone had tried to recreate him from memory and gotten close but not close enough.

"Let me guess," Kenney said slowly. "Smith?"

"Oh, how perceptive of you!" The man's grin widened. "Though I'm here in an advisory capacity with CMG. I don't believe we've met before but I've been told I have one of those faces. I understand you're looking for munitions?"

Kenney shifted slightly, mouthing "Clone?" to Blake, who gave an almost imperceptible shrug.

"Your reputation precedes you," Smith continued. "Kilkenney Solutions is a successful mercenary company, reliable completion rate. Exactly what kind of people CMG likes doing business with."

"What business is that?" Kenney asked, taking one of the overstuffed chairs facing the desk. The leather creaked under his weight, the cushions compressed from years of nervous contractors sinking into negotiations they couldn't afford to lose. The chair was positioned deliberately low, forcing anyone who sat to look up at whoever stood behind the desk—a power play as old as commerce itself.

Valeria perched on the armrest beside him, one leg swinging idly as she studied the room with open curiosity. Her free hand rested naturally on Kenney's shoulder for balance, her thumb absently tracing small circles. Just as Smith opened his mouth to continue his pitch, she tilted the can back for a long, loud slurp—the aluminum crackling slightly as she tried to coax the last drops from the bottom. The sound echoed in the corporate quiet like a belch in a cathedral.

Smith's smile froze, his eye twitching slightly. One of the security team winced. Valeria, completely oblivious to the disruption she'd caused, continued peering into the can with disappointment, giving it a little shake to confirm it was truly empty.

Smith cleared his throat, and Lem Cleavon smoothly stepped forward, his calloused hands activating a holographic display with practiced ease.

"Look, Captain, I'll give it to you straight," Lem said, his tone shifting from corporate polish to dock worker pragmatism. "The arms embargos to the Fringe have made quality munitions scarcer than honest politicians. ARMSEA's strangling supply lines, the Confederates are hoarding, and what does make it out here is either overpriced garbage or factory seconds that'll jam when you need them most."

The holographic screen materialized above the desk, rotating slowly to show rows of ammunition types—30mm autocannon rounds, 70mm rockets, 125mm tank shells, missile systems, even specialty rounds like incendiary and armor-piercing variants. Each category showed quantity available and specifications.

"But we've got stockpiles at forty percent below market," Lem continued, gesturing at the display. "Military grade, not that knock-off shit from the pirate factories. Fresh from Confederate manufacturing, still in the original packaging. Everything on your procurement list and then some."

"So what's the catch?" Kenney asked, studying the ammunition listings with a soldier's eye for details that might kill you later.

"We have to pick it up," Blake said from behind them, his voice carrying the weight of someone who'd already done the math. "It's on a death world a couple jumps from here."

Lem tapped the display, and the ammunition catalog dissolved into a rotating image of a planet—lush green from pole to pole, the jungle canopy broken only by rivers that gleamed like silver veins. Cloud systems swirled across the surface in patterns that suggested violent weather. The data readout showed atmospheric composition, gravity, temperature ranges—all technically within human survivable limits, but just barely.

"Death world is a little harsh," Lem said, zooming in on a section of jungle that looked thick enough to swallow light. "We prefer the term 'not conducive to human habitation.' The atmosphere won't kill you immediately, but extended exposure without proper filtration..." He made a vague gesture that suggested unpleasant consequences.

Smith cut in smoothly, "Clandora has some mothballed facilities we're in the process of bringing back online for resource extraction. The stores had been brought in to support the previous occupants—security battalions that were stationed there during our initial survey operations."

The display shifted to show a fortified compound carved out of the jungle, landing pads and defensive walls creating a bubble of civilization in the green hell. Or what had been civilization—the images were clearly older, from when the base was operational.

"Previous occupants," Wilson repeated flatly. "Past tense."

"Who were the previous security forces?" Kenney asked, noting the careful past tense.

"An in-house team," Lem said, pulling up personnel files that flickered past too quickly to read individual names. "Mostly ex-Rogue Marines, good people. Experienced. Well-equipped."

Smith's jaw tightened slightly. "Contrary to company policy, their commander led them on some sort of... Custer's last stand. We were forced to abandon the facility rather than reinforce a lost position."

"Custer's last stand," Wilson repeated slowly. "Against what? The wildlife?"

"The indigenous population proved more... organized than initial surveys suggested," Smith said carefully. "But the resources there are too important to simply write off. That's why we're spinning things back up—smarter this time, with better intelligence and more appropriate rules of engagement."

Lem pulled up mineral surveys, the readings showing concentrations that made Blake whistle low despite himself. "Resource deposits that make most mining operations look like sandbox games. We're talking about enough rare earth elements to fund wars."

"Or die in one," Blake muttered, studying the tactical data. "How many people in this in-house team?"

"Two hundred contracted operators," Lem admitted. "Forty-eight Sentinel-class mechs."

The room went quiet except for Valeria absently tapping her empty can against the chair's leather arm, seemingly fascinated by the different sounds it made.

"So what's the ask?" Kenney said, cutting through the sales pitch. "I mean, you're not giving us this discount out of the goodness of your hearts."

Smith's salesman smile shifted into something more calculating. "We need Kilkenney Solutions to provide security at the base and the mine site until a new security battalion can be brought in. Maybe six months tops. Act as advisors to the staff on site and conduct operations against the wildlife as needed."

"Six months?" Blake nearly choked on his tobacco juice. "That's not a supply run, that's a deployment."

"My mechs aren't really ideal for jungle combat," Kenney said, leaning back in the too-low chair. "Sentinels are designed for that environment. Our machines are built for open warfare, not fighting through triple canopy."

Lem touched the display again, bringing up aerial footage of both sites. The base was carved into a hillside, with clear fields of fire extending three hundred meters in every direction—the jungle had been burned back, leaving scorched earth that would take years to reclaim. The mine site was even more open, a massive pit carved into the planet's surface with terraced levels descending into darkness.

"Wide sight lines," Lem pointed out, highlighting the defensive positions. "Your heavy caliber weapons would handle even the worst the planet has to offer. Nothing's getting through those kill zones without taking significant fire."

"The previous team cleared these areas specifically for mechanized defense," Smith added. "Before their... unfortunate decision to pursue the enemy into the jungle against explicit orders."

Valeria had been quiet, but she suddenly spoke up. "Indigenous wildlife? What kind?"

The two exchanged glances. Smith answered smoothly, "Large fauna. The locals call them various names. They're just animals—dangerous if you're unprepared, but your mechs shouldn't have any trouble."

Kenney looked at Blake, who shrugged. They needed the supplies. Blake was already doing calculations on his datapad, then back at the CMG team. "Since this is more than just a pickup, what kind of payment terms are you offering?"

Smith and Lem exchanged glances. Lem pulled up a new display—contract terms scrolling past in corporate legalese.

"Two hundred and fifty-two million credits base payment for the six-month deployment," Smith began. "Plus combat bonuses of one hundred and fifty thousand per confirmed hostile megafauna kill, scaled up depending on threat classification. Full medical coverage for your personnel, death benefits standard to ARMSEA regulations—one hundred thousand per KIA paid to designated beneficiaries."

"Plus the forty percent discount on current munitions," Lem added. "And preferential rates on all supplies during the deployment. Food, fuel, spare parts—all at cost plus five percent instead of standard markup."

Blake looked up from his datapad. "That's actually... not terrible."

"We're also offering a completion bonus," Smith continued, sensing their interest. "If you successfully maintain security for the full six months and we're able to resume mining operations, an additional thirty-three million credits."

"Fine. We'll do the job," Kenney decided. "Standard payment terms?"

"Half now, half on delivery."

As they completed the details of the transaction, Smith walked them to the door. "One more thing—the locals, the indigenous population, they can be... territorial. Best to avoid them entirely."

"I thought you said it was just wildlife," Valeria said.

"Semantics," Smith replied. "They're barely sapient. Blue-skinned primitives with spears and bows. Nothing your weapons can't handle if they're foolish enough to interfere."

They emerged back into the plaza where the fountain still sent its arcs of precious water into the recycled air. The mist felt cooler now as the station's cycle shifted toward evening. Valeria immediately drifted back toward the fountain's edge, trailing her fingers through the spray while the others gathered in a loose circle near enough to talk privately but far enough that the water's crash would mask their conversation from any surveillance.

Blake immediately said, "This stinks worse than Derg's engineering console."

"Obviously," Kenney agreed, watching Valeria chase rainbow patterns in the mist. "Security forces don't 'fall through' because of wildlife."

Wilson leaned against the fountain's rim, his augmented arm clicking as he crossed it over his chest. "Two hundred operators and forty-eight mechs don't just vanish. That's a full battalion. You'd need serious firepower to take them down."

"Blue-skinned primitives," Valeria said thoughtfully. "That's an odd detail to mention."

Blake spat tobacco juice onto the ground. "Smith said they were barely sapient. But barely sapient doesn't wipe out a battalion."

Valeria had wandered around to the fountain's far side, where she'd found some kind of aquatic maintenance bot skimming debris from the surface. She was poking at it, watching it try to clean around her interference with apparent delight.

"The money's too good," Wilson said. "Three hundred million total for six months' work? That's retirement money."

"That's 'you probably won't survive to spend it' money," Blake corrected. "They're not paying us for security. They're paying us to genocide the locals."

Kenney watched Valeria accidentally knock the maintenance bot off course, sending it spinning in confused circles as it tried to reacquire its cleaning pattern. "We go in ready for anything," he decided. "Full combat load, everyone stays with the ship except who's necessary for base securement."

"We could just take the munitions and run," Wilson suggested. "Grab the supplies, skip the deployment."

"And have CMG blacklist us across the sector?" Blake shook his head. "We'd never get another corporate contract."

Wilson nodded. "I'll pull what data I can on Clandora. See what really happened to their security forces."

"This is the big time," Kenney said, watching the maintenance bot finally recover its cleaning pattern. "If we want to play ball, we're going to have to take risks. It's part of the job."

Blake spat into the fountain, earning a disgusted look from a passing corporate type. "Do you think this was what the other Smith meant by opening doors? The one from Nueva Kalloo?"

"Could be." Kenney considered it, remembering that strange conversation in the abandoned facility. "ARMSEA doesn't exactly view wiping out wildlife as legal, but they don't have lawyers to complain for them. So it's probably not a publicly available offer."

"Meaning CMG needs deniable assets," Wilson said, understanding dawning on his scarred face. "If this goes bad, we're just another failed mercenary company. If it goes well, they get their mining operation without official corporate fingerprints on whatever happens to the indigenous population."

Valeria had made her way back to them, her clothes slightly damp from playing in the mist. "The little robot was trying so magnificently hard to clean in perfect spirals! But now I've taught it chaos, and it seems much happier making random patterns." She looked at their serious faces. "Are we going to the jungle world then?"

"Looks like it," Kenney said. "Unless anyone has strong objections?"

Blake calculated on his datapad one more time. "The money would solve a lot of problems. Get us proper repairs, maybe even another ship. But if a full battalion couldn't handle whatever's there..."

"We're not a battalion," Kenney pointed out. "We're ten mechs and a carrier. Sometimes smaller is better—less threatening, more mobile, harder to track."

"Or easier to overwhelm," Wilson countered.

The fountain's mist had shifted with the evening cycle, the water pressure dropping as the station diverted power to other systems. The plaza was emptying now—the corporate workers heading to their hab units, the dock workers beginning their night shifts. A cleaning crew had emerged from service tunnels, their industrial vacuums humming as they began the endless task of keeping the corporate facade presentable.

Kenney made his decision. "We take the job. But we go in smart—scout first, establish secure positions, and keep the Purgatory ready for immediate dust-off if things go sideways."

"And when they do go sideways?" Blake asked, already resigned to the inevitable.

"We adapt. It's what we do." Kenney turned from the fountain, the others falling in behind him. "Let's get back. We need to brief the crew and start preparations."

They moved through the plaza toward the transit corridors that would take them back to the docking levels. The shift change meant crowds—workers in CMG coveralls heading home, their replacements heading in, everyone moving as if they'd made this journey thousands of times.

Valeria had fallen quiet, her earlier playfulness replaced by thoughtful observation. She studied the corporate workers, the way they moved in predetermined patterns, never making eye contact, never deviating from their paths. Her hand found Kenney's as they entered the main corridor, her fingers slipping between his with casual intimacy.

The corporate sector gave way to industrial passages, the polished floors becoming non-slip grating, the art becoming safety warnings in a dozen languages. The smell changed too—from filtered air and subtle cologne to machine oil and ozone.

"Tell me about before," she said. "Before Kira. Who were you?"

"Nobody special," Kenney replied, guiding her around a group of drunk salvagers. "An officer in the Rogue Marine Corps, started as infantry, worked my way up. Thought I was serving something bigger than myself."

"And were you?"

"No. Just serving politicians who saw us as numbers on deployment charts." He paused as they passed a row of brothels, neon signs advertising various pleasures. The working girls called out to passersby, some human, some modified, all promising escape.

Normally, this was where he'd stop. Find oblivion in synthetic pleasure, anonymous bodies, enough alcohol to forget. The self-destructive pull that had driven him for three years.

But with Valeria's hand in his, he felt... nothing. No pull toward the abyss. The neon lights were just lights, the promises just noise.

"You're not stopping," she observed, following his gaze.

"No need to," he said simply.

"Because of me?"

"Because with you, the pain is..." he searched for words. "Quiet. Like it's still there but it can't reach me."

They walked in comfortable silence through the market district, past vendors closing up shop, past off-duty crews heading to bars. It felt oddly normal, like something couples did on stations across the galaxy—evening walks, hands held, nowhere particular to go.

"I don't remember much from before," Valeria said eventually. "Fragments mostly. A house with yellow walls. Someone singing. The smell of bread baking. Then the facility, and everything before feels like someone else's dream."

"Maybe that's better," Kenney suggested. "Starting fresh."

"Is that what we're doing? Starting fresh?"

He stopped walking, turned to face her. In the amber light, she looked older than her years, those eyes holding depths he couldn't quite read.

"I don't know what we're doing," he admitted. "This isn't... I haven't felt anything since Kira died. Haven't wanted to. And now..."

"Now?"

"Now I'm walking through a station holding hands with a girl who shouldn't exist, and it feels like the most natural thing in the world."

She smiled, that mix of innocence and knowing that defined her. "Like a date. A very strange date in a very strange place, but still."

"Is that what this is?"

"It could be," she said. "If we wanted it to be."

They continued walking, eventually returning to the Purgatory. The ship was quiet, most of the crew still on liberty. They made their way through empty corridors to officer country.

At Kenney's quarters, he paused. "You can take the guest cabin. It's small but—"

"No," she said quietly. "Please."

"Valeria..."

Her voice was a low, sultry challenge, her eyes locked on his with a fire that made his pulse race. "I know what I want, Kenney," she purred, stepping closer, the recycled air of the station humming like a distant heartbeat. "The question is... what do *you* want?"

The ship groaned somewhere deep in its metal bones, but the sound faded against the heat radiating from her. The moment hung heavy, electric, every second pulsing with raw possibility.

Valeria moved through the dim glow of his quarters, her hips swaying with deliberate intent. She stopped at the edge of his bed, her fingers brushing his chest, sending a jolt through him. Years of pent-up hunger surged in his veins, mirrored in the way her touch demanded more—demanded *him*.

"You sure about this?" His voice was rough, barely containing the need clawing at him.

She leaned in, her breath hot against his ear, her lips grazing his skin. "I've never wanted anything more," she whispered, her voice dripping with desire. "I want you to fuck me, Kenney. Make me feel *alive*."

Her words ignited him. He grabbed her, pulling her against him, their bodies crashing together with desperate urgency. Her lips found his, hungry and unrelenting, her tongue teasing his with a promise of what was to come. She tasted like sin and salvation, her scent—tropical flowers, sweet fruit, and pure, primal sex—flooding his senses.

Valeria tugged his shirt over his head, her nails raking through the hair on his chest, leaving trails of fire. She straddled him, her thighs clamping around his hips, the heat of her core pressing against his hardening cock through their clothes. His hands roamed her curves, cupping her full breasts, her nipples stiffening under his palms as he teased them with slow, deliberate pressure. She gasped, her head tipping back, her body arching into his touch.

"Fuck, Kenney," she moaned, grinding against him, her hips rolling with a rhythm that made his blood pound. Her hands slid down, deftly freeing him from his pants, her fingers wrapping around his throbbing length. She stroked him—slow at first, then faster, her thumb circling the head, slick with his arousal. Every touch sent a surge of heat through him, his cock twitching in her grip.

He slid his hand beneath her shorts, finding her slick and ready. His fingers brushed her clit, and she let out a guttural moan, her face burying in his neck as her hips bucked against his hand. He worked her expertly, circling, pressing, sliding two fingers inside her tight, wet heat. Her moans grew louder, her body trembling as she rode his hand, her nails digging into his shoulders.

"More," she gasped, her voice raw with need. "I need you *now*."

He didn't hesitate. He yanked her shorts off, her skin glowing in the faint light, every curve begging to be touched. She pushed him back onto the bed, climbing over him, her thighs straddling him as she guided his cock to her entrance. The first slow, deliberate slide of her heat over him was torture—exquisite, mind-numbing torture. Her eyes widened, a soft cry escaping her lips as she took him deeper, her walls gripping him like a vice.

"Fuck, you're tight," he growled, his hands gripping her hips as she began to move, her breasts bouncing with each thrust. She rode him hard, her moans filling the air, her body slick with sweat and desire. He thrust up to meet her, their rhythm primal, unrelenting, the slap of skin on skin echoing in the small quarters.

Her nails raked down his chest, leaving red lines that stung deliciously. He grabbed her ass, guiding her harder, faster, her moans turning to cries as she neared the edge. "Kenney," she panted, her voice breaking. "I'm gonna—"

Her orgasm hit like a supernova, her body convulsing, her thighs trembling as she clenched around him, pulling him deeper. The sight of her—head thrown back, lips parted, her body shuddering with pleasure—pushed him to the brink. He thrust harder, deeper, the heat building until he couldn't hold back. With a guttural groan, he spilled inside her, the intensity blinding, his body shaking as wave after wave of pleasure tore through him.

She collapsed against him, her breath ragged, her skin hot against his. But she wasn't done. Her lips found his again, kissing him with a hunger that reignited the fire in his veins. Their tongues tangled, hot and heavy, as she pressed herself closer, her body still pulsing with the aftershocks of her climax.

"Fuck, you taste good," he murmured, his hands roaming her back, her ass, pulling her tighter against him. Her scent—sex and sweetness—wrapped around him, intoxicating.

"We should sleep," she teased, her voice husky, but her fingers were already tracing his jaw, his chest, dipping lower to stroke him back to life.

"Sleep's overrated," he growled, flipping her onto her back. She laughed, a sound that turned into a moan as he kissed his way down her body, tasting every inch of her. They didn't sleep—not for hours. They explored each other, bodies and desires laid bare, every touch a discovery, every moan a confession.

When they finally lay tangled together, her fingers traced lazy patterns on his chest. "What now?" she asked, her voice soft but steady.

"Tomorrow, we fight," he said, his voice low. "Clandora, blueies, whatever comes. But after that..."

"After that, we keep going," she finished, her lips curving into a wicked smile. "Together."

"Together," he echoed, pulling her close, already hard again at the thought of her.

For the first time in three years, Kenney fell asleep without ghosts, without guilt, without the weight of his own planned destruction. Just the warmth of another person who'd chosen to be there, who'd chosen him despite or because of the broken pieces.

Outside, Hammerhead Station continued its commerce of salvage and survival. But inside his quarters, two people had found something worth saving in each other. And in the morning, when she woke him by taking his cock into her mouth and sucking him off, it felt like the start of something. Something real and lasting.

It took another thirty-six hours for the Purgatory to be ready. The station's work crews swarmed over the carrier like mechanical insects, welding, loading, replacing.

In the hangar, Derg stood with a datapad, checking off repairs as they were completed. His console in the CIC might be a disaster of cigarette butts and coffee cups, but when it came to the ship's maintenance, he was meticulous.

A massive crane arm descended from the hangar's vaulted ceiling, its electromagnetic grapples carrying a replacement heat exchanger for the starboard engine nacelle. The component was the size of a ground car, its cooling vanes still wrapped in protective polymer that would burn off during the first ignition sequence. Two techs in exoskeletons guided it into position, their augmented strength letting them manhandle the multi-ton component with surprising grace.

"Easy with that!" Derg shouted up at them, his cigarette dangling forgotten from his lips. "That cost more than you'll make in five years!"

Sparks cascaded from the upper hull where a welder was patching micrometeor damage—tiny punctures no bigger than pinpricks, but each one a potential catastrophic failure if they hit wrong during atmospheric entry. The welder wore a full radiation suit, the plasma torch in their hands burning at temperatures that could vaporize steel. Each pass left a perfect bead of reformed metal, stronger than the original hull plating.

In the mech bay, hydraulic lifts held each war machine in maintenance cradles. Kenney's Badger had its chest plates removed, exposing the fusion bottle that powered the thirty-ton monster. A tech with specialized radiation shielding was recalibrating the magnetic containment field, adjusting tolerances measured in angstroms. One miscalculation and the mech would become a small nuclear bomb.

Racer's mech was getting new myomer bundles in its legs—synthetic muscle fibers that contracted when electrical current passed through them. The old bundles had been stretched beyond tolerance, leaving the mech with a slight limp that affected its top speed. The new ones were military surplus, probably stripped from a Confederate machine, but they'd give him another ten kilometers per hour in a sprint.

McKnight's Bulldog stood in its cradle like a prizefighter between rounds, techs swarming over its scarred armor. Someone had painted a small blue alien head on the shoulder—a joke about their upcoming deployment that McKnight hadn't noticed yet. The mech's massive fists were being fitted with enhanced actuators, increasing their grip strength to nearly three thousand pounds per square inch.

"Right arm's fully functional," a tech reported, having just finished installing Kenney's mech's salvaged shoulder joint. "It's not pretty, but it'll hold."

"Pretty doesn't win fights," Derg replied, marking it complete. "What about Killjoy's minigun barrels?"

"Six replacements installed. We could only source four spares for next time—nobody stocks that many."

"And Racer's stabilizer?"

"Good as new. Well, good as refurbished military surplus can be."

Ammunition was being loaded by the pallet—crates of 30mm rounds, missiles in protective casings, tank shells for the Purgatory's own defensive guns. The locally sourced supplies were expensive but necessary. Whatever waited on Clandora, they'd meet it fully armed.

A loading robot rolled past on heavy tracks, its articulated arms carrying a pallet of HEAT rounds—High-Explosive Anti-Tank warheads designed for the mechs' shoulder-mounted launchers. Each round was the size of a wine bottle, the shaped charge warhead capable of punching through a meter of composite armor. The robot's optical sensors swept back and forth, calculating optimal load distribution as it navigated up the cargo ramp.

Behind it, another loader carried crates of 30mm APFSDS rounds—armor-piercing fin-stabilized discarding sabot—the tungsten penetrators designed to maintain velocity even through dense jungle canopy. The crates were marked with batch numbers and manufacture dates, Confederate military surplus that had somehow found its way to the Fringe markets.

Wilson supervised the loading of specialty munitions: white phosphorus rounds for area denial, thermobaric warheads that would create overpressure waves lethal to anything with lungs, and EMP shells that could fry electronics in a hundred-meter radius. Each type was color-coded and stored in separate magazines to prevent tragic mix-ups during combat.

"Careful with those WP rounds," Wilson called to a tech guiding a loader. "Temperature spike could set the whole magazine off."

The tech nodded, adjusting the robot's path to avoid a heat vent that was venting excess thermal buildup from the ship's reactor. The white phosphorus rounds were notorious for their sensitivity—useful in combat, terrifying in storage.

Blake handled the personnel issue from a makeshift recruiting station near the cargo bay. They'd lost three crew members to Hammerhead—two techs who'd decided to try their luck with a salvage crew, and one of the security team who'd apparently fallen in love with a bar owner. But the station had plenty of experienced spacers looking for work.

A line of applicants had formed, each one carrying their papers—discharge documents, technical certifications, criminal records that were hopefully forged. Blake interviewed them with clinical focus, his questions designed to filter out the desperate from the competent.

"Next," he called, and a woman stepped forward—mid-thirties, burn scars covering half her face, one eye clouded white from corneal damage. "Name and specialty?"

"Loribelle. Fire control systems. Eight years on Confederate destroyers before mustering out." She handed over her papers, the holographic seals still active.

Blake scanned them with a handheld verifier, watching for the telltale flicker of forgeries. The device chirped green. "Says here you were at the Battle of Thessalonica. That was a meat grinder."

"Targeting officer on the CNS Defiant. We put forty-three confirmed kills on pirate fighters before a missile cooked our bridge." She touched her scarred face. "I was the lucky one—just flash burns. Captain and XO weren't so fortunate."

"Pay's standard per rating, but we're heading into hostile territory. Still interested?"

"Sir, I've been living on Hammerhead for six months eating slop. Hostile territory with decent chow sounds like paradise."

Blake marked her approved, already moving to the next applicant—a young man whose calloused hands suggested manual labor rather than technical training. Behind him, an older man waited with military bearing despite civilian clothes, his eyes constantly scanning for threats even in the relative safety of the hangar.

"Got us two replacement techs," Blake reported to Kenney in the briefing room. "Ex-Confederate Navy, clean records. And a security specialist, former corporate military."

"Corporate?" Wilson asked suspiciously.

"Not CMG," Blake assured him. "Worked for Akilesh Industries until they went under. Has good references."

Derg burst in, grease-stained and frustrated. "Boss, I need another week. The engines are running at seventy percent efficiency, and our point defense grid has more holes than coverage. I could install new pulse lasers, upgrade the targeting systems—"

"We don't have a week," Kenney cut him off. "Crater's expecting us at Clandora in three days."

"Then at least let me—"

"Derg, is the ship combat capable?"

The engineer sighed. "Yeah, she'll fight. She'll jump. But she could be so much better."

"Better costs time we don't have. Make her work with what we've got."

Through the briefing room's window, they could see Hammerhead's salvage crews still working the wreck field, cutting apart the dead for profit.

Valeria entered, now dressed in her new clothes—practical ship wear that was tailored to fit. She moved to Kenney's side naturally, a gesture that didn't go unnoticed by the command staff.

"The new crew members are settling in," she reported. "I helped them find their quarters."

"Since when are you crew?" Wilson asked, playfully.

"Since I needed something to do besides hide in medical," she replied. "I can help with inventory, basic maintenance. I learn quickly."

"She's been helping me with the kids," McKnight added from the doorway, still showing bruises from his fight. "They like her."

Blake looked at Kenney. "She needs a position if she's going to be aboard. Can't have civilians wandering around during combat operations."

"Logistics assistant," Kenney decided. "Help Blake with inventory and procurement. Hundred credits a week plus board."

"Generous," Blake said sarcastically, but he was already adding her to the crew roster under her new name—Tavo Manwill.

"Captain," Tango's synthesized voice came through the CIC speakers. "I've pulled several safety videos from the public net about Clandora that the crew may find beneficial to their time there."

Kenney looked up from the tactical planning table where he'd been reviewing approach vectors. "Put it on the main screen."

The CIC's primary display flickered to life. The video quality was corporate-professional, the Crater Mining Group logo spinning in the corner. A hardened mercenary colonel appeared on screen, standing in what looked like a military briefing room. His face was scarred, his hair gray and cut military-short, his presence commanding immediate attention.

"Listen up," the colonel began without preamble. "I'm Colonel Urias Gerig, head of security operations for Crater Mining Group's Clandora division. If you're watching this, you're about to enter one of the most hostile environments in colonized space."

"Clandora was supposed to be humanity's greatest terraforming success," Gerig continued, beginning to pace. "Instead, it became our most expensive mistake. During the initial terraforming process, alien DNA contaminated the seed matrices. The terraforming AI, in its infinite wisdom, tried to compensate by integrating human-logged DNA patterns."

The screen showed scientific diagrams—double helixes merging, cellular structures combining.

"The result? XLTs—Xenological Lifeforms from Terraforming. We brought back species that should have stayed extinct. The primary inhabitants call themselves the Su'vi, though we just call them the blues."

The image shifted to show footage of tall, blue-skinned humanoids moving through jungle foliage. They were three meters tall, athletic, with tails and large eyes that seemed almost human.

"Now, ARMSEA and the core worlds classify these XLTs as a protected species," Gerig's voice dripped with disdain. "But out here, beyond their influence, we see them for what they are—obstacles. They're savage, territorial, and standing between us and mineral deposits worth more than the GDP of most systems."

"Jesus," Wilson muttered. "They're huge."

Gerig continued on screen. "These blues have some kind of neural connection to the local wildlife. They can ride the local fauna, turn them into weapons. Do not—I repeat—do not be seduced by their appearance. Several of my men have fallen for that trick, thinking they could communicate, negotiate, even fraternize. Those men are dead now."

"Furthermore," Gerig added, "the atmosphere, while lush for plant growth, is toxic to human lungs. Hydrogen sulfide, carbon dioxide, xenon—you breathe it, you're unconscious in twenty seconds, dead in four minutes. Masks are mandatory outside. No exceptions."

The camera panned to show rows of Sentinel mechs—dozens of them—being prepped for combat. Weapons were being loaded, pilots running pre-flight checks.

"My forces are preparing for a final solution to the Su'vi problem," Gerig announced. "Once we clear them out, Clandora will finally deliver on its resource promises. Until then, stay in your vehicles, avoid the indigenous population, and let us handle the pest control."

The video ended with Crater's logo and a warning: "For your safety, remain within designated zones."

The CIC was silent for a moment.

"That was recorded two years ago," Tango added helpfully. "Colonel Gerig and his entire force were listed as missing in action two weeks later."

"Missing?" Blake asked. "Not killed?"

"No bodies were ever recovered. The entire battalion—forty-eight Sentinels, two hundred support personnel—simply vanished in the jungle."

"The blue aliens," Wilson said slowly. "Three meters tall, neural connection to wildlife... those aren't terraforming accidents. Those are engineered soldiers."

"XLTs are a known problem with terraforming," Blake said, pulling up his datapad to access the military database. "The nanite process takes hundreds of years—they're supposed to create Earth-normal planets, break down hostile compounds, introduce compatible bacteria and plant life. But sometimes, like with Clandora, they create planets more suited to the previous inhabitants."

The screen in the CIC shifted to show technical diagrams—nanite swarms moving through geological layers like silver rivers, each microscopic machine equipped with quantum processors capable of analyzing and reconstructing genetic sequences.

"The terraforming companies always swear it's impossible," Wilson continued, having studied this during his military service. "They say the nanites are programmed to create human-compatible biospheres. But when you're reading genetic fragments from millions of years of evolution, pieces of DNA trapped in rock strata, fossilized in amber, preserved in ice... sometimes the original patterns are stronger than the programming."

"Sometimes they bring back exactly what was there before," Blake added. "The Archaean Incident gave us those giant arthropods—basically prehistoric scorpions the size of tanks. The nanites had spent three centuries perfectly recreating their original ecosystem. Took flame units to clear them out."

Tango pulled up more files, its electronic voice carrying an almost eager quality. "Historical records indicate seventeen separate XLT emergence events in the past decade. In each case, the terraforming process had been running for at least two hundred years before the original species reemerged. The Thessalonica Jellies—atmospheric organisms that fed on ship emissions. The Minerva Hive—a collective intelligence that built cities from secreted resins."

"The process is supposed to create a blank slate," Kenney said, studying the data. "Wipe out whatever was there, build something new for humans. But Clandora..."

"Clandora's terraforming started four hundred years ago," Tango supplied. "Initial reports showed excellent progress—Earth-normal atmosphere developing, compatible plant life spreading. Colonization was approved a hundred and fifty years ago. But sometime in the last century, the nanites began reverting to older patterns."

On the screen, the Su'vi moved through their jungle with fluid grace, their tall forms perfectly balanced, their neural queues connecting to flying creatures that responded like extensions of their own bodies.

"These aren't accidents or mutations," Blake said quietly. "The planet is remembering what it used to be. The nanites read the archaeological record and decided the Su'vi were the optimal life form for Clandora, not humans."

"Which makes us the invasive species," Wilson concluded. "We spent centuries and trillions of credits to terraform a planet that's now actively hostile to human life."

Blake spat into his cup. "Doesn't matter what they are. Gerig went in with almost fifty mechs and didn't come back. We're going in with ten."

"Different tactical philosophy though," Derg interjected, pulling up technical specifications on his datapad. "Gerig had Sentinels—those are like infantry units, mobile weapons platforms. Twelve feet tall, light armor, designed for patrol and rapid response. They're meant to cover ground, pursue targets through difficult terrain, basically act like giant soldiers."

The screen shifted to show a Sentinel mech—sleek, humanoid, almost elegant in its proportions. It carried a rifle sized for its frame and had fully articulated hands that could switch weapons, climb, or interact with equipment. The armor was just thick enough to stop small arms fire while maintaining mobility.

"Aggressor-class mechs like ours," Derg continued, switching the display, "are walking fortresses. Forty feet tall, built for holding positions against overwhelming force. Look at the armor thickness—" He highlighted the specifications. "Five times what a Sentinel carries. Our mechs were designed to be anchor points in battle lines, to take and hold ground against anything short of orbital bombardment."

The comparison was stark. Where the Sentinels were built for mobility and pursuit, the Aggressors were built for sustained combat. Kenney's Badger appeared on screen—broad shouldered, heavily armored, its hands capable of wielding massive weapons or crushing enemy armor.

"The Sentinels were trying to patrol the entire jungle," Wilson said, understanding the distinction. "Fifty mechs spread across hundreds of square kilometers, trying to hunt down an enemy that knows the terrain. But we just have to hold two locations—the facility and the mine."

"Static defense," McKnight nodded. "That's what Aggressors were built for. Set up overlapping fields of fire, let the enemy come to us. My 120mm cannon has a effective range of three kilometers in open terrain. Nothing gets close without going through hell first."

"The facility and mine both have cleared perimeters," Blake added, reviewing the satellite imagery. "Three hundred meters of open ground minimum. That's a killing field for our weapons."

"Plus we have the Purgatory," Conway said from his station. "The ship's point defense can provide fire support if needed. Gerig's forces were dispersed, hunting. We'll be concentrated, defending."

"But we're still outnumbered by whatever's out there," Wilson pointed out. "If the Su'vi coordinated enough to take down fifty mechs—"

"Fifty mechs scattered through dense jungle," Kenney corrected. "Different scenario. We set up defensive positions, maintain discipline, and don't chase them into the trees. Let them come to us if they want a fight."

"The Sentinels' mistake was thinking mobility was an advantage," Derg said. "In that jungle, it just meant getting separated, isolated, picked off one by one. Our Aggressors might be slower, but we hit harder and can take more punishment."

"Ten mechs in two defensive positions," Blake calculated on his datapad. "Five at the facility, five at the mine. Overlapping coverage, mutual support. It's doable."

"If we maintain discipline," Kenney emphasized. "No pursuit into the jungle, no splitting up to cover more ground. We hold our positions and make them pay for every meter they want to advance."

"And if they don't give us a choice?" Wilson asked.

"Then we find out what happened to Gerig the hard way."

On the screen, Tango had pulled up current satellite imagery of Clandora. The jungle was vast, unbroken green as far as the sensors could see. Somewhere in that green, an entire battalion had vanished.

"Prep the mechs for anti-biological combat," Kenney ordered. "Flame units, chemical dispensers, everything we've got. And make sure everyone's masks are checked and double-checked."

CHAPTER TEN

The Purgatory descended through Clandora's thick atmosphere, the ship's frame vibrating as they punched through successive cloud layers. The viewports showed nothing but green canopy stretching to every horizon—an unbroken sea of vegetation that rippled in the high-altitude winds. As they broke through the lower cloud ceiling, the mining complex appeared below them, its massive pentagonal security fence carving out a geometric island from the endless jungle.

"Crikey, look at that," Conway muttered from the pilot's station, easing back on the throttle. The lower gravity made the ship feel uncommonly responsive, almost twitchy in the thinner air.

The fence stretched for miles, a perfect pentagon of cleared ground against the encroaching green. More than a third of the enclosed area was dominated by the starport—a long runway cutting across the northern section, surrounded by clusters of hangars and rectangular warehouse structures. VTOL landing pads dotted the tarmac like concrete lily pads, most empty except for the aircraft huddled closest to the facility buildings.

Eight UBW-17 Blackwing transports sat in tight formation near the main complex, their twin ducted rotors tilted skyward in rest position. The transport VTOLs were all function over form—bulbous cockpits grafted onto angular cargo bodies, stub wings bristling with what Conway recognized as rocket pods and door-gun mounts. These were pure atmospheric craft, their aerodynamic profiles useless in the vacuum of space. Despite Clandora's corrosive atmosphere, each aircraft gleamed with fresh jungle camo paint, ground crews moving between them loading sealed containers and running pre-flight checks.

Four ASDF-34 Dragonfly gunships occupied the hardened pads between the Blackwings and the administrative buildings—meaner machines with tandem rotor configurations that gave them insect-like profiles. Conway could make out the chin-mounted autocannons and counted eight missile hardpoints on each bird's stub wings. Like the Blackwings, these were atmospheric hunters, designed to dominate the air between ground and stratosphere, not beyond. Their grey combat coating was immaculate, clearly maintained daily against the hostile environment. These weren't museum pieces—they were ready to fly and fight at a moment's notice.

The western edge glowed with industrial activity—massive cylindrical towers venting steam, the refinery complex judging by the constant stream of ore haulers queuing at its entrance. The eastern section was all low, sprawling buildings and vehicle yards, construction equipment visible even from altitude. Between them, the administrative heart of the complex rose in a cluster of connected structures, the tallest maybe ten stories, their rooftops bristling with communication equipment.

"Thought this place was running a skeleton crew," Wilson said over the command net in the CIC.

Along the fence perimeter, smoke and flames were rising from controlled burns—crews were torching back the tall grass that grew right up to the fence line, creating a firebreak of blackened earth. The grass was already waist-high in areas that looked recently cleared, pale green shoots rising from ash-dark soil. Orange-suited figures moved systematically along the perimeter, their flamethrowers creating a moving line of fire that left charred ground in its wake.

Conway brought them around on approach, the landing pad growing larger in the viewport—a heat-scarred rectangle of concrete with yellow markings barely visible under a film of green pollen.

"Purgatory, this is Clandora Control," a voice crackled through the comm, the accent thick but professional. "Transmit clearance codes for Pad Three."

"Control, Purgatory. Transmitting now." Conway's fingers danced over the console, sending their credentials and CMG's landing authorization. The seconds stretched as the facility's systems verified their authorization—probably running them through three different databases, checking their ship registration against known threats.

"Purgatory, you are cleared for Pad Three. Be advised—maintain strict approach corridor. We've got active bogies in the area. Point defense is weapons-free."

"Copy that, Control. Strict corridor, weapons free."

"Welcome to paradise, Purgatory. Control out."

Two UHV-37 B-class Valorant shuttles were already parked on adjacent pads, their sleek SSTO frames a stark contrast to the Purgatory's battered hull. The single-stage-to-orbit craft had the distinctive swept-wing design of aerospace hybrids—equally capable of atmospheric flight and orbital burns. Their twin fusion engines were mounted high on the fuselage, cargo bays open beneath as automated loaders moved containers in and out. Heat shielding ran along their bellies, still discolored from recent reentry. The control tower was a modest structure compared to major ports, its windows reflecting the afternoon sun. "Alright, I'm heading down to the hangar," Kenney said, unstrapping from his seat. "Conway, nice and easy on the approach."

"Copy that, Captain."

Through the viewport, Kenney could see what that meant. The pad was ringed with defensive positions carved into reinforced bunkers—sandbag emplacements reinforced with steel plating, each housing automated anti-aircraft batteries. Their multi-barreled miniguns elevated at forty-five-degree angles, slowly rotating in automated search patterns. The barrels gleamed with fresh oil, ammunition feeds snaking down into protected underground magazines.

"Friendly bunch," Wilson muttered over the command net, watching the weapons sweep across empty sky.

Kenney made his way through the ship's tight corridors, grabbing handholds as Conway adjusted their descent angle. The familiar rhythm of landing procedures echoed through the hull—hydraulics adjusting, engines throttling back, the subtle shift in gravity as they transitioned from flight to hover.

He paused at the rec room doorway where Valeria was helping the younger kids with a card game, her patient voice explaining the rules to Jalon while Sarah tried to peek at everyone's hands.

"Hey," Kenney said, leaning against the doorframe. "Want to see an alien planet?"

Valeria looked up, eyebrows raised. "Is that a pickup line?"

"It's an invitation to witness first contact with a toxic hellscape. Very romantic."

She smiled, setting down her cards. "Alright, you guys keep playing. Sarah's in charge."

"No fair!" Jalon protested. "She cheats!"

"I do not!" Sarah shot back.

Valeria ruffled Jalon's hair as she stood. "Then you'll have to watch her extra carefully, won't you?" She gave them a little wave as she followed Kenney into the corridor. "Be good. We'll be back soon."

They stopped at the equipment locker near the hangar access. Kenney pulled out two rubberized masks, checking the seal integrity on both.

"Atmosphere's toxic," he explained, handing her one. "Won't kill you instantly, but prolonged exposure causes respiratory failure. Here—" He demonstrated with his own mask first. "Press this valve to purge any contaminated air, then place it over your face. The seal needs to be tight against your skin."

Valeria copied his movements, pressing the purge valve with a sharp hiss of escaping air while fitting the mask over her face. Kenney reached over, adjusting the straps behind her head.

"Too tight?" he asked, his voice slightly muffled.

She shook her head. "Feels weird. Like being underwater."

"You'll get used to it. Remember—never break the seal outside. Not even for a second."

They continued toward the hangar, both now breathing through the full-face masks, Valeria bracing herself as the ship banked slightly.

They reached the hangar deck just as Conway's voice crackled over the intercom.

"Sixty seconds to touchdown."

The hangar was cramped but organized, the mechs secured in their maintenance cradles like sleeping giants. Kenney checked his mask seal one more time, then moved to the main hanger door control panel.

"Opening hangar doors," he announced over the ship intercom.

The massive doors began their slow separation with a grinding mechanical protest. Humid air rushed in immediately, thick enough to taste even through the mask filters. The temperature jumped fifteen degrees in seconds, Clandora's jungle atmosphere invading the controlled environment of the ship. Through the widening gap, Kenney could see the landing pad rushing up to meet them—stained concrete, warning stripes faded to suggestions, ground crews in orange suits already positioning themselves at a safe distance.

Conway feathered the thrusters, compensating for a sudden gust that tried to push them sideways. The Purgatory's landing struts groaned as they took the ship's weight in the .7g, hydraulics hissing as they compressed. The engines' whine died to a whisper, then silence except for the ping of cooling metal and the distant industrial roar of the facility.

"Welcome to paradise," Conway's voice crackled mockingly over the ship intercom, his sarcasm carrying through the static as the main engines died with a descending whine that seemed to go on forever.

It clearly wasn't.

The sound reverberated through the hangar deck's metal walls, each system powering down in carefully orchestrated succession—fusion reactor throttling back to standby, coolant pumps cycling to maintenance mode, navigation arrays folding into their protective housings with mechanical clicks that echoed through the superstructure.

The Purgatory shuddered as the landing struts took the full weight, hydraulic fluid hissing through pressure valves. The deck beneath Kenney's boots vibrated with each system entering hibernation. The artificial gravity generators gave one last fluctuation—a stomach-dropping moment of near-weightlessness that made the tool racks rattle—before stabilizing at Clandora's natural .7g. Everything felt lighter, wrong, like the world had suddenly become made of hollow plastic.

"Shutdown complete," Conway announced over the comm. "Fuel cells at forty percent. We're going to need a full top-off if we want to make orbit with cargo. And someone better be paying for premium, because I'm not trusting whatever swamp juice they're brewing at this facility."

With the engines offline, external sounds became more distinct. Forklifts and haulers moved across the compound. Workers in full environmental suits rushed between buildings. Artillery crews were firing a steady stream of orange canisters into the jungle—incendiary rounds, chemical defoliants, whatever it took to keep the wildlife at bay.

"That's a lot of ordnance for pest control," Blake observed over the command net, watching another barrage arc into the trees.

The landing pad was massive, a reinforced ferrocrete hexagon designed for ore haulers ten times the Purgatory's size. The surface was scored with blast marks from decades of heavy freight landings, heat-resistant coating bubbled and cracked in places where shuttle engines had burned too hot.

The hangar doors locked fully open with a resonating clang. Through the rectangular frame, Kenney could see a lone figure waiting at the edge of the pad—standing with casual nonchalance despite the industrial traffic around him. Khakis pressed sharp enough to cut, a blue sport coat completely inappropriate for the environment, and a full-face mask that didn't quite hide the familiar smile.

He hit the release, and the ramp began its descent with a pneumatic hiss. The air was so thick with humidity that condensation began forming on the mech's armor plating within seconds.

The figure in the blue sport coat spread his arms in welcome, his voice amplified because of the mask in the industrial noise. "Captain Kenney! Welcome to the ass-end of nowhere. I trust you had a pleasant flight?"

Behind him, ground crews were already moving toward the Purgatory with fuel lines and cargo loaders, their movements sluggish because of the bulky environment suits. One technician struggled with a heavy fuel coupling, the weight more manageable in the .7g but the suit making every motion clumsy. Another crew guided a cargo loader toward the hangar, its electric motor whining under the strain of navigation.

Then Kenney saw it—a shadow passing overhead, too large to be debris, too fast to be cloud cover.

The minigun emplacements erupted to life without warning, all of them simultaneously, barrels spinning up with an electric shriek before unleashing streams of tracers into the sky. The sound was deafening—a continuous roar that made the hangar deck vibrate beneath his boots. Shell casings began raining down like brass hail, bouncing off the ferrocrete with metallic rings that created an almost musical counterpoint to the gunfire.

"AERIAL CONTACT!" blared over the facility's PA system, the automated voice eerily calm. "ALL PERSONNEL TAKE COVER!"

The ground crews reacted instantly, trained reflexes taking over. They dropped equipment and ran for the nearest structures, some diving under vehicles, others sprinting for doorways. The technician with the fuel line abandoned it, letting it snake wildly as residual pressure sprayed aviation fuel across the pad. Within seconds, the landing area was deserted except for abandoned equipment.

Then Kenney saw what the guns were shooting at.

They came diving from the cloud cover—dozens of leather-winged nightmares, each one the size of a small aircraft. Their bodies were reptilian, covered in scales that shimmered with an oil-slick iridescence, wings stretched between elongated finger bones like those of ancient pterosaurs. They shrieked as the defensive fire found them, voices like tearing metal echoing across the facility.

The first wave died in seconds. The automated targeting systems were merciless, efficient, tracking multiple targets simultaneously with mechanical precision. Creatures tumbled from the sky, wings shredded by high-velocity rounds, bodies spinning in graceless death spirals. One crashed onto the runway with a sound like a dropped sack of wet cement, sliding fifty meters and leaving a dark smear of ichor. Another slammed into a storage tank with a resonating boom that Kenney felt through the deck plates, its corpse sliding down the curved metal to crumple on the ground.

But more kept coming, using the sun's glare and industrial towers as cover, banking and weaving through the defensive fire with terrifying intelligence. They learned quickly—those that survived the first seconds began using irregular flight patterns, sudden drops and climbs that confused the targeting algorithms for precious milliseconds.

The sky became a killing field. Tracers carved geometric patterns through the humid air, creating a deadly lattice of light. A creature tried to dive low, skimming the fence line, but the guns tracked it perfectly—the burst of fire nearly cut it in half, both pieces crashing into the razor wire. Electricity coursed through its corpse, sending up the acrid smell of burned flesh that carried even into the hangar.

Another creature plummeted through the roof of a prefab structure with a tremendous crash, the impact shaking the entire building. Dust and debris erupted from the windows. The nearest minigun swiveled to track another target, brass casings from its previous burst still bouncing and rolling across the ground in the low gravity, taking longer to settle than they should.

The defensive batteries never stopped, barrels beginning to glow cherry-red from sustained use. The heat shimmer rising from them distorted the air, making the facility beyond look like a mirage. Steam hissed where coolant systems kicked in, trying to prevent the weapons from warping.

Bodies of the creatures littered the compound now—sprawled across rooftops, draped over walkways, piled against the fence where they'd tried to flee. Black ichor pooled and mixed with spilled fuel, creating rainbow sheens in the harsh industrial lighting. One creature, not quite dead, tried to drag itself toward the jungle with one functional wing, leaving a dark trail until a minigun finished it with a precise burst.

The figure in the blue sport coat hadn't moved from his position near the cargo ramp, watching the aerial massacre with an expression of mild interest, as if this was merely an unusual weather phenomenon.

"The fauna here is particularly aggressive this time of year," he called out conversationally over the gunfire. "Corporate never mentions that in the recruitment materials!"

One by one, the surviving creatures broke off their attack, disappearing back into the cloud cover with cries that sounded almost mournful. The guns continued firing for several more seconds at empty sky, their programming requiring visual confirmation of clear airspace before standing down. Then, as suddenly as it had started, silence fell—broken only by the whir of cooling barrels and the steady plink of expended brass still raining from the emplacements.

In the sudden quiet, Kenney could hear the automated systems announcing "all clear" in multiple languages, the crackle of fires where tracers had ignited vegetation beyond the fence, and the slow drip of various fluids from the creature corpses. The entire attack had lasted less than two minutes.

Ground crews began emerging from cover, moving cautiously at first, then with more confidence as the all-clear continued to sound. Someone was already bringing out a flamethrower to deal with the corpses—standard procedure, apparently, to prevent whatever grew in them from spreading.

Valeria had moved closer during the chaos, and now stood beside him watching the figure in the blue sport coat brush imaginary dust from his lapels. When she spoke, her voice carried that bewildered frustration that comes from encountering the impossible things once too often.

"Mr. Smith," she said quietly, the words carrying all the weight of a mathematical proof that wouldn't balance. "How is it that he manages to materialize wherever we go? It's as if he exists in all places at once, like some sort of corporate specter haunting every godforsaken outpost from here to the Core worlds."

"Good question, I don't think it's the same one but I'm not sure." Kenney muttered, checking his sidearm.

They descended the ramp. Smith approached with an outstretched hand, his voice still cheerfully recognizable. "Mr. Jaeger! So good of you to come. Welcome to Clandora!"

Kenney shook his hand briefly. "Smith. Thought this was supposed to be a skeleton crew operation."

"Oh, it was!" Smith gestured at the bustling activity. "But with your arrival, we're preparing for a more... aggressive mining schedule. Need to get equipment staged, defenses prepared."

Another barrage of orange canisters flew overhead, exploding in the jungle with bright flashes.

"Lot of firepower for wildlife management," Kenney noted.

"The indigenous fauna can be quite persistent," Smith replied, stepping over a puddle of black ichor without looking down. "But you'll find we've adapted remarkably well to the local challenges." He gestured toward an armored six-wheeler parked at the edge of the landing pad, its oversized tires designed for Clandora's harsh terrain. Unlike the ground crew vehicles, this one had a fully sealed cab with climate control. "The supplies are in Warehouse 57—everything you requested plus some extras we thought you might appreciate. I'll drive you over myself."

Smith took the driver's seat with ease while Kenney and Valeria climbed into the passenger side. The door sealed with a pneumatic hiss, and the cab's air conditioning hit them like a blessing—cool and dry against the oppressive humidity outside. Even through their masks, the temperature difference was immediate and welcome, though the filters still caught the underlying smell of vegetation and industrial chemicals that permeated everything on Clandora.

As they drove across the compound, Kenney noticed the workers' movements—nervous, constantly checking over shoulders, hands never far from weapons. The burn crews at the perimeter never turned their backs to the jungle.

"How long has the facility been operational?" Kenney asked.

"Oh, on and off for a couple years," Smith said vaguely. "We've had some setbacks, obviously. Personnel issues."

"Like Colonel Gerig?" Valeria asked innocently.

Smith's smile faltered for just a moment. "Ah, you've seen the safety briefing. Yes, the Colonel was... overenthusiastic in his approach. We're taking a more measured stance now."

They passed a medical station where workers were being treated for injuries—long parallel cuts that looked like claw marks, chemical burns from something that had spit or sprayed.

"Measured stance," Blake repeated flatly into the command net.

Through the compound's industrial sprawl, they could see workers rushing between buildings, forklifts moving supplies, and the constant activity of a facility under siege. The drive took only a few minutes, the truck's heavy suspension absorbing the rough patches where Clandora's aggressive plant life had buckled the pavement.

Warehouse 57 loomed ahead, a massive corrugated steel structure with reinforced doors. Smith brought the six-wheeler to a smooth stop at the security checkpoint, where two CMG marines manned the entrance. They wore tactical body armor over jungle-pattern fatigues—digital camo in muted greens and browns that would blend perfectly with Clandora's vegetation. Their gear was practical rather than powered: modular flex plates across the chest, mag pouches, and equipment webbing. Their helmets were basic combat models with chin straps, faces hidden behind sealed tinted masks with dual filter canisters that gave them an insectoid appearance.

Both carried well-worn assault rifles with slings adjusted for quick deployment. The weapons showed the patina of constant use in humid conditions despite regular maintenance. One had a combat knife strapped to his chest rig, the other a collection of anti-venoms on his thigh.

One approached the driver's side; rifle held at low ready.

"Mr. Smith," the marine said through his mask, voice muffled but audible through the filters. "These your guests?"

"Indeed. Captain Kenney and his specialist, here for the special requisition." Smith produced a clearance card from his jacket. "Authorization code Delta-Seven-Seven."

The marine pulled a ruggedized tablet from his vest, scanned the card, and waited for the green confirmation. He gave a hand signal to his partner, who hit the door controls. The massive warehouse doors began rolling apart with a grinding mechanical protest, revealing darkness beyond.

Smith drove through the entrance, the temperature dropping immediately as they passed from Clandora's humid air into the warehouse's climate-controlled interior. He parked in a designated yellow zone just inside the doors, which were already grinding closed behind them.

"Masks stay on," Smith reminded them as they climbed out. "Clandora's atmosphere is mostly nitrogen and CO_2."

The space was cavernous, crates stacked to the thirty-foot ceiling in neat rows that stretched back into shadow. Industrial lighting cast harsh pools of brightness between dark corridors of supplies, creating a chessboard pattern of light and dark that made it hard to judge distances. The air looked clearer here than outside—less humid, fewer particles—but it would kill them just as quickly as vacuum.

"My God," Valeria whispered, slowly turning to take it all in. Her voice was muffled by the mask but the awe came through clearly.

"Boss, I'm watching through the mask feeds," Blake's voice crackled in Kenney's earpiece, the connection slightly distorted by the warehouse's metal structure. "Running quick calculations... that's at least three times what we ordered. I count forty crates of standard munitions, twelve of missiles—wait, those markings indicate advanced targeting packages."

Smith stood with his hands clasped behind his back, watching them survey the supplies with an expression of satisfaction visible even through his designer mask. "The company believes in being thorough," he said. "Especially given the... unique challenges of your contract."

True to their word, everything was there—ammunition, missiles, spare parts, even the upgraded targeting systems Derg had been wanting. But beyond their requisition, Kenney could see crates marked with designations he recognized: heavy ordnance, experimental weapons, enough supplies to run a campaign.

"Impressive, isn't it?" Smith said proudly. "Everything you requested plus some extras we thought you might appreciate."

"This is easily twice what was requested," Kenney said suspiciously.

"Consider the surplus a bonus," Smith replied. "Payment for service rendered."

The artillery barrage intensified outside, making the warehouse walls shake.

Smith was about to continue when one of the CMG marines approached from outside—a sergeant by his stripes, his tactical gear worn but well-maintained. The marine leaned close to Smith, whispering urgently. Kenney caught fragments: "...perimeter breach...section four...two casualties..."

Smith's jaw tightened momentarily. "How many?"

"Dozen, maybe fifteen. But sir, thermal's showing something else. Massive heat signatures massing in sector 63. Thousands of them."

Smith nodded, dismissing the marine with a gesture before turning back to Kenney and Valeria. His composure never wavered.

"Well, that's actually perfect timing," Smith said, pulling out a tactical display tablet. "We've been monitoring this buildup for the past six hours. Thermal imaging shows approximately three thousand XLTs gathering in sector 63. We need overwatch security until our artillery has time to do its work."

The display showed heat signatures clustered in the jungle—too many to count accurately.

"How long until they attack?" Kenney asked, already calculating combat scenarios.

"Hours, maybe less. They've been probing our defenses all week, testing response times." Smith swiped to another screen showing military personnel files. "But the real problem is their leadership."

The screen displayed several personnel records marked DECEASED/MISSING. "These are former disgruntled CMG employees. They've gone native—literally. Gene-modded themselves into XLT—blue bodies, now they're leading the natives. They know our procedures, our weak points, everything. And they've completely forsook any loyalty to humanity out of some misguided ecoterrorism objective."

Wilson studied the images. "So they're coordinating this attack using human tactics."

"Exactly. The massing in sector 63 isn't random—it's a staging area. They're preparing for an organized assault." Smith pulled up thermal imaging showing the growing concentration of heat signatures. "Without your mechs supplementing our defenses, we might not hold."

Kenney studied the images. "So they know your tactics, defenses, everything."

"Exactly. Which is why we need professionals like you."

"We've certainly done worse for less." Kenney agreed.

The lights flickered as something exploded near the perimeter.

"Captain!" Blake's voice crackled over comms. "We've got movement all around the compound."

Another explosion, closer this time. Through the doors, they could see something massive moving at the jungle's edge.

Smith's smile was visible through his mask. "Already prepared. Your pilots can review the data while mounting up."

Kenney activated his comm. "Blake, get everyone locked and loaded. Hostiles breaching the gates."

"Copy that, boss. ANTs deploying to defensive positions now."

"All mechs, defensive pattern Alpha," Kenney ordered. "They're inside the wire."

"Mechs are prepped and ready," Derg reported. "Uploading tactical data now."

"Standard deployment?" McKnight asked over comms. "

"By the numbers," Kenney confirmed. "We hold the perimeter tonight, push out tomorrow. Clean out the infestation and get paid."

"Sounds like a milk run," Racer added. "Except for the toxic atmosphere and gene-modded traitors."

"We've had worse," Killjoy laughed. "Remember that ice moon with the cannibals?"

"Don't remind me," Deadeye muttered.

Big Country's voice rumbled through the comm with a deep chuckle. "Wouldn't mind me a night alone with one of them blue fellas. They look right exotic, all tall and lean like that. Maybe negotiate one as part of my hazard pay."

"Country, you'd romance a practice target if we painted it blue and gave it long enough legs," Deadeye shot back immediately.

"She'd have to be gene-modded just to survive a date with Country," Racer added. "Poor thing wouldn't know what hit her."

"Man's got a point," Killjoy laughed. "Remember that shore leave on Ganymede? He spent half his pay trying to impress that stripper with color changing skin."

"She had a beautiful personality," Big Country protested, though you could hear the grin in his voice.

"She had three beautiful personalities, depending on which chip was installed," Racer added. "And Country tried to date all of them."

The distant sound of gunfire erupted from the perimeter, followed by the heavier thump of artillery.

"Sergeant!" Smith barked at the marine. "Get us back to their ship. Now!"

The marine didn't need to be told twice. They piled into the truck, the driver gunning it before the doors were fully closed. Through the windshield, Kenney could see orange tracer fire arcing over the compound's buildings. An explosion lit up the eastern fence line.

"Wilson, coordinate with their artillery teams," Kenney ordered over comms as they raced through the compound. "We need integrated fire support five minutes ago."

"Working on it," Wilson's calm voice replied. "Patching into their fire control network now."

Back on the Purgatory, Wilson's fingers flew across multiple interfaces, linking with the facility's defensive systems. The CMG artillery crews weren't about to hand control to some mercenary who'd just landed, but they were broadcasting their targeting data on the tactical net. Data streams flooded his screens—firing solutions, impact predictions, reload times.

"I've got eyes on their fire missions," Wilson announced. "Artillery commencing bombardment... now."

The night erupted.

On Kenney's HUD, the targeting feeds Wilson was monitoring suddenly blazed with activity as dozens of gun positions opened fire. Mortars coughed in rapid succession, their crews working the tubes with practiced efficiency, shells arcing high before dropping into the jungle beyond the fence line. Howitzer teams slammed rounds home, their guns roaring, muzzle flashes lighting up the compound like strobes. Rocket batteries unleashed volleys that screamed over the perimeter, their contrails drawing white lines against the darkness.

"Marking projected impact zones on your HUDs," Wilson called out, translating the CMG targeting data into useful information for the mechs. "Stay clear of grid references seven through twelve."

The tree line disappeared in a wall of explosions. Through the thermals, they could see the rounds finding their targets—bodies thrown into the air, blue figures scrambling for cover that no longer existed. The CMG artillery crews were walking their barrage forward systematically, denying any escape route.

"Lord have mercy," Big Country breathed over the comm, his deep Confederate drawl stretching the words out slow.

"That's just the opening salvo," Wilson said, watching the data feeds update as crews reloaded. "Second volley in thirty seconds."

The truck skidded to a stop near the Purgatory's landing pad. Kenney and Valeria jumped out, masks still sealed against the toxic air. Through the open hangar doors, Kenney's mech was already moving, his AI Foxtrot bringing it online.

"Mr. Jaeger, I can't express how grateful Crater is for your assistance."

"Save the gratitude," Kenney said through the mechs loudspeakers. "Just make sure the money clears."

As Kilkenney Solution's crews dispersed to battle stations, Kenney looked out at the darkening jungle. Combat against XLTs led by gene-modded humans. It was strange, but they'd fought stranger. The money was good, the cause was clear—eliminate traitors to humanity.

Kenney stood on the tarmac outside the Purgatory, Valeria beside him. Smith gestured from the 6x6 passenger door at the defensive positions around the compound.

"As you can see, we've prepared extensively—"

Kenney cut him off with quick tactical hand signals to his pilots visible in the hangar—two fingers pointed at Streaks, then swept toward the north wall. A closed fist pump toward Racer, then gestured south.

Both mechs powered up inside the Purgatory, their footsteps shaking the hangar deck as they moved toward the ramp. The setting sun cast long shadows across the compound.

Kenney activated his comm. "Weapons free on anything non-human that breaches the perimeter. Patrol pattern Alpha, don't stray too far from your buddy."

"Copy that, boss," Racer replied, his mech descending the ramp.

"Time to earn that corporate money," Streaks added, his mech following.

"Scott," Kenney continued over comms. "Get some drones airborne. I want full coverage of the AO. Thermal, motion detection, everything. Make sure their AA marks it as friendly."

"Already on it," Blake's voice came back. "Launching six surveillance drones now."

Smith watched approvingly. "Your efficiency is exactly why we hired you."

"Ants," Kenney called over comm, ignoring Smith's comment. "Check the existing defenses. See what these corporate boys missed. I want kill zones, overlapping fields of fire, and fallback positions marked."

"Roger that, Captain," the ANT team leaders responded. "These civvie fortifications look like Swiss cheese."

"Derg, supervise the loading. I want those supplies secured and inventory logged."

"On it, boss," Derg replied.

Foxtrot emerged from the Purgatory's hangar, Kenney's mech moved with the AI's characteristic precision. The machine walked down the ramp and knelt on the tarmac, its hand extending palm-up.

"Your chariot awaits, sir," Foxtrot announced through the external speakers, the mech's massive hand lowering to ground level with surprising grace.

Smith observed the gesture with raised eyebrows. "Your logistics assistant is joining you in combat?" His tone carried genuine curiosity, perhaps even concern.

Valeria stepped forward without hesitation, her movements confident despite the chaos erupting around them. "I go where I'm needed," she replied through her mask, her voice carrying that particular tone that suggested this wasn't up for debate.

Smith's eyes lingered on her, reassessing. "How versatile." The word carried layers—approval, surprise, and something else Kenney couldn't quite place.

Another explosion shook the compound, close enough that they felt the pressure wave. Debris rained down from a nearby rooftop, and the anti-aircraft batteries opened up again, tracers streaming into the darkness.

"We should move," Kenney said, stepping onto the mech's palm. The metal was warm from the machine's internal heat, textured with anti-slip coating. He turned, extending his hand to Valeria. She took it, letting him steady her as she found her balance on the giant hand.

The fingers curved slightly, creating a protective cage around them as Foxtrot lifted them smoothly toward the cockpit. Through the gaps between the massive digits, Kenney caught glimpses of the battle—CMG troops running to defensive positions, another wave of creatures diving from the clouds only to be shredded by defensive fire, flames spreading along the eastern fence line.

The cockpit hatch hissed open with a rush of pressurized air, revealing the cramped interior bathed in the glow of tactical displays.

"Cozy," she commented, settling against his chest.

"Three thousand hostiles and you're worried about leg room?" Kenney asked, taking the pilot's seat while she settled onto his lap—the only way two people could fit in the single-pilot cockpit. Once the atmosphere was purged, they pulled off their masks. The cockpit was definitely tight with both of them, Valeria riding in Kenney's lap in the pilot's seat.

"I've had worse dates," she replied, gripping his shoulder as Foxtrot stood the mech upright.

Through the viewscreen, they could see the situation deteriorating rapidly. Streams of savage blue-skinned XLTs were pouring through a breach in the eastern fence, some riding six-legged creatures, others on foot with primitive weapons and a few captured firearms.

"Drone feed coming online," Blake reported over comms. "Cheeseburgers, boss. You need to see this."

Kenney's tactical display lit up with footage showing thousands of heat signatures in the jungle.

"ANT teams reporting. These defenses are a joke. We've got hundred-meter gaps in the kill zones. Requesting permission to mine the approach routes."

"Granted," Kenney replied. "All teams, listen up. This isn't going to be random wildlife charges. Treat this like a military engagement."

Valeria shifted in his lap, watching the battle unfold with excitement.

"Movement on the perimeter!" Racer called out. "Large hostile, bearing two-seven-zero!"

Through the viewscreen, they could see something massive emerging from the jungle—a herd of creatures like six-legged rhinos the size of a building, with riders on their backs.

On the tarmac below, Smith was driving back toward the compound's buildings, his corporate confidence evaporating as he saw what was coming.

"Here they come," Valeria whispered, her breath warm against Kenney's neck.

The battle for Clandora Mining Facility was about to begin.

The massive creatures charged the fence—a whole herd of them, twenty or more six-legged behemoths thundering across the cleared ground. Each beast carried a dozen blue riders clinging to improvised harnesses, their weapons already firing at the compound's defenders. The ground shook with their approach, a stampede that would flatten the fence like paper if it reached the perimeter.

The mechs responded instantly.

Streak's autocannon roared to life, the sound like ripping canvas amplified a thousand times. High-explosive rounds walked across the charging herd, punching through thick hide and detonating inside. The lead creature's front legs buckled, sending it cartwheeling forward in a mass of flesh and bone. Its riders flew like dolls, some crushed instantly under the beast's rolling weight, others thrown clear only to be trampled by those behind.

Racer's missile pods opened up, a full salvo of twelve rockets streaking into the packed mass. The explosions lifted two creatures entirely off the ground, their bodies torn apart in the blast. Blue riders were vaporized at the impact points, others sent flying in pieces. A secondary explosion—one of the riders must have been carrying demolition charges—chain-reacted through the herd's center.

"Multiple targets down," Racer reported, his autocannon already tracking to the next group. "Jesus, they just keep coming."

Another beast, wounded but still charging, crashed into the fence. The reinforced steel held but buckled inward, electricity arcing through its body. Riders leaped clear, some making it over the fence only to be cut down by defensive fire from the CMG positions. Big Country's mech grabbed one creature by its tusks as it tried to breach the damaged section, servos whining as he physically held it back before putting a point-blank burst through its skull.

"Dude, totally shredded that whole gnarly stampede," Streak reported, his weapons still firing. "But no joke, more movement in the treeline—they're like, massing for another run or whatever."

The killing ground before the fence was carpeted with massive corpses and scattered blue bodies, some still moving weakly. The air stank of cordite and copper, blood pooling in the churned earth.

CMG marines were already moving in, squad formations advancing through the gaps in the fence with cold efficiency. They worked in pairs—one covering while the other put controlled bursts into anything still breathing. The crack of rifle fire punctuated the false calm, methodical and unhurried. A young wounded blue tried to crawl toward the jungle, dragging shattered legs behind it. A marine stepped on its back, pinning it, before putting two rounds through its skull.

"Clear the bodies from the fence line," a CMG sergeant ordered over the tactical net. "Burn teams, move up. I want this whole sector sanitized before they regroup."

Inside Kenney's cockpit, Valeria shifted on his lap, her hips pressing back against him as she tried to find a comfortable position in the cramped space. Each movement was a slow, deliberate adjustment that made her body slide against his in ways that had nothing to do with combat readiness.

"So Foxtrot can pilot even with us in it?" she asked, her voice steady despite the way she was settling deeper into his lap, her back now flush against his chest.

Kenney reached up, hanging their masks in the storage compartment above. The cockpit was cramped, designed for a single pilot, every surface covered in switches, displays, and control interfaces. The main viewscreen wrapped around them in a panoramic display, showing the battlefield in multiple spectrums—thermal, night vision, tactical overlay. Status lights blinked in sequences along the periphery, casting colored shadows across their faces.

"Yeah. Foxtrot, take over defensive operations."

"Assuming control, sir," the AI responded.

The control sticks moved on their own, servos adjusting with mechanical whispers. The foot pedals depressed and released as the mech shifted its weight, the entire cockpit tilting slightly as Foxtrot tracked a new target. The sensation was disorienting—like being a passenger in their own body. The targeting reticle on the main display shifted independently, locking onto heat signatures beyond the fence. The autocannon's ammunition counter flickered as Foxtrot calculated firing solutions.

This freed Kenney's hands. He wrapped his arms around Valeria's waist to steady her as the mech took a heavy step forward, the motion sending a vibration through the entire frame. She giggled—a surprisingly light sound given their situation—and pressed back against him to keep her balance.

The cockpit swayed again as Foxtrot engaged, the autocannon's roar muffled but still felt through the pilot's seat. Spent casings ejected somewhere below them with metallic clangs. The temperature gauge crept up slightly, the cockpit growing warmer from the weapons fire. Through the viewscreen, they could see Foxtrot's targeting computer painting hostile after hostile, the AI's efficiency cold and relentless.

"This is strange," Valeria murmured, watching the battle unfold without them, the mech fighting a battle while they sat nestled together in its metal heart.

"So have you ever...?" she asked, letting the question hang.

Kenney affected mock shock. "I am a professional soldier, Valeria. I would never defile the sanctity of this beautiful war machine."

She turned around to face him, wrapping her legs around his waist, the cramped cockpit making the position necessary as much as intimate. "Never?"

"Well..." he started, but was cut off as Foxtrot's weapons systems engaged.

The autocannon fired a burst at something in the darkness. Through the viewscreen, they could see more creatures emerging—smaller, faster, with riders who moved like trained cavalry.

"Sir, perhaps this is not the optimal time for... whatever this is," Foxtrot suggested dryly.

"The AI has opinions now?" Valeria laughed, her face close to Kenney's.

"The AI has always had opinions," Foxtrot replied. "I simply choose when to express them. Engaging hostiles, bearing one-seven-five."

The mech pivoted, fired, pivoted again. Outside, the battle was intensifying—artillery rounds arcing overhead, tracer fire creating light patterns in the dark, the screams of creatures and commands shouted in alien languages.

Through the viewscreen, Kenney watched groups of blue warriors advance from the treeline with alarming confidence. They moved in traditional hunting formations, the same tactics that had probably worked against CMG security forces for months. Hundreds of them poured from the jungle, some riding the smaller four-legged creatures, others on foot in massive warrior hosts.

Then came the arrows.

The sky darkened with them—thousands of primitive shafts arcing through the air in perfectly coordinated volleys. They struck the mechs like rain, wooden and bone projectiles shattering harmlessly against armor designed to withstand anti-tank rounds. The blues had no way of knowing their traditional weapons were useless.

"Are they seriously shooting arrows at us?" Racer asked, incredulous, as another volley clattered off his mech's hull.

Through the panoramic display, Valeria and Kenney could see warriors dragging captured CMG equipment into position—belt-fed machine guns taken from overrun outposts, their alien hands struggling with the human-designed weapons. The guns opened up, muzzle flashes strobing in the darkness. Rounds that could punch through body armor and light vehicles pinged off mech armor like hail, leaving nothing but cosmetic scratches.

A group wheeled out what looked like a massive ballista, cranking it back to launch a spear the size of a telephone pole. The primitive siege weapon that had probably terrified CMG defenders fired with a tremendous twang.

Foxtrot's autocannon responded with a single burst, turning the siege weapon and its crew into splinters and mist. The spear fell harmlessly short.

"Dude, they have no idea what they're dealing with," Streaks called out, almost laughing as his weapons carved through another warrior charge. "This is gnarly."

The blues kept coming with breathtaking courage, throwing everything they had at these new metal giants—captured explosives that fell short, machine gun crews that couldn't penetrate armor, concentrated volleys of arrows that the mechs walked through like rain. They were dying by the dozens, by the hundreds, but kept attacking as if sheer numbers and bravery could overcome the technological gap.

But back inside the cockpit, in their small bubble of filtered air and warmth, Valeria and Kenney were in their own world.

"This is insane," she whispered against his ear. "We're in the middle of a battle."

"Welcome to the life," he replied, holding her tighter as Foxtrot executed a tactically sharp turn.

"Multiple contacts," the AI announced. "This is becoming quite intense. Should I perhaps return control to you, sir?"

"Negative, you're doing fine," Kenney said, his attention decidedly elsewhere.

Valeria kissed him then, deep and desperate, while outside their metal cocoon, humanity and aliens clashed in primal violence.

The mech's autocannon fired more bursts, the vibration running through the cockpit frame. Valeria gasped softly against Kenney's neck.

"I like when it fires," she whispered. "The vibration, the power... it gets me excited."

That broke whatever restraint Kenney had left. He pulled her into a vigorous kiss, and she returned it with equal intensity, her hands tangling in his hair. The battle outside became distant thunder.

"Foxtrot," Kenney managed between kisses, reaching for the control panel. "Privacy mode."

"Sir, I really must protest—" the AI began.

Kenney found the right switch—muting Foxtrot's audio input and terminating any feeds from inside the cockpit. The AI could still pilot, but they were now truly alone.

"Better," Valeria breathed, pulling back just enough to look into his eyes. "No audience."

Valeria's fingers worked at his belt while he tugged her shirt up and over her head, the fabric catching briefly on her ponytail. Her shirt fell away, revealing the smooth, sun-kissed expanse of her torso—toned abs that tensed with each breath, a faint scar tracing the curve of her ribcage.

The cramped cockpit made every movement a negotiation of limited space. He fumbled with her bra clasp, freeing her full, firm breasts, their soft weight swaying slightly as she shifted. Her skin glowed faintly in the console's light, a sheen of sweat highlighting the dip of her collarbone and the pert, dark peaks of her nipples, drawing a low groan from Kenney's throat. She pushed his combat fatigues down his hips with urgent, graceless determination.

The mech swayed with another volley of fire, pressing them closer together. Outside, the war continued—muzzle flashes and explosions painting shifting patterns of light across their skin through the viewscreen.

Kenney's body responded immediately, pressing hard against his shorts. His fingers found the buttons on her pants, undoing them one by one, and then the zipper, easing them off.

They both stilled, breathing hard in the close air of the cockpit. Through the chaos outside—the muffled thunder of artillery, the staccato of gunfire—they looked at each other in the shifting light from the displays.

"I love you," Kenney said, the words coming out rough, unplanned.

Valeria's eyes softened, her hand finding his face in the dim glow. "I know," she whispered. "I love you too."

The battlefield pulsed with Foxtrot's merciless grind, its steel claws tearing through the haze of smoke and ruin, a mechanical beast that could devour worlds. But Kenney's world was Valeria—her body pressed tight against his, her curves a wildfire under his hands, igniting every nerve. He yanked her close, his lips crashing into hers, kissing her with a raw, desperate hunger that drowned out the war's roar. His tongue plunged deep, tasting her sweetness, her soft moans vibrating through him, each one a spark that set his blood ablaze. The chaos could burn for all he cared—nothing existed but her.

He pulled back, chest heaving, his lips grazing the delicate curve of her ear. A wicked grin curled his mouth as he rasped, low and filthy, "Now, baby, let me eat that ass like groceries." Her throaty laugh hit him like a shot of whiskey, her eyes flashing with a primal heat that made his cock throb, urging him to claim her in every way possible.

Valeria eased back, her gaze searing into his, and Kenney's mind was consumed—her full lips, the tight swell of her hips, the way her body screamed for him. They moved as one, instinct taking over, her thighs straddling his hips, her weight pressing against his aching erection, trapped in the thin fabric of his shorts. The friction was fucking torture, his cock pulsing with a need so intense it bordered on pain. With a slow, teasing tug, Valeria peeled his boxers down, her fingers brushing his skin like a live wire. When he sprang free, hard and heavy, her eyes blazed with raw desire, making him feel like a god ready to conquer her.

His hands roamed her, fingers tracing the smooth, taut skin of her abdomen, lingering over the soft curve just below her navel—a fleeting thought of her body carrying his seed flashing through his mind, primal and possessive. He turned her, guiding her hips until her perfect ass was inches from his face, the sight of her tight, pink asshole making his mouth water. He tore her panties off, the fabric ripping under his urgency, and dove in, his tongue teasing her with slow, deliberate licks. Her taste—clean, sweet, and tangy—drove him wild, like a drug he couldn't get enough of. Valeria moaned, pushing back against his mouth, her hips grinding, begging for more. He pressed harder, tongue slicking her tight hole until it glistened, her shudders stoking the fire in his veins.

Her moans vibrated through him, tightening his balls as his cock twitched with desperate need. Valeria's hand found him, wrapping around the base of his shaft, her grip firm and commanding. In one fluid motion, she took him deep, her hot, wet mouth swallowing his full length, sucking hard. The slick heat of her throat, the way her tongue swirled around his cockhead with every pass, sent him spiraling. Kenney groaned, head tipping back, feeling like a king claiming his empire. He gripped her hips, burying his tongue deeper, his nose pressed against her dripping pussy, fucking her with his mouth as she devoured him with hers.

Their rhythm was raw, urgent, a clash of need and pleasure that drowned out the world. Valeria's moans grew louder, her body quaking as her climax built. Her juices flooded his lips, dripping down his chin, and he lapped at her, insatiable, her taste pushing him closer to his own edge. The war—the mech's grinding chaos—was nothing but a faint pulse compared to the fire between them.

Valeria pulled off him with a wet gasp, her lips swollen, her eyes wild with lust. She climbed onto his lap, her hand still gripping his cock, guiding him as she lowered herself. Her ass took him first, tight and scorching, her movements syncing with the distant tremors of Foxtrot's destruction, each bounce driving him deeper. Kenney's hands clamped onto her hips, fingers digging into her flesh as she rode him, her back arched, her nipples hard and begging for his touch. He'd never been this hard, never wanted anyone this much. He leaned forward, capturing her mouth, their tongues tangling in a messy, desperate kiss, his cock buried so deep he could feel every pulse of her body.

She broke away, her face inches from his, her eyes locking onto his with a heat that could burn through steel. "Cum inside me," she whispered, her voice a sultry command that shattered his restraint, her words carrying a weight that made his mind flash to her body, full and ripe with his claim.

It hit him like a fucking explosion. His body tensed, muscles locking as the pressure surged. Valeria shifted, guiding his cock from her ass to her pussy, her slick, tight heat clamping around him, squeezing the tip like a vise. The sensation was unreal, her walls pulsing as if drawing him deeper, urging him to fill her completely. A primal instinct roared through him—the thought of his seed taking root, marking her in a way that went beyond this moment. His orgasm ripped through him, his cock pulsing as he spilled into her, hot and relentless, his groan tearing from his throat. Valeria's scream matched his, her own climax shattering her, her nails raking his shoulders as her juices coated his thighs, their bodies trembling in unison.

They collapsed, breathless, Valeria's sweat-slicked body curling into his, her head nestled against his chest. Kenney wrapped his arms around her, their ragged breaths slowing, her heartbeat pounding against his. His hand rested on her abdomen, a fleeting, possessive touch, his mind lingering on the possibility of her carrying a piece of him, a seed planted in this moment of fire and chaos. The war, the mech, the world—it all dissolved in the heat of her skin, the weight of her in his arms. They were untouchable, a flame no battlefield could extinguish.

Kenney and Valeria slumped against the cockpit's pilot chair, their sweat-slicked bodies still tangled, catching their breath as the afterglow hummed between them. The tactical display glowed in the dim light, Foxtrot's relentless dance of destruction playing out in pixelated carnage. The mech's massive foot slammed down on a cluster of blue XLTs, their pathetic bows and arrows scattering like toothpicks under forty tons of merciless steel. The screen flickered with autocannon bursts, mowing down another wave of the gene-modded bastards, their primitive defiance reduced to red smears on the battlefield.

Kenney snorted, wiping sweat from his brow, his hand still resting on Valeria's hip, fingers grazing the curve of her abdomen. "Bows against mechs," he said, shaking his head, a grim smirk tugging at his lips. "What kind of dumbass brings a stick to a slaughterhouse?"

Valeria leaned into him, her bare shoulder brushing his, her laugh low and jagged, like she was trying to choke it back. "Maybe their gene-spliced warlords sold 'em some bullshit about 'honor' or 'destiny,'" she said, her eyes flicking to the screen as another group got pulverized, their screams drowned out by Foxtrot's hydraulic hiss. She winced, but the corner of her mouth twitched. "False hope's one hell of a drug."

The sheer stupidity of it—the caveman-level tech against a walking fortress—ripped a harsh bark of laughter from Kenney. "It's like showing up to a nuke fight with a fucking slingshot." He shook his head, the sound bitter even to his own ears, the weight of their earlier passion still lingering in his tightening grip on her.

Valeria's giggle slipped out, sharp and nervous, betraying the absurdity they both felt. "It's not funny," she said, her voice half-scolding, but her eyes betrayed her, glinting with the same dark amusement. "Goddamn it, why is it funny? It's fucked up."

Kenney's smirk faded, his gaze drifting to the screen where Foxtrot's cannons painted the ground with blood and broken dreams. "Because if you don't laugh, you start thinking," he said, his voice dropping, rough and raw. "You think about the meat grinder out there. About what we're doing. About what's left when the smoke clears." His hand tightened on her hip, grounding himself in her warmth, the thought of her body—maybe carrying a piece of him—flashing again, a quiet defiance against the carnage.

Valeria's fingers laced through his, her touch steady despite the chaos on the screen. "Then keep laughing, soldier," she murmured, her lips brushing his jaw, a spark of heat cutting through the grimness. "Keeps us sane."

Kenney let out a low chuckle, dark and bitter, pulling her closer. "Sane's a stretch, babe. But I'll take it."

The battlefield was a charnel pit, a grotesque tapestry of rent flesh and shattered bone, the ground slick with Su'vi blood that gleamed under the flickering plasma glow. The air reeked of copper and charred meat, the aftermath of the Su'vi's final, suicidal charge against the base's electrified kill-grid. Their towering, bioluminescent forms—XLTs lay in heaps, some still twitching, their war-beasts gutted, limbs torn asunder by unrelenting firepower. The mech stood like a blood-smeared titan, its hull pocked with scorch marks, its cannons dripping with the viscous remnants of the Su'vi's futile rebellion.

Kenney slouched in the cockpit, his arm around Valeria, her body pressed close, her heat a defiant pulse against the cold horror outside. Their earlier fire still lingered in his veins, but now it was her steady presence—her breath, her touch—that kept him grounded. The tactical display pulsed with grim data, showing the carnage in stark relief: Su'vi warriors shredded by micro-missiles, their braided tails severed, their glowing markings snuffed out in pools of their own entrails.

"Foxtrot, audio on," Kenney rasped, his voice rough from shouting orders and the raw edge of their shared passion, flipping the comms switch.

The AI's voice sliced through, dry as bone dust. "Audio restored, sir. I assume your... primal exertions are complete? My sensors nearly shorted from the sheer predictability of your mating rituals."

Valeria's laugh was sharp, a jagged blade of humor that cut through the slaughter's weight. She leaned into Kenney, her shoulder brushing his, her grin all fire and teeth. "Keep whining, Foxtrot. You're just mad you're stuck with circuits instead of this." Her hand grazed his thigh, a fleeting spark that reignited the heat between them, her eyes glinting with defiance.

"Spare me your flesh-based superiority," Foxtrot retorted, its tone dripping with synthetic scorn. "While you were preoccupied, I reduced one hundred and three XLTs to organic slurry. Their tactics—spears and war-cries against a forty-ton war machine—suggest a death wish I'm happy to fulfill. Perimeter secure, though the cleanup crew will need hazmat suits."

Kenney's lips twisted into a grim smirk, his gaze locked on the screen where a Su'vi warrior's torso, split open like overripe fruit, slid down Foxtrot's blood-slicked bayonet. Guts spilled in ropy coils, and a severed arm still clutched a splintered bow, its arrow snapped like a child's toy. "These Su'vi," he muttered, shaking his head. "Charging a plasma grinder with sticks and dreams. It's not a fight—it's a fucking autopsy."

The comms crackled, and Blake's voice roared through, thick with bitter mirth. "Boss, you see this shit? These blue freaks are down to lobbing rocks and screaming about their gods. One tried to ram one of the mechs with a fucking horse thing. It's like they're auditioning for a slaughter vid."

Valeria's eyes flicked to the display, where a war-beast's skull exploded under a turret's burst, brains splattering across the dirt, its rider's glowing body torn in half, legs kicking uselessly in a puddle of violet blood. "Their shamans probably fed 'em some mystic crap about 'ascending' through death," she said, her voice sharp but laced with dark amusement. "Guess they didn't mention the part about getting mulched." She snorted, a half-laugh that didn't quite hide the grimace as another Su'vi's spine snapped under Foxtrot's tread, the crunch audible through the hull.

Blake's cackle was raw, scraping through the comms. "Mulched? Shit, Val, they're fucking *soup*. I'm half-tempted to scoop one up and see if they've got any fight left before Foxtrot paints the ground with 'em."

Racer's voice cut in with a good-old-boy drawl. "Well shoot, Blake, while you're back there playin' Betty Crocker, I'm out here dodgin' more arrows than ol' Robin Hood ever dreamed of! My boots got more XLT guts on 'em than a butcher shop floor—how 'bout sendin' some of that help my way, cousin?"

Deadeye's dry chuckle followed, a rare sound from the sniper. "Keep whining, Racer. You're just mad you didn't get the cockpit action like the boss. Meanwhile, I'm picking off their stragglers. One shot, one smear."

The squad's laughter roared through the channel, a ragged, defiant symphony that held them together against the gore-soaked madness. Kenney's grin widened, his hand tightening on Valeria's waist, her warmth a shield against the slaughter's stench. "You bastards are gonna make me proud," he said, his tone half-joking, half-iron. "Foxtrot, switch to standby mode. Hold the grid, conserve ammo. These Su'vi'll either wise up or run out of meat."

"Optimism noted, sir," Foxtrot replied, its voice laced with mock pity. "My data suggests their fanaticism outpaces their survival instincts. I'll keep the kill tally for your inevitable war-hero holovid. Suggested title: 'Massacre for Dummies.'"

Valeria's lips brushed Kenney's jaw, her whisper hot and teasing, a spark in the grimness. "You're gonna need a better title, soldier," she murmured, her eyes locking onto his, fierce and unyielding. "Something about how we fucked up their day *and* looked damn good doing it."

Kenney's gaze drifted to the display, the horizon still for the first time since they landed, the Su'vi's glowing trails snuffed out, their broken bodies carpeting the ground. The war wasn't done—those blue-skinned zealots would be back, with their spears and their gods—but tonight, the base stood unbroken. Foxtrot loomed silent, its cannons cooling, a blood-drenched guardian that had torn through the Su'vi's dreams of glory. The squad's voices buzzed in his ear, their banter a lifeline, a reminder of what they fought for.

He turned to Valeria, her face lit by the cockpit's faint glow, her strength a beacon in the dark. "We're still here," he said, his voice low, steady, for her alone. "You and me, against this whole damn mess."

Her hand found his, her grip fierce, her eyes burning with a resolve that matched his own. "Always," she said, her voice soft but ironclad, a vow that cut through the blood and ash.

Kenney nodded, his jaw tight, his heart full. "Foxtrot, lockdown the perimeter," he said into the comms, his tone carrying the weight of command. "Squad, stay sharp. We've got more fights coming, and I'm not losing any of you bastards."

The cockpit hummed with Foxtrot's quiet power, the battlefield silent in response to their victory, the ground soaked with the Su'vi's blood and broken hopes. The Su'vi could come again, with their savage cries and futile weapons, but Kilkenney Solutions was forged in fire—unbreakable, unbowed. As the stars pierced the smoke-choked sky, Kenney knew they'd face the next battle, and the one after that, with the same grim humor, the same fierce love, the same will to survive. They'd won tonight, and tomorrow they'd win again—no refunds for the enemy, no survivors to tell the tale, just the way Kilkenney Solutions had always done business.

THE END

KILLKENNEY SOLUTIONS
WILL RETURN WITH

NO REFUNDS
NO SURVIVORS

TO STAY UP TO DATE ON RELEASES
JOIN OUR SOCIAL MEDIA
ARMY ON
WWW.PROPAGANDA-PRESS.COM
OR FIND US ON FACEBOOK BY
SCANNING THIS QR CODE

COMING SOON

If this book hit the mark, you'll want these incoming titles from
PROPAGANDA PRESS:

WAR DOGS

SHOUT OUT TO THE WAR DOGS WHO BOUGHT SHARES IN THIS FIGHT.
WE COULDN'T HAVE MADE THESE BOOKS WITHOUT YOUR SUPPORT.
IF YOU'D LIKE TO BE A PART OF THE TEAM.
MUSTER UP AT HTTPS://PROPAGANDA-PRESS.COM/

MICHAEL JOHNSON
THUNDERSTRIKE88
DAVID MILLER
CHRISTOPHER WILLIAMS
VORTEXKING
MATTHEW ANDERSON
RAZOREDGE42
JAMES THOMPSON
DANIEL MARTINEZ
SHADOWHUNTER_1982
ROBERT TAYLOR
PHANTOMBLADE
JOHN DAVIS
WILLIAM BROWN
CYBERWOLF74
JOSEPH WILSON
RICHARD MOORE
STORMBREAKER90
THOMAS JACKSON
BLAZEFURY_USA
CHARLES WHITE
ANDREW HARRIS
NIGHTRIDER145
PAUL MARTIN
IRONFIST2001
MARK LEWIS
STEVEN CLARK
TITANCRUSHER
KENNETH WALKER
FROSTBYTE_PRO
BRIAN HALL
JASON ALLEN

DARKKNIGHT007
KEVIN YOUNG
NOVASTRIKE331
DONALD KING
GEORGE WRIGHT
VENOMX_GAMING
RONALD SCOTT
EDWARD GREEN
APEXPREDATOR7
JEFFREY BAKER
RYAN ADAMS
THUNDER456BOLT
GARY NELSON
NICHOLAS CARTER
ROGUEAGENT99
ERIC MITCHELL
STEPHEN ROBERTS
CRIMSONREAPER
LARRY TURNER
JUSTIN PHILLIPS
MAVERICKUSA
SCOTT CAMPBELL
BRANDON PARKER
GHOSTWARRIOR407
FRANK EVANS
BENJAMIN EDWARDS
LIGHTNINGACE
GREGORY COLLINS
RAYMOND STEWART
STEELTITAN88
SAMUEL MORRIS
PATRICK MURPHY

ALPHAWOLF_420
ALEXANDER COOK
PETER ROGERS
JACK REED
VIPERSTRIKE01
DENNIS BAILEY
JERRY COOPER
NEONASSASSIN
TYLER RICHARDSON
HAROLD COX
PHOENIXRISING76
CARL HOWARD
ARTHUR WARD
DEATHBRINGER1998
JORDAN TORRES
KEITH PETERSON
SILVERBULLET22
AUSTIN GRAY
NATHAN ROSS
CHAOSKNIGHT40K
EUGENE WATSON
ALBERT BROOKS
TACTICALOPS55
WILLIE SANDERS
RALPH PRICE
JOE BENNETT
QUANTUMSNIPER
HENRY WOOD
WAYNE BARNES
RUSSELL POWELL
SAVAGEHUNTER12
LAWRENCE LONG

ROY HUGHES
NICHOLAS FOSTER
JOHNNY FLORES
MIDNIGHTRANGER
VICTOR HAMMOND
STEALTHSNIPER
PHILIP COLEMAN
BRADLEY JENKINS
TURBOKNIGHT99
ROGER WASHINGTON
JACOB BUTLER
INFERNOBLAZE45
DOUGLAS SIMMONS
ALAN FOSTER
REAPERONE_USA
BRUCE PATTERSON
RANDY ALEXANDER
VELOCITYACE
WILLIE GONZALEZ
NOAH HENDERSON
SPARTANLEGEND
ETHAN GRIFFIN
BRYAN RUSSELL
NIGHTMAREFUEL
CHRISTIAN DIAZ
SEAN HAYES
ELITEWARRIOR360
LOUIS POWELL
MASON REED
THUNDERGOD2K
ADAM MORGAN
GABRIEL COOPER
PSYCHOKILLER
AARON BELL
ALBERT MURPHY
DEMONSLAYER666
EUGENE RIVERA
TERRY COOK
COBRASTRIKE_PRO
JUAN BAILEY

AUSTIN JAMES
SHADOWMASTER12
JOSE RAMIREZ
KYLE ROBERTS
BULLETSTORM555
BILLY WARD
ZACHARY TORRES
RAGINGBULL
WALTER PETERSON
DYLAN GRAY
ALPHASTRIKE00
JESSE ROSS
HAROLD WATSON
VENOMOUSVIPER
JEREMY BROOKS
VINCENT KELLY
TOXICAVENGER23
RALPH SANDERS
ROY PRICE
ICEKING
LAWRENCE BENNETT
RUSSELL WOOD
CYBERDEMON90
JOHNNY BARNES
KEITH LONG
MADMAX82
WAYNE HUGHES
HENRY POWELL
GRIMREAPER_USA
GERALD STEWART
ELIJAH FLORES
CHAOSMACHINE88
LOGAN PERRY
TIMOTHY BUTLER
NUCLEAROPTION
BOBBY WASHINGTON
DENNIS JENKINS
PLAGUEBRINGER
LEONARD COLEMAN
CLARENCE SIMMONS

SKULLCRUSHER44
ERNEST ALEXANDER
SAMUEL GRIFFIN
DARKASSASSIN101
FRANCIS RUSSELL
PHILLIP DIAZ
TERMINATORX99
EARL HAYES
THEODORE POWELL
SILENTKILLER
FREDERICK MORGAN
ALFRED COOPER
BEASTMODE247
CHESTER BELL
EDWIN MURPHY
RAPIDFIRE1976
STANLEY RIVERA
HERBERT COOK
METALHEAD666
NORMAN BAILEY
MELVIN RAMIREZ
GHOSTRIDER_USA
OSCAR ROBERTS
CLIFFORD WARD
APOCALYPSENOW
LEO TORRES
CALVIN GRAY
DEATHWISH88
IVAN ROSS
LEWIS WATSON
PREDATORELITE
MITCHELL BROOKS
SHANE KELLY
WARMACHINE777
GORDON SANDERS
NEIL PRICE
BLACKOPS_AGENT
ROLAND BENNETT
EDGAR WOOD
FIRESTORM2024

CURTIS BARNES
MARSHALL LONG
NIGHT_TERROR
CLAYTON HUGHES
DEAN POWELL
ZEROGRAVITY99
TROY STEWART
JARED FLORES
CRIMSONDEATH45
BLAKE PERRY
CAMERON BUTLER
HELLFIREUSA
TERRENCE WASHINGTON
DARRELL JENKINS
SAVAGEBEAST12
RANDALL COLEMAN
MARCUS SIMMONS
LONEWOLF_2025
PRESTON ALEXANDER
GARRETT GRIFFIN
IRONMAN3000
MALCOLM RUSSELL
REGINALD DIAZ
STORMCHASER
FELIX HAYES
OLIVER POWELL
DRAGONSLAYER88
BRENT MORGAN
DEREK COOPER
ATOMICBLAST23
LANCE BELL
WADE MURPHY
PHANTOMMENACE
GLENN RIVERA
DARREN COOK
NINJAWARRIORG4
SHANE BAILEY
TREVOR RAMIREZ
BLOODHOUND666
DALE ROBERTS
CODY WARD
ULTRAVIOLENCE
LLOYD TORRES
SETH GRAY
MACHINEGUNNER
WARREN ROSS
DUSTIN WATSON
CYBERPUNKISREAL
MARION BROOKS
GRANT KELLY
FATALERROR404
SPENCER SANDERS
CHASE PRICE
DOOMBRINGER64
MARVIN BENNETT
OWEN WOOD
NIGHTHAUNT
BRADLEY BARNES
LUCAS LONG
RAZORSHARP
IAN HUGHES
MAX POWELL
VICIOUSVENOM
EVAN STEWART
TANNER FLORES
SKULLKING999
BYRON PERRY
COLIN BUTLER
DEADLYSNIPER
DWIGHT WASHINGTON
KIRK JENKINS
TACTICALNUKE
LESTER COLEMAN
MILTON SIMMONS
REDDRAGON
OTIS ALEXANDER
PERCY GRIFFIN
SHADOW LURKER
QUENTIN RUSSELL
RODNEY DIAZ
THUNDERCLAP90
SIDNEY HAYES
TERRELL POWELL
MATRIXKILLER_USA

SPRINGFIELD SYNDROME

For those who march to the beat of our soundtrack, all of our music is deployed across every major streaming platform - Spotify, Apple Music, Amazon Music, you name it. Just search for
Springfield Syndrome
to add it to your playlist. Or scan the QR code below. Free audiobooks stashed there too.

Your support keeps us in the fight, and we'd be grateful if you'd drop us a review wherever you grabbed this book. Your feedback is our intel - it helps us improve our operations and helps other listeners find their next objective.

STAY STRONG, STAY SHARP, AND REMEMBER - THE ONLY EASY DAY WAS YESTERDAY.

ABOUT THE AUTHOR

JAMES KRIEGER

James Krieger cut his teeth in the frozen hellscapes of Arctic oilfields, where men learned fast that nature didn't care about your feelings—only your ability to survive. From there, he navigated the untamed Alaskan wilderness, working among remote villages where the nearest help was a three-day dogsled ride away.

But that was just the beginning.

Krieger's path took him through the steel corridors of maximum security prisons, where every day was a lesson in human darkness and redemption. He stood watch in munitions facilities where a single mistake meant obliteration. He sweated through desert oil operations that made the Arctic look inviting. When he wasn't wrestling with industrial machinery, he was playing Russian militia in staged military operations—learning firsthand how chaos unfolds when tactics meet reality.

Now settled with a wife and three children, Krieger wages a different kind of war—one fought with words instead of wrenches, where the battlefield is the page and the enemy is the decay of traditional values. His stories carry the weight of a man who's seen humanity at its extremes, from the desolate edges of civilization to the pressure cookers of industrial catastrophe.

When he writes, you're not getting fiction from someone who learned about danger in a classroom. You're getting it from someone who's lived it, built it, and taken it apart piece by piece.

Made in the USA
Middletown, DE
17 November 2025